precious *and* fragile things

MEGAN HART

precious *and* fragile things

ISBN-13: 978-0-7783-2924-4

PRECIOUS AND FRAGILE THINGS

For questions and comments about the quality of this book please contact us at Customer_eCare@Harlequin.ca.

www.MIRABooks.com

Printed in U.S.A.

First, to my friends and family
who read this book in its many stages—thank you.
It's a better book because of you.

To my agent Laura Bradford
for not curling her lip when I first told her about the book,
and for believing in it all along.

To Superman—
I wouldn't be able to do this without you.
Thanks for catching the kids.

To my spawn—
I love you both, even if I did throw you out the window
as "research."

As always, I could write without music,
but I'm ever so grateful I don't have to. Much appreciation goes
to the following artists whose songs made up the playlist for this
book. Please support their music through legal sources.

"Give it Away"—Quincy Coleman
"Take Me Home"—Lisbeth Scott and Nathan Barr
"Everything"—Lifehouse
"This Woman's Work"—Kate Bush
"You've Been Loved"—Joseph Arthur
"Iris"—Goo Goo Dolls
"Look After You"—The Fray
"The End"—The Doors
"One Last Breath"—Creed
"A Home for You"—Kaitlin Hopkins, Deven May
"Over My Head"—Christopher Dallman

And a special thanks to Jason Manns,
whose version of "Hallelujah" wasn't there when I started the book
but was there all through the end.

January

1

This was the life she'd made.

Cheese crackers crunching beneath her boots. A tickling and suspicious stink like milk that had been spilled in some unfound crack coming from the backseat. An unfinished To Do list, laundry piled and waiting for her at home, two over-tired and cranky children whining at her. This was her life, and most of the time Gilly could ignore these small annoyances that were only tiny details in the much larger overall picture. Embrace them, even.

But not today.

Please, shut up. For five minutes. Just shut up!

"Give Mama a few minutes" is what Gillian Soloman said instead, her voice a feathery singsong that belied her growing irritation.

"I'm thirsty, Mama!" Arwen's high-edged, keening whine stabbed Gilly's eardrums. "I wanna drink now!"

Count to ten, Gilly. Count to twenty, if you have to. C'mon, keep it together. Don't lose it.

"We'll be home in fifteen minutes." This would mean nothing to Arwen, who didn't know how to tell time, but to Gilly it was important. Fifteen minutes. Surely she could survive anything for fifteen more minutes, couldn't she? Gilly's voice snagged, ragged with the effort of keeping it calm, and she drew in a breath. She put a smile on her face not because she felt like smiling, but because she didn't. Kept her voice calm and soothing, because an angry tone to the children was like chum to sharks. It made them frenzied. "I told you to bring your water bottle. Maybe next time you'll listen to me."

Gilly made sure she'd signed the check in the right place and filled out the deposit envelope appropriately. Looked over it again. It was only a check for ten bucks and change, but if she messed up the amount written on the envelope, the credit union could and would charge her a fee. It had happened before, unbalancing her checkbook and causing an argument with her and Seth. The numbers blurred, and she rubbed her eyes.

"Mama? Mama? Mama!"

Gilly didn't even bother to answer, knowing the moment she said "what?" that Arwen would fall into stunned silence, nothing to say.

Fifteen minutes. Twenty, tops. You'll be home and can put them in front of cartoons. Just hold it together until then, Gilly. Don't lose it.

From the other seat came Gandy's endless, wordless groan of complaint and then the steady *thump-kick* of his feet to the back of Gilly's seat. *Bang, bang, bang,* the metronome of irritation.

"Gandy. Stop kicking Mama's seat."

For half a second as her pen wavered, Gilly thought about abandoning this venture altogether. What had she been thinking, making "just one more" stop? But damn it, she needed to cash this check and withdraw some money from the ATM to last her through the week, and since she'd already had to stop to pick up her prescription at the pharmacy...

"I wanna drink now!"

What do you want me to do, spit in a cup?

The words hurtled to her lips and Gilly bit them back before they could vomit out of her, sick at the thought of how close she'd come to actually saying them aloud. Those weren't her words.

"Fifteen minutes, baby. We'll be home in fifteen minutes."

Thump, thump, thump.

Her fingers tightened on the pen. She breathed. She counted to ten. Then another five.

It wasn't helping.

Last night: she fumbles with her house key because Seth locked the door leading from the garage to the laundry room when he went to bed. She stumbles into a dark house in which nobody's left on any lights, carrying handfuls of plastic bags full of soap and socks and everything for other people, nothing for herself. She'd spent hours shopping, wandering the aisles of Wal-Mart, comparing dish towels and bathroom mugs just so she had an excuse to be by herself for another hour. She took the long way home with the radio turned up high, singing along with songs with raunchy lyrics she can't listen to in front of the kids because they repeat everything. Scattered toys that had been in their bins when she left now stub her toes, and she mutters a curse. In the bedroom, lit only by the light from the hall so she doesn't wake her sleeping husband, the baskets of clean, waiting-to-be-put-away laundry have been torn apart by what, a tornado? Clothes all over the floor, dumped as though she hadn't spent an hour folding them all.

Even now as she remembered, Gilly's fingers twitched on the ATM envelope and rage, burning like bile, rose in her throat. Seth's excuse had been "I needed clean pajamas for the kids." She'd gone to bed beside him, stiff with fury, the taste of blood on her hard-bitten tongue.

She'd woken, still just as angry, to the sound of Seth slamming dresser drawers and his plea to help him find a pair of clean socks, though of course they were all in the very basket he'd trashed the night before. In the shower Gilly had bent her head beneath lukewarm water that too quickly ran to chill. She'd been glad when he didn't kiss her goodbye.

At breakfast the children each wanted something different than what she'd put on the plate in front of them. Shoes wouldn't fit on feet, coats had gone AWOL, and every pair of Arwen's tights had managed to get a hole. The cat got loose, and the children cried, no matter how much she tried to reassure them Sandy would be just fine.

They'd been late to Gilly's doctor appointment. On any other day being on time would've meant a fifteen-minute wait. Today, the sour, scowling nurse informed them they'd almost forfeited their appointment. Arwen pinched her finger in a drawer, and Gandy fell off the rolling stool and cracked his head. Both children left the office in tears, and Gilly thought she might just start to cry, too.

The day didn't get better. There was whining, there was fussing, there were tantrums and yelling and threats of timeouts. And of course, though she'd spent hours in Wal-Mart the night before, she'd still forgotten to buy milk. That meant a trip to Foodland. That meant children begging for sugary cereals she refused to buy. More tears. Pitying looks from women in coordinated outfits without stains on the front and well-behaved children who didn't act like starving beggars. By the time they'd finished their grocery shopping, Gilly was ready to take them both home and toss them into bed. She'd made one last stop at the ATM.

One last stop.

"Mamaaaaaa!"

The whining rose in intensity and persistence. The kicking continued, ceaseless. Like all of this. Like her life.

Count to ten. Bite your tongue. Keep yourself together, Gilly. Don't lose it. Don't lose it.

Gilly made herself the Joker. She wouldn't have been surprised to feel scars rip open on her cheeks from the smile she forced again. "Ten more minutes, baby. Just ten. Let Mama do this, okay? Now listen. I'll be right back."

She turned in her seat to look at both of them, her angel-monsters. Arwen's eyes had gone squinty, mouth twisted into a frown. Gandy had snot dribbling from his nose and crusted goo at the corners of his lips. He'd spilled a juice box all over his pale blue shirt. They looked like the best of her and Seth combined. This was what she had made.

"I'll be right back," Gilly said, though frankly she wanted to start running down the highway and never look back. "You both stay here and keep your seat belts *on.* You hear me? Seat belts on. Do not get out of your seats."

Good mothers didn't leave their children in the car, but the ATM was only a few feet away. The weather was cold enough that the kids wouldn't broil inside a locked vehicle, and she locked them in so nobody could steal them in the five minutes it would take her to finish her task. Besides, she thought as she slid her ATM card into the machine and punched in her PIN, dragging them both out into the freezing, early evening air would surely be worse than leaving them warm and safe in the Suburban.

Frigid wind blew, whipping at her hair and sending stinging pellets of winter rain that would've been less insulting as snow against her face. She blinked against it, concentrating on punching in her PIN number with fingers suddenly numb. She messed up. Had to cancel, do it again.

Slow down. Do it right. One number at a time, Gilly. It'll be okay.

She deposited the check, withdrew some cash, shoved her receipt and her card into her wallet and got back in the car. The kids had been silent when she opened the door, but within thirty seconds the whining began again. The steady kicking. The constant muttering of "Mama?" Gilly swallowed anger and tried desperately to scribble the amount of her withdrawal from the ATM in her checkbook, because if she didn't do it now, this minute, she would forget and there'd be another overdraft for Seth to complain about, but her hands shook and the numbers were illegible. She took a deep breath. Then one more. Willing herself to stay calm. It wasn't worth losing her temper over any of this. Not worth screaming about.

Five minutes. Please just shut up for five minutes, or I swear I'll…

Not go crazy. Not that. She wouldn't even think about it.

Gilly put the truck in Drive and pulled slowly out of the parking spot. The strip mall bustled with activity, with Foodland getting its share of evening foragers and the office supply store just as busy. Gilly eased past some foron in a minivan who'd parked askew, brake lights on, and mentally threatened them with violence if they dared back out in front of her.

This part of the strip mall had been under construction forever—the promise of a popular chain restaurant and a couple upscale additions had made everyone in Lebanon salivate at the thought of getting some culture, but in the end poor planning and the economy's downturn had stalled the project. They'd only gotten as far as building a new access road, slashing like a razor on a wrist through what had previously been a tidy little field. Gilly stopped at the stop sign and looked automatically past the empty storefront to her left, though all that lay at the end of the road in that direction were dirt and Dumpsters.

The passenger door opened, and Gilly looked to her right. She blinked at the young man sliding across the bench seat toward her. He slammed the door and grunted as he kicked his duffel bag to the floor. For one infinite moment, she felt no terror, only confusion. "Where did you—?"

Then she saw the knife.

Huge, serrated, gripped in his fist. She didn't even look at his face. And she wasn't confused any longer.

Cold, implacable fury filled her and clenched her hands into numbness. All she'd wanted to do was go home, put the kids to bed and take a hot bath. Read a book. Be alone for a few precious minutes in peace and quiet before her husband came home and wanted to talk to her. And now…this.

The tip of his knife came within an eyelash of her cheek; his other hand gripped her ponytail and held it tight. "Go!"

There was no time for thought. Gilly went. She pounded her foot so hard on the accelerator the tires spun on ice-slick ground before catching. The Chevy Suburban bucked forward, heading for the traffic light and the road out of town.

He has a knife. The press of steel on flesh, parting it. Blood spurts. There is no smell like it, the smell of blood. That's what a knife can do. It can hurt and worse than that.

It can kill.

Gilly's hands moved on the steering wheel automatically.

With little conscious thought, she flicked her turn signal and nosed into the line of traffic. Night had fallen. Nobody could see what was happening to her. Nobody would help her. She was on her own, but she wasn't alone.

"I'll do what you want. Just don't hurt my kids."

No smile this time, but it was the same voice she'd used just minutes ago with her children. It was her mother's voice, she thought. She'd never noticed. The realization sent a jolting twist of nausea through her.

"Mommy?" Arwen sounded tremulous, confused. "Who's that man?"

"It's okay, kids." This was not her mother's voice, thank God. It was the one Gilly used for things like shots and stitches. Things that would hurt no matter what she said or did. This voice broke like glass in her throat, hurting.

Gandy said with a two-year-old's wisdom, "Man, bad."

The man's gaze shot to the backseat as if he only now noticed the kids there. "Shit." He moved closer. He gripped the back of her seat this time, not her hair, but the knife stayed too close to her neck. "Turn left."

She did. The lights of the oncoming cars flashed in her eyes, and Gilly squinted. Slam on the brakes? Twist the wheel, hit another car? A checklist of choices ticked themselves off in her brain and she took none, her fury dissolved by the numbness of indecision and fear. She followed his barked orders to head out of town, away from the lights and the other cars. Away from safety. Away from help.

"Where do you want me to go?" The big SUV bounced with every rut in the road, and the knife wavered that much closer to her flesh. She'd bleed a lot if it cut her. She didn't want her children to see her bleed. She'd do anything to keep them from seeing that.

The man looked over his shoulder again. "I'll tell you when to turn."

The Suburban headed into farm country, past silos and barns, dark and silent. Gilly risked a look at him. She took a deep breath, spoke fast so he'd listen. "I have sixty dollars in my purse. You can have it. Just let—"

"Shut up and drive!"

No other traffic passed them, not even a car coming the opposite direction. Salt and grit spattered against the windshield, smearing it. She turned on the windshield wipers. She didn't oblige him by driving fast.

If he didn't want money, what did he want? Her mind raced. The truck? The vehicle wasn't the kicky, sexy sort of car she'd always assumed people wanted to steal. It was far from new but well-maintained, and had cost an arm and a leg, but she wasn't attached to it.

"Look, if you want the truck, you can have it."

"Shut up!" The knife again dipped close to her shoulder, close enough to brush the fleece of her jacket. The blade glittered in the green dashboard light.

He didn't want the truck. He didn't want the money. Did he want…her?

Both children wailed from the backseat, a sound that at any other time would have set her teeth on edge. Now it broke her heart. The road stretched out pitch-black and deserted before them. No streetlamps out here in Pennsylvania farm country. Nothing but the faint light of electric candles in the window of a farmhouse set off far down a long country lane.

"What do you want?" Her fingers had gone past numb to aching from holding on so tightly to the steering wheel.

He didn't answer her.

"Just let my kids go." She kept her voice low, not wanting

Arwen and Gandy to hear her. "I'll pull over to the side and you can let them out. Then I'll do whatever you want."

Only fifteen minutes had passed. She'd have been home by now, if not for this. The man beside her let out a low, muttered string of curses. The knife hovered so close to her face she didn't dare even turn her head again to look at him. Ahead of them, nothing but dark, unwinding road.

"Just let my kids go," Gilly repeated, and he still didn't answer. Her temper snapped and broke. Shattered. "Damn it, you son of a bitch, let my kids go!"

"I told you to shut up." He grabbed the back of her neck, held the point of the knife against it.

She felt the thin, burning prick of it and shuddered, waiting for him to slice into her. He only poked. No worse than a needle prick, but all it would take was a simple shift of his fingers and she'd be dead. She'd wreck the car, and they'd all be dead.

Just ahead, lights coming from a large stone farmhouse settled on the very edge of the road illuminated the pavement. A high stone wall separated the driveway from the yard. Though the snow this winter had so far been sporadic, two dirty white piles had been shoveled up against the wall.

Yanking the wheel to the right, Gilly swerved into the driveway. Gravel spanged the sides of the car and one large rock hit the windshield hard enough to nick the glass. She slammed on the brakes using both feet and sent the truck sliding toward the thick stone wall and concrete stairs leading to the sidewalk.

Into the slide or away from it? She couldn't remember, and it didn't matter. The truck was sliding, skidding, and then the grumble of antilock brakes shuddered through it. The truck stopped just short of hitting the wall. Gilly's seat belt locked against her chest and neck, a line of fire against her skin. The carjacker flew forward in his seat. His head slammed into the windshield and starred the glass before he flew against the side window and back against his seat.

Gilly didn't waste time to see if the impact had knocked him out. She stabbed the button that automatically rolled her window completely down, and with a movement so fast and fierce it hurt her fingertips, unbuckled her seat belt and whirled over the center console to reach into the backseat. Arwen was crying and Gandy babbling, but Gilly didn't have time for speech. She reached first to the buckles on both booster seats and flung the freed seat belts with such force the metal hook on one of them smacked the window.

The inside lights had been on when they pulled into the driveway, but now the porch lights came on, too. It would be only moments before whoever lived in the house came to the door to see who was in their driveway. Gilly had driven past this house and barn a thousand times, but she'd never met its occupants. Now she was going to trust them with her children.

"No tears, baby." She pulled Gandy back with her over the center console.

The carjacker groaned. A purpling mark had appeared on his forehead, a starburst with beading blood at the center. More blood dripped from his nose to paint his mouth and chin. His eyes fluttered.

"I love you," she whispered in Gandy's sweet little boy ear as she lifted him out the driver's side window. She heard his cry as he fell to the frozen ground below, but hardened her heart against it. No time, no time for kissing boo-boos. Arwen balked and protested, but Gilly grabbed her daughter by the front of her pink ballerina sweatshirt and yanked her forward.

"I love you, honey." She heard the man starting to swear. She'd run out of time. "You take Gandy and you run, do you hear me? Run as fast as you can inside the house!"

Gilly shoved her purse strap over Arwen's shoulder, grateful the bag had been on the floor in the backseat. Wallet. Phone. They'd be able to call Seth. The police. Incoherent thoughts whirled.

Then she shoved her firstborn out the window, noticing the girl wore no shoes. Irritation, irrational and useless, flooded her, because she'd told Arwen to keep her sneakers on, and now her feet would get wet and cold as she ran through the snow.

Gilly had her hand on the door handle when he grabbed her again.

"Bitch!" The man cried from behind her, and she waited for the hot slice of metal against the back of her neck. Time had gone, run away, disappeared. "You'd better drive this motherfucker and drive it fast or I'm gonna put this knife in your fucking guts!"

He reached over, yanked the gearshift into Reverse and slammed down on her knee. The engine revved. The truck jerked backward. Gravel sprayed. Gilly twisted in her seat, reached for the wheel, struggled for control, fought to keep the truck from hitting the kids. The headlights cast her children in flashes of white as they clutched each other in the snow. The back door opened and a Mennonite woman wearing a flowered dress and a prayer cap planted on her pinned-up hair appeared. Her mouth made a large round O of surprise when she saw the truck spinning its wheels and hopping backward onto the road like a rabbit on acid. When she saw the weeping, screaming children, she clutched her hands together and ran to them, her own feet bare. Gilly would never forget the sight of her children in the rearview mirror as she sped away. She couldn't see their faces, only their silhouettes, backlit from the porch light. Two small figures holding hands in the dirty, drifted snow.

"Drive!" commanded the man who'd taken over Gilly's life, and she drove.

It took her at least a mile to realize he hadn't stabbed her. His slamming hand had bruised her knee, which throbbed, and he still had her tight by the back of the neck, but she wasn't cut. The truck slid on a patch of black ice and she didn't fight it. Maybe they'd skid and wreck, end up in a ditch. She couldn't think beyond what had happened, what was still happening now.

Her babies, left behind.

"Not the way it was supposed to go down. Fuck. Fuck. Fuck!"

He repeated the word over and over, like some sort of litany, not a curse. Gilly followed the curves in the road by instinct more than attention. She shuddered at the frigid night air from the open window and kept both hands on the wheel, afraid to let go long enough to close it.

"Damn, my fucking head hurts."

Blood covered his shirt. He let go of her to reach toward the floor and grab a squashed roll of paper towels. He used a few to dab at the blood. Then he pointed the knife back at her. It shook this time.

"What do you want from me?" Her voice didn't sound like her own. It sounded faraway. She felt far away, not here. Someplace else. Was this really happening?

He snorted into the wad of paper towels. "Just drive. And roll up the fucking window."

She did as he ordered, then slapped her hand back to the wheel. They'd only gone a few more miles, a few more minutes. Ahead, a traffic light glowed green. She sped through it. Another mile or so, and she'd hit another light. If it was red, what would she do? Stop and throw herself out of the car as she'd thrown her children?

She risked a glance at her abductor. He wasn't even looking at her. She could do it. But when she got to the light, it didn't oblige by turning red, or even yellow. Green illuminated the contours of his face as he turned to her.

"Turn right."

Now they were on a state road, still deserted and rural despite its fancy number. Gilly concentrated on breathing. In. Out. She refused to faint.

The man's voice was muffled. "I think you broke my fucking nose. Christ, what the hell were you doing?"

Gilly found her voice. Small, this time. Hoarse, but all hers with nothing of anyone else in it at all. "You wouldn't let me stop to get my kids out."

"I could've cut you. I still could." He sounded puzzled.

Gilly kept her face toward the road. Her hands on the wheel. These were things that anchored her, the wheel, the road. These were solid things. Real. Not the rest of this, the man on the seat beside her, the children left behind.

"But you didn't. And I got my kids out."

He made another muffled snort. The wad of bloody paper towels fell out of his nose, and he made no move to retrieve it. He'd dropped the knife to his knee. Not close to her, but ready. Gilly had no doubt if she made any sudden moves he'd have it up at her face again.

"Well, shit," he said, and lapsed into silence.

Silence. Nothing but the hum of the road under the wheels, the occasional rush of a passing car. Gilly thought of nothing. Could think of nothing but driving.

Her mind had been blank for at least twenty minutes before she noticed, long enough to pass through the last small town and onto the night-darkened highway beyond. When was the last time she'd thought of nothing? Her mind was never silent, never quiet. She didn't have time to waste on daydreams. There were always too many things to do, to take care of. Her thoughts were always like a hamster on a wheel, running and running without ever getting anywhere.

Tomorrow the dog had a vet appointment. Arwen had kindergarten. Gandy needed new shoes. The floor in the kitchen badly needed a mopping, which she meant to do after paying the last round of bills for the month…and if she had time she wanted to finish reorganizing her closet. And through it all, the knowledge that no matter how many tasks she began, she'd complete none of them without being interrupted. Being demanded of. Being expected to take care of someone else's needs.

Tonight a man had held her at knifepoint and threatened to take away that tomorrow with its lists and chores and demands. If nothing else, no matter what else happened, how things turned out, Gilly would not have to heave her weary body out of bed and force herself to get through one more day. If she was really unfortunate, and a glance at the twitching young man beside her told her she might be, she might never have to get out of bed again.

The thought didn't scare her as much as it should have.

He shifted. "I need to get to Route 80."

"I'm not sure…"

"I'll tell you."

In a brief flash of light from the streetlamp, she saw his forehead had furrowed with concentration. Gilly looked to the road ahead, at the lights of oncoming cars and the lit exit signs. The man ordered her to take the exit for the interstate, and she did. Then he slumped in his seat, head against the window, and the sound of his tortured breathing filled her ears like the sound of the ocean, constant and steady.

In the silence, uninterrupted by cries and demands, Gilly let her mind fall blank again as she drove on. Her rage and terror had passed, replaced by something quiet and sly.

Relief.

2

Thud, thud. Thud, thud. Thud, thud. The truck's wheels passed over asphalt cracks with a sound like a beating heart. For an hour or so her abductor had told her which roads to take, what highways to follow. Some were small, obscure back-country lanes, some major four-lane roads, all of them dark and fairly clear of traffic. She didn't know if he meant to dodge pursuit, was lost, or had a plan. He'd listened to the radio for a while, switching stations, pausing at a commercial for the built-in navigation service that came with all the newer model cars.

He'd run his fingertips over the dash. "You got that?"

"No. It was only an option when we bought the truck, and we didn't take the option."

On the radio, the soft-voiced operator assured the sniveling woman that she was going to be just fine. The commercial narrator reminded everyone what a lifesaver the service was. The man had seemed pleased and switched the station, finally settling on the weather. They were predicting snow. His eyes had closed several miles back. His breathing had slowed, joined with the heartbeat of their passage, to soothe and lull her further into blankness.

Into quiet.

When Gilly was growing up, her best friend's house had been full of constant noise. Danica had four brothers and a sister, plus a dog, a cat, a bird and several tanks full of fish. Her parents yelled a lot, mostly to be heard over the rest of the roar. Gilly loved spending time at Danica's house, but she'd often come home from a visit with her head whirling, slipping into her solitary bedroom and putting her head under the pillow to muffle even the silence that almost always greeted her.

It wasn't until she'd had kids of her own that Gilly realized noise was normal. Most families lived with it. Shouts, laughter, calling to each other from room to room. The burble of the radio, television. These were the sounds of normal families. She'd come to appreciate the noise of normality, but could never quite relish it the way she now savored the silence in the car. It had been a long, long time since she'd been in silence like this, been granted the choice to stay silent, herself.

Gilly drank the quiet like it was wine, and felt nearly as drunk from it. No whining, no complaining. Nobody asking to stop to pee or to change the radio station. Nobody ignoring directions. Nobody grumbling she was going too slow or too fast. Nothing but an occasional sigh from the man in the driver's seat beside her, or the clink of metal to remind her he still had the knife ready at his side.

The man beside her came awake with a snort and flailing arms. The knife hissed through the air scant inches from her hand and arm, then knocked against the center console, rattling it. Gilly swerved across the center line and back, heart pounding. The man sat up and scrubbed at his face with the hand not wielding the weapon.

"Fuck!"

Gilly shifted in her seat and repositioned her hands on the wheel. She didn't say anything. Her abductor muttered and tapped the hilt of the blade in his hands, then apparently decided to pretend he hadn't been sleeping at all. Maybe he thought she hadn't noticed.

"Where are we?" he blurted as if he didn't realize she ought to be the one with the questions.

Gilly told him by tilting her head toward the road sign they'd just passed. They'd been on the road for two hours. Her thoughts drifted briefly to Arwen and Gandy. Had Seth picked them up yet? Were they home, safe in bed? It was past their bedtime, and Arwen was impossible in the mornings if she didn't have enough sleep….

"I asked you a question!"

The rap of the knife's blade against her shoulder made the car jerk beneath her startled hands. Gilly yelped, though he'd only tapped her with the flat of it. She steadied the massive truck, visions of rolling the huge vehicle punching any other thoughts from her head.

"Pay attention!"

"Sorry," she said, but she didn't sound it. She tried again. "Sorry."

She told him out loud, though by now they'd passed another sign. She watched him scowl at the white letters on the green background, and wondered if he couldn't read. He pulled a crumpled piece of paper from his pocket and held it up, turning on the map light to look at it.

"We need Route 80." He shook the paper at her. "You didn't go the wrong way, did you?"

The unfairness of the accusation stung her into response. "You're the one telling me which way to go!"

She regretted her outburst when he bared his teeth, blood grimed in the cracks, and lifted the knife.

"I have a knife." His voice was hoarse.

"I know you do."

"Don't talk to me like I'm some kind of fucking idiot."

If he was going to cut her, he wouldn't do it while she was driving. He'd make her pull over first. Wouldn't he?

"Sorry."

"Okay." He seemed to think they'd reached some sort of mutual agreement. Gilly didn't know what it might be, but she wasn't going to argue.

"We haven't passed Route 80 yet."

He held up the soiled scrap of paper again. "That's where we need to go."

"We haven't even made it to State College," Gilly said, not pointing out they'd have been long past there if he hadn't made her take such a crazy, circuitous route.

Gilly waited to hear what he'd say next. He didn't speak. The tires thudded. She felt him staring.

"We're going to need gas," she said at last, since even though she loved the quiet, craved it, it frightened her. "Depending on how far we're going."

He leaned close to her to look at the gas gauge. She expected a whiff of sweat, of dirt. An angry or scary odor, something bad.

He smelled like soap and cold air. For the first time she noticed he didn't even wear a winter coat, only jeans and a worn hooded sweatshirt with a zipper. In the green dashboard illumination she couldn't tell the color, but everything on him was dark. Hair, eyes, the growing scruff of a beard she could just make out. A quick glance at his feet revealed huge and battered hiking boots.

"Fuck." He leaned back into his seat. The knife seemed forgotten at his side, but she wasn't sure she could trust that impression. One sudden move and she could find herself with four inches of steel inside her.

Later, when it was all over and she could be totally honest with herself, Gilly would think it was that clean scent of soap and fresh air that let him keep her. That and the silence. People assumed it was the knife, and she never disabused them of that notion, but Gilly knew the truth. He smelled good, and he didn't talk much. It was wrong…but right then, it was enough.

They drove a few more miles in the silence before he sighed heavily and rubbed his eyes. "How much longer before we have to stop?"

She looked at the gauge. "We have less than a quarter of a tank."

Her captor made a muffled sound of disgust. "Next gas station, stop."

They weren't on a particularly populous stretch of road, but it wouldn't be long before they found a station. He leaned forward again to punch the button on the radio and found only static. He punched the button to play the CD. The familiar words of a lullaby, albeit one unconventional and untraditional, blared from the speakers.

"What the hell is this?" He turned down the volume.

Her smile felt out of place but she couldn't stop it. *"Bat Boy: The Musical."*

He listened for a moment longer to the words, a mother's gentle promise to nurture the unloved and unwelcome bat-child found in a cave and brought to her home. The song was one Gilly liked to sing along with, but she didn't now. When it was over and the next song from the campy rock musical had taken over, he stabbed the button on the stereo to turn it off.

"That's weird," he said bluntly. "You listen to that with your kids in the car?"

She thought of Arwen, who hadn't seen the show but loved to sing along with the songs too. "Yes."

He shook his head. "Damn. What's it about?"

His voice had a smoker's rasp. He talked slowly, as if choosing each word was a mental strain, but he didn't slur his words or use bad grammar. His voice matched the rest of him, unkempt and battered.

"It's about Bat Boy." Gilly's eyes scanned the road signs, looking for one that showed an exit or gas station ahead. "It's… it's just fun."

"Who the hell is Bat Boy?"

She hesitated, knowing already how the answer would sound. "He's half human, half bat. They found him in a cave down in Virginia."

"You're shitting me." Even his curses were clipped and precise, as though he was speaking written dialogue instead of his own thoughts.

"It's a story," she said. "From the *Weekly World News*. I don't think it's real."

He laughed. "No shit."

"There's a gas station ahead. Do you want me to pull over?"

She tensed, waiting for his answer. He shrugged, leaned forward to check the gas gauge again. "Yeah."

She signaled and slowed to exit. Her heartbeat accelerated and her palms grew moist. Anxiety gripped her, and a sense of loss she refused to acknowledge because she didn't want to think what it meant.

Apparently he remembered the knife, for now he pulled it up and waved it at her again. "Don't forget I have this."

As if she could. "No."

Ahead of them was the parking lot, busy even at this time of night. Bright lights made Gilly squint. She pulled the truck up to the pumps and turned off the engine. She waited for instructions, though normally being told what to do chafed at her. Now she felt as though she could do nothing else but wait to be told what to do. How to do it.

He leaned close enough to kiss her. His breath smelled like Big Red gum. "Give me the keys."

Gilly pulled them from the ignition and passed them into his palm. His fingers closed over hers, squeezing. She winced.

"If you so much as flick the headlights, I will gut you like a deer. You got that?"

She nodded.

"I'll pump." He waited, looking at her. She saw a flicker of apprehension flash across his face, so fast she wasn't sure she saw it at all. He held up the knife, but low so anyone looking at them wouldn't see it through the windows. "Don't get out of the car. Don't do anything. Remember what I said."

She expected him to ask for money. "I don't have my purse."

He made that sound of disgust again, and now he sounded contemptuous, too. "I don't need your money."

He folded the knife and put it into a leather sheath on his belt, slipped the keys into his pocket, then opened his door and went around to the pump, using the keyless remote to lock the door. He fumbled with the buttons and the handle, finally getting the gas to start. Then he went inside.

Gilly sat and watched him. After a moment, stunned, she realized this was the second time he'd let his attention slide from her. She sat a moment longer, seeing him choose items from the cooler, the racks of snacks and the magazine section.

From this distance she had her first good look at him. He was tall, at least six-two or -three, if she judged correctly. She'd seen his hair was dark, but in the fluorescent lights of the minimart it proved to be a deep chestnut that fell in shaggy sheaves to just below his shoulders. He didn't smile at the clerk and didn't appear to be making small talk, either, as he put his substantial pile of goods on the counter. He motioned to the clerk for several cartons of cigarettes, Marlboro Reds. He was spending a lot of money.

He didn't hurry. He didn't look nervous or wary. She could see the knife in its leather sheath from here, peeking from beneath the hem of his dark gray sweatshirt, but this *was* rural Pennsylvania. Deer-hunting country. Nobody would look at it twice, unless it was to admire it.

Outside, the gas pump clicked off. Gilly shifted in her seat. Inside the market, her abductor pulled an envelope from his sweatshirt pocket and rifled through the contents. He offered a few bills to the clerk, who took the money and started bagging the purchases.

This was it. She could run. He wouldn't chase her. If he did, he couldn't catch her.

She could scream. People would hear. Someone would come. Someone would help her.

She breathed again, not screaming. The white-faced and thin-lipped woman in the rearview mirror could not be her. The smile she forced looked more like the baring of teeth, a feral grin more frightening than friendly.

Time had slowed and stopped, frozen. She'd felt this once

when she'd hit a deer springing out from the woods near her house. One moment the road had been clear, the next her window filled with tawny fur, a body crushing into the front end of the truck and sliding across the windshield to break the glass. She'd seen every stone on the street, every hair on the deer's body before it had all become a haze.

Today she'd felt that slow-syrup of time stopping twice. The first when the man slid across the seat and pointed a knife at her head. The second time was now.

She wasn't going back. Not to the vet appointments, the ballet practice, the laundry and the bills. She wasn't going back to the neediness, the whining, the constant, never-ending demands from spouse and spawn that left her feeling on some days her head might simply explode. She didn't know where she was going, just that it wasn't back.

When he opened the driver's side door, he looked as startled as she must have been when he made his first appearance into her life. "I…I didn't think you'd still be here."

Gilly opened her mouth but said nothing.

His eyes cut back and forth as his mouth thinned. "Move over."

She did, and he got in. He turned the key in the ignition and put the truck in Drive. Gilly didn't speak; she had nothing to say to him. With her feet on the duffel bag he'd squashed onto the passenger side floor, her knees felt like they rubbed her earlobes. He pushed something across the center console at her: the latest edition of some black-and-white knockoff of the *Weekly World News,* not the real thing. The real thing had gone out of publication years before.

"You care if I smoke?"

She did mind; the stench of cigarettes would make her gag and choke. "No."

He punched the lighter and held its glowing tip to the cigarette's end. The smoke stung her eyes and throat, or maybe it was her tears. Gilly turned her face to the window.

He pulled out of the lot and back onto the highway, letting the darkness fall around them with the softness and comfort of a quilt.

3

"Roses don't like to get their feet wet." Gilly's mother wears a broad-brimmed straw hat. She holds up her trowel, her hands unprotected by gloves, her fingernails dark with dirt. Her knuckles, too, grimed deep with black earth. "Look, Gillian. Pay attention."

Gilly will never be good at growing roses. She loves the way they look and smell, but roses take too much time and attention. Roses have rules. Her mother has time to spend on pruning, fertilizing. Tending. Nurturing. But Gilly doesn't. Gilly never has enough time.

She's dreaming. She knows it by the way her mother smiles and strokes the velvety petals of the red rose in her hand. Her mother hasn't smiled like that in a long time, and if she has maybe it was only ever in Gilly's dreams. The roses all around them are real enough, or at least the memory of them is. They'd grown in wild abundance against the side of her parents' house and along gravel paths laid out in the backyard. Red, yellow, blushing pink, tinged with peach. The only ones she sees now, though, are the red ones. Roses with names like

After Midnight, Black Ice, even one called Cherry Cola. They're all in bloom.

"Pay attention," Gilly's mother repeats and holds out the rose. "Roses are precious and fragile things. They take a lot of work, but it's all worth it."

The only flowers that grow at Gilly's house are daffodils and dandelions, perennials the deer and squirrels leave alone. Her garden is empty. "I've tried, Mom. My roses die."

Gilly's mother closes her fist around the rose's stem. Bright blood appears. This rose has thorns.

"Because you neglected them, Gillian. Your roses died because you don't pay attention."

"Mom. Your hand."

Her mother's smile doesn't fade. Doesn't wilt. She moves forward to press the rose into Gilly's hand. Gilly doesn't want to take it. Her mother is passing the responsibility to her, and she doesn't want it. She tries to keep her fingers closed, refusing the flower. Her mother grips her wrist.

"Take it, Gillian."

This is the woman Gilly remembers better. Wild eyes, mouth thin and grim. Hair lank and in her face, the hat gone now in the way dreams have of changing. Her mother's fingers bite into Gilly's skin, sharp as thorns and bringing blood.

"You love them," Gilly's mother says. "Don't you love them?"

"I do love them!" Gilly cries.

"You have to take care of what you love," her mother says. "Even if it makes you bleed."

Gilly woke, startled and disoriented. She didn't know how long she'd slept, how far they'd gone. Didn't know where they were. She rolled her stiff neck on shoulders gone just as sore and stared out to dark roads and encroaching trees. Steep mountains hung with frozen miniwaterfalls rose on both sides.

A train track ran parallel to the road, separated by a metal fence.

Had she seen these roads before? Gilly didn't think so. Nothing looked familiar. The man took an unmarked exit. They rode for another hour on forested roads rough enough to make her glad for four-wheel drive, then turned down another narrow, rutted road. Ice gleamed in the ruts, and the light layer of snow that had been worn away on the main road still remained here. A rusted metal gate with a medieval-looking padlock blocked the way.

He pulled a jangling ring of keys from the pocket of his sweatshirt and held them out to her. "Unlock it."

Gilly didn't take the keys at first. It made no sense for her to defy him. In the faint light from the dashboard his narrowed eyes should have been menacing enough to have her leaping to obey his command even if the threat of the knife wasn't. Yet she sat, staring at him dumbly, unable to move.

"Get out and unlock the gate," he repeated, shaking the key ring at her. "I'm going to drive through. You close it behind me and lock it again."

She didn't move for another long moment, frozen in place the way she'd been so often tonight.

"You deaf?"

She shook her head.

"Just fucking stupid, then. I told you to move. Now move your ass," he said in a low, menacing voice, "or I will move it for you."

This morning she'd stood in her closet, picking out clothes without holes or too many stains, jeans with a button and zipper instead of soft lounge pants with an elastic waist. She'd dressed to go out in public, not like the stay-home mom she was. She'd wanted to look nice for once, not dumpy and covered in sticky fingerprints.

She should've worn warm boots, not the useless chunk-heeled ones that hurt her feet if she stood too long. No help for it now. She'd chosen fashion over function and now had to face the consequences. Gilly got out of the car. Immediately she slipped on some ice and almost went down, but managed to keep upright by flailing her arms. She wrenched her back, the pain enough to distract her from the tingling in her drive-numbed legs.

Frigid air burned her eyes, forcing her to slit them. Her nose went numb almost at once, her bare fingers too. The padlock had rusted shut, and the key wouldn't turn. Her fingers fumbled, slipped, and blood oozed from a gash along her thumb. It looked like ketchup in the headlights. Gilly clasped her hands and tried to warm them, tried to bend her fingers back into place, but they crooked like talons.

At last the key turned with a squeal, and the hasp popped open. She slipped the lock off and pushed the gate forward. Ice clinked and jingled as it fell off the metal. The gate stuck halfway open, grinding, and she pushed hard, her feet slipping in the icy ruts. Her palms stung against the cold metal; she had a brief vision of the movie *A Christmas Story* and the boy who stuck his tongue to the pole, but fortunately her hands didn't stick. She grunted as she shoved once more. More pain in her back, her hands, her freezing face, her cramped toes. The gate groaned open the rest of the way, and the truck pulled through.

It didn't stop right away and for one panicked moment Gilly thought he was going to leave her behind. Then the red glare of the taillights came on, bathing everything in a horror-show haze. Once open, the gate wouldn't close. Gilly pulled the sleeves of her jacket down over her palms to get a better grip and protect her hands, but that only made them slip worse. She tugged, hard, and fell on her ass.

The truck revved. Gilly got to her feet, slipping and sliding. He hadn't stabbed her. He wasn't going to drive away and leave her here to freeze, either. She ran anyway as best she could on frozen toes. Her fingers slipped again on the door handle. Gilly climbed back into the truck and slammed the door.

He drove for another thirty minutes along a road so twisted and potholed Gilly had to grip the door handle just to keep herself upright every time the truck bounced. Trees pressed in on them. Some branches even snaked out to scrape along the truck's side. At one point, the battered driveway took a steep pitch upward. The tires spun on loose gravel. They were climbing.

At last, the man stopped the truck in front of a battered two-story house, bathing it in the twin beams of the bright headlights. *House* was too flattering a term. It was more like a shack. A sagging front porch with three rickety steps lined the front. Green rocking chairs, the sort with legs made from a single piece of bended metal, lined the porch. Gilly had seen chairs like that in 1950s pictures of her grandparents vacationing in the Catskills.

He turned off the ignition. Darkness clapped its hand over her eyes. Gilly blinked, momentarily blind.

"Get out," the man said without preamble.

He opened the door and stepped into the glacial night air, then shoved the keys into the pocket of his ratty sweatshirt, slammed the door shut and headed toward the house without hesitation. He quickly blended into the dark.

Without the light of the headlamps to guide her, the distance from the truck to the front porch became instantly unnavigable. She already knew the ground here was frozen and hard. At best she'd fall on her ass again. At worst, she'd end up with a broken leg.

Gilly put her hand on the door. Tremors tickled her, and her fingers twitched on the handle. Her feet jittered on the duffel bag. Only her eyes felt wide and staring, motionless while the rest of her body went into some strange sort of Saint Vitus' dance.

She was dreaming. Was she dreaming? Was this real? In the dark, the silent dark, Gilly had to press her twitching fingers to her eyelids to convince herself they were open. Like a blind woman she felt the contours of her face, trying to convince herself that it was her own and uncertain, in the end, if it was.

The slanting shack began to glow from the four windows along its front. The light was strange, yellow and dim, but it gave her the courage to open the door. The meager glow was just enough to allow Gilly to make her stumbling way to the front porch steps, and then through the door he'd left open.

She entered a small, square room with a sooty woodstove on a raised brick platform between the two windows along the back wall. Now she could see why the light coming from the windows seemed so odd. Propane, not electric, lights illuminated the room. She wrinkled her nose against the smell, which reminded her of summer camp.

Despite the stains and dirt on the carpet she could see it was indisputably green. Not emerald, not hunter, but mossy and dull. The color of mold. The furniture grouped around the woodstove was faded brown plaid with rough-hewn wooden arms and feet. The two long sofas facing each other across a battered coffee table looked in decent enough condition, but the two chairs beside them had seen better days. Time or rodents had put holes in the plaid fabric, and stuffing peeked out here and there. The scarred dining table had four matching chairs and a fifth and sixth that didn't match the set or each other. Someone long ago had tried to make it pretty with an arrangement of silk flowers, now dusty and only sad. A larger camping lantern, newer than the wall sconces but unlit, also sat upon the table.

To her right Gilly saw the kitchen, separated from the living room by a countertop and row of hanging cabinets. Through the narrow gap between them she saw another table and chairs. Off the kitchen she thought there might be a mudroom or pantry. She glimpsed the man standing at the refrigerator, mumbling curses. Maybe at the emptiness, maybe at the stench of mildew and age that she could smell even from here.

Gilly closed the door behind her with a solid, remorseless thud.

"Smells like a damn rat died in the fridge."

Gilly wasn't positive he spoke to her or just at her. She swallowed her disgust at the thought and looked around the room again. Through the door immediately to her left she spied a linoleum floor and the glint of metal fixtures. A bathroom. The doorway farther back along the wall hinted at a set of steep, narrow stairs. That was it. Upstairs must be bedrooms.

"I need to take a piss," he told her matter-of-factly. Carrying a large battery-powered lantern, he brushed past her and into the bathroom. Next came the sound of water gushing, then a toilet flushing. At least the facilities worked.

Her own bladder cramped, muscles that had never been the same since her pregnancies protesting. When he came out, she went in. He'd left her the lantern. She peed for what felt like hours. At the sink, washing her hands, a stranger peered out at her from the cloudy mirror. A woman with lank hair, dark to match the circles under her eyes, and skin the color of moonlight. She looked like her mother.

She'd run away just like her mother.

She tried for dismay and felt only resignation. Her eyes itched and burned, and not even splashing cold water helped. She breathed in through her nose, out through her mouth, her stomach lurching. She didn't puke. Eyes closed, Gilly gripped the sink for one dizzy moment thinking she would open them and find herself at home in front of her own mirror, all of this some insane fantasy she'd concocted out of frustration. Wishful thinking. Maybe crazy would be better than this.

When Gilly came out of the bathroom, she found the man sitting at the dining room table. He'd lit the lamp there and spread out a bunch of wrinkled papers. He held his head in his hands like the act of reading them all had given him a headache.

Gilly cleared her throat, then realized she hadn't used her voice since they'd stopped for gas. Four, five hours ago? Less than that or longer, she had no idea. She waited for him to look up, but he didn't.

He ran his fingers again and again through the dark lengths of his hair, until it crackled with static in the cold air. Gilly waited, shifting from foot to foot. Awkward, uncertain. Even if she did speak, what could she possibly say?

He looked up. Under the thin scruff of black beard, his face had fine, clean lines. Thick black lashes fringed his deep brown eyes, narrowed now beneath equally dark brows. He wasn't ugly, and she couldn't force herself to find him so. With a shock, Gilly realized he wasn't much younger than she was, maybe three or four years.

"My uncle," he said suddenly, looking up at her.

Gilly waited for more, and when it didn't come she slipped

into one of the battered chairs. She folded her hands on the cold wood. It felt rough beneath her fingers.

He touched the pile of papers, shoving a couple of them toward her. "This was my Uncle Bill's place."

Gilly made no move to take the papers. She found her voice, as rusty as the gate had been. "It's…quaint."

His brow furrowed. "You making fun of me?"

She expected anger. More knife waving. Perhaps even threats. Anger she could handle. Fight. She could be angry in response. Instead she felt hollow shame. He'd spoken in the resigned fashion of a man used to people mocking him, and she *had* been making fun.

"Was it a hunting cabin?"

"Yeah." He looked around. "But he lived here, too. Fixed it up a little at a time. I used to come here with him, sometimes. Uncle Bill died a couple months ago."

Condolences rose automatically to her lips and she pressed them closed. It would be ridiculous to express sorrow over a stranger's death, especially to this man. Her fingers curled against the table. Surreal, all of this.

You're not dreaming this, Gilly. You know that, right? This is real. It's happening.

She knew it better than anything and yet still couldn't manage to process it. She stared across the table. "He left you this cabin?"

"Yeah. It's all mine now." He nodded and gave her a grin shocking in its rough beauty, its normality. They might've been chatting over coffee. This was more terrifying than his anger had been.

She looked around the room, like maybe it might look better with another glance. It didn't. "It's cold in here."

He shrugged, pulling the sleeves of his sweatshirt down over his fingertips and hugging his arms around himself. "Yeah. I could light a fire. That'll help."

"It's late," Gilly pointed out. She'd been about to say she needed to go to bed, but she didn't want him to get the wrong idea. Fear flared again as she watched him run his tongue along the curve of his smile. He was bigger than she was and certainly stronger. She wouldn't be able to stop him from forcing her.

"Yeah" was all he said, though, and made no move to leap across the table to ravish her. He blinked, cocking his head in a puppyish fashion that might have been endearing under other circumstances. "Let's go to bed."

Stricken, Gilly didn't move even when he pushed away from the table and gestured to her. Her throat dried. *Lie back and enjoy it,* she thought irrationally, remembering what a friend of hers had said a blind date gone horribly wrong had told her to do. Gilly's friend had kicked the would-be rapist in the nuts and run away, but Gilly had given up the chance for running back at the gas station. Even if she ran, now, where would she go?

He went to the propane lamps and lowered the flames to a dim glow, then jerked his head toward the steep, narrow stairs. "Beds are upstairs. C'mon."

On wobbly legs she followed him. She'd been right about the stairs. Dark, steep, narrow and splintery. Festooned with cobwebs and lit only by the lantern he carried.

The stairs entered directly into one large room that made up the entire upstairs. More propane sconces, wreathed in spiderwebs furry with dust, lined the walls beneath the peaked roof. The windows on each end were grimy with dirt and more cobwebs. A waist-high partition with a space to walk through divided the room in half widthwise. A low, slatted wall protected unwary people from falling down the stairs.

"Beds." He pointed. "You can have the one back there."

He meant beyond the partition. Gilly realized he didn't intend to follow her when he handed her the lantern. She passed the double row of twin beds, three on each side of the room, then went through the open space in the middle of the partition. On the other side were a sagging full-size bed, a dresser, an armoire and an ancient rocking chair. A faded rag rug covered the wooden plank floor.

"Cozy," she muttered and set the lantern on the dresser.

The man had already crawled into one of the beds on the other side. Gilly, mouth pursed with hesitant distaste, pulled back the heavy, musty comforter. The sheets beneath were no longer white, but still fairly clean. Nothing rustled in them, at least nothing she could see.

She unlaced her useless boots and slipped them off with a sigh, wriggling her toes. She hadn't realized how much they hurt until she took off her boots. Without removing her coat, Gilly crawled into bed and pulled the knobby cover up to her chin. The thought of putting her head on the pillow made her cringe, and she pulled her hood up to cover her hair.

His voice came at her out of the dark. "What's your name, anyway?"

"Gillian. Gilly."

"I'm Todd."

She heard the squeak of springs as he settled further into the mattress. Then exhaustion claimed her, and she fell asleep.

4

What finally woke Gilly was not a warm body burrowing next to hers and the stench of an overripe diaper. Nor was it the sudden blaring of a television tuned permanently to the cartoon channel. What woke her this morning was the numbness of her face.

She hadn't slept without nightly interruption for more than five years but now her eyes drifted open slowly. Gradually. Bright morning sunshine dimmed by the dirt on the window glass filled the room. She'd rolled herself into the covers, cocooned against the bitter winter air. Her hood, pulled up around her hair, had kept her head warm enough. Her face, though, had lain exposed all night. She couldn't feel her cheeks or her nose or her lips.

The night rushed back at her. Her heart thumped, and her mouth behind the frozen lips went dry. Gilly sat up in the sagging double bed, fighting to untangle the covers that had protected her through the night.

She managed to push them off. On stiff legs she got out of bed and hugged her coat around her. Her boots were gone.

Everything in the dusty attic room shone with an unreal clarity that defied the fuzziness of her thoughts. How long had she slept? The sudden, panicked thought she might have slept for more than just one night, that she'd been gone for days, forced her into action.

In the light of day she could no longer take solace in the dark to hide her actions, to excuse her decisions. She'd made a terrible mistake last night. She could only hope she had the chance to fix it.

Gilly pounded down the stairs, breath frosting out in front of her. She hurtled into the living room and stumbled over her own feet. She caught herself on the back of the hideous plaid sofa.

From the kitchen, Todd swung his shaggy brown head around to look at her from his place at the stove. "You all right?"

She didn't miss the irony of his concern. "Yeah. Thanks."

By the time she walked across the living room and entered the kitchen, her stomach had begun to grumble like thunder. The last thing she'd eaten was half a granola bar Arwen had begged for and then refused because it had raisins in it. Gilly swallowed against the rush of saliva.

"Hungry?" A cigarette hung from Todd's mouth and wreaths of smoke circled his head. He lifted a spatula. "I'm making breakfast. Take your coat off. Stay awhile."

Gilly wrinkled her nose at the stench of smoke and didn't laugh at what he'd obviously meant to be funny. With her stomach making so much noise she couldn't pretend she wasn't hungry, though she didn't want to admit it. "I'm cold. What time is it?"

Todd shrugged and held up a wrist bare of anything but a smattering of dark hair. “Dunno. I don’t have a watch.”

Her stomach told her she’d slept well past eleven. Maybe even past noon. It grumbled again, and she pressed her hands into her belly to stop the noise.

Gilly looked around the kitchen. The propane-powered appliances were old, like the chairs on the porch, straight out of the 1950s. Green flowered canisters labeled Flour, Coffee, Sugar and Tea, and a vintage table and chairs set stuck off in one corner prompted her to mutter, “You could make a fortune on eBay selling this stuff.”

Todd swiveled his head to look at her again. “What?”

“Nothing.”

From the stove in front of him came the sound of sizzling and the smell of something good. A wire camping toaster resting on the table held two slices of bread, a little browner than she preferred. Her stomach didn’t seem to care.

“Toast,” Todd said unnecessarily. He pointed with the spatula. “There’s butter and jelly in the fridge.”

All this as casual as coffee, she thought. All of this as though there was nothing wrong. She might’ve woken at a friend’s house or a bed and breakfast. She shuddered, stomach twisting again. She fisted her hands at her sides, but there was nothing she could grab on to that would stop the world from turning.

“Christ, move your ass! Put it on the table,” Todd said, voice prompting as if she was an idiot.

She jumped. The command got her feet moving, anyway. Not from fear—he didn’t sound angry, just annoyed. More a point of pride, that she wasn’t so scared of him she couldn’t move, or so stupid she couldn’t figure out how to eat breakfast.

Remembering his comments the night before, Gilly hesitated to open the refrigerator. She expected to recoil from the smell of dead rodents and had one hand already up to her nose in preparation. The interior of the appliance was not sparkling; age would prevent that from ever being true again. But it was clean. The caustic but somehow pleasant scent of cleanser drifted to her nostrils. Food filled every shelf, crammed into every corner. Jugs of milk and juice, loaves of bread, packages of bologna and turkey and deli bags of cheese. The freezer was the same, bulging with packages of ground beef and chicken breasts. No vegetables that she could see, but plenty of junk food in brightly colored boxes, full of chemicals and fat. The sort of food she bought but felt guilty for serving.

"You went shopping."

"Even bastards gotta eat," Todd said.

Gilly pulled out the jumbo-size containers of jelly and margarine, not real butter, and set them on the table. She shifted on her feet, uncertain what to do next. She wasn't used to not being the one at the stove. The bare table beckoned, and she opened cupboards in search of plates and cups, pulled out a drawer to look for silverware. The tiny kitchen meant they needed complicated choreography to get around each other, but she managed to set the table while Todd shifted back and forth at the stove to give her room to maneuver.

When at last she'd finished and stood uncertainly at the table, Todd turned with a steaming skillet in one hand. "Sit down."

Gilly sat. Todd set the skillet on the table without putting a hot pad underneath it, but Gilly supposed it wouldn't matter. One more scorch mark on the silver-dappled white veneer would hardly make much of a difference.

Todd scooped a steaming pile of eggs, yellow interspersed

with suspicious pink bits, onto her plate. Gilly just stared at it. She smelled bacon, which of course she wouldn't eat, and which of course he couldn't know.

Instead she spread her browned toast with a layer of margarine and jelly and bit into it. The flavor of it burst on her tongue, igniting her hunger. She gobbled the rest of the bread and left only crumbs.

A teakettle she hadn't noticed began to whistle. Todd left the table to switch off the burner and pull two chipped mugs from one of the cupboards. Into each he dropped a tea bag and filled the mugs with the boiling water, then pushed one across the table at her.

He took his chair again and settled into the act of eating as naturally as if he'd known her all their lives. He ate with gusto, great gulps and lip smacking. His fork went from the plate to his mouth and back again, with little pause. Watching him, Gilly was reminded of the way their dog crouched over his bowl to keep the cat from stealing the food. Her stomach shriveled in envy. One piece of toast wasn't going to be enough.

He paused in his consumption long enough to look up at her. "You not eating? There's plenty. I made extra."

The sudden loud gurgle of her stomach would make her a liar if she said no. "Maybe some more toast."

The smooth skin of his brow furrowed. "You don't like eggs?"

Gilly pointed to the skillet. "Ah…they've got bacon mixed in with them."

Todd licked his lips. The gesture was feral and wary, as though she was trying to trick him and he knew it, but wasn't sure how to stop her. "Yeah?"

"I don't eat bacon," Gilly explained. Her stomach gurgled

louder. She'd no more eat the breakfast he'd cooked than she would kick a puppy, but the smell *was* making her mouth water.

"Why not?"

"I'm Jewish," she said simply. "I don't eat pork."

Todd swiped his sweatshirt sleeve across his lips. "What?"

Gilly was used to having to explain herself. "I don't eat bacon. I'm Jewish."

Todd looked down at his plate and shoved the last few bites of pig-tainted eggs around with his fork. When he looked up at her, she noticed his eyes were the same shade as milk chocolate. "You don't look Jewish."

The comment, so ripe with anti-Semitism, was one she'd heard often and which never ceased to rankle. "Well, you don't look crazy."

He cocked his head at her, again lining the rim of his lips with his tongue. From any other young man the gesture might have been sensual or even aggressively, overtly sexual. On Todd, it merely made him look warily contemplative. Like a dog that's been kicked too many times but keeps coming to the back door, anyway. Mistrustful, waiting for the blow, but unable to stop returning.

"Uncle Bill always made the eggs that way up here," he said finally. "He called them camp eggs. But I can make you some without bacon, if you want."

She wanted to deny him that kindness, to keep him as the villain. Her stomach gurgled some more, and she couldn't. "I'll make them."

She pushed away from the table, heat stinging in her cheeks. Why should she feel guilty? He was the bad guy. He'd held a knife on her, kidnapped her, stolen her vehicle. Put her kids in danger.

"Can you use this skillet, or…" His voice trailed off uncertainly from behind her. "Or do you need one that didn't have pig in it?"

Again she thought of a kicked dog, slinking around the back door hoping for a moment of kindness, and the heat burned harder in her face. That she doubted there was any utensil in this cabin that hadn't at some point touched something nonkosher didn't really matter. He was trying to be considerate. This, like his concern when she'd tripped, was scarier than if he'd shouted and threatened. This made him…normal.

And if he was normal, what did that make her?

"No, I can just wash it out. That one will be fine."

He scraped the remains of the skillet onto his plate and handed it to her. She washed it, then opened the fridge and pulled out the cardboard carton of eggs. She opened two cupboards before she found a bowl and rinsed it free of any dust that might have gathered. She cracked the first egg into it, checking automatically for blood spots that would make it inedible.

The skin on the back of her neck prickled. He was watching her, and of course. What else would he look at but this woman in his kitchen, a stranger he'd stolen? Gilly broke another egg with crushing fingers, bits of shell falling into yellow yolk.

"How long have you been Jewish?"

It wasn't the question she'd expected. "My whole life."

Todd laughed. "I guess that's about how long I've been crazy."

Crazy.

She'd thrown out the term offhandedly, the way most people did, not meaning it. The way Todd had, himself. His tone had told her he didn't think he was crazy. Not really. Gilly didn't think he was crazy, either. Gilly knew crazy.

Crazy was having a chance to escape and ignoring it, not just once, but many times. Crazy was wanting to escape in the first place.

Her stomach lurched into her throat, bile bitter on the back of her tongue. She swallowed convulsively. She wasn't hungry anymore. She beat the eggs anyway and poured them into the skillet along with some margarine. The smooth yellow mess curdled and cooked. Gilly knew she wouldn't be able to eat it now no matter how hollow her stomach. She removed the eggs from the stove and turned off the flame.

She sipped in a breath, forming her words with care, keeping her tone light and easy. Casual as coffee. "Where are we, by the way?"

"My uncle's cabin. I told you last night."

Keeping her back to him, Gilly gripped the edge of the counter. "No. I mean…*where* are we? We drove a long time. I fell asleep. I don't know where we are."

A beat of silence. Then, "I'm not telling you. Jesus, you think I'm stupid enough to do that?"

Last night he'd held a knife to her and she'd been angry; this morning, faced with the kindness of breakfast and his sullen but nonaggressive tone, Gilly had to dig deeper than her fear to find even a thread of fury. She drew in a breath and then another. She gripped the counter so hard her knuckles turned white and one nail bent and cracked.

She turned to face him. "Todd. That's your name, right? Todd, you have to take me back. Or take me someplace. Let me go."

He wasn't looking at her. He shook his shaggy head and got up from the table to stalk to the living room with a handful of paper napkins he used to build up the fire in the sooty woodstove. He went to the table and picked up a bulging folder, then took it to the woodstove where he crouched in front of its warmth, sifting through the papers. Every so often he threw one of them into the blaze.

"Please," Gilly said from the kitchen.

Todd ignored her, bent to his task with a single-minded self-absorption. He muttered as he worked, but she couldn't make out the words. Gilly moved to the living room, wanting to draw closer to the fire's warmth but feeling as though it was up to her to keep a proper distance between them. There had to be something for her to say or do to make him listen.

If she ran away now, would he chase her? Gilly's head felt fuzzy, her thoughts mangled, but everything in the cabin seemed too sharp, too clear. Looking at things straight on hurt her eyes. She couldn't blame exhaustion since she'd had the longest night's sleep she'd had since before being pregnant with Arwen.

She'd felt this way before, when the pain of childbirth had made time stretch on into an unfathomable and interminable length. When the drugs she'd been taking for a sinus infection had made her feel as though she were constantly floating. Now it was the same, every minute lasting an hour, her head a balloon tethered to her shoulders by a gossamer thread that could snap at any minute.

You did this to yourself, Gillian. You know you did. Now you pay the price.

It was her mother's voice again, stern and strong. Gilly thought of the dream she'd had while driving. Roses and thorns and blood and love.

The fire warmed the room and she shrugged out of her coat. She hung it on the back of a chair. "Todd."

Todd shuffled his pile of papers together and held them out to her. "Read this."

Her first instinct was to say no, but wouldn't it be better to do what he wanted than to antagonize him? Gilly sat on the plaid couch and took the offered papers. The first was a bank statement. The name at the top of the account was Todd Blauch. The previous balance was for a little more than five thousand dollars. One withdrawal had been made a couple weeks ago for the entire amount. That explained the envelope at the minimart.

She explained what that meant. He gave her that look again, the one that said he knew she mocked him, he just wasn't sure how cruelly. "I know that."

"You told me to read them."

"I know *that* one," he said. "I need help with the ones under that one."

She took a look. The legal-size sheets would have been incomprehensible to her even without the crumpling and staining. It was some sort of legal document. A will. All she could really make out were the names Bill Lutz and Todd Blauch. There was a bunch of mumbo jumbo about property lines and taxes. Deeds.

"Is it the will saying you've inherited the cabin?"

Todd sighed. "Yeah. But there's too many words on that paper. Lots of little words always mean there's something they can catch you on."

"I'm pretty sure that's all it says," Gilly told him. "But I'm not a lawyer."

"That would've been my luck," Todd muttered. "To get stuck with a lawyer."

"You're not stuck with me."

Todd stuffed the papers back in his folder. "Shit, Gilly."

"You took my boots." It wasn't a question.

He stared at her sideways, head cocked and his thick dark hair hanging over one eye. "Yeah."

"So I couldn't run away."

He shrugged but didn't answer.

Gilly screwed up her courage with a deep breath. She lifted her chin, determined her voice would not tremble. "Do you want sex?"

He looked as stunned as if she'd slapped him across the face. Her words propelled him from the couch. Todd turned from her, facing the woodstove, his shoulders hunched.

"Jesus. No!"

"If that's what you want," she continued, her voice a calm floating cloud that did not seem to come from the rest of her, "then I will let you do whatever you want…if you let me go…."

He whirled around, and to her surprise, his tawny cheeks had bloomed the color of aged brick. "I don't want to fuck you!"

Gilly shook her head, immensely relieved but inexplicably offended. "What do you want me for, then?"

"I didn't want you at all, I just wanted the fucking truck. Jesus fucking Christ. Shit!" He smacked his fist into the palm of his hand with each invective. "What the hell?"

She pressed her hands tightly together to prevent them from trembling, but nothing could stop the quaver in her voice. "I just thought…"

He tossed up his hands at her, forcing her to silence. He lit a cigarette, staring at her while the smoke leaked from his nose in twin streams like the breath of a dragon. The steady glare was disconcerting, but she forced herself to meet it.

"You think I stole you?" Todd said slowly. "I mean, you look at me and you think I'm a guy who takes women?"

"You *did* take me!"

"Yeah, well," he said, "I didn't mean to."

I didn't mean to.

It was one of the things Seth said when he wanted to sound like he was apologizing but really wasn't. Gilly hated that phrase so much it automatically curled her lip and made her want to spit. The noise forced from her throat sounded suspiciously like a growl.

"How could you not mean to? I was in the truck. You got in with a…with a knife!" Her words caught, her voice hoarse. "How was that an accident? What happened? Did some big wind come up and just blow you into my car?"

"I didn't say it was an accident. I just said I didn't take you on purpose!"

"There's no difference!" Gilly cried.

Todd stared at her long and hard. "There is a fucking difference."

Shouting would solve nothing and might, in fact, make things worse. Gilly made herself sound calm and poised. "I want you to let me go, Todd."

"Can't."

His simple answer infuriated her. "What do you plan to do with me, then?"

He shrugged, sucking on the cigarette until his cheeks hollowed. "Hell if I know."

"Someone will find me."

He stared at her, long and hard, through narrowed eyes. Todd didn't look away. Gilly did.

"I don't think anyone *will* find you," he said. "Not for a while, anyway, and by then…"

"By then, what?" She stood to face him, but he only shrugged. She softened her tone. Cajoled, tempting that boot-kicked dog closer with a piece of steak. "Look. Just give me my boots. I'll hike down to the main road and…hitch a ride. Or something. Find a gas station."

He snorted laughter. "No, you won't. You'd never make it. Christ, it's…" He stopped himself, wary again, as if telling her the distance would give her any sort of clue where they were. "It's too far."

"I'd make it," Gilly said in a low voice.

"No," Todd said. "You wouldn't."

Images of a mass grave, multiple rotting bodies, filled her brain. Gilly swallowed hard. Fear tasted a little like metal, but she had to ask the question. "Are you going to kill me?"

Todd started. "No! Jesus Christ, no."

There was no counting to ten this time, nothing to hold her back from rising hysteria. "Because if you are, you should do it now. Right away! Just do it and get it over with!"

Todd flinched at first in the face of her shouting, then frowned. "I didn't bring you here to kill you. The fuck you think I am, a psycho?"

Gilly quieted, chest heaving with breath that hurt her lungs. Her throat had gone dry, her mouth parched and arid. Todd stared, then shook his head and laughed.

"You do. You really do think I'm crazy. Fuck my life, you think I'm a fucking psycho."

Gilly shot her gaze toward the front door and expected him to step in front of her, but Todd just tossed up his hands.

"Go, then," he said derisively. "See how far you get. People die all the time in the woods, and that's ones smart enough to have the right gear with them. You don't have gear, you got nothing. See how long it takes your ass to freeze."

"The police," she offered halfheartedly. "They'll be looking for me."

"Where?"

He had a point, one she didn't want to acknowledge. "They can trace things. The truck, for one."

"The fuck you think this is, CSI?" Todd shrugged. "Maybe. Maybe not."

Gilly looked again to the door and then at the floor in defeat. "Please. I'll give you whatever you want."

"You can't give me what I want," Todd said.

Gilly went to the front windows and looked out at the yard. Her truck was there, but she had no keys. The forest ringing the patchy, rocky grass looked thick and unwelcoming, the road little more than a path. He was right. She wouldn't get far. Running out there would be stupid, especially without shoes.

She had to be smarter than that.

"I need to clean up," Gilly said finally. "Brush my teeth, wash my face…"

She trailed off when he walked past her. He picked up a plastic shopping bag from the dining room table, and for the first time she noticed there were many of those bags on the chairs and beneath the table. He tossed her the first one.

It landed at her feet, and she jumped. Gilly bent and touched the plastic, but didn't look inside. He'd bought more than groceries.

"Go ahead." Todd poked at the other bags on the table. "Look."

"What's all this for?" Gilly sifted through a stack of turtleneck shirts, one in nearly every color.

Todd pushed another handful of bulging plastic sacks toward her. "I had all my stuff with me. You didn't have anything."

Gilly pulled out a pair of sparkly tights. She said nothing, turning them over and over in her fingers. They were her size. She didn't even know they made sparkly tights in her size. She looked up at him.

Todd shrugged.

She let the tights drop onto the rest of the pile and wiped her now-sweating palms on her thighs. Her heart began to pound again.

"All of this… You bought enough to last for months," she said finally.

Todd stubbed out his cigarette in a saucer on the table and lit another, flicking the lighter expertly with his left hand. He sucked deep and held it before letting the smoke seep from between his lips. "The fuck am I supposed to know what a woman needs? You needed shit. I bought it."

Gilly steadied herself with one hand on the back of a chair. "I won't be here for months."

Todd flipped the lid of his lighter open and shut a couple of times before sliding it back into his pocket. Without answering her, he stalked to the woodstove and piled a few logs on the fire it didn't need. His faded flannel shirt rode up as he knelt, exposing a line of flesh above the waist of his battered jeans.

If she could stab him there, he'd bleed like any other man. The thought swelled, unbidden, in her mind. She could run at him. Grab his knife. She could sink it deep into his back. For one frightening moment the urge to do it was so strong that Gilly saw Todd's blood on her hands. She blinked, and the crimson vanished.

Gilly sifted through the contents of the bags. He'd bought soap and shampoo, toothpaste. Shirts, sweatpants, socks, a few six-packs of plain cotton underpants in a style she hadn't worn in years. No shoes, no gloves or scarf, no hat.

She rubbed her middle finger between her eyes, where a pain was brewing. It seemed he'd thought of just about everything. Nothing fancy, all practical, and probably all of it would fit her. She thought she should be grateful he hadn't bought her something creepy like a kinky maid's outfit. She thought she should be happy he'd bought her clothes and wasn't going to skin her to make a dress for himself, that's what she should be grateful for.

Gilly gathered as many of the bags as she could. "Is there a shower?"

"Outside. There's a tub in the bathroom."

The plastic shifted and slipped in her fingers as she took the bags and went into the bathroom. She shut the door behind her. There was no lock. The room's one small window slid up easily halfway, but then stuck. She would never fit through it. And if she did, where would she go? How far would she get with no coat or gloves and nothing but socks on her feet, with no idea where she was or how to get anywhere else? Todd was right, people died all the time in the woods.

"You didn't bring any water?" This comes from Seth, looking surprised. "But you always bring everything."

Not this time, apparently. Gilly shifts baby Gandy on one hip and watches Arwen toddle along the boardwalk through the trees. There are miles of boardwalk and lots of stairs at Bushkill Falls, and who knew it would take so long to walk them, or that there'd be no convenient snack stands along the way? Gilly's thirsty too, her back aches from carrying Gandy in the sling, her heart races as Arwen gets too close to the railing.

Gilly is the planner. The packer. The prepared one. Seth is accustomed to walking out the door with nothing but his wallet and keys, and if he slings the diaper bag over his shoulder it's without bothering to look inside. He trusts her to be prepared. To have everything they could possibly need and a lot of stuff they won't.

"I can't believe you didn't pack water," Seth says, and Gilly fumes, silent and stung, her own throat dry with thirst.

That had been an awful trip. Walking for miles to see the beauty of the waterfalls that she'd have enjoyed more without the rumble of hunger and a parched mouth distracting her. And that had been along set paths, no place to get lost, in temperate autumn. What would happen to her if she set out without shoes into the frigid mid-January air and tried to make her way down a mountain, through the forest, without having a clue about where she was going?

No. She had to plan better than that. Be prepared. Because once she started, there'd be no going back.

First, she'd get cleaned up. The tub, a deep claw-foot, was filthy with a layer of dust and some dead bugs. The toilet was the old-fashioned kind with a tank above and a pull chain. It would've been quaint and charming in a bed-and-breakfast.

Gilly set the bags on the chipped porcelain countertop and pulled out a package of flowery soap. Her skin itched just looking at it. Further exploration brought out a long, slim package. A purple, sparkly toothbrush. The breath whooshed from her lungs as if she'd been punched in the stomach. Gilly let out a low cry, holding on to the sink top to keep her buckling knees from dropping her to the ground. Shudders racked her body, so fierce her teeth clattered sharply.

He'd bought her a toothbrush.

The simple consideration, not the first from him, undid her. Gilly pressed her forehead to the wall, her palms flat on the rough paneling. Sobs surged up her throat and she bit down hard, jailing them behind her teeth. She cursed into her fists, silent, strangled cries she didn't want him to overhear. She didn't want to give him that.

Count to ten, Gilly. Count to twenty if you have to. Keep it in, don't let it out. You'll lose it if you let it out.

You'll lose you.

Gilly clutched at her cheeks and bit the inside of her wrist until the pain there numbed the agony in her heart. He'd given her opportunity to escape, and she hadn't taken it. Had been unable to take it.

She was crazy, not him. She was the psycho. It was her.

Quickly, she ran water from the faucet. It was frigid and tinged with orange, barely warming even after a minute, though it did turn clear. She splashed her face to wash away tears that hadn't fallen. When she could breathe again she forced herself to look in the mirror. Her eyes narrowed as she assessed herself.

She'd dreamed of her mother speaking words she'd never said. Never would've said. Gilly didn't need a dream dictionary to parse out what the dream meant, her mother with the flowers that had sometimes seemed to mean more to her than her family. Blood. The responsibility of roses.

Looking at her face now she saw her mother's eyes, the shape of her mother's mouth. She'd heard her mother's voice, too.

"I am not my mother." She muttered this, each word tasting sour. She didn't believe herself.

Her ablutions were brief but effective. Staring at the clothes in the bags, Gilly felt herself wanting to slip into disconnectedness again. It was tempting to let the blankness take over. She forced it away.

She changed her panties but kept her bra on. Apparently he hadn't thought to buy her one. She put her own jeans back on, her own shirt. She didn't want to wear the clothes he'd bought her. She wanted her own things, even if the hems of her jeans were stiff with dirt and her shirt smelled faintly of the juice she hadn't realized was spilled on it. She folded the rest of the clothes and shoved them back in the bags.

Gilly combed her hair and tied it back with the ponytail holder from her jeans pocket. It was Arwen's. Her fingers trembled as she twisted the elastic into her hair. They'd stopped by the time she finished using the sparkly toothbrush.

Todd had put more wood in the stove, and now the room was almost stifling. He sat on the couch, staring at nothing. Smoking, tapping the ashes into an old coffee can set on the table in front of him.

"Feel better?" he asked without looking at her.

"No."

Todd sighed. "I'm not an asshole, Gilly. Or a psycho. Really."

She didn't say anything.

He looked at her, anger smoldering in his dark eyes. The sight made her step back toward the insignificant safety of the bathroom. Todd got up from the couch and made as though to step toward her.

"You afraid of me?"

She shook her head, not quite able to voice the lie. She was suddenly terrified. In her hands the plastic crinkled and shifted, and she clutched the bags in front of her like a shield.

"Shit," Todd said. "This is all a bunch of shit."

Then he stormed to the front door and out, slamming it behind him. A few minutes later she heard the truck's engine roar into life. Gilly dropped the bags and ran to the window, but he'd already pulled away.

5

Gilly had always prided herself on keeping cool in an emergency, but now she flew to the door, flung it open, ran out onto the freezing front porch. The truck had disappeared. She ran after it anyway.

She couldn't even hear it by the time she crossed the snowy yard and reached the gravel that began the rutted road. Rocks dug into her sock-clad feet and she hopped, slapping at her arms to warm herself in her long-sleeved but thin shirt. She ventured a few steps down the road, which grew immediately shadowed by the trees.

A layer of snow, perhaps two inches deep, interspersed with rocks and ice, blanketed the ground. It hadn't been a good winter for snow. Bitter-cold temperatures had abounded since late October, and one large storm had closed schools across the state, but that was all. None of it had melted, and piles of it were still all over the place, but no more had fallen. Gilly looked at the moody gray sky, clouds obscuring the sun. This spot was up high. Close to the sky. The wind pushed at the trees and lifted the tips of her hair. Was she going to run?

She looked again down empty road and knew she wasn't. Not like this, anyway. Not unprepared. Sparkly tights would not protect her feet. He hadn't bothered to tie her up when he left, but he hadn't needed to.

"Moss," she muttered aloud, turning back toward the cabin. "Something about moss."

Growing on a side of a tree. Something about finding and following a stream. She knew snippets of information about how to find her way out of the woods, but nothing useful.

The smartest thing to do would be to steal the truck and drive away, something she'd have to do when he got back. With that in mind, Gilly headed back into the cabin. She closed the door behind her and looked down at her muddy socks. She stripped them off and dug around in the plastic bags until she found another pair. They had kittens on them. Sparkly, glittery kittens.

Socks in hand, Gilly sank onto the floor and cradled her face in her hands. She didn't cry. Her feet and hands were cold, and she shuddered, wrapping her arms around herself. The floor was filthy, but she couldn't seem to care. How had she ended up here, in this place?

Quiet. Everything was quiet around her. Her knees ached, her thighs cramped, and a chill stole over her in the overheated room. Still, Gilly didn't move. She had nowhere to be, nothing to do, nobody tugging on her for attention. She was still. She was silent.

She sat that way for a long time.

Without a watch or a clock, Gilly had no way of knowing how long Todd had been gone. At last she could no longer stand even the luxury of idleness. She had to *do* something.

With nothing to keep them occupied, her hands opened and shut like hysterical puppets. Gilly paced the room, step by step, measuring her prison with her footsteps. There had to be a way, some way to take advantage of his absence. In the end, she could think of nothing, could make no decision.

She understood without hesitation she was breaking down, that she'd broken down the moment at the gas station when she'd stayed in the truck instead of escaping. Her split from reality was shameful but not surprising; that she'd wondered for years if she would one day step off the deep end did not, now, make her feel better about having taken the dive.

She was too strong for this, damn it. Had always forced herself to be too strong. No fashionable Zoloft or Prozac for her, no trips to the therapist to work out her "issues," nothing but sheer determination had kept her functioning. And yet now...now all she could think about was her mother.

Gilly had grown accustomed to hearing her mother's voice. Dispensing advice. Scolding. She knew it was really her own inner voice. She hadn't realized until a day ago that she'd used it out loud, too.

She thought of her mom now, not hearing her voice but remembering it, instead.

"We're normal," her mother says. "You think we're not, but we are. Other families are just like this, Gillian. Whether you believe it or not."

Gilly doesn't believe it. By now she's spent too much time at Danica's house. She understands that most other people's mothers don't spend days without showering or brushing their teeth, without getting out of their nightgowns. Most mothers are able to get up off the floors of their bedrooms. They don't cry softly, moaning, over and over and over again while rocking. Most people's mothers wear bracelets on their wrists, not scars.

A cliché has prompted her mother to say it. Spilled milk, a puddle of it on the table and the floor. Gilly knocked it over with her elbow and would've cleaned it up before her mom even noticed, but it's one of the days Marlena has made it out of the dim sanctuary of her bedroom. She weeps over the spill, gnashing her teeth and pulling at her hair as she gets on hands and knees to mop up the spill with the hem of her skirt.

"This is normal, Gillian," her mother mutters over and over. "You think this isn't, you think we aren't. But we are!"

Gilly had stood watching as blank faced as she felt now.

This is different. You're not her. This isn't like that.

But it was worse, wasn't it? What Gilly had allowed to happen, no, what she'd *chosen to do* was worse than anything her mother had ever done. Because Gilly couldn't blame any of this on being crazy. She'd worked too hard against insanity.

A plastic bag tangled in her ankles as she paced, and Gilly paused to kick it away. She looked at all the things he'd bought her and kicked those, too. Scattering the brightly colored turtlenecks made her feel better for a moment, gave her some power.

She gathered up the clothes and stuffed them back in the bags. Gilly looped the handles over her arms and took all the stuff upstairs. She was moving on autopilot, but having something to do made her feel calmer. Allowed her to think.

She pulled open the top drawer on the dresser and prepared to put away the clothes. Inside she found a sheaf of photographs, some in frames but most loose. She picked up the top one.

A dark-haired boy stared out at her. He stood beside a tall, bearded man wearing a blaze-orange vest and holding a gun. The boy was not smiling. Gilly traced the line of his face with one finger. It was Todd.

He was in other photos, too, in some as young as perhaps eight and others as old as sixteen. It was the younger faces that grabbed her attention. Something about him as a boy seemed so familiar to her, but she couldn't quite figure out why.

Gilly put the pictures away and used the other drawers to store the things Todd had bought for her. In the chest at the foot of the bed she found sheets, blankets, pillowcases. These were cleaner than those on the bed and fragrant with the biting scent of cedar. She stripped the bed and made it up again. Smoothing the sheets and plumping the pillows gave her hands something to do while her mind worked, but when the task was over her mind was as blank as it had been before.

In the kitchen, she opened cupboards and saw the supplies he'd bought in the hours she'd been asleep. Beneath the sink she found bottles and cartons of soap, sponges, bleach. They weren't new, but they'd work. She rolled up her sleeves and bent to the task.

The day passed that way, and Gilly lost herself in the work. At home, Gilly was lucky if she got to fold a basket of laundry before being pulled away to take care of some other chore. Floors went unmopped for weeks, toilets went unscrubbed, furniture went undusted. Gilly hated never finishing anything. She'd learned to live with it, but she hated it. She felt she could never sit, never rest, never take some time for herself. Not until she was done, and she was never done. Later in her life, with spotless floors and unrumpled bedspreads, she might look back to this time with wistful nostalgia. But she doubted it. She hated never finishing anything.

Most of her girlfriends complained about it incessantly, but Gilly liked cleaning. Not just the end results, but the effort. Making order out of chaos. For her, it was much the same feeling she'd heard long-distance runners or other athletes describe. When she was cleaning, really working hard, Gilly could put herself into "the zone."

Everything else faded away, leaving behind only the scent of bleach and lemon cleanser, the ache of muscles worked hard and a blank, serene mind. It wasn't a state she often reached. Always, there were too many distractions, too many interruptions. Too many demands on her time.

Now, today, the dirty cabin and time reeled out in front of her without an end to either of them. By concentrating on one small part at a time, the task didn't seem so daunting. Todd had cleaned the fridge before loading it with groceries, but the rest of the kitchen was a disaster. Gilly started with the counters, then the cupboard fronts, the stove. She cleaned the scarred table of as much grime as she could. She discovered the pantry, as fully stocked as the fridge and cupboards, and through it the door to the backyard. She scrubbed the floor on hands and knees and dumped buckets of black water off the back porch, forming a dirty puddle that quickly froze.

Early-falling dark and the grumbling of her stomach forced her to stop. Gilly surveyed her efforts. The kitchen would never be fresh and new, but it was now, at least, clean. Her back ached and her fingers cramped, stiff and blistered from the scrub brush, but satisfaction filled her. She'd accomplished something, even if it was irrelevant and useless to her situation.

She went to the windows. Snowflakes flirted through the sky, promising a storm. As she watched, the soft white flakes grew thicker. Maybe they weren't just flirting after all.

She thought of Arwen and Gandy. Who was with them? Did they miss her? And Seth, dear, sweet Seth who couldn't find his own pair of socks...what must he be going through?

She thought of the stack of bills waiting to be paid and the poor dog missing his vet appointment. Laundry, baskets of it overflowing, and dishes piled in the sink. The house would be falling apart without her.

When Gilly was pregnant with Arwen, her grandmother had given Gilly a sampler. Embroidered in threads of red and gold, it read simply: "There is a special place in Heaven for mothers." Gilly had thought she understood the sentiment, but it wasn't until after Arwen's birth, as her daughter grew from baby to child and Gandy came along, that Gilly really did understand. She'd embraced motherhood with everything inside her, determined to be the kind of mother she'd always wanted but hadn't had.

Good mothers cooked and cleaned and read stories to their children before bed. They sang songs. They played the Itsy Bitsy Spider until their fingers fell off, if that was the game that made their babies giggle. They changed diapers, filled sippy cups, sewed the frayed and torn edges of favorite blankies to keep them together just another few months. They gave up everything of themselves to give everything to their children.

Good mothers did not run away.

Gilly pressed her fingertips to the cold glass. She'd wanted to run away. How often had she thought about simply packing a bag, or better yet, nothing at all? Just leaving the house with nothing but herself.

Gilly understood having children meant sacrifice. It was the only thing about motherhood she'd been certain of before actually becoming a mother. Impromptu dinners out, going to the movies, privacy in the bathroom, had all become luxuries she didn't mind foregoing, most of the time. She didn't even mind the grubby clothes, which were far more comfortable than the pinching high heels and gut-busting panty hose she'd worn when she worked. Gilly cherished her children. Lord knew, they drove her to the edge of madness, but wasn't that what children did? Staying home to raise them had become the most challenging and rewarding task she'd ever undertaken. She'd conceived her children in love and borne them in blood, and her life without them wouldn't be worth living. It was just the constant never-endingness of it that some days made her want to scream until her throat burst.

She loved Seth, the solid man she'd married more than ten years before. Seth did his share, when he was home, of bathing and diapering and taking out the garbage. Yes, he needed reminding for even the simplest tasks and no, he never quite managed to complete any of them without asking her how to do it, but he tried.

She had a good life. Her children were healthy and bright, her husband attentive and generous. They lived in a lovely house, drove nice cars, went on vacation every year. She had as many blessings as a woman could want. If there were still days Gilly thought she might simply be unable to drag herself out of bed, it wasn't their fault.

They were her life. They consumed every part of her. She was a mother and a wife before she was a woman. Feminism might frown on it, and Gilly might strain against the shackles of responsibility, but when it came right down to it, she'd lost sight of how else to be.

The hours of cleaning had cleared her mind. Everyone would believe a knife to her head had made her toss her children out the car window, and nobody would question that fear for her life had kept her moving. Only Gilly would ever know the real and secret truth. She'd wanted to escape, but not from Todd. From her precious and fragile life. From what she'd made.

Gilly opened the pantry door and surveyed what she found.

She ran her hands along the rows of canned spaghetti, the jars of peanut butter and jelly, the bags and cartons of cookies and snacks. He'd bought flour, sugar, coffee, pasta, rice. Cartons of cigarettes, which she moved away from the food in distaste. He'd stocked the cabin with enough food for an army...or for a siege.

Gilly took a box of spaghetti and a jar of sauce from the shelf and closed the pantry door behind her. He'd already told her he didn't plan to let her go and warned her of the risks of trying to leave on her own. Two choices, two paths, and she couldn't fully envision either of them. Yesterday she'd been ready to toss her kids out a window to get away from them, and Todd had appeared. Now she felt tossed like dandelion fluff on the wind.

Gilly slapped the box of pasta on the counter. She found a large pot and filled it with water, then a smaller one. She lit the burners on the stove with an ancient box of matches from the drawer and set the water boiling and the pasta sauce simmering. She stood over them both, not caring about the old adage about watched pots. The heat from the stove warmed her hands as she stared without really seeing.

There was a third choice, one she'd already imagined even though now her mind shuddered away from the thought. If she could not manage to convince Todd to voluntarily let her go, and if she couldn't somehow be smart and strong enough to escape him, there was one other option. And, of the three choices, it was the one Gilly was sure would work.

Some pasta sauce had splashed on the back of her hand, rich and red. She licked it, tasting garlic. The water in the pot bubbled, and she opened the box of spaghetti, judged a handful, then tossed in the whole box. Dinner would be ready in a few minutes, and Todd was likely to return soon.

If she couldn't change his mind or break for an escape, Gilly thought she might just have to kill him.

6

Todd walked in the door just as Gilly finished setting the table with a red-and-white-checkered cloth and a set of lovely, Depression-era dishes and silverware she'd found in the drawer. Though the silver was tarnished and several of the plates cracked or chipped, she could only imagine what pieces like this would sell for in an antiques shop. Hundreds, maybe thousands of dollars. He paused in the doorway to sniff the air. Again, he reminded her of a hungry, loveless dog hanging around the kitchen door.

"Smells good." He jingled the pocket of his sweatshirt, then took out her keys. He tossed them on the counter.

Gilly purposefully kept her eyes from them. "I hope you're hungry," she said flatly. "I made a lot."

Todd pulled out his chair with a scrape that sent chills up her spine, like fingernails on a chalkboard. "Fucking starving."

Gilly poured the spaghetti into the strainer she'd put in the sink. Clouds of steam billowed into her face and she closed her eyes against it. She scooped some onto a plate and went to the table, taking the seat across from him.

Todd didn't serve himself, just stared at her expectantly. With a silent sigh she got up from her seat and took his plate to the sink, plopped a serving of spaghetti on top and splashed it with the sauce. She tossed a piece of garlic bread beside the spaghetti and handed it to him.

"Thanks." At least he did have some manners.

They ate in silence interrupted only by the sounds of chewing and slurping. Surreptitiously Gilly watched the movement of his mouth as he gobbled pasta. A few days' worth of beard stubbled his tawny cheeks, the dark hairs glinting reddish in the light from above.

"This is good." He wiped his mouth with the napkin she'd folded next to his plate. "Really good."

"Thank you." Cleaning had made her hungry. She'd polished off a large plateful herself and now sat back, her stomach almost too full.

Todd burped loud and long, the kind of noise that at home would have earned a laugh followed by a reprimand. Gilly did neither. She sipped some water, watching him.

"Where did you go?"

"Out."

She hadn't really expected him to tell her. She sipped more water and wiped her mouth. Todd eyed her, his mouth full. He chewed and swallowed.

"Why'd you do this?" Todd twirled another forkful of spaghetti but didn't eat it.

"To be nice," Gilly said. There was more to it than that.

Todd's eyes narrowed. He knew that. "Why?"

Only honesty would suffice. Gilly took a deep breath.

"Because I'm hoping that if I'm nice to you, you'll let me go home."

Todd sat back in his chair, tipping it. "I can't. You know my name. You know where we are. You'd tell someone. They'd come."

Desperation slipped out in her voice. "I don't know where we are, remember? You could blindfold me. Take me someplace far away, dump me off."

Todd shook his head.

Her voice rose with tension. "I won't tell anyone your name. Or anything. I'll say I don't know anything, I swear to you. If you let me go, I'll..."

"Don't you get it? I can't ever let you go now. Not ever." His hands clutched the tabletop. His face twisted in loathing. "Don't you get it?"

"No! I don't! You don't want me here, so just..." Her voice broke, softened, slipped into a murmur. "Please, Todd. Please."

Again, he shook his head. His voice got lower, too. "You say you won't tell them anything, but even if you mean it, I know you will. You'll have to. They'll keep at you and keep at you. It's what they fucking *do,* Gilly."

"Who?"

"Them. The cops. Your therapist. Your fucking husband, I don't know. Someone will want to know where the fuck you were, and with who, and you can't tell me you won't break down and tell them. You'll spill it all, and I'll be totally fucked. And I'll tell you something," Todd said, voice lower still, his body stiff and tense, "I won't go back to jail."

Gilly wasn't surprised Todd had been to jail. He must've seen the lack of shock in her expression, because he looked first ashamed, then defiant. He lifted his chin at her.

"I mean it. Not going back. Ever. I can't."

"You should've thought of that before," Gilly said under her breath but loud enough for him to hear her.

"You think I fucking didn't?"

Gilly shrugged. "I don't know what you thought. But you have to see that no matter what happens, you're going to get caught, Todd. Whether you let me go or I get away."

He studied her, dark eyes pulling her apart and leaving big gaps in the seams of her composure.

"No. I'll do…whatever I have to." The words were clipped and tight, his expression hard.

Gilly had thought the same. Whatever she had to, to survive. To get away from here and back to her family. If Todd was as desperate as she was—but she couldn't let herself think about that right now. Couldn't let herself be afraid.

Time spun out as they stared each other down. From the corner of her eye, Gilly spotted a glint of metal on the counter beside them. Though she tried not to let her eyes flicker, something in her gaze must have given her away. She saw it in his eyes, the sudden wariness that showed he knew what she was thinking.

Todd launched himself across the table as Gilly pushed back in her chair so hard it toppled to the floor. His fingers, not clenched now but stretched into grappling talons, scratched at her neck but didn't gain purchase.

Gilly would've hit the floor if the wall hadn't been so close behind her. Instead, she cracked the back of her head hard enough to see stars. She rolled along the short length of wall until she reached the opening to the living room. Her feet twisted on themselves and she almost fell, but her hand, grasping, found the edge of the counter, and she stayed upright. Her fingers clenched over the bundle of keys.

Todd moved fast, with swift, athletic grace, but Gilly had the thoughts of her children to fuel her. She turned, swiftly, as he grabbed at her. Keys bristled between her knuckles, and she sliced at him, hard. The metal slashed his cheek. He clapped a hand over the wound, which gushed bright blood.

He caught her just inside the living room and knocked her feet out from under her. Gilly hit the floor on her hands and knees, the keys still gripped tight in her fist. With a low growl, Todd grabbed her ankles and yanked her closer, scrabbling at the back of her shirt but not quite able to catch her.

Gilly rolled, kicking, as he loomed over her. Todd's eyes glittered, fierce, the blood on his face like war paint. He grabbed the front of her shirt, tearing it.

She kicked him in the nuts. Her foot didn't connect squarely, hitting part of his thigh, but it was enough. Todd went to his knees with a strangled groan.

Gilly got up and ran.

Adrenaline exhilarated her. She flew to the front door and leaped through it, leaving it hanging open. She'd misjudged the stairs and the icy ground beyond, and so went sprawling onto her hands and knees. Rocks tore her pants and her skin. She didn't drop the keys even though the sharp metal sliced her.

Gilly got up, palms bloodied, and ran for the truck. She heard Todd shouting and cursing on the porch behind her. She didn't stop to look around.

The lightly falling snow had turned into thick, soft blankets of white, hiding the treacherous ice beneath. Gilly slid but kept herself from falling this time. She hit the driver's side full on, hard enough to send spikes of agony into her shoulder and dent the door. The keys scratched the paint like four claws as she grabbed the door handle to keep from falling. He'd locked it. Her numb fingers fumbled with the key-ring remote.

"Don't do this!" Todd cried from the porch. A sudden gust of wind tore his words to tatters.

Gilly ripped open the door and pulled herself into the driver's seat. Her palms stung as she gripped the wheel and plunged the keys into the ignition. She had to do this now, because she hadn't before. Because she'd been crazy before, crazy stupid. She'd let this man drive her away from her home, her husband, her children.

The Suburban roared into life. Gilly kept her foot steady on the accelerator. Her right knee, already bruised from when he'd hit her there before, had taken the worst of her fall and now throbbed with every motion. Blood slicked her palms and her hands slipped until she forced her frozen fingers to curl. She yanked the gearshift into Reverse and the truck revved backward, narrowly missing the tree that loomed in her rearview mirror.

Drive.

Her wet feet slipped on the gas pedal and light from the headlights swung wildly as she forced the truck through the snow. She hadn't realized it had gotten so deep. The vehicle slid a little, bouncing in the ruts when she jammed the gas pedal.

Her heart hammered. Everything in front of her was black, and the headlights weren't helping much. She tried to remember how long this road was, where it turned, how far to the gate, and couldn't. All she could do was drive.

On her left, the mountain. On the right of the narrow, ice-slick road, a steep incline. A line of trees reared up in front of her as the road bent. Gilly braked, forgetting in her panic everything she'd ever learned about driving. The truck went into a long, slow slide. It seemed impossible she'd actually hit the tree row, not in slow motion.

Her mind was in slow motion. Her reactions. too. But not the truck. It mowed down the trees with a vast and angry crashing that pounded Gilly's ears. The big vehicle tilted, throwing her against the door, and slammed back to the ground with a thud that jarred her to the bone. She had time to think she was going to be okay before she looked out the side window and saw the side of the mountain reaching for her.

The Suburban veered into the wall of rock. Metal screeched. Gilly, not wearing a seat belt, was flung forward into the steering wheel hard enough to knock the breath out of her. It didn't end there—the truck shuddered and groaned, sliding on ice and snow.

She was going over.

Gilly had no breath to scream. She did have time to pray, but nothing came but the sight of her children's faces. That was prayer enough.

The Suburban jolted off the road and over the edge, nearly vertical at first and then with a huge, thumping slam, it came to rest with the hood crumpled against a tree. The airbag didn't even go off, something she only noticed when she could see, very clearly, the bent and broken trees barely managing to keep the truck from sliding down the mountain. The horn bleated and died. The interior lights had come on and the pinging noise signifying an open door sounded although all the doors were closed.

Everything blurred. She tasted blood. Warmth coated her lap and dimly, Gilly was embarrassed to think she might've wet herself. It wasn't urine but more blood gushing from a slice in the top of her thigh. She groaned, the sound of her voice too loud.

The door opened. Gilly screamed, then, thin and whistling but with as much force as she could muster. In the next minute Todd yanked her from the driver's seat, shoving her against the metal. Gilly swung and missed.

"Let me go!"

"You crazy dumb bitch! The fuck you think you're doing?" Todd shook her.

Beside them, the truck groaned. The trees snapped. The metal behind her back shifted and moved, and Todd yanked her a few steps toward him. Gilly fought him but couldn't get free.

Nothing seemed real. The pain in every part of her wasn't as bad as knowing she'd tried and failed to escape. She fought him with teeth and the talons of fingernails Arwen had painted pale blue only yesterday.

Todd dodged her swinging fists and her teeth. He slapped her face, first with his palm. Then, when she didn't stop flailing at him, with the back of his hand so hard her head rocked back. Gilly fell into the snowy brush and was instantly soaked. Red roses bloomed in front of her eyes.

"You dumb bitch," Todd said again, this time into her ear. He'd lifted her though she was suddenly as limp as a rag doll.

He'd hit her. Nobody had hit her that way in a very long time. Blood dripped from her mouth, though everything was so shadowed she couldn't see it hit the snow.

Todd's fingers dug into her arms as he jerked her upright and shook her. Everything was dark and cold around them, and the sound of creaking branches was very loud. The lights from the truck abruptly dimmed.

"Wake up. I can't get your ass up this hill if you're deadweight."

Gilly blinked and struggled feebly. "Don't...hit me... again."

"I don't *want* to hit you, for fuck's sake." Todd sounded disgusted. "Just get your ass moving. What happens if that tree won't hold, huh? You want to get wiped out by that truck when it goes crashing down the rest of this hill? Look up there, how fucking far we have to get back up to the lane!"

Gilly didn't look. She couldn't, really. Turning her head made bright, sharp pain stab through her. Besides, it was too dark. The headlights were pointing the other way, down the steep slope, and as she watched they guttered and went out, followed an instant later by the ding-ding alert of the interior light cutting off.

"Ah, fuck," Todd muttered in the sudden silence. "Just stay still. Don't move."

As if she could've moved. Gilly, limp, went to her knees when Todd let her go. The snow was soft and thick but not deep enough to cradle her. Rocks and bits of broken branches stabbed at her.

"All right. Let's go. Get up. I can see," Todd said, and jerked her by the back of her collar.

Gilly couldn't. Everything was still black. She scrabbled along the slope with Todd yanking her hard enough to pull her off her feet a few times.

This was a nightmare. It had to be. Right? Pain and darkness and fear.

They got to the top of the slope and Todd paused, breathing hard. Now instead of rocks and broken trees, gravel bit into Gilly's skin as she went to her hands and knees. It was easier to get to her feet, though, when Todd yanked the back of her collar again.

Somehow they made it back to the clearing and the cabin, still ablaze with light that hurt her eyes after so many long minutes in darkness. Gilly was beyond fighting him by then. She barely made it up the front steps and into the living room. She definitely didn't make it up the steep, narrow stairs to the second floor. Todd, cursing and muttering, did that by yanking and pushing her.

With rough hands he forced her toward the bed she'd slept in. When he tried to take off her shirt, Gilly found the strength to fight him again. Todd shouted out another slew of curses.

"Stop fighting me!"

But she would not. If this was a nightmare, she was going to keep swinging and scratching, even though every movement made her cry in pain. Todd, finally, ripped her shirt completely down the front, pushed her onto the bed and yanked at her pants, too.

Gilly kicked out as hard as she could. Maybe Todd dodged it, maybe she missed. She couldn't tell. All she knew was he grabbed her by the upper arms, fingers digging deep into her flesh, to yank her to her feet.

"I'm trying to help you!" Todd shouted into her face, breath hot and spittle wet on her cheeks. Then, "Oh, shit. Don't you pass out on me, Gilly."

But Gilly did.

7

Gilly woke up blind. She lurched upright, clawing at her face. "My eyes!"

Her eyes were merely gummed shut, not blind. Her head ached in the dull, persistent manner that meant no amount of aspirin would stop it. The cold air stung a long gash on her cheek. She put trembling fingers to it and felt that the wound's curve from the left side of her jaw all the way to the corner of her eye. The crash had taken its share of skin and blood from her face, which felt puffy and tender. Her chest ached from impact with the steering wheel, but, though she sensed bruises, nothing appeared to be broken.

She wore a thick flannel nightgown that had rucked up about her thighs. She hated nightgowns for just that reason. She touched the soft fabric with her jagged, broken fingernails and shivered with distaste.

Gilly tested her limbs one at a time, cataloging aches and pains that ranged from mild to agonizing. Her neck hurt the worst. The pain when she looked to the left was excruciating enough to twist her stomach. The gash on her thigh proved to be shallow but ugly, sore to the touch and still oozing blood and clear fluid.

Still, she was alive. There was that.

A shuffle of feet from the stairs told her he was coming. She spoke before she saw him. "What time is it?"

"Does it matter?"

He'd paused at the top of the stairs but she could see him through the partition. Gilly rubbed at her temples but the throbbing didn't ease. "No. I guess it doesn't."

Todd took a few steps closer. "How are you?"

"Bad."

"You're a mess," he said flatly. "You know that?"

Gilly shrugged slightly. It was the greatest motion she could make without ripping herself open. It wasn't slight enough; she ached and more pain flared.

"The fuck were you thinking?"

She looked at him. "I want to go home."

"Yeah, well, I want a million dollars."

Gilly blinked at this attempt at…humor? Sarcasm? He'd said it with a straight face, so she couldn't be sure. "My head hurts. My neck, too. I think I strained something. And this cut on my leg needs stitches."

"No shit. You're lucky you didn't get hurt worse. That was some crash." Todd let out a low whistle. "Nice shiner."

Gilly got out of bed and went to the dirt-encrusted attic window. Her entire left side felt rubbed raw. She winced at every step but could walk.

Everything outside was white. Snow piled against the cabin in drifts that looked nearly waist high. One giant drift reached almost to the windowsill.

No. Oh, no.

"All of this in one night?" she cried, incredulous. She put her hands to the cold glass.

Todd moved to her side. She shrank from him, but he didn't seem to notice. He leaned forward to peer out the window.

"It snowed all night and all morning, too. It stopped about an hour ago. Sky's still gray. I don't think it's finished yet."

"The truck?"

He shrugged. "Totaled. Halfway down the mountain, unless that tree broke. Then that bitch is all the way at the bottom, and you can forget about ever getting it back."

She knew that already but let out a gusting sigh that became a small moan. "Oh, no."

"Hope you have good insurance."

Another joke Gilly didn't find amusing. She pressed her face to the glass, eyes closed, and let out another small, despairing sigh. "Does that even matter now?"

Todd laughed and moved away from her. "Probably not. You shouldn't have tried to run away. That was stupid."

Gilly looked at him. She searched his face for sign of a threat, but what would she do even if she saw it? Run? Fight? She'd failed miserably at both.

"You gave me no choice. I have to get home to my kids. My husband's probably worried sick."

Todd shrugged. "Neither one of us will be going anywhere until this snow melts. Not without the truck. We're pretty much fucked."

Gilly went back to the bed and sat. "I want to go home."

His face went hard, the soft, dark eyes bitter. He threw her own words back at her. "Maybe you should've thought about that before."

Don't lose it…

But it was already lost.

"Fuck you! You think I don't know that? Fuck you, Todd!" Gilly shrieked, lurching to her feet with fists flailing.

If she'd aimed for his face she probably wouldn't have hit him, but one of her wild swings caught him just under the eye. Todd stumbled back, muttering curses. The wound she'd inflicted on him earlier broke open, oozing blood. Gilly stood her ground, fists clenched and teeth chattering, ready to batter him again.

He reached out, quick as a cat, and grabbed her shoulders. He shook her like one does a naughty child, or a pet, each shake emphasizing a word. "That's twice. Don't do it again."

"Or what?" she cried. "What could you possibly do that's worse than what you've already done?"

Todd stared at her with a flat black gaze for too long before answering, "I could do worse."

He let her go so suddenly she stumbled back, her aggression puffed out like a breath-blown match. They were at a standoff. Gilly rubbed the sore spots his fingers had left, just a few more to add to the plethora already aching all over her.

Without another word, Todd went down the stairs. She went to the window again and stared out at the vast expanse of blankness. Even the trees had been covered in heavy quilts of white, blurring their lines and making them nothing more than vague humps. She wasn't going anywhere until that melted. Perhaps as early as March or as late as April, but April was three months away.

Her throat was dry. She needed a drink. Gilly looked around the walls of the prison she'd inflicted upon herself. A wave of dizziness washed over her and she sat on the bed, then put her head on the pillow, hoping it would pass. She'd caught every flu bug Arwen brought home from kindergarten, from the nastiest stomach virus to the most persistent of colds. No amount of hand washing had seemed to help, and she was wary of overusing hand sanitizer, fearing the creation of a superbug more than risking the chance of catching yet another case of the sniffles. She'd been on antibiotics, on and off, for the past few weeks, to get rid of a bad sinus infection. Now she felt even worse, aching from head to toe and shivering with chills. She got up just long enough to slide back beneath the covers again and closed her eyes against the pain stabbing her behind the lids.

If there was any relief for her, it had the same source as her anxiety. She felt sick; she could lie down without fear of little hands plucking at her, little voices calling her name. The last time she'd taken herself to bed, unable to stand up without the world spinning, Gandy had decided to remove all the DVDs from their cases and, for some reason known only to his toddler brain, stick them in and out of the jumbo-size tub of margarine she used for making grilled cheese. That had been the day she called Seth, desperate for him to come home early from work, and he had.

There'd be no Seth to rescue her this time.

Desperation gnawed at her, a frenzied yearning to burst into action. She forced herself still, resting. Nothing to be gained by wild action; she'd learned that lesson the hard way. She thought of the snow outside, and she thought of Todd.

She supposed the real question was what did she think he would do to keep her, if he couldn't or wouldn't let her go? Did she think he would kill her if he had to? She remembered the desperation in his cry "I won't go back to jail!" And she thought that yes, he might. He might be slow of thought, and he might be kind at heart, but something had happened to him that made him what he was today. Gilly didn't think Todd had brought her here to kill her, but she did believe he would if he felt he had to.

But hadn't she determined that she'd do the same? If the chance arose, if she was left with nothing else. The thought of it now sent a shudder cascading up and down her spine, like cold fingers stroking the nape of her neck. She'd tried to change his mind, and she'd tried to escape. Both had failed. But what would happen if she killed him? The third option that had seemed so matter-of-fact and to-the-point didn't feel that way now.

Even if she managed to bring herself to kill him, she was still trapped in this cabin without a phone, without a map, without proper clothes. No vehicle, that was her own stupid fault. Even if he died, there was nothing for her to do until the snow melted. She snuggled deeper into the cave of warmth her body heat created beneath the blankets. It turned out she had a fourth option.

Waiting.

8

Three days gone. She'd never been away from her babies for that long. Not to visit a friend, not to go on a girls' weekend away, not even to a scrapbooking seminar.

In her college days and just after, before meeting Seth, Gilly had been a traveler. She'd stayed in youth hostels or taken summer jobs at tourist destinations in different states. She'd jaunted on spur-of-the-moment trips based on whatever cheap airfare she'd found. Once she'd bought a companion ticket on an ocean liner from an elderly woman whose friend had been unable to make it at the last minute. The woman's name was Esther and though Gilly had been nervous about sharing a cabin with a stranger, the two of them had hit it off superbly. They'd kept in touch for years, until Esther passed away. Gilly hadn't traveled like that in a long, long time and probably never would again.

Seth traveled sometimes for work. He came home with the news of a conference or business trip, how many days he'd be gone, what time his flights left and returned. He made his plans and took the trips without a second thought about who'd pick up Arwen from kindergarten or take Gandy to preschool. Who'd feed and walk the dog, sign for deliveries. Pay the bills or take care of the loads of laundry. Seth decided he was going, and he went.

A trip for Gilly would take weeks of planning and countless favors called in from friends to juggle her children's schedules and her time commitments. The effort it took for her to step out the door for a trip to the grocery store by herself would be magnified to such extent even a few days spent in a spa getting hot-stone massages and foot rubs from handsome, oiled men in loincloths wouldn't be worth the hassle.

This was not even close to a hot-stone massage. Paused at the bottom of the stairs, Gilly looked across the room at Todd sitting at the table, still sorting through his folder of papers. He had a cigarette in one hand and sucked in long, deep draws of smoke he held for an impossibly long time before letting it seep from his nostrils. His hair fell forward as he bent over the papers, but she could still see the wounds she'd inflicted on his face. The cuts were evidence she'd done what she could to get away, but small consolation compared to her aches and bruises.

She'd stayed upstairs for what felt like an hour but might've been two. Might've been fifteen minutes. She didn't have a watch, the cabin had no clocks, and the daylight outside was set permanently to twilight. More snow drifted down in spurts, dandruff brushed from a giant's shoulders.

Todd looked up when her foot creaked on the bottom step. He closed the folder and stood. "Hi."

Walking stiffly so as to jar her sore muscles as little as possible, Gilly limped into the living room. She kept a wary distance, but Todd acted as though he'd never raised a hand to her. He came around the couch but stopped when she took a step back.

"I got your stuff," he said.

"What stuff?" Gilly asked. She didn't think he was capable of being particularly subtle, but she *was* wary of some sort of trick she couldn't anticipate.

Todd hesitated, then gestured at the front door. "Your stuff. From the truck. I got what I could, anyway. It was fuckall tough. That little tree's not going to hold it much longer. But…I thought you might want stuff out of it before it hits the bottom of the mountain."

Gilly's aching knees buckled. The doorway saved her from falling as she gripped it with her sore hand. He'd brought her things.

She moved on stumbling feet, three, four, five steps, to crouch by the pile of miscellaneous junk Todd had brought back from the wreck. Most of it *was* junk. A scattering of plastic toys. A stray sock that had been missing for months and was now too small for either of the kids. A sippy cup, thick with the remnants of some red juice. Gandy's blankie, many times repaired and badly in need of a wash. He'd be missing it by now. Crying for it, unable to sleep.

Gilly grabbed it. Held it to her face. Breathed in the scent of her son. She made a wordless noise of grief into the fabric.

You're never going to see him again. Or Arwen, or Seth. This is what you did, Gilly. This is what you deserve.

"Gilly?"

Todd's hand came to rest on her shoulder, and she shook it off. Clutching the blankie to her chest, she glared up at him. "Don't. Just don't!"

Todd held up both hands, face grim. "Fine. Jesus. What a bitch."

He slouched away, boots heavy and clomping on the bare boards of the floor. Gilly crouched over her meager pile of belongings. The detritus of motherhood. Tiny, mismatched pieces of her heart.

She found her iPod, safe in the soft eyeglass case she used to transport it, the earbuds still wrapped around it. He'd also brought the black CD case bulging with discs she only listened to while driving. Bat Boy, scratched probably beyond repair.

Behind her, Gilly heard Todd pacing, but she didn't look. She held the CD close to her. She'd bought this disc with Seth at one of the last few shows this cast had performed at an off-Broadway theater, four days after the Twin Towers had fallen.

"We took the ferry," she said.

Todd's boots stopped thumping.

Gilly bent her head over the disc. Her fingers left misty marks on the silver back. "We parked in the lot and took the ferry across. It was full of people going to volunteer to help. There was a federal marshal on board. I could see his gun. I looked out across the water and saw the smoke."

Gilly closed her eyes, her memories clutched in bruised and aching hands.

"There were posters everywhere. Pictures of people who were still missing, with numbers to call. When we got to the other side, there were parking lots blocked off by wire fencing, filled with pallets of water. I saw a bundle of axes, maybe twenty of them, leaning against the fence."

"The fuck are you talking about?" Todd asked, but softly.

Gentle. It was the way someone might speak to someone standing on a ledge or a bridge.

Gilly opened her eyes. She gathered up what he'd brought to her, careful not to lose anything. "It was the worst thing I'd ever seen."

"You messing with me again?"

She stood and looked at him. "No. I'm not. I'm trying to tell you that I've seen bad things."

"Yeah?" Todd frowned. "Well, so have I."

"I thought at the time that was the worst experience I'd ever have. Seeing what had been left behind. The grief of people who'd lost someone they loved. The bravery of the ones who'd traveled from all over to help dig out the dead. I thought it was the very worst thing, and it was bad…" She looked up at him. "But I think this is worse."

Todd took a step back, mouth thinning. "Why don't you shut up now, Gilly."

"Yes," she said faintly and held her things close to her. "Yes. I think I will."

Todd scuffed a boot on the floor. It left a black mark on the boards she'd so painstakingly swept earlier. "I'm making dinner. Come have some."

Gilly shook her head. "No."

"You should eat something."

Her stomach, empty, was nonetheless too shriveled for hunger. The thought of food made her feel sick. "Why?"

Todd's mouth opened and closed. He scowled, then tossed up his hands and turned on his heel to stalk to the kitchen. Gilly watched him go, then stood, juggling her belongings, and went upstairs.

She put everything he'd salvaged in the top drawer of the dresser she was nauseated to realize she thought of as "hers."

Then she climbed into bed and burrowed under the blankets with the iPod.

Though it didn't look broken, the iPod wouldn't turn on. It gave a low, chugging *whir* when Gilly pressed the button. She slapped it into her palm as if she was tamping a pack of cigarettes, once, then harder. The screen lit, then shut off. She tamped it again. This time, the Apple logo showed up as the unit rebooted or did whatever it was doing.

She slipped the earbuds in and thumbed the controls. It was an old model, inherited from Seth after he'd upgraded, but that had never mattered. It had enough space on it to store some music and photos. She scrolled to the picture slideshow she'd loaded to show Seth's parents the last time they'd visited. In moments the bright and bouncy music, some instrumental piece that came with the photo software, came on. So did the photos.

Arwen in pink tights and a ballerina sweatshirt, curly dark hair pulled into pigtails, showing off a hole where her front tooth had been. Gandy dressed like Scooby Doo, holding an empty pumpkin pail, chocolate smeared on his face. Photo after photo of her children, each one precious and remote, unforgettable and unreachable.

And finally, Gilly wept.

9

Gilly woke again to the morning sun and frozen cheeks. She hunched the covers up around her face to warm it. From the other side of the barrier she heard the low, familiar rumble of male snoring.

It was early, judging by the slant of sunlight made brighter by its reflection off the snow. Her entire body still hurt, possibly worse than it had the day before. Her bruises had bruises. Joints popped and crackled as she stretched. Her stomach wasn't too happy, either. She hadn't eaten much of anything, but the thought of food made her swallow a gag.

Her head hurt. Gilly had been prone to headaches her entire life, most of them tension related, but this was a bad one. Pain cradled her skull and spiked her eyes from the combination of infected sinuses, lack of food and anxiety. She'd never been diagnosed with migraines, but now she blinked away what sure as hell looked like an aura.

Groaning seemed worthless, but she did it anyway. No cease

from the snoring on the room's other side. Gilly pressed her thumbs to the magic spots just above the bridge of her nose, willing the pain to go away. It didn't, but it did ease a little. Long experience told her that eating would help, even if she didn't feel like it. A hot shower would, too, but she was out of luck on that one.

She flung the covers off and swung her legs over the bed. Her head spun and her stomach rocked alarmingly. Clenching her jaw didn't help her headache, but she refused to puke. Absolutely refused. Raw bile burned in her throat, and she swallowed convulsively, over and over.

Breathe, Gilly. In. Out. Keep it together.

She must've groaned louder because suddenly Todd appeared, leaning on the partition. "You okay?"

She didn't dare speak, and so only nodded. She pressed her thumbs more firmly against her forehead. The throbbing subsided. Sheer willpower kept her stomach's contents inside it rather than all over the floor.

"You don't look good."

"I don't feel good."

He didn't say anything. Gilly looked up at him. Sleep had mussed his hair and still clouded his eyes. He wiped a hand across bristled cheeks. "You gonna puke?"

"No!" Her indignation chased the last of her sour stomach away.

"Just asking. You look kinda pale."

"I'm always this color."

He raised his eyebrows at her. "If you say so."

"I just need to eat something." Gilly pushed past him and hobbled down the stairs. In the kitchen, she toasted bread and poured cereal. The single half-gallon container of milk was almost empty. She swished it around thoughtfully before pouring it. There'd be no more for a long time after this was gone. She poured it anyway.

Todd had bought the kind of sugary cereals she never bought at home because she knew they'd rot her kids' teeth or give them cancer or send them into hyperactive spirals. Now Gilly dug into the bowl and crunched the sweetness. She gobbled it. She watched the colored cereal turn her milk the color of a tropical sunset.

Todd appeared at the bottom of the stairs. He wore a loose-fitting pair of sweatpants, slung low across his hips. When he lifted his arm to scrub at his face she saw the tan expanse of his belly, not taut and buff but soft and slightly curved. A long, angry scar dimpled the skin.

"It's starting to snow again," Todd remarked as he looked out one of the back windows. "Goddamn, look at that coming down. Fucking snowpocalypse out there."

Gilly filled her bowl again and kept crunching. Famine had replaced her earlier nausea. The sweet cereal made her teeth ache.

"There's no more milk," she said when he entered the kitchen, and waited to see what he would say.

"There's five gallons outside in the lean-to," Todd replied. "As long as it's cold like this, it'll stay frozen out there."

Gilly felt somehow defeated in her defiance. "You've thought of everything."

Todd got a bowl from the cupboard and sat across from her to fill it with Lucky Charms. He shrugged. "Didn't want to get caught needing something I didn't have."

Gilly pushed her bowl away, suddenly no longer so hungry. "You planned this."

His spoon stopped halfway to his mouth, then lowered. "I had a plan, yeah. And then it changed. I wasn't sure what the hell was going to happen, so I tried to make sure I was ready for whatever. Lucky for us, huh?"

He had that wary look in his eyes again. Gilly toyed with the floating rainbow chunks in the bright pink milk. She watched him lift the spoon to his mouth, watched him chew.

"It was a pretty piss poor plan." Todd shrugged, pretending it didn't matter. "I didn't plan on you."

"You took my truck! How could you not plan on me? Why not just steal a car if you wanted one so bad?"

"First, you obviously don't know how fucking hard it is to steal a car in the middle of a busy parking lot, duh. If I even knew how to hot-wire one which I fucking don't. And…I didn't know you had kids in the back, okay?" Todd pushed back from the table, and his spoon clattered to the floor. He stalked to the sink and hunched over it, his hands splayed on the green countertop. "I didn't see the kids. When you went to the money machine, I just saw you."

Gilly thought back to what seemed like so long ago. "I left them in the truck to run to the ATM for one second."

"I thought I'd just take the truck and tell you to drive someplace quieter, then make you get out," Todd continued. "The fuck were you thinking? Leaving your kids in the car. Don't you know you're not supposed to leave your kids alone in the car?"

"Don't you…don't you question my parenting skills!" Gilly cried. "You don't know anything about it!"

"I didn't know they were in there."

His voice shuddered and his face twisted. Gilly sat motionless. It would have been easy for her to pity him, to soften her heart. But she did not.

"I'd never hurt a kid." His mouth pulled down in distress. "I might be a fuck-up, but I'd never hurt a kid!"

She believed him, strangely enough. "That's a damn good thing, Todd. Because if you'd harmed one hair of my children's heads, I would've…I *would* have killed you."

Saying it aloud, she knew it was true. There'd have been no hesitation. If he'd hurt her kids, she'd have done it.

He turned to face her, his eyes wide. "Shut up."

She leaned forward, hands flat on the table, one on each side of her cereal bowl. Her voice was steadier than she expected. Full of truth. "I would have killed you."

He wet his lips, thinking. Then he scoffed. "No, you wouldn't have."

His easy dismissal irritated her. "Yes. I would."

He stared at her, frowning. "You have no idea how hard it would be to kill somebody. You're not hard like that, Gilly. I can tell."

Under any other circumstances, his comment would have been a compliment. Now she was as insulted as if he'd called her a vile name. Her eyes bored into his. "If you hurt my children, nothing in this world could have kept you safe from me."

Todd's gaze flickered. He put his hands on the table, too, and leaned to look into her eyes. "You're full of shit."

He was wrong about her—she did know how hard it was to kill. Her mother, at the end, had begged for Gilly to put a pillow over her face, to give her pills, to turn up the drip on the morphine until it sent her off to sleep for good. Her mother, sallow and scrawny by then, with nothing left of the beauty Gilly had always envied, had wept and pleaded. She'd called Gilly names and raged with breathless whispers, the loudest she could make. She'd demanded.

Gilly hadn't killed her mother, but she'd wanted to.

Gilly leaned forward, too. She could've kissed him, if she'd chosen. Or bitten him. "I'm a mother and I would do anything for my children. I *would* kill you. Believe it."

She had never meant anything more.

"Mothers don't love their children that much." Todd stood and shrugged. "It's something they made up for TV. You don't have a clue about killing."

"Do you?" she shot back, and was instantly afraid of the answer.

"Are you asking me if I ever killed someone?"

Did she want to know?

"Yes," Gilly said.

Todd gave her no answer other than a shake of his head.

Gilly swallowed hard, choking for a second on the breath she'd been holding. "Would you kill me?"

"Aw, hell! I already told you that's not why I brought you here, Jesus."

"I didn't ask if you wanted to kill me. I asked if you would." She didn't like this side of herself, the relentlessness, but she didn't stop herself. "If I run away again, and you catch me, will you kill me? Will you kill me anyway? Because someone will come, Todd. Someone will find out where I am, and come for me. You know they will."

He ran both hands through his hair, gripping his head for a moment before replying through gritted teeth. "Shut the fuck up, okay?"

She moved closer, tiny compared to his height, but pushing him back with every step she took. "I want to hear you say it. I want to know. I deserve to know!"

"Why?" He backed away, shaking his shaggy head, the dark hair swinging like the mane of some wild stallion. "Why the fuck do you deserve a fucking thing from me?"

"Because you took me!" The words tore her throat.

"At the gas station I thought you'd leave and it would be all over. You'd call the cops, they'd come, whatever. I figured that was it. I went in the store and bought my shit, the whole time thinking I was gonna come back out and find you gone. I thought for sure I was screwed, but you stayed in the truck. Why didn't you get out? Why the hell didn't you get out?"

"Why didn't you make me get out?"

"Fuck if I know. I figured…what the hell, if you didn't get out, you wouldn't tell the cops…I dunno. Christ, you scared the shit out of me, Gilly. That's all. I didn't know what the hell to do with you. You had the chance to get out and you didn't…." Todd's grin reminded her of the Big Bad Wolf. All teeth. "You're as crazy as I am."

Crazy meant medication, hospitals, long narrow corridors smelling of piss and human despair. Crazy was her mother, locked away in a room with only her mood swings for company. It was the grit of shattered glass underfoot and the smell of spilled perfume.

"No, I'm not." Her words weren't as convincing this time.

Todd snorted and turned back to the window with the same easy knack he had of pushing away the tension, making it appear that it hadn't happened at all. "Man, it's really coming down. We might get another foot, at least."

Gilly stood and took her bowl to the sink. She had to push past him to get there, but he stepped aside and didn't crowd her. Side by side they stared out the window.

"So," she said. "What happens now?"

Todd shrugged again. "I don't know."

Gilly wanted to slap him. Instead, she rinsed her bowl and spoon and set them to dry in the drainer. He didn't move, only watched her.

"I won't stop trying, you know," she whispered. "To get away, I mean."

"I'll always stop you."

"No," Gilly said. "One day, you won't."

10

Short days passed into long nights. Gilly's body ached, but she forced herself to appreciate every ache and pain and hobble around the cabin to keep her stiff muscles limber. She didn't think there'd be another chance for escape, but if one came she didn't want to be too disabled to take it.

Todd didn't say much to her, and if he noticed Gilly keeping her distance from him, he didn't show it. Again, she was struck at how easy he was about all of this, how commonplace he made it. While every gust of wind scraping a tree branch on the house startled her into jumping, Todd barely glanced up. When she padded past him to the kitchen to forage for something to eat, he called out casually for her to grab him a beer.

She did, not sure why. The bottle, a longneck, chilled her palm as she brought it to him. She watched while he took a pocketknife, much smaller than the one he'd threatened her with, and used the bottle-opener part to open it. He tipped it to his lips, drinking it back with a long sigh.

"Want one?" he said. "There's a couple in the fridge, couple of six-packs on the back porch in cans. I should've bought more."

"No."

Todd lipped the bottle's rim and drank again. His throat worked. She was looking at him but her gaze fell on the knife on his belt. He watched her looking and tipped the bottle at her.

"Might be good for you," Todd said.

Gilly felt her mouth go tight and hard. "To get drunk?"

"Might loosen you up."

"I don't need to be loose," Gilly muttered, and turned her back on him.

In the kitchen she opened drawer after drawer. He'd taken away all the sharp knives. She went through the cupboards, too, aware he'd come to watch her. Todd leaned in the doorway, one ankle crossed over the other, beer in his hand.

"What are you looking for?"

She slammed a drawer, making the silverware inside jump. She shrugged. She didn't really know. Todd laughed, and Gilly glared at him over her shoulder.

"Have a beer," he said. "It'll make you feel better, really."

"I don't drink." She pulled down a glass and filled it with cold, clear water that must've come straight up from a hundred feet underground. It went down the back of her throat like a shot, delicious, and sent a spike of pain to the center of her forehead.

Todd took a long pull from the bottle and set it on the counter next to him. "How come?"

Gilly blinked slowly and rinsed her glass from the faint

imprint of her lips. She dried it with a hand towel and put it back in the cupboard. She didn't answer.

"Whatever," Todd said, and went back into the living room, where he lit a cigarette and fiddled with the small radio he'd pulled from someplace when she wasn't watching.

At first it blatted static interspersed with gospel music. Finally, after several minutes fidgeting with the knob, Todd tuned in a station playing some contemporary music. The song ended and the disc jockey came on.

"…worst blizzard in twenty years…" The static broke the words into burps and fizzles, but the message was clear. More snow had fallen on the region than in twenty years, and more was predicted.

"Fuck me," Todd murmured. "More damned snow."

She'd already paced the length and width of this place while he was gone. There wasn't enough room to keep between them. She could find privacy in the bathroom, though not for long since he had to share it, or upstairs, where she'd lain for hours listening to random songs on her increasingly finicky iPod. Here in the living room, though, he was too close even when he was across the room.

Gilly went to the window. Crossing her arms over her chest, she rubbed her elbows even though she wasn't cold. He'd filled the woodstove with logs and it had heated the downstairs, at least. Heat was supposed to rise but maybe the vents were blocked or something, because upstairs stayed cold enough to show her breath.

She couldn't see much through the glass. The propane lanterns that illuminated the room didn't quite reach outside. She couldn't see the snow falling, but she could hear it. It sounded like a mother shushing a ceaselessly cranky child.

Shh. Shh. Shhh.

Todd clicked off the radio with an annoyed grunt. "Good thing I got the supplies when I did. Uncle Bill always said to shit when you had the paper."

Gilly didn't turn. "How eloquent."

She'd spoken thick with sarcasm, but Todd only laughed. "He had a way with words, all right. He liked 'em. Big ones, especially."

She flicked a glance toward him. "I wouldn't say *shit's* a particularly big word."

"Nah. I mean he liked other big words. Like *stygian* and *bumptious* and *callipygian*." He laughed, shaking his head. "That means you have a nice ass."

"It doesn't!"

"Sure it does. You can look it up if you want. Uncle Bill kept a list of words he ran across that he didn't know. He'd look them up in the dictionary and write them down. He said a man who could use big words had something over the man who didn't." Todd paused. "Obviously I don't much take after my uncle. Of course, Uncle Bill always said it was good to know your own faults, too."

She wasn't sure if he were being self-deprecating or simply brutally honest. "He's right."

"He *was* right," Todd said. "Now he's just dead."

Gilly had nothing to say to that but "I'm sorry."

Todd snorted. "Why? You didn't even know him. No point in being sorry about something you didn't do."

"Is that something else your uncle Bill said?"

"As a matter of fact, he did."

Moments of silence passed with nothing but the sound of the snow outside and her own heart beating its slow tempo in her ears. Gilly stared out into the darkness, seeing nothing. Thinking of everything.

"I'm hungry," Todd said.

She wasn't, and didn't answer. Gilly shut her eyes and leaned her forehead against the glass. The cold soothed her bruises.

Shh. Shh. Shhh.

"How about some dinner?"

"No, thanks." Her stomach turned over again at the thought of food, her throat so tight she wouldn't be able to swallow anyway. And even if she did, it felt like all of it would come right back up.

"I meant," he said, "how about making *me* some dinner."

Oh, no, he did not just ask me that.

"No." Gilly twisted to face him for a moment, her face set in the look her husband called Wrath of the Gorgon. It was usually enough to send her family scattering, but not Todd. He just tilted his head to stare.

"No?" Todd said as though he hadn't heard her.

"No," Gilly repeated, and turned back to the window.

Shh.

Tears licked at the back of her eyelids, burning them. She swallowed another lump in her throat. Her fingers clutched tight into fists, her broken nails digging without mercy into her palms.

"What do you mean, no?"

She heard him get up from the table and braced herself for his touch. She already knew he had no trouble using his hands to get what he wanted. Well, he could force her into the kitchen if he wanted. Make a puppet of her, forcing her hands to cook, if that was important enough to him. Gilly thought about the promise she'd made to herself that she'd get out of this alive, but three months was a long time to serve as someone's slave. She'd be damned if she would. Gilly straightened her spine and kept her face against the glass.

"I'm not hungry. If you are, you can make yourself something to eat. I won't do it for you."

He let out a low, confused snuffle. She pictured him shrugging, frowning, though she hadn't turned around to see it. "Why not?"

One. Two. Three.

She wouldn't make it to ten. "Because I'm not your wife and I'm not your mother. I'm not here to take care of you."

"But..." She heard the struggle in his voice as he tried to understand. "But you made dinner for me before, the other day when I came back."

"I made dinner for *me,*" Gilly said. "And I made enough for you while I was at it. It's an entirely different thing. I was trying to be nice."

"Why don't you try to be nice now?"

His question was simple, and she had a simple answer.

She turned to look at him. "Because there's no point in it, now, is there?"

She waited for him to speak. Instead, he left the room and went to the kitchen. She smelled garlic and ground beef, good smells that should've made her hungry but only sent bitterness surging onto her tongue. She heard the clatter of dishes and silverware, the sound of the kitchen chair scraping on the linoleum. Later, a belch.

Gilly stayed looking out at the night, eyes not seeing the dark outside or the reflection of her face in the glass facing her. She looked beyond those things to the faces of her children and drew strength from them, and she listened to the soft sound of the snow covering the world outside.

Shh. Shh. Shhh.

11

She'd woken earlier than him again. Gilly listened to the soft sound of Todd's snoring from beyond the partition. Though an initial slow stretch proved her aches and pains had eased a little, her stomach rocked and her head pounded. Somehow this was worse than feeling as though she'd been beaten with a mallet.

Why bother getting up? You have no place to go. Nothing to do. Nobody needs you. Go back to sleep. When's the last time you stayed in bed so long?

Gilly couldn't convince herself to get up. She'd given up the luxury of sleeping in for babies, and it was one she missed the most. Admitting to herself she was enjoying not having to get out of bed felt wrong, but she forced herself to own it. She'd never been the sort to poke herself on purpose with pins, but something about this pain felt right.

She still didn't get up.

Lethargy weighted her limbs. Beneath the layers of quilts,

warmth cocooned her. She shifted her legs and the soft flannel of the nightgown rubbed against the heavy fleece sweatpants she wore beneath it. Turning onto her side, face snuggled into the pillow, Gilly sighed and drifted.

When her leg cramped and her hip ached, she turned onto her back. When that position started to hurt, she rolled to her other side. She didn't sleep, not really, no matter how much she wanted to. She did dream, though. Random patterns of memory and thought, currents of imagination painting pictures in her brain.

Long, lazy nights spent making love. Burrowing deep under blankets against the light of morning, against the chill of winter air. Snuggling up tight against naked flesh, the sound of Seth's voice and low laughter warming her as much as the layers of quilts. Pressing against him. Loving him.

How long had it been since they'd spent a day like that together, staying in bed for hours? Enjoying each other's company beyond just sex? Would she ever have the chance again?

Her stomach gurgled, more in hunger than nausea this time. Gilly ran her tongue over her teeth and wrinkled her nose at the film there. She hadn't showered or bathed, *really* bathed in four days.

Until Todd built up the fire for the day, the cabin would stay cold. There was nothing else to do but brave it. She flung off the covers and jumped out of bed. Her head pounded harder at the motion, but she forced herself to continue.

With a quick glance over the partition at still-sleeping Todd, Gilly slipped the heavy flannel gown over her head and tucked it under her pillow, then tugged the covers over it. She grabbed the turtleneck shirt and sweater from the rocking chair next to the bed and pulled them both on. Later, she'd be reduced to short sleeves and sweating even, but for now she wanted both the protection of "real" clothes, not pajamas, and as many layers as she could.

Todd muttered in his sleep, rolling onto his belly and pulling the pillow over his head as she walked past him. The floor creaked and she paused, but he didn't wake. Downstairs, Gilly used the poker on the red coals until they flared and then put on a log. She warmed her hands for a few minutes at the stove and watched the huff of her breath shine silver and ephemeral before disappearing.

She hated being cold. Really hated, not just disliked. Growing up, the house had always been chilly and dark. Gilly had vowed she'd never live that way, shivering and piling on sweaters to stay warm. And yet here she was, covered in goose bumps with the tip of her nose an ice cube.

"Bleah," Gilly muttered.

The room warmed, slowly. Her stomach rumbled. She was no more eager to move from her spot near the stove than she'd been to get out of bed, but eventually she forced herself to get up and wander into the kitchen on toes still too miserably cold for her good humor.

She finished her breakfast, more sugary cereal, with no sign or sound of Todd from above. Strangely, the sweetness again settled her stomach. She craved coffee, which was also odd since even at home she usually preferred tea.

She washed her bowl and spoon and set them in the drainer to drip dry. So domestic, so normal. Gilly paused, hands still in the sink, fingers ringed with bubbles. She tried hard to find some outrage or anger or fear, but none came.

As a kid, the only constant in their house had been inconstancy. From one day to the next Gilly was never sure whether her dad would be home or traveling, if her mother would be a bright and smiling TV-perfect mom, baking cookies, or something rather less pleasant. Gilly could adapt to anything. Even, it appeared, this.

With her bowl and spoon washed, Gilly had nothing else to do. Todd had brought her sparkly tights and flannel pajamas, but he hadn't brought her anything to read. A search of the large armoire in the corner revealed a large selection of board games including Monopoly, Parcheesi and Trouble. Decks of cards, poker chips, a checkerboard with a plastic Baggie of checkers stacked on top. She found a hinged box full of spent shotgun shells and stared at it for a long time as though looking would give her some clue as to why anyone had saved them, but in the end she couldn't think of any reasons that made sense. On one of the shelves she discovered a stack of *Field & Stream* and *People* magazines from the 1980s.

Princess Diana stared out at her from one cover, Mel Gibson from another. She touched the slick paper and ran her fingers over his piercing blue eyes. *Sexiest Man Alive.* Would anyone think so now? Probably not after the adultery and anti-Semitic rants.

"Morning." Todd startled her out of her reverie. "You been up long?"

"A little while."

He yawned and stretched, showing the pale worm of his scar twisting across his belly. His face had scabbed. He was healing. They both were.

"Still snowing?" he asked, not waiting for a reply before looking out one of the back windows. He glanced over his shoulder at her. "It's ugly out."

Gilly shrugged. Did it matter? What would be a few more inches on top of what had already fallen?

Todd yawned again and scrubbed at his hair. "I thought we were supposed to have whatchamacallit. Global warming."

Gilly gathered a handful of magazines and closed the armoire door. "That's what they say."

"They." Todd laughed, shaking his head. "Who's they, anyway? Bunch of scientists sitting around yanking their cranks, figuring out stuff to scare everyone. That's what I think. You eat already?"

She nodded and Todd padded into the kitchen. He ate breakfast while Gilly read about celebrities and fads from thirty years ago. The room grew warmer as he added more wood to the stove. Gilly shed her sweater, at last warm if not exactly cozy.

Perhaps an hour passed while Gilly read. During that time, she was aware of Todd drifting around the room. She kept her eyes on the pages as he walked aimlessly from window to window. He checked the stove, adding logs and pushing them around with the poker until sparks flew. He went out onto the front porch, letting in a burst of air that ruffled the pages and raised goose bumps on her flesh.

At last, irritated, Gilly snapped. "Can't you find something to do?"

Todd flopped on the sofa across from her and sighed. "There *is* nothing to do."

He looked so much like Arwen when she said the same thing that Gilly bit her lip against a chuckle. Todd drummed out a beat on the arm of the couch, something rhythmic and annoying. Gilly ignored him, concentrating on the magazine, but Todd wouldn't be ignored. He shifted, muttered, wriggled, thumped. At last she set aside the issue in her hands; Princess Di slithered off the couch and onto the floor.

"Why don't you go have a beer," she said. "Or something."

He paused in the incessant motion and raised a brow. "I thought you didn't drink."

"I don't. Doesn't mean you can't."

He glanced toward the kitchen, then back at her with a raised eyebrow. "Why, you want me drunk?"

"Oh, God, Todd. Why on Earth would I *want* you drunk?"

"Maybe so I'll pass out."

He didn't say the rest, that she'd use the chance to escape, but Gilly knew what he meant. It was unreasonable to feel stung that he might be as wary of her as she was of him, but Gilly sniffed anyway. "Actually, no. I don't like being around drunk people. Does one beer make you drunk?"

"Not usually." He grinned and thumped his feet on top of the coffee table, shifting the pile of magazines she'd finished.

"Could you not do that? You're making a mess." She bent to pick up all the magazines and stacked them neatly, then looked up to see him staring at her curiously.

"Does it make a difference?" Todd said.

Gilly stood, stretching against the lingering bumps and bruises. "Yes. It does."

Todd put his feet down with a thud and a frown. "Sorry."

For once he'd been the one to say it, and Gilly looked him over. "It's just nicer if things are clean, that's all."

"Yeah, well, nothing stays..." Todd began and stopped. He scowled. "Yeah. I guess so."

Restless, Gilly stretched again. The passage of time struck her. She'd lost track of the days. "What's today?"

"Friday. I think. Right? Fuck if I know."

Friday. At home she'd be spending the day cleaning and cooking in preparation for Shabbat. By nightfall she'd be exhausted, but seeing the faces of the ones she loved in the light of the Sabbath candles always rejuvenated her. Gilly looked forward to Friday nights for just that reason.

She baked fresh challah, the Jewish Sabbath bread, every week. Her stomach muttered at the thought. She didn't remember seeing any yeast in the kitchen, but she might be able to find something. If her ancestors had survived fleeing Egypt with only unleavened bread to take with them, Gilly Soloman could make do.

The heat from the woodstove didn't quite reach the pantry. Her breath plumed out in great gusts as she searched the shelves. Todd's more recent purchases, many of them still in plastic grocery bags, cluttered the front of the shelves, but further back were items that had probably been there as long as the magazines.

Her fingers were growing numb. "Todd!"

He appeared in the doorway after a moment. "Yeah?"

Gilly waved her hand at the chaos. "Get this stuff all put away, will you? You can't just leave it like this."

"Why not?"

She gave him an exasperated sigh. "Because it's a mess, that's why. Who raised you, wolves?"

She'd meant the question as rhetorical, but by the way his expression slammed shut she knew she'd touched a sore spot. "Sorry."

He set his jaw but brushed past her. The pantry wasn't really big enough for the two of them. As he began taking cans and jars out of the bags, Gilly felt the heat radiating from him. He was his own furnace.

She stepped away, uncomfortable with the contact. "I'll go work in the kitchen. Shut the door so the heat doesn't come out."

He grunted in reply but kept unpacking. She gave him a look. Todd made an exasperated sputter.

"What? You think I'm that much of a douche bag that I don't even know enough to keep the freaking door shut?"

She didn't answer that, just went into the kitchen and closed the door behind her. Gilly opened cupboards, pulling out ingredients she'd need as she found them and organizing the ones she didn't. Uncle Bill must have used the cabin fairly frequently, for it was well stocked with staples like salt and spices, and lots of nonperishable goods. Todd had also made good choices in his grocery buying. Not just all sugar cereals, cigarettes and booze like she'd thought.

It chilled her, a little, how methodical he'd been about shopping. Making sure there was enough of everything. She should be grateful for it now, considering the circumstances, but he hadn't known they'd be snowed in when he'd bought it all, which only further hit home how long he'd intended to be here.

Todd emerged from the pantry blowing on his hands and shivering. He shut the door behind him. The look he gave her was defiant but proud. "It's all done."

Gilly didn't shame him by checking, which is what she'd have done for one of the kids. But he wasn't a child, much less one of hers. "Thanks."

"What are you doing?"

"I'm going to make challah, if I can find the right ingredients," she said.

His puzzled look told her he had no clue what she was talking about.

"Bread," she explained. "For the Sabbath."

Thankfully he didn't ask her more, and so she didn't have to explain a whole lot. He did look skeptical, though. "Bread?"

"We'll see how it turns out," Gilly told him. "I don't suppose you bought any yeast?"

To her surprise, he had. Not the sort of thing she'd have expected to find in a bachelor's mountain hideaway, but he went back into the pantry and came out with several packets.

"Eggs," Gilly said, looking in the fridge. "Butter. Margarine will do, I guess."

She found both and set them on the table. Todd watched as she found a bowl and mixing spoons. Gilly laid out the ingredients carefully, working from inadequate memory and hoping for the best. They'd have to do without poppy seeds, but if everything else turned out okay she supposed that was all right.

"Do you want to crack the eggs?" She asked him what she always asked Arwen and Gandy. To her surprise, Todd said yes.

She gave him the eggs, and he first made a well in the flour before he cracked them into the bowl. Then he expertly separated the final egg yolk from its white and plopped the golden glop in with the rest.

"You've done this before," Gilly said.

He shrugged. "I've had a lot of jobs. Worked in a bakery for a while. At a diner. I guess I can cook okay."

Gilly kneaded the dough, then set it aside to let it rise. She remembered seeing something in the pantry, an item she'd thought a strange choice. "We…we could make some chocolate chip cookies. If you want."

He gave her a guarded expression. "Why?"

Why did she want chocolate chip cookies, or why was she being nice? Gilly wiped carefully at the sprinkles of flour on the table. "Because I feel like it."

The grin began on the left side of his mouth, where it twitched his lips until it reached the other side. "I make good cookies."

"So do I."

She hadn't intended a challenge, but there it was. Todd brushed the hair out of his eyes and looked at her thoughtfully. Gilly lifted her chin, staring back.

"Mine are better," Todd said.

"Why don't we find out?" Gilly asked.

Wasting the eggs and butter seemed foolish when both knew there could be no more until the snow thawed. Todd didn't mention it, so neither did Gilly. Both gathered what they needed with an unspoken agreement not to peek while the other worked.

Gilly's recipe had come straight off the back of the store-brand chocolate chips she bought in bulk from the warehouse club. It was only a little different from the one on the package Todd had bought. With the exception of walnuts, which she despised and Todd hadn't bought anyway, she'd made the same kind of cookies for years with fine results.

She measured and mixed from memory, handing off the measuring cups and spoons without a word. There weren't any rubber scrapers and the wooden spoons looked to be of questionable cleanliness, so she mixed the dough with a metal fork that clanked against the edge of the bowl in a steady rhythm. As with cleaning, the mixing and making put her mind on auto-pilot.

Todd took a half-used jar of ground ginger from the cupboard. She heard him humming under his breath as he mixed and scraped. Ginger?

"Wanna lick?"

She turned to see him holding out a fingerful of dough. Gilly shook her head. "No, thanks. I don't want to get salmonella."

Todd shrugged. "You don't know what you're missing."

Gilly had sneaked spoonfuls of cookie dough and risked food poisoning more times than she could count, but she wouldn't have taken the sweet, sticky dough off his finger if he'd held his knife to her head again. It might be a matter of stilted, silly pride, but it was her pride. "No, thanks."

"Okay." He put his finger in his mouth and licked the dough. He made a groaning noise of pleasure and dipped again into the bowl for another fingerful.

Gilly shivered as she watched him. Something about Todd was as raw as the cookie dough he sucked off his finger. What made it worse was that he did these things as innocently and unselfconsciously as a child. He finished with the second glob of dough and held out a third to her.

"Sure you don't want any?"

Her voice shook just a little, probably unnoticeable to him. Gilly concentrated on her own mixing bowl. "I said no."

They put the cookies on trays that had seen better times and slid them into the oven. The timer on the oven wasn't digital and took some figuring, but she managed to set it. Fifteen minutes was a very long time to sit and stare at each other. Todd thumped out a pattern on the table with his fingers, caught her looking and smiled sheepishly. He turned his hands palm up and shrugged.

"I'm a spaz. Sorry."

Gilly herself hadn't moved, though she'd felt as restless as his dancing hands had proved Todd to be. "My son is like you. Can't stop moving. It's like he runs on batteries that never wear down."

"Like that rabbit in the commercials," Todd offered.

She smiled before she could stop herself. "Yeah, like that."

"I used to drive my teachers crazy," Todd confided. He laughed and tapped out another rhythm on the tabletop, but consciously this time.

"I'm sure you did."

The timer dinged, then, saving her from having to make more conversation. Both sets of cookies came out golden-brown and smelling like heaven. Todd unceremoniously dumped his on a tea towel, cursing when he burned his fingers on the edge of the ancient blackened cookie sheet. Gilly used a spatula to pry hers from the sheet, then set them carefully on a pink ceramic plate.

"Milk," Todd said. "Gotta have milk."

"I'll get it."

She needed something fresh to breathe, some space. Gilly left the kitchen and went through the pantry to the back door, then the rickety back porch and the lean-to. Ten half-gallons of milk in white plastic jugs were lined up on one of the shelves alongside some packages of bacon, sausages, lunch meat, some cheese. Everything wore a thin silver coating of frost.

After the stifling warmth of the kitchen, the air out here was cold enough to burn. Her earlobes and the tip of her nose had gone almost instantly numb, and she was losing sensation in her fingers.

Despite all that, the cold felt good. Cleansing. Gilly didn't want to admit that she'd enjoyed the past hour, that it had actually been...pleasant. She searched inside her for the hate but, just as she had earlier, came up empty. Like joy and terror, anger was too fierce an emotion to sustain for long.

Gilly grabbed a half gallon of milk and went back inside. Todd had put two of each type of cookies on two plates and set them on the table. He'd even set out glasses.

Gilly ran the milk under the water for a few minutes until it was at least no longer frozen solid. It filled the glasses in crystalline white chunks. Todd laughed.

As it turned out, his cookies were better.

Later, as night descended, she asked him for some candles. He gave her two, squat and half-burned and ugly. She lit them with the blessings that ushered in the Sabbath. Gilly waited for the calm that always filled her, but all that came was a sense of emptiness and sorrow.

12

Gilly marked the passage of time by the aching of her heart. Each day seemed like an eternity. How long had it been since she'd smelled Gandy's hair or helped Arwen tie her shoes? How long since Seth had kissed her on the way out the door, his mind already on his job and hers on how nice it would be when nap time came? Too long.

Gilly ducks into the pantry when the kids are mesmerized by relentlessly running cartoons. In the dark and quiet she breathes in deep. Scents of cinnamon and spices. Wooden floor cool under her toes. The door has a lock on it because Gandy will sneak sweets if she doesn't keep an eye on him. She locks it now and sits on the step stool she keeps there so she can reach the highest shelves.

She only wants a few minutes' quiet. Some time to herself. She's not hungry, not thirsty, but she is bone-achingly tired. She wants to take a nap but when she tried to lie down on the couch, Gandy had made her his personal trampoline. She can't go upstairs and leave them alone down here while she sleeps. They'll destroy the house.

She wants to simply sit and breathe but the patter of small feet happens almost at once. They're tuned to her, those precious angel-monsters. She might as well put up a red alert when she goes to the bathroom, because they're instantly there. A phone conversation is a certain beacon, bringing them clinging to her legs as she tries to get in a word with friends. And, oh, she dare not sit down at the computer to check her emails before little voices beg for time on the online pet store or whatever games the cartoon shows are promoting.

"Mama?" The knock comes. Shadows shift under the door as two small humans pace back and forth. "Mama? Mama? Mama!"

And for a few seconds she pretends she doesn't hear them. Doesn't answer. For one long, eternal moment, she hopes they will simply give up and go away.

"What do you want for breakfast?" Todd's words startled her out of her thoughts.

She left the window and slid into a seat at the kitchen table. "Nothing."

He turned from the stove and looked at her critically. "C'mon. You got to eat something."

"I'm not hungry." She wasn't. Her appetite had ebbed and flowed, changing drastically over the past week. She blamed stress. She went from the edge of starvation to having her stomach want to leap from her throat at the very thought of eating anything at all, much less the skillet of eggs he was frying.

"You got to have a good breakfast if you want to get through the day." His words sounded so scholarly, so fourth-grade teacherly, so damned smug.

She wanted to give him the finger.

"I'm serious," Todd said. "Breakfast is the most important meal of the day."

"Who told you that?" she asked cruelly. "Your dear sainted mother?"

The skillet clattered against the burner rings. Todd switched off the propane with a sharp and angry twist of his wrist. "No. Not from her."

The word dripped with a vehemence so thick Gilly could practically see it. She found herself apologizing to him again for remarks she'd made about his upbringing. "Sorry."

The set of his shoulders said the apology hadn't been accepted. Gilly told herself she didn't care. It was nothing to her if she hurt his feelings. Situation and circumstance should have given her the perfect reason to forget the sort of fake politeness she'd always hated and never been able to stop herself from offering.

Todd shook himself slightly, then set the eggs on the table. "Eat."

"I'm not hungry," Gilly repeated. "What are you going to do, force me?"

He cocked his head. "Uncle Bill always said if you had to force someone to do something it probably wasn't worth making them do it."

More words of wisdom from Uncle Bill. Gilly sat back in her chair and fixed him with a glare. "Oh, really?"

He stabbed a pile of yellow fluff with his fork. Before he brought it to his lips, he paused. Searched her gaze with his own in a manner so forthright it brought heat to stain Gilly's cheeks.

Todd pointed with his fork to the snow-laden window. A drift had formed outside, one large enough to nearly cover the glass. "Even if I *wanted* to let you go, I couldn't."

"But you don't *want* to." She teased out this truth between them as though he'd tried to deny it.

Todd set down the utensil with its uneaten clump of egg still clinging to it. His eyes glinted but his voice remained soft when he answered her. "I can't go back to jail, Gilly. I just can't. Don't you get it?"

"I get it."

Todd paused, gaze not shifting from hers. Serious. "And if I get caught for this, that's what would happen. They'd put me back in jail. I'd rather die."

Her fingers tapped a random pattern on the faded tabletop before she stopped them. Her voice went tight and hard, unsympathetic. "You should have thought about that before you kidnapped me."

His sigh was so full of disgust it made her flinch. "I didn't kidnap you."

Gilly shoved away from the table and went to the sink. Nothing outside but white. She gripped the edge of the counter, forced herself to lower her voice. "Don't act like you picked me up in a bar during fifty cent draft night."

She'd had moments like this before, days when every little thing worked at her like a grain of sand against an eyeball. One minute close to tears, the next ready to scream until her throat tore itself to bloody shreds. Seth knew to stay out of her way when she was like this, blaming it on her hormones or menstrual cycle with a man's bland acceptance that the mysteries of a woman's body could be blamed for everything. Her temper was hot but brief, and Gilly had learned to hold it in as best she could. She had to.

Her mother had screamed a lot, when she wasn't facing Gilly with cold silence that was somehow worse than the shrieking accusations. Her mother had alternated between rage and despair with such little effort Gilly hadn't known until adulthood there could be a difference in the emotions.

Counting to ten. Counting to twenty. Biting her tongue until it bled. Sometimes, most times, those tactics worked. It hurt, holding in all that anger, but she wasn't going to put her kids through what she'd gone through as a child. Some days that had meant hiding in the pantry, clinging to the very last shreds of her patience with everything she had, just to keep herself from flying apart.

She wasn't feeling very patient now. Not even counting to a hundred was going to work. Angry words wanted to fly from her lips, to strike him, to wound. She bit the inside of her cheek. Pain helped her focus. Fury wouldn't help her. Todd was right about the snow and their situation. He couldn't let her go, and she couldn't realistically, practically or logically escape. It was keep her temper or lose her mind.

"You should just kill me," she said through clenched jaws, knowing even as she said it she was poking him too hard.

Todd shook his head, facing away from her. He hunched over the table, stabbing at his plate with the tines of his fork. "Shut up."

But she couldn't. The words tumbled out, bitter and nasty. Harsh. "You could've let me freeze to death out there. You wouldn't have to worry about me, then. You should've left me in the truck. Then I'd be dead and you'd have nothing to worry about."

"I said," Todd muttered tightly, "shut up."

She'd never pulled the legs off daddy longlegs, never tied a can to a puppy's tail. Gilly had never been the sort to tease and torture. But now she found a hard, perverse and distinct pleasure in watching Todd squirm.

"The only way you'll ever be safe is if I'm dead," she continued, gleeful, voice like a stick stabbing him in tender places.

"So you should just do it. Get it over with. Save us both the hassle—"

"Shut up, Gilly."

She slapped the counter hard enough to make some dishes jump. "Do it or say you'll let me go!"

He stood and whirled on her, sending her stumbling back against the sink. The chair clattered to the floor. The cold metal pressed against her spine; her elbow cracked painfully on the counter's edge.

"I only wanted the truck. I told you that. I was going to dump you off by the side of the road, but then you had the kids in the back. I didn't want to hurt the kids. I just wanted to come up here and stay away from people, to get away! I didn't want to keep you, for fuck's sake! But now here you are, right? Right up in my fucking face. Yeah, I could've left you out there to freeze, but I didn't. But that doesn't make me a hero, right? Just makes me an asshole. I'm fucked no matter what. So why don't I just kill you, Gilly? Why don't I? Because I don't. Fucking. Want to."

She'd thrown her hands up in a warding-off gesture, but Todd didn't touch her. He raked one hand through his hair instead and backed off. It would've been easier if he'd hit her. She was waiting for it. She was pushing him to do it. She wanted him to hit her, she realized with sickness thick in her throat.

"Uncle Bill died. He left me this place, and the money. Five grand," Todd said in a low, hoarse voice. A broken voice. "Not a whole lot of money, but nice. I was doing okay without it. I was making it. Doing whatever I had to, to get by. Working shit jobs, never doing anything but work and sleep. Shitty apartment, piece-of-shit car, mac-and-cheese for dinner four times a week. And not the good kind," he added, this affront clear. "The four-for-a-dollar crap from the dollar store."

Gilly remembered the flavor of that kind, made with water instead of milk when her bank account had run low. She could taste it now, the flavor nostalgic and gritty on her tongue. It wasn't necessarily a bad memory.

"The money was going to make a difference, pay some bills, so that was good. I thought I might actually get ahead for once instead of always being behind. But it didn't get released right away. Some bunch of legal shit I had to sift through and I didn't know how. But I was doing okay."

He shot her a narrow-eyed look, emphasizing it. "I was doing *okay.* Then they fired me at the diner for being late. I was late because my car broke down. My buddy Joey DiSalvo was going to sell me a car, real cheap, but he needed a thousand bucks. It was everything I had. I mean everything. Rent, food, everything. But no car, no job. That son-of-a-bitch took my money and ran off…."

The words tumbled out of him in a rush, breathless, but with the same precise manner she'd noted about him before. As though every word he spoke had been carefully thought out before he pronounced it.

Todd paced the worn linoleum. There wasn't really enough room for him to do that, not without bumping against her, but he didn't seem to notice or care. He stalked to the pantry door and slipped a crumpled pack of Marlboros from his shirt pocket. Without pause, he lit a cigarette from the stuttering flame from his lighter and drew the smoke deep into his lungs. It streamed forth from his nostrils as he paced. Her eyes watered at the acrid stench as he passed.

He talked and smoked, the cigarette tipping against his lip but never falling out of his mouth. "They fired me because I was late," he repeated. "One time. One fucking time. They wouldn't give me a second fucking chance, you know?"

"Because you'd been in jail." The sight of him fascinated her. She was no less angry than she'd been a few moments before, but Todd had a way of defusing her fury that Seth, despite their years together, had never mastered.

Todd slammed his fist against the cupboard, rattling the dishes inside. Gilly jumped. "Yeah. Because of that. You want to know what I did? I robbed a liquor store because I owed some guys some money. I thought it would be an easy gig, right? Bust in, get the cash, get the fuck out. The state doesn't need that money, why the fuck do we pay all those taxes, right? Old man doing inventory wasn't supposed to be there. But he was. Shit, Gilly, my fucking gun wasn't even real. I bought it at a garage sale. It was a fucking *lighter.*"

"You robbed a store. Did you think that was someone else's fault, too, like it was my fault I have kids?"

Todd's lip curled, his dark eyes glinting. "You don't know shit about a damn thing."

"I've never robbed a liquor store, I know that." Gilly pointedly waved a hand in front of her face to disperse the smoke stinging her eyes and coughed, though she doubted Todd would care.

His gaze through the wafting smoke became assessing. "You don't know what it's like to be poor. That's what I know."

She thought of college, living on ramen noodles and dollar-store macaroni-and-cheese to make ends meet, but always knowing she could go home if she really needed to. And of how living in near poverty was often better than going home. "There are plenty of disadvantaged people who don't turn to crime."

He sneered again, taking another drag on the cigarette.

This time instead of letting the smoke seep from his nostrils he held it in his mouth and let it drift out one side. "I wasn't *disadvantaged*."

"No?"

"I was royally screwed, that's what I was."

She raised her eyebrows at him. "What happened? Kids make fun of you at school because you didn't have the right clothes?"

"Sometimes." Todd's gaze went flat. "Sometimes for other things."

It was her turn for a curled lip. "Poor baby."

"You don't know anything about what my life was like. Don't even try. You can't even guess." Now his voice shook, just barely, and he swallowed hard before turning away.

She couldn't, actually. She had no experience with people who thought living on the other side of the law was fair compensation for the slights society had made against them. Her voice was hard and humorless, though not quite as poking as it had been before.

"Everybody thinks their lives are hard, Todd. It's human nature to think you're special. Especially when you're not."

She'd meant that to hurt him, but it seemed to miss the mark, because Todd didn't even flinch. He leaned toward her much as she had done to him earlier. Smoke laced the hot breath caressing her cheek. Gilly forced herself to stand still, to meet his eyes. To not turn away. She'd put herself in this place. She had to face it.

"*Your* life didn't seem too hard. Nice car. Wallet full of money." He reached out and flicked the pendant dangling from her neck. "Nice husband to buy you pretty jewelry. Nice kids. You had it *real* hard, Gilly. Poor fucking you. Poor little rich girl."

Guilt raged through her, because what he said was true. She couldn't deny it. She'd let him steal her from that good life, the good man and the children who were her reason for everything. Gilly slapped his hand away.

"Don't touch me."

Todd drew back. He threw the remains of the cigarette on the floor and ground it out with the toe of his boot. He rested for a minute, sagging against the counter, and slipped his hands into the pockets of his jeans. "It was the first time I'd ever robbed a place. But I got into a lot of trouble as a kid. He…the judge said…maybe some time behind bars would change my attitude."

"Did it?" The question was rude, but Gilly couldn't take it back.

"Hell if I know." Todd shot her a grin then, shocking in its unpredictability. "Guess not."

Gilly shook her head, unbalanced by his shift in attitude. "Stealing my truck wasn't too smart."

"You got stupid people and smart people," Todd said with another of his dangerously charming and artless shrugs. "I'm just not smart."

He was no genius, she knew that. Yet something about his reply told her that he'd been told he was stupid so many times that it had become the truth, rather than the other way around. He'd been told it, and he believed it. He had become it.

"Didn't you think they'd trace the truck?"

He snorted. "Trucks get stolen all the time. I had a buddy who was going to take care of it for me. Not DiSalvo, that piece of shit. Some other dude. Said he'd give me a good deal on a trade-in. I'd have been out of it and into something else before anyone even knew where to start looking for it. It would've been in a hundred pieces, sold for parts."

He sounded so confident and made it sound so plausible, she thought he might be right. Not that it mattered, now, with her Suburban probably in a hundred pieces at the bottom of a mountain ravine instead of a junkyard. "Forgive me if I don't feel bad for you."

Todd lit another cigarette and puffed the smoke at her. He cocked his head again, the puppyish tilt of it at odds with the harshness of the smoke curling from his nostrils. "C'mon, Gilly. I haven't been such a prick to you, have I?"

"You've been a real Prince Charming," Gilly muttered. She had a headache, and her stomach had begun its incessant churning again. She was frustrated and annoyed, but no longer in a raging fury. She only wanted to lie down and go back to sleep.

Todd reached out as casually as if he were plucking a flower and grabbed a handful of hair at the back of her head. Faster than a moment, he'd pressed her against him. Todd's fingers twisted in her hair, the pressure just on the edge of becoming pain.

"I could have hurt you. Could've pulled over the side of the road and gutted you like a deer." Todd nuzzled his cheek against her neck in the sensitive part just below her ear, though there was nothing sensual about the caress. Nothing sexy. Beneath the harsh smell of tobacco smoke, she caught the scent of soap and flannel. His lips brushed her ear when he whispered, "But I didn't, did I?"

"Don't." Unable to move away from him with his hand fixed in her hair, Gilly stiffened her spine against a shiver.

"Even though you act like that's what you want me to do." His fingers curled tighter, knuckles pressed to the back of her skull. Her scalp protested, skin smarting. "Is that really what you want?"

Gilly closed her eyes.

"Answer my question," he said without letting go. When she didn't answer, he tugged sharply until she looked at him. "Haven't I been good to you, Gilly?"

"No, you haven't," Gilly muttered, bracing herself for more pain that didn't come.

"I didn't want you here." He put his forehead on hers. His deep brown eyes bored into hers, hardly even blinking. "I even tried to let you escape. But you didn't go."

She twisted her head, fighting him. He was too big, too strong. She felt the strength of him in every movement. She could not wriggle free. He was violating her more surely than if he'd forced his tongue into her mouth or his hand between her legs.

"Why didn't you go when you had the chance, huh? Why not just run away to the hubby and the kiddies and the nice, white house with the yard and the dog—"

"Fuck you!" The words tore out of her.

"Don't feel good, does it? Being judged? Seems to me like you should be thanking me, not treating me like I'm something gross you stepped in."

"You don't know me." Gilly ground the words from between clenched jaws.

"You know what I think? I think," Todd said slowly, deliberately, his gaze pinning her like a beetle to a board, "I'm the best thing that ever happened to you."

Gilly stopped struggling.

He let her go. Gilly stumbled back, whacking her elbow on the counter again. More pain. She forced back a gag.

"I want to be nice to you," Todd told her. He sat at the table with his back to her. He stubbed out his smoke, then began to eat his eggs. "But you make it really fucking hard."

Gilly left the kitchen and walked to the front door. The back of her head still smarted, but her cheek fairly burned from the caress he'd put on it. She scrubbed at the flesh with her hand, the long sleeve of the sweatshirt he'd bought her fleecy-soft against the skin.

She paused by the scarred wooden table, staring without really seeing the faded plastic flowers. Roses. They were roses, faded and plastic and not real. As she wished none of this was real.

Slowly, methodically, she pulled the sweatshirt over her head. She folded it carefully, one arm over the other, then into a bulky square. She set it on the table.

Her hands went to the waist of her sweatpants. She'd had to tie the string in a double tight knot to prevent the large pants from falling off her hips. From the kitchen came the clatter of dishes in the sink. Gilly didn't pause. Her fingers worked the string, and all the while she stared at the flowers.

Roses needed lots of care. A lot of responsibility. Love wasn't enough, you had to trim them, water and fertilize them. Roses were precious and fragile things that took a lot of time and effort to grow and sometimes, no matter how much time you gave them, they still failed.

Gilly wore no shoes, only a thick pair of white athletic socks. She slid her sweatpants down over her thighs, her ankles, and over the socks, which came off with a small twist of each foot. Goose bumps rose on her skin, though with the woodstove going the room was quite warm. She was left in her panties and bra, her own that she'd been wearing the day he took her, and a cotton T-shirt that had Princess on the front in tacky rhinestone letters.

She folded the sweatpants and put them with the sweatshirt, then added the socks to the pile. She slipped the T-shirt over her head and stood nearly naked. Still staring at the flowers. Thinking about roses.

She heard the back door open as Todd went out through the pantry and to the lean-to for something. Gilly touched her breasts, her belly, the triangle of pink material between her legs. This was what was hers. She'd brought these things with her, and she didn't owe him anything for them.

The frigid air outside forced a gasp when she stepped out onto the front porch. Gilly didn't bother to shut the door behind her. She went down the rickety steps into the knee-deep snow outside.

It was cold. Very cold. She shuddered and kept walking, fixing the picture of roses in her mind. Her feet went numb so fast she could easily forget she wasn't wearing boots. Her hands reached out as though she were blind, though everything in front of her was as crisp and clear as if she were viewing it all through a magnifying glass.

She didn't know what she was doing, or why, just that his touch had made her feel unclean. Fire could burn it away; ice could sear her clean. She stumbled and went to one knee. The snow, when she threw out her hands to catch her fall, covered her arms all the way to the shoulders.

Hadn't he been good to her? Hadn't he been nice? He'd bought her clothes, he hadn't hurt her. She thought of the pale worm of a scar twisting across the softness of his belly, of cigarette smoke curling dragonlike from his nostrils, of the way his eyes glowed when he grinned. Gilly's stomach rose again at the feeling of his cheek on hers. Not because it had been repulsive, but because it had not.

He's right. You were glad to let him take you away. You wanted to be taken away, so you wouldn't have to run. Because then you could blame someone else for what you really wanted. He's right, you did this. This is all you, Gillian. All you.

She let out a small cry, unable to tell if it was of anger or despair. She forced herself to her feet. Chunks of ice littered the snow, and she'd cut her hand on one of them. A crimson rose, her blood, bloomed on the otherwise pristine surface of the drift. She swept it away with her hand, punching at it. Her fist broke through the thin crust of ice, smearing the blood into the soft snow beneath.

He'd taken her, but she'd allowed it. Nothing could ever change that. No amount of screaming, no number of accusations or lies. Todd hadn't done this to her, she'd done it to herself.

How many times did you wish for someone or something to take you away? How many times did you imagine how nice it would be to get sick, really sick, so you could be hospitalized and have someone else take care of you for a change?

The thoughts penetrated her mind over and over as she scrubbed herself with snow. Her skin turned pink, then red, and still Gilly forced her deadened hands to scoop more and rub it all over.

"The fuck are you doing?"

Todd grabbed her up out of the snow. His fingers must have dug into her skin, but she didn't feel them. He shook her so hard her teeth rattled. Gilly got to her feet and kicked out at him, feeling nothing as her bare toes crunched on his shin.

"Jesus Christ, Gilly!"

"Let me go!" The chattering of her teeth made the words a gobbledygook.

"You're out of your goddamned mind! You're crazy, you know that?"

She swung at him, but feebly, and he held her off as easily as if she hadn't even tried. "Don't touch me!"

"It's freezing out here, you dumb bitch. Get inside." Todd yanked her arm, his fingers pinching down on numbed flesh.

Gilly resisted with a strength that surprised them both. She slipped from his grasp and went sprawling back into the snow. Todd grabbed her up again, shrugging out of his battered gray sweatshirt and wrapping it around her shoulders. Gilly had no more strength to fight.

"Let me go," she thought she whispered, but neither one of them heard.

When he saw she couldn't walk he scooped her up. In the movies he would've strode through the snow cradling her against his chest without faltering. But this was not the movies, it was real life, and Gilly was no anorexic starlet. Todd stumbled and went onto one knee, dropping her.

He ground out a curse and picked her up again. He staggered up the steps and tripped through the open doorway. Gilly spilled out of his arms and onto the living room floor next to the table.

"Goddamn it." Todd grabbed her under the arms and dragged her in front of the woodstove, her heels thumping on the floorboards as she hung limp in his grasp. He began chafing her hands. "The fuck was that all about?"

She couldn't explain, not even to herself. Sheer stupidity had made her go out there, and it made no sense. It had felt right, that was all. She yelped as the feeling began returning to her hands and feet, and swatted him away.

"Don't touch me!"

He backed off, hands in the air. He went to the table and grabbed up the pile of clothes she'd left there. He came back, knelt beside her, tried to wrap her in the clothes. She shoved him away and struggled into them by herself.

"Don't touch me," she repeated. "Ever again."

He backed off again and pulled out another smoke. She felt his eyes on her as he lit up. The curl of smoke rising from the tip of the cigarette wavered in the air. His hands were shaking.

"You scared the shit out of me," he said.

Now that she was warming up her teeth chattered incessantly. She'd been out there for perhaps only fifteen minutes, but that was long enough for the first angry red patches to appear on the backs of her hands and probably other places, too. She hitched closer to the stove. Shudders racked her body.

"I want to go home." It wasn't what she'd thought she was going to say.

"I know you do."

"I miss my kids," she whispered. "And Seth."

He sighed. "I know. But you can't."

A sob hitched from her chest, burning her throat. "I want to go *home,* Todd. Where it's warm. With my family. I want to tell them that I'm sorry…I shouldn't have let you keep me…."

She sank to the floor, pressing her face to the faded rug. It smelled of dust and age. She closed her eyes, aware of the rug's nubbly surface making grooves in her skin but too tired to care.

From somewhere very far away she heard him say her name, but then she didn't hear anything else.

13

His hands were on her again, but Gilly couldn't fight them. He held her too tightly. A mountain of blankets covered her, suffocating. She kicked at them, writhing, and whimpered in gratitude at the blessed blast of cool air that covered her.

"Water," she begged, and he pressed a glass to her lips.

It choked her and she gagged. Bile burned her throat and tongue. He was there with a basin, whispered soothing things to calm her as she retched. He pushed the hair back from her forehead and gave her a cool cloth for her forehead.

Gilly sank back on her pillow, exhausted. The headache that had been plaguing her for weeks had become agonizing again. Even blinking made her head throb worse than a thumb hit by a hammer.

She remembered her stupid run out into the snow, and looked at her hands. They were still red and chapped, but it didn't look like she'd lose any fingers. She wiggled her toes under the heavy weight of the blankets, relieved to feel them all.

Todd sat back, watching her, the expression in his dark eyes veiled. "You okay?"

She nodded, though fresh pain flared behind her eyes at the movement. Gilly pressed her thumbs just inside the curve of her eye socket. It didn't help.

"Advil," she managed to say. Then as an afterthought, "Please."

"I have aspirin." Todd left and returned a few minutes later with a gigantic bottle in one hand. "This okay?"

Aspirin would barely touch the horrendous throbbing, but Gilly took the two white pills he shook out and offered. "Two more."

Todd looked at the bottle and squinted. "It says…"

"I know what the dose is," Gilly said, careful not to raise her voice and send spears of agony ripping through her head. "It's not enough. It won't help me."

"I don't want you to OD on me," Todd said, but he shook out two more pills into her outstretched hand.

She struggled to sit up. Todd slipped a hand behind her elbow to help her, and she stiffened. "Don't."

He dropped her arm as though her words had burned him. "Jesus, sorry."

Gilly shifted herself upright, which helped relieve some of the pressure. She took the cup of water he offered and swallowed the aspirin, fighting back the urge to puke it all up again.

Already she felt herself drifting again. Her eyes became heavy lidded, her limbs leaden. Gilly let herself sink back into sleep.

"You want to go up to bed?"

She did, but didn't want him to take her. Gilly opened her

eyes. The room blurred. She forced herself to sit and waited until everything around her stopped spinning.

"I can do it," she said quietly when Todd made a move to help her.

She made it to the kitchen where she drank a full glass of cold water, then refilled it and took it with her upstairs. Her former aches and pains had intensified along with the throbbing agony in her head. She thought again of her old wish to be taken so ill she'd need nursing. She put the cup close at hand on the dresser, then slipped into bed.

Her cheeks flushed, hot with fever or, more likely, embarrassment at her run out into the snow. She'd been stupid, not even trying to get away. Not even sure what she was trying. Todd must think she was nuts, and…well, wasn't she?

Her chest felt tight, her throat ticklish. Gilly coughed experimentally and groaned at the throb in her temples. She didn't think she'd be able to sleep, but she did, and dreamed.

Not of her mother, or of Seth and the children. Not even of Todd. Gilly dreamed of fields of roses, vast acres of red blooms and green stems. Beautiful, vibrant roses protected by thorns. She grabbed and grabbed again until blood ran slick and hot from her fists, and it was the same as dreaming of all of them.

14

She woke again, this time to darkness. She'd thrown off the layers of blankets and now chills assaulted her. Gilly shuddered, twisting against the pillow and struggling to pull the covers back up. Just as she did, her cheeks flared with sudden, urgent heat.

She understood in the back of her mind that she was feverish but could do nothing about it. She seemed to float in the darkness, and without the bed beneath her to anchor her to the earth, Gilly wondered if she might have just floated all the way to heaven.

She groped for the cup of water. Her fingers tipped the cup, spilling it onto her pillow. She pressed her cheek against the welcome wetness, but all too soon even that brief chill was gone. The heat from her face was so great it dried the tiny spill in no time.

She thought about calling for Seth, knowing even as she did so that he wouldn't come. She couldn't exactly remember why and didn't want to try. Where were her pills, the extrastrength antibiotics and heavy-duty decongestants that worked to make the pain in her head disappear?

She must be sicker now. Was she at home? Gilly had the sudden fear that her wish had come true. That she'd been hospitalized, taken from her children. Who was with them if she was here?

She cried their names, reaching into the blackness as though she might find their faces there beneath her fingertips. She found only frigid air and emptiness. Gilly plunged her hands back beneath the covers, hugging herself and burying her face in the pillow.

Someone had wrapped her in cotton. The thickness of it, the weight, surrounded her, pressed in on all sides. Someone had covered her eyes with gauze, so that even the blackness had taken on a fine white haze. Someone had gloved her hand, so that all she touched seemed faraway and unrecognizable.

Hands stroked her forehead. Fingers ran a delicate pattern down her cheek. Gilly turned her head, her hand trapped beneath the cotton and the gloves, unable to fight off the caresses she did not want.

"No," she mumbled. "The drugs…it's not safe…."

Antibiotics interfered with the effectiveness of birth control pills. She couldn't let Seth make love to her, not this cycle, not without some other protection. They hadn't used other protection in years.

"No," Gilly muttered as she gained the strength to push at the hands now slipping beneath her shoulders. "Don't touch me."

Not until after her next period, when the cycle would be unaffected. But when would that be? Thinking was hard, the effort enormous and ineffective, because she couldn't remember anyway. Two weeks? One? A few days?

"Don't touch me!" She found the force of will to say, and the hands underneath her slipped away and left her alone.

She had to get to the children. Baby Gandy was crying for her. Gilly's breasts tingled with a surge that meant it was feeding time.

Then she realized it was not baby Gandy sobbing for her to nurse him, but Arwen crying out for her. "Mama!" Then it was the two of them, crying her name over and over, the sound of it agonizing to hear.

She had to go to them, had to get to her babies. Gilly struggled free of the covers anchoring her to the bed. Even the darkness would not prevent her from finding them.

Her hands paddled at the air, swimming through it, but gaining no purchase. Her legs were leaden. She couldn't move them. She managed to push herself out of bed.

She hit the floor with a thud that jarred her head so badly she cried out. The ceaseless cries of "mama" stopped abruptly, and a sob of despair threatened to rip from her throat. Something was wrong with her babies. She had to get to them, *had* to.

The wood floor scraped at her cheek. Gilly pushed against it with little result, too weak to sit up, much less stand. Her breath whistled in her lungs, forcing her to cough until bright sparks flashed in her vision.

She couldn't breathe. Gilly gasped for air, but it felt like soup in her lungs, thick and suffocating. She struggled, choking and coughing, flopping on the floor.

Her mind cleared a little, and she remembered where she was. But she *had* heard someone saying "mama." She hadn't imagined it. Gilly pushed again at the floor, but couldn't really move.

The dark began to turn gray, but not because the sun was coming up. Fringes of red flickered in the gray. She was going to pass out.

She'd been sleeping a long time, she could sense that. Dozing in and out for hours. Maybe even days. But now true unconsciousness threatened, and Gilly fought it as though it were a physical being. The red fringes thickened and clung together, taking over the gray.

The darkness had been difficult, frightening but not terrifying. It was natural, part of the night. The gray and red were horrifying in their casual replacement of the simple darkness; the gray and the red were not outside of her, they were in her mind.

Her arms stiffened even as she twitched. Every meager breath she managed to take sounded like a freight train, rumbling. Gilly wheezed, unable to do anything more now than clutch at the pain in her head, squeezing her temples with frozen fingers.

She was losing the battle. She could not get up from the floor; she could not get to her children. She'd abandoned them. Even as unconsciousness threatened, her thoughts became clear.

The gray and the red had been replaced by blackness, black as ink, as tar, as eternity. Not the darkness of night, but of the void. Gilly fought it, too, but fared no better. She closed her eyes but the blackness followed her even there.

She would never see her children or Seth again. Whatever sickness she'd been fighting for the past few weeks had taken root and bloomed. Without medicine to battle it, and with the circumstances to aid it, it was going to overtake her.

She coughed again, feebly, unable to bring up the mess in her lungs stealing her ability to breathe. Gilly choked and choked, unable to stop.

Slow down. One breath at a time. Breathe in slow, breathe out slow.

It didn't help. Her breath was too thick. It lodged in her throat, refusing to get down into her lungs. The floor beneath her spun.

Was this it? The blackness filled her vision from side to side so there was nothing left. Gilly couldn't win.

Gilly dives to the bottom of the lake on a dare to retrieve a weighted ring. She makes it to the muddy bottom, finds the garish-colored piece of plastic, but the search has taken her too long. She hasn't gone more than a quarter of the way back to the surface before her lungs begin to burn. Halfway back her legs stop kicking hard enough to get her back to the surface in time.

She sees daylight, golden as it slants through green water, and beyond that the shimmery image of the wooden raft moored at the lake's center. She glimpses her friend's faces, watching, laughing, pointing. Gilly lets go of the weight, feels it knock against her ribs and snag the lilac nylon of her bathing suit. She reaches to the sky, grasps for the air, but cannot reach it.

What of all the boys she'll never kiss? The songs she'll never hear? She'll never finish school, marry, move from her parents' house. Regret and yearning give her enough strength to kick once, twice more, but it isn't enough. A flurry of bubbles, the last desperate few, escape her lips like butterflies dancing in the breeze.

Only one of her friends has seen her distress. David Phillips reaches one of his long arms down into the water and hauls Gilly out by her hair. She breaks the surface choking and gasping, breathing in deep. Shaking while everyone laughs. For the rest of the day, she endures the good-natured teasing of the group at losing the weight and thus the dare, but Gilly won't so much as dip a toe in the water for the rest of that summer.

She'd only nearly drowned then, but she was going to drown now. This time there would be no hand reaching down to pluck her to safety. This time, she had so much more to regret losing.

She heard her name and thought it part of the dream. The voice came again, louder this time. Hands grasped her own and pulled. Gilly didn't fight the touch this time, recognizing they were saving her from drowning. From dying.

A light shone in her eyes, and at first she thought it must be the hand of God. She blinked, and the golden glow revealed Todd's face instead. Gilly felt instant relief and disappointment at the same time.

"Don't die, Gilly." Todd's fingers bit into her wrists as he hauled her upright. "Don't die, please, don't die…."

He didn't put her back on the bed. He lifted her, and Gilly had time to think she must've lost weight, because he didn't stagger beneath her this time. Despite everything, she smiled. Would she be skinny, now?

He must have seen her smile and taken it for something else. "Jesus, Gilly. Don't you fucking die on me!"

"…easier for you…" she wheezed.

They were in the stairway now, her feet and head thumping on the narrow walls with every step.

"Shut up." He grunted with the effort of carrying her. So she wasn't skinny, after all.

"…what you want…"

"It's not what I want, goddamn it!" At Todd's shout pain flared again behind her eyes, but Gilly welcomed that pain as a good sign. She wasn't slipping away any more.

He plopped her down on the ugly plaid couch; her head

banged on the arm. He left her to light the propane lantern on the table. Gilly managed to stay upright, though without the support of his arms she barely had the strength. All at once it seemed like someone had taken a huge vacuum cleaner and sucked the garbage right out of her lungs and nose. She could breathe again, albeit with a wheezing, grumbling snort, but she *could*.

If she could breathe, that also meant that she could cough. The first bout brought up a bunch of gunk that she spit into the palm of her hand, not caring how disgusting that was. Mothering had made her immune to bodily fluids. She'd had worse on her fingers. The second bout of coughing brought a fine spray of blood from her lips.

The green mucus disgusted her, but the blood scared her. With trembling hands she took the wad of paper towels Todd handed her and wiped her hand and mouth. She waited to see if more blood would come, perhaps a gout of it, but it didn't. It looked even worse on the paper towel, small blots of crimson against the white paper. She crumpled it in her fingers so she wouldn't have to see.

He hovered over her. "Are you going to be all right?"

"I need a doctor."

He shook his head. "I can't get you one."

"I need medicine."

He held up his hands helplessly. "I don't have any. Just aspirin."

Another cough swelled in the back of her throat, but she was afraid to let it out. She swallowed convulsively to get rid of the tickle. The feeling of thick snot draining down the back of her throat sickened her, but vomiting would be worse than the coughing.

Another round of chills racked her, clattering her teeth.

More pain stabbed behind her eyes and in the hollows beneath them. In her cheeks, too, and her ears, which popped mercilessly with every swallow. Gilly rocked with the pain, body jerking. Todd paced the floor in front of her, each stride long enough to take him out of her area of view and then back into it again as he turned. With nearly every step his calf rubbed against the couch until not even the shaking and the pain in her head could stop her from yelling, even though her shout came out as no more than a hissing whisper.

"Stop that. You're shaking me."

He stopped and dropped to his knees beside her. "I don't know what to do."

She was sick, sicker than she'd ever been in her adult life, and yet she *still* had to be the one in charge. To take care of herself. Resentment burbled in her, but she didn't have the strength to do anything about it.

"Blankets" was all she managed to get out before another round of coughs ripped through her. "Hot tea..."

Todd put his hand gently on her arm, timidly, as though afraid she would order him to take it off. She didn't have the strength for it, and now it didn't seem like such a big deal. Like so much else that had happened over the past few days, what difference did it make any longer?

When he saw she wasn't going to yell, he bent forward to look at her. "You got to tell me what to do."

Wasn't that what she was doing? Gilly clenched her jaw to keep herself from biting her tongue. "Get me some blankets, some hot tea. Some more aspirin."

"Okay."

An idea struck her like a hammer between the eyes, so hard and strong she gasped and coughed. "The truck!"

"It's wrecked," Todd said. "I can't drive it anywhere. Shit, it might be totally gone, I told you that."

"Not drive," Gilly managed. "In the truck. Medicine. It's in the center console. You didn't bring it."

"I didn't know," he started, sounding defensive, but Gilly shushed him.

She'd stopped at the pharmacy just before going to the ATM. Her prescription, the decongestants and antibiotics, were in the truck. She gripped his arm, her fingers slipping and falling away without strength. "Just go. Try. I have pills in there. They'll help."

He left her, and was back in a moment with an afghan he tucked around her tightly. Todd tucked the edges around her, smoothing them. And after that, Todd didn't come back for a long time.

Gilly closed her eyes. Sleep took her again almost instantly, but it was fretful. She twisted on the couch, coughing relentlessly every time it seemed she'd drift off. Her neck and back cramped from the force of it, and shudders still swept over her.

Had she ever felt this bad? If she had, she couldn't remember it. There'd never been time to be sick when she was a kid, not when she had to be awake and alert to take care of her mother, who was hardly ever well. Even in later years, when Gilly came down with everything the kids did and often twice as hard, she didn't get "sick days."

"He's not coming back," her mother said, clear as sunlight, unmistakable.

Gilly's eyes opened, and she screamed in a breathless whistle. She was alone. She fell back against the arm of the couch, unable even to weep.

She didn't know how much time passed before cold air

caressed her. She heard the clomp of boots. The next whistle came not from her throat but the teakettle. Todd brought her a mug of tea and held it to her mouth. It burned her mouth and she winced, and the tea itself was bitter, but she sipped anyway. He slipped a couple of pills into her mouth and she washed them down.

"What else can I do?"

The warmth of the tea and blankets eased her chill; or perhaps the aspirin was helping with her fever, she didn't know. His fingers were chilly on her forehead, and that felt just fine. Gilly let her eyes close again.

"I need to sleep. Give the medicine time to work."

She sensed him leaving, but sleep wouldn't take her. The couch was old and lumpy, and her head rested at an awkward angle. The blankets that had given her such welcome warmth now lay on her like stones. Briars had bloomed in her throat, dry and scratching.

She coughed again and he was there, helping her to sit and holding out another wad of paper towels to catch what came out of her mouth. She ought to have been embarrassed, but couldn't seem to manage.

The soft fringes of his hair brushed her cheek as he slipped a pillow behind her head to ease the awkward position. Gilly turned her face away, accepting the comfort he offered but even in her delirium unwilling to accept the man who gave it. Todd tucked the blankets tighter around her and then sat on the couch facing hers.

"You shouldn't have run out in the snow," he said. "And the truck…I got the stuff out, but it's really gone, now. The tree broke when I closed the door. It's at the bottom of the mountain."

Hot tears leaked from beneath Gilly's closed eyelids and

slipped down her cheeks. She didn't speak. Todd sighed. She heard the smack of his lighter and smelled the smoke.

It made her start to cough again. The few moments of clarity she'd had began to fade again. Gilly slipped back into the twilight world.

15

She thought several days passed, but she wasn't sure. Gilly left the couch only when Todd dragged her into the bathroom to use the toilet. He didn't leave her, even there. He brought her soup and tea and medicine, and he changed the cool cloths on her forehead when the fever dried them. The more he offered her, the more she took until she had given herself up to him entirely.

This was what she'd wanted, but not the way she wanted it. After having her children there'd been nurses in the hospital who'd brought her food and helped her to pee. One kind nurse had even lifted Gilly's breast with steady efficiency to help her learn to nurse Arwen, an intimacy that Todd hadn't had reason to employ. As for the rest of it, it wasn't much different than allowing him to drive away with her. Her reasons for letting him were the same. Lying on the couch, Gilly didn't have to think. She didn't have to remember that she was missing her children, that her husband must be sick with grief at losing her.

Her illness gave her detachment a legitimacy she would not otherwise have allowed herself. She'd finally been granted her wish, an illness so deep she was unable to care for herself.

The days passed, one blurring into the other, while she slept and dreamed. There were times when she truly did not know where she was, or who Todd was, times when his comforting hand on her brow became Seth's, or even her mother's.

Gilly wept in the throes of these fever dreams, because her mother had died more than twelve years ago, before she and Seth had married, before Gilly had become a mother herself and could talk about the joys and sorrows of motherhood with her.

Gilly didn't want to die. In fact, she refused. Not like this, not from a stupid, simple bout of flu. Not in a cabin with a man she couldn't trust and wouldn't like. Not away from her family.

The power of her will had been a driving force in her since childhood and the secrets she'd had to keep about her mother's illnesses. It had seen her through high school, when good grades and snack cakes had substituted for slumber parties and prom dates. And in college, when success had frightened her more than failure.

It would save her now, too.

February

16

There came a day when her head no longer threatened to explode every time she moved, and her throat didn't constantly scratch with the urge to cough. She was far from well, but she recognized with vivid relief that she felt better. She no longer needed him, and as he put an arm beneath her to help her up, she spoke in a dull, flat voice.

"Please don't touch me."

Todd's fingers twitched briefly on her shoulder, and then he withdrew. "I was just…"

She spoke stiffly, not looking at him, her chin lifted to keep her voice from trembling. "I'm better now. You don't have to do that."

His breath hissed from between his lips, and he sat back. "Thanks, Todd."

"What?"

He hadn't smoked around her during the worst of her illness since it made her erupt into violent coughing, but now he pulled out a cigarette and lit it. "Thanks, Todd. For helping me while I puked my guts out. Thanks, Todd, for taking me to the can so I didn't have to piss myself. I could've left you to choke on your own snot."

The spot on the inside of her cheek was still sore, but she bit it anyway. "But you didn't. So…thank you."

Todd grunted and cocked his head to peer at her. "Jee-sus. Women are all the same. Ungrateful bitches."

Gilly set her jaw. "I said thank you."

"Yeah, I could really tell you meant it. You know what your problem is, Gilly? You're too fucking prideful," Todd snapped, and stalked away. He went to the kitchen and slammed some cupboard doors but didn't take anything out. He went out through the pantry and the lean-to, slamming the door behind him.

Gilly sat rigidly on the couch, her hands clenched together in her lap. He'd called her ungrateful, and he was right. He *had* helped her during the worst illness she could ever remember having. Just as he hadn't left her in the snow to freeze, just as he hadn't stabbed her through the heart. She might've died without him. Not wanting that to be fact didn't make it any less true. Pride kept her from gratitude. Still, wasn't that all she had left?

17

After that, he left her alone. Gilly had spent so many days lying on the sofa she itched for a change. She managed to set herself up in one of the armchairs with the pile of blankets and a pillow for her head, but once seated she had no more strength to do anything else. She spent the day there, and the closest Todd came to her was when he bent to put more logs on the fire.

He ate in the kitchen, alone, without offering to bring her anything. When she hobbled to the kitchen table and had to put her head down to keep herself from fainting, he ignored her and left the room. That night she managed only a glass of water and a handful of stale saltine crackers.

Facing the steep stairs by herself was a more daunting task. She almost broke down then, but stopped herself from asking for his help. She felt his eyes on her as she put her foot on the first step, and it was only his gaze that allowed her to straighten her back and take the next step. Another step had her head reeling. She put both hands on the railing. One more step and she had to sit to catch her breath.

Gilly nearly cried, wanting only to slip into bed and sleep. She slapped at the tears, forcing them away, and then she took another step. By the time she reached the top of the stairs, she was on her hands and knees. Crawling, she crossed the attic room and made it only halfway before she collapsed in exhaustion.

Just a little bit farther. You can do it. You can get yourself into that bed, and then you can sleep again. But you can't sleep here.

She pushed herself on her arms with a low groan, her head spinning. She'd left the pills downstairs, and at the realization let out a low groan. Her forehead again touched the dirty wooden planks. Dust made her sneeze until harsh, barking coughs replaced it. The world grayed, but she forced herself to stay conscious.

She hadn't realized Todd had followed her until he spoke. "You okay?"

"Fine," she managed to say.

"You're dumber than I am." Todd crouched next to her and put a gentle hand between her shoulder blades. "C'mon. Let me help you."

She assumed he'd simply pull her upright, but Todd waited. Gilly looked at him through swollen eyes and the fringe of her hair, greasy and unkempt. She licked cracked lips. "Why?"

Why should I? Why would you want to? Gilly wasn't sure what she meant.

Todd sat back on his heels and cocked his head at her again as though looking at her from an angle would help him understand her better. "Wouldn't you do the same for me?"

Gilly managed a hoarse noise that sounded as dusty as the

floor beneath her. Todd smiled a little. He pushed his hair out of his eyes with a quick flick of his fingers.

"Maybe not. Okay, so you'd let me choke to death on my own snot. I get it." He shrugged.

Gilly, still on hands and knees, blinked slowly. The truth pricked her. A thorn.

"I know you think I'm some sort of monster," Todd said after a moment when she didn't say anything.

He didn't look at her. He shifted his weight, his boots sliding on the wood. She could count the threads hanging from the hem of his jeans. The cracks in the leather of his boots.

"Well…maybe you're right," he continued. "Maybe I am. But I ain't going to let you just…die. You can't lay here on the floor like this. If you want to get into bed, I'll help you. But you got to tell me you want it."

Screw you.

The words formed in her brain but not on her tongue. She'd always hated being told what to do. Gilly blinked again, knowing to fight this was useless and ridiculous and petty. She felt his touch between her shoulder blades again.

She nodded.

He put his hands under her armpits and lifted. Not gently. The room spun as he hoisted her upright and walked her to the bed where he let her fall ungracefully. Todd stood back, watching as Gilly squirmed into the blankets.

"You need anything?"

She managed a croaking reply. "No."

He flicked his hair from his eyes again. "I'm going downstairs. If you need something, holler."

She closed her eyes. "Okay."

She listened to the sound of his boots, heavy on the floor, and the thud of him going down the stairs. The softness of the bed cradled her, and there was no denying it was better than the couch had been. Better than the floor, where she'd still be if Todd hadn't come to check on her.

She wanted to think of him as a monster, but she knew the real monster here wasn't Todd.

18

The next day was better. Her vision was clearer, her head not so heavy. She woke feeling refreshed, and though her legs still wobbled when she got out of bed, Gilly could walk.

In a cabin as small as this, she couldn't avoid him forever. It seemed trivial and childish not to speak to him when they were no more than a few inches apart at the breakfast table. Especially when he pushed the sugar across to her as she stirred her tea.

"Thank you." Gilly cleared her throat and tried again. "Thank you, Todd."

He grunted, shoveling oatmeal into his mouth. "Whatever."

She reached out hesitantly, hating herself for it but unable to stop herself from being decent. "I mean, thank you for… everything. You didn't have to."

He stared at her. "Lots of things I didn't have to do."

She nodded. "But you did."

"Ain't life funny that way?" Todd asked her, then shot her one of his wolflike grins. He gave his next words an exaggerated Pennsylvania Dutch accent. "One great big fuckup, ain't?"

His comment almost made her laugh but, in the end, did not. "Yeah. It sure is."

Todd shrugged, looking down. His face had started healing. The wounds she'd inflicted might not leave any scars, but Gilly would never look at him without remembering how she'd made him bleed.

Nobody would blame her. Probably not even Todd. But as she watched him get up from the table and take her plate with him to the sink, Gilly blamed herself.

"Anyway," she said. "Thanks."

Todd shrugged, his back to her, and put on the kettle. He brought down two mugs, two tea bags. He opened the cupboards, searching until he found a package of chocolate sandwich cookies, the chocolate chip ones they'd made long gone. He opened the package, arranged the cookies on a flowered plate and slid it across the table in front of her.

"Here," he said gruffly.

"No, thanks. I'm not hungry." Her stomach still hovered on the edge of nausea even as her mouth squirted saliva at the sight of the junk food.

A faint smile tugged the corner of his lips. "Why aren't women ever hungry?"

"I'm really not," she said, but took a cookie anyway. White frosting edged her fingertip and she licked it off. The sweetness was almost too much, but after a second it settled her stomach.

"Right." Todd leaned his rear on the counter and crossed

his arms over his chest. "How about just a salad? You want that instead?"

Gilly frowned. "No. Yuck."

He laughed at that and turned off the gas just as the kettle began to whistle. He refilled their mugs, then sat. Today he wore a white tank top beneath an unbuttoned, snap-front Western shirt. He'd rolled the sleeves up to his elbows.

For the first time, Gilly noticed the tattoo on the inside of his left arm, halfway between his wrist and his elbow. Black ink, stylized numbers. At first she assumed it was a piece of Japanese calligraphy of the sort that had become so trendy over the past few years, people getting inked with words they didn't know how to read. Or maybe it was tribal ink, another trend she'd never understood unless it was by someone with Native American heritage. Jews weren't supposed to get tattoos, anyway, but if she'd ever considered getting something permanently embedded in her skin, it would be something that made sense to her personally, not something everyone got just because it was popular.

She saw it more clearly when he stretched his arm to grab a couple of cookies from the plate. Not calligraphy and not tribal markings, though the numbers had been drawn in a highly stylized form that made them almost indecipherable.

1 of 6

It took her a few seconds to puzzle out what it meant, sort of like trying to read a custom license plate, or that funky cross-stitch piece that said Jesus when you looked at it one way and looked like nonsensical blocks the other. As with those things, once she'd figured it out there was no way to not see it, of course. Gilly snorted lightly, feeling stupid.

"One of six," she said aloud.

Todd jumped. His hand hit his mug, sending it to the floor

where it shattered. Hot tea splattered. Gilly jumped, too, at the sound, and the sudden motion sent a wave of dizziness through her.

Todd stood. "Shit. Look at that."

He sounded too distressed for a simple accident—even though the mug had broken, the cupboard was stocked with at least a dozen more. It bore the name of a bank and she didn't see how it could possibly have any sentimental value. Todd kicked at a shard of porcelain, sending it skittering across the floor as he went to the sink for a dish cloth.

"Be careful," Gilly said automatically when he bent to wipe at the spill. "Use the broom, first."

He paused, head down, shoulders hunched. "I can clean up a broken mug."

"I'm not saying you can't. I just meant..."

"I know what you meant." He stood and tossed the towel into the sink while Gilly watched, helpless to understand.

Todd went through the pantry, out to the lean-to, and came back with an ancient, straggly straw broom. The handle had been painted with whimsical designs and looked utterly out of place here in this cabin that didn't look like it had seen a woman's touch in a long time, if ever. In his other hand he gripped a red metal dustpan that looked as old as the chairs on the front porch. He put it on the floor and held it with his boot as he swept up the mug. The straw broom left dirt marks on the floor she'd scrubbed not so long ago, and Gilly made an inadvertent noise of protest.

Todd looked up at her, brow furrowed. She opened her mouth to complain about the mess he'd made of what had been a relatively clean floor, but stopped herself. He wasn't hers to scold.

He finished with the mug while she sipped at her tea and

nibbled the cookie his scorn had forced her to take. Sitting while someone else cleaned was such a novelty she had to enjoy it, at least a little, even though she didn't want to. But when he left again to return the broom and dustpan, Gilly couldn't stay in her seat.

She took the dish towel, dampened it, and swiped at the smudges he'd left behind. She looked up at the sound of his boots and discovered him staring down at her. She got up to rinse out the towel, though the water from the tap was too cold to make it easy to clean it.

"Thanks," Todd said.

"You're welcome."

She wrung out the cloth and let it hang over the edge of the sink. "I can make you another cup, if you want. The water's probably still pretty hot."

"Nah." Todd hovered between her and the table. "I'm good."

He'd pulled his sleeves down, a fact Gilly noticed but didn't comment upon. They stared at each other until he straightened up. He was always taller than she thought he was, probably because he slouched a lot. Taller and with broader shoulders. He took up a lot of space but just now Gilly didn't feel threatened.

"Going out for a smoke," Todd said, though he'd never bothered to either warn her or ask permission in the past.

She watched him go out the front door. Then she got the broom again and made sure nothing remained on the floor to cut their feet. He'd returned by the time she was rehanging the broom, but if he minded her cleaning up after him, Todd didn't say.

19

She was down to the last few pills and probably didn't need them, but took them anyway. Medicine that was supposed to make other people wakeful always knocked her out, so she stayed in bed. Besides, beneath the blankets she was warm, and under their protection she didn't have to face Todd.

The more she slept, the easier sleep seemed to find her. Gilly, who hadn't gone one night through without interruption in more than five years, now spent more than half the day in bed, creeping downstairs only to use the toilet and sneak a few slices of stale bread while Todd was outside smoking or chopping wood for the stove. She was back upstairs before he came in, and when he came into the attic to stand over her, staring, Gilly closed her eyes and pretended to be dreaming. She'd always been a vivid dreamer, but now her dreams became more real to her than her life.

Sometimes she dreamed of things that had already happened. Her wedding to Seth, dancing in a high school musical, falling off her bike and cutting her leg badly enough to need stitches. Other things she dreamed of had never happened and likely never would—appearing on Broadway in the role of Annie Oakley, flying, attending Harvard.

She dreamed of her children, the sweet scent of their skin and the softness of their cheeks as she cuddled them. The days of nursing them as infants, when their tiny mouths puckered so sweetly against her breast and their fingers curled around hers. Those dreams left her aching and desperate to sleep again, both to escape and embrace the dreams.

And she dreamed of roses. Always roses, never tulips or daffodils or lilies, all flowers she actually had in her yard. Giant fields of roses and herself in the middle of them, watching them bloom and die over and over while she tried to grab them up and never succeeded. She didn't know what a dream dictionary would say about the symbolism of roses. She knew what they meant to her.

When night fell and Todd again climbed the stairs, this time to go into his own bed, Gilly waited until she heard the soft rumble of his snores before she went down again to use the toilet. She was back under the blankets in less than ten minutes.

As a child it had never made sense to her, why her mother complained of being so tired all the time when she barely got out of bed. How her mother could be still for so long without moving. Gilly understood her mother much better now.

Gilly drifted that way, until morning when a glance from her pillow showed nothing but white outside the window. Nothing had changed. Maybe nothing ever would.

Her lethargy grew deeper every day. She woke to eat and

use the bathroom, but spent as little time as possible at either of those activities before returning to the sanctity of her bed. Beneath the covers, she was protected from the world.

20

"You gonna sleep your whole life away?"

Gilly cracked open one bleary eye and peeled her face from the pillow. Apparently, at some point during the night, she'd drooled. She swiped her gummy tongue across equally sticky lips and teeth.

"…time…?" She mumbled.

"Time for you to get your lazy ass out of bed." Todd leaned against the dresser and sniffed loudly, then recoiled. "Clean yourself up. You reek."

Gilly shook her head and rolled over. "Go away."

"Get out of bed, Gilly."

"No!"

Gilly pulled the covers over her head, ignoring him. Todd muttered a string of curses under his breath and clomped away. Then he came back.

"I ain't going to ask you again," he told her. "Get out of bed."

Gilly untangled her hand from its citadel of blankets and waved her middle finger at him. "No, and fuck off."

"Goddamn it, Gilly," Todd said. "You are one impossible bitch! The fuck is wrong with you?"

"I want you to leave me alone," Gilly told him, and wriggled farther down beneath the blankets. "Just go away and leave me alone."

"So you can rot up here? No fucking way."

She pulled the pillow over her head, knowing it was immature and doing it anyway. "I'm tired. Let me sleep."

"You been sleeping for three days!"

"Leave me alone!" Shouting hurt her throat and made her cough, though even she couldn't pretend to still be sick.

"No way."

Todd grabbed the covers and tore them away from her, ripped the pillow from her hands and threw it on the floor. Gilly flailed at him, grabbing without effect at the sheets as he tugged them away, too. Red-hot rage filled her, and she screamed, a wordless roar of anger like shards of glass in her already wounded throat.

Without hesitation, Todd reached down and grabbed the front of her nightgown. The cloth tore as he pulled her from the bed. Gilly fought him, twisting in his grip. Her feet hit the floor and her ankle turned, sending tingling sparks of pain flaring up her leg. She bit out a curse, her words as harsh as his, and punched him in the stomach.

Todd barely flinched as he backhanded her across the cheek without letting go of the front of her gown. Gilly reeled, hand to her face. Bright blood dripped from the corner of her mouth and stained her fingers. The gown ripped completely from her neck to her waist, exposing the shirt and sweatpants she wore beneath, and she fell back onto the bed.

"You son of a bitch," she said, incredulous, showing him the crimson stain. "You hit me! Damn you, you hit me!"

"Get up."

He had struck her before and there'd been a time she'd actually wished for him to hit her, but that felt surreal compared to this. She rubbed the blood on her fingertips. "You're an asshole."

His eyes narrowed. "Get up or I'll crack you again."

Apparently, she didn't move fast enough for him. He reached down and grabbed her by the front of her shirt with both hands and hauled her upright. Gilly managed to smack him in the face.

Todd grunted, face turning from the force of her blow. When he looked back at her with glistening eyes, his mouth had gone pinched and thin. His nostrils flared.

"I told you not to do that."

"You hit me!" she cried, dangling in his grip, noticing even in her distraught state at how his nose wrinkled and he turned his face from the gust of her sour breath. "You! Hit me!"

Todd's eyes didn't widen. "And I'll fucking do it again if you don't get your shit together."

Gilly blinked, swallowing a retort. He was so much bigger he'd lifted her onto her tiptoes, and in socks she couldn't do any damage by stepping on his toes or kicking his shins, either. She couldn't even get another good strike at his face, if she was going to be so stupid.

"You going to be sensible?" he asked.

She didn't nod or shake her head, but Todd must've seen something in her face because he let go of the front of her shirt. Gilly kept her feet, mostly because he took hold of her upper arm. His fingers could almost encircle her bicep, bunching her sleeve.

"C'mon," Todd said. "Downstairs."

She dug in her feet and tried to turn back toward the bed. "I'm tired. I want to stay in bed."

"No." He pulled her harder. "You can't stay up here all the time. You got to take care of yourself."

"You said you wouldn't," Gilly muttered.

Todd didn't let go of her arm. "Wouldn't what?"

"Make me do anything I didn't want to do."

He grunted. "For chrissake, Gilly, you stink. You haven't changed your clothes in a week. When's the last time you brushed your teeth? How can you stand it?"

She couldn't, actually, now that she was fully awake and aware of it. But she wouldn't let him know that. She tried to pull her arm away, but his grip was too tight.

"You're hurting my arm."

"I know."

"Just leave me alone," Gilly begged with a glance at the bed. "Why do you care?"

"You can't sleep all the time," Todd told her, punctuating his words with a shake. "If you're not sick, you can't stay in bed all day. You can't just fucking…fade away."

"I'm not fading away, I'm waiting!" Gilly shouted.

Todd dropped her arm and stepped away from her. He didn't need to ask her what she was waiting for. "You said you didn't need me to take care of you anymore. Then you got to take care of yourself."

"Why do you care?" Gilly repeated.

"You ain't no good to anybody up here," Todd said. "Not me, not yourself…not them, either."

"Don't. Don't you talk about them."

He sighed and rubbed at his eyes. "I'll make you a deal. You promise to come downstairs and act like a human being…"

"And what? You'll let me go?" Gilly sniffed, rubbing the spot on her arm where the bruise would appear.

He shook his head. "No, I'm not going to let you go, for fuck's sake, Gilly, that's getting pretty old. But you want to run out in the snow again? Be a dumbass? Be my guest. See what happens this time, see if I save your sorry ass one more time."

"What about when the snow melts, Todd? What then?"

His gaze wavered for a second before he shoved her away from him and stalked to the center of the room, head hung low. When he swung around to look at her, his dark eyes were large in his face, his mouth a pensive frown.

"Why can't you just like me?" he asked her. "I ain't done anything real bad to you, Gilly. Not real bad."

"I won't ever like you. Don't you see I can't?"

"Why not?" Todd held out his hands, giving her that kicked-dog look. "Why?"

"Because you're my enemy." Gilly pulled the torn pieces of her gown back together with one hand, the fabric a useless shield but one she couldn't put down. Her mouth stung when she spoke, but the blood had ceased dripping. "Because you are keeping me from the things I love."

He sighed as if the weight of the world had come to rest on his broad shoulders. "We could get along better than we do."

"No!" She recoiled, grimacing.

"I didn't mean like that," he said quietly.

"I know you didn't. The answer's still no."

He looked angry again. "We're stuck here, Gilly. Ain't no way around it. We're fucking stuck out here in the middle of no place up to our assholes in snow. That's the way it is. Don't keep pushing me into being something you wish I was just so you can feel better about what *you* did."

It wasn't the statement of a stupid man but of an insightful one, and Gilly wondered at what the people in his life had done to him, and for how long, to convince him he was so dumb.

"I don't *want* to hurt you," Todd said. "I don't *want* to."

But he would. The words unsaid nevertheless hung between them, loud and clear.

She turned her face away. "When the snow melts, I'm going to try to get away. Are you going to tie me up?"

"I'm not that kinky," Todd said, "though a girl did ask me once to put on her panties."

This was serious and she hated he was making a joke of it. "The only thing keeping me here is the snow. You know that."

"Ah, fuck me. Yes. I know it." Todd scowled.

"So, what happens when the snow melts?" She asked the question more quietly this time, not pushing so hard. Truly curious. She wanted to know the answer.

"I knew an old hound dog once," Todd said after a pause. "He wasn't mine—I never had a dog. He belonged to this guy who lived down the street from one of the places they put me after…one of the places I lived as a kid."

Despite herself, Gilly lifted her face to meet his unwavering gaze. Todd's voice was solid, deep, precise even in its uneducated manner. He stood with his feet planted slightly apart, hands at his sides. Telling her.

"This dog was one mean son of a bitch. The guy kept him outside on a chain, and that dog would run so fast to bite your ass he'd choke himself right off his own feet. Every day, I'd walk by that dog on my way to school, every fucking day he'd try to get me. But he never did."

Todd laughed, low. "The guy that owned him could've just kicked that dog when he saw him, but he never did. That guy always made sure that dog had plenty of food and water, and he gave him chew toys and rawhide bones. And every night, when that guy came out to feed the dog, he'd pat him on the head and scratch him behind the ears. And the dog, that ass-biting dog, always growled.

"The guy loved that dog, even though the dog never loved him back, and never thanked him for all the nice things he did for it. Then one night, when the guy went out to feed the dog and pat him on the head, the little fucker didn't bother growling. This time, he took a big chunk right out of the guy's hand."

Her throat had gone dry during the telling of his tale. "What happened then?"

Todd smiled, an empty expression that bared his teeth and did not reach his eyes. "The guy went inside his house and got his shotgun, and he blew that little fucker's head right off."

There was no mistaking the meaning of his story, but Gilly wasn't afraid of it. "Which one of us is the dog?"

"I don't know, Gilly," Todd said. "I guess we'll just have to wait and see."

21

She got out of bed on her own the next morning. Washed and dressed. Sat across the table from him and ate her breakfast. She did not speak.

Todd didn't seem to mind. He ate as heartily as he ever did, and after breakfast lit up a cigarette as if it was dessert. Gilly waved away the smoke hanging in front of her face and coughed deliberately, but Todd either didn't notice or did not care.

"You giving me the silent treatment?" he asked her finally, when she got up to put her dishes away.

Gilly paused before answering. "I don't have anything to say to you."

"How about good morning?"

She repeated the words without enthusiasm. Todd got up from the table and touched her shoulder to turn her to face him. Gilly moved without resistance, her gaze on the ground.

"Gilly. Look at me."

She did so grudgingly.

"We got to go through this again?"

She shook her head and tried to turn her face away. "No."

He lifted her chin so she had to continue looking at him and asked her the question he'd asked her once before. "You afraid of me?"

"No."

"You're not a good liar," Todd said, and let her go. He followed her to the living room. "Will you just stop for a minute?"

She whirled to face him. "Can't you just let it go? What do you want from me?"

"Just thought we were going to try and be friends, that's all. Seems better than not being friends." Todd shrugged. The tip of his cigarette glowed red as he drew the smoke deep into his lungs.

"I never said I was going to be your friend." Lip curling on the word, Gilly crossed her arms in front of her.

"You just gonna keep being that growling dog, ain't you?" Todd grinned. "Okay. I'll just keep patting you on the head…."

"And maybe one day I'll bite you," Gilly retorted.

"Maybe one day you will," Todd conceded. "Or maybe, one day, you'll just stop that growling."

"I don't think so." She went to the front window, watching the snow outside. A rabbit hopped along the white drifts, leaving behind its footprints. Then it was gone.

"Ah, Gilly, why not?" He sounded so sincerely curious, she turned to face him.

"The idea is ridiculous."

"How come?"

He wanted to know, so she told him. "We have nothing in common. There's nothing about our lives that would ever have brought us together."

"Not true. We did get brought together."

"Not by my choice!"

Todd made a thoughtful face. "Not by mine, either, but it happened. What, you can only be friends with someone you met on purpose? The fuck kind of fun is that? You must not have many friends if that's how you go about it."

"You have a lot of friends?" she asked, sounding snide, expecting the answer to be negative.

Todd shrugged. "Depends on what you consider a friend. I know a lot of people. And most of them I didn't meet on purpose. But yeah, some of them are friends. Some are douche bags who run off with my money and turn me to a life of crime."

He was making another joke. She saw it in his eyes and the slight tilt of his lips, though his voice was dead serious. Gilly realized suddenly she envied Todd his sense of humor, even amongst all of this. His ability to somehow laugh at what was going on. She'd had a great sense of humor, once upon a time, but she hadn't been able to find the humor in lots of things for a long time. Certainly not this, now.

"We would never be friends under any circumstances, and this situation is certainly not conducive to friendship," she said stiffly.

"Huh. You like big words just like Uncle Bill." Todd shrugged. "This situation is all we got. How fortuitous for both of us to have made each other's acquaintance. See? I know some big words, too."

"It doesn't matter, Todd," Gilly said tiredly.

"Now who won't let it go?" Todd drew in another deep lungful of smoke, watching her with narrowed eyes. Thinking. "You sure are stubborn."

Gilly lifted her chin. "I've been called worse."

"I bet." Todd shrugged. "Well, I guess it's up to me, then."

She eyed him suspiciously. "What's up to you?"

"Guess I got to prove to you I really am a nice guy." Todd smiled. "Prove we can be friends. You and me, besties. It'll be great. Maybe we can even braid each other's hair."

His eyes glinted with humor even in the face of Gilly's answering glower. In fact, he laughed out loud, right into her face. Gilly crossed her arms.

"Keep dreaming," she said.

"Ah, c'mon. Not even if I make you a friendship bracelet?" Todd fluttered his eyelashes at her.

He looked so utterly harmless and innocent Gilly almost laughed out loud, but she cut it off, tight. Locked it up. "No. Forget it. Not happening."

"You could at least think about it."

"No. I can't." She watched the light of his humor fade. "Really, Todd. You should understand that."

He nodded, just barely, after a long minute of looking at her. "Yeah. Sure, sure. I get it."

Why now did she feel that she was the one in the wrong again? She held her apology, a pearl on her tongue created from the sand of their argument. "We'll never be friends, Todd."

"We'll see," Todd said. "Maybe we'll be something else."

22

Danica is Gilly's best friend until their junior year of high school, when Danica's braces come off and she replaces her glasses with contact lenses. A perm, a tan, a few pounds lost and an inch in height had transformed her over the summer from a band geek into a hottie, and the boys have noticed. That would be fine, but Danica notices, too.

They've shared most everything over the years. Secrets, dreams. They'd practiced kissing their pillows during sleepovers at Danica's house, and she's the only person Gilly's ever told about her crush on their gym teacher, Mr. Grover, in seventh grade. Danica has a lot of brothers and sisters, but Gilly has none. Danica's her sister. Her best friend.

At first, Danica's new popularity with the opposite sex is sort of a boon to Gilly, who's had her share of giggling crushes and notes passed to her in study halls but never really had a boy like her. Not like her, like her, not the way she liked him. Now, walking the halls of school before the bell rang for homeroom, Gilly follows Danica and the boys follow them both. Surely one or two of them will look Gilly's way when they see her friend is busy with the others.

And sure enough, one does.

Not the one Gilly likes. That's Bennett Longenecker, who looks like he just stepped out of one of those teen movies. Perfect hair, perfect skin, perfect teeth, perfect smile. He likes Danica, of course, but he's nice enough to Gilly because he also has a perfect personality. Gilly swoons inside whenever he looks her way, which is just often enough to keep her pleasantly tingly all throughout the school day and sometimes even into the evening.

The boy who likes her has the unfortunate name of Reginald Gampey. He was named for his dad and his grandfather, and he goes by Reg...but it doesn't help. With a name like Reginald Gampey he's destined for thick glasses, an overbite and bad acne. Being a brainiac might've made up for it but he lacks even the smarts to be considered one of the class's top students.

And, he likes Gilly.

He manages to become a part of the little crowd of those who hang out before and after school. Danica and her admirers, Bennett, who seems to soak up all the adoration directed his way without really absorbing it. Gilly. Another girl, Marie. And Reg.

Things are bad at home again. They'd been okay for a while, but over the summer when Danica was growing breasts, Gilly'd been dealing with her mother's increasingly difficult behavior. Mom didn't want Gilly going to the pool or out with friends, to the movies, out late at night. She wanted to know where Gilly was all the time, to keep her from "trouble." The only trouble Gilly had was hiding the fact that her home life was so shitty.

Danica knows something's up—she's been Gilly's best friend since grade school, after all. But things have changed. Looking back now, Gilly thinks there would've been distance between them without the boys and the new look. But back then Gilly doesn't notice or doesn't want to see how Danica's eyes slide past her, or how Danica doesn't laugh at Gilly's old jokes, or how she mostly just ignores her whenever she can and makes up excuses about how she's too busy to hang out.

The night of the Homecoming dance that fall, the plan is to go as a group date. A lot of the kids from school are doing it rather than springing for limos and corsages. It probably was Danica's idea anyway, so she doesn't have to choose which one, single boy can take her. Reg had asked Gilly but with the group date thing in place she has a reason to say no.

Gilly's having a great time. She slow-dances with Bennet once and a couple other boys. Even Reg, though the way he gazes so longingly into her eyes unnerves her. The DJ plays all the best songs and afterward, the plan is to go out to the local diner to eat and stay out a whole hour after curfew.

"I don't think you should come," Danica says. "Don't you have to get home to your…mom?"

"My dad's with her."

Danica shrugs, so much said in that artless response. "I think you should find someone else to hang out with, Gilly."

"Tonight?" Gilly asks, stunned.

Danica looks at her. Another shrug. "Just…all the time. I think you should find a new best friend."

Then she goes off with the rest of their friends, leaving Gilly to stand with Reg, who offers to drive her home. She lets him, too. Lets him feel her up in the front seat, parked in front of her parents' house. Lets him French-kiss her.

She lets Reg think she likes him, until Monday at school when she tells him the same thing Danica had said to her. "I think you should find another girlfriend."

Gilly never asked Danica what had prompted the change in their long friendship. She never had the courage. She played it off, pretended it didn't matter, but for the rest of that year she watches Danica laugh and joke with everyone else but her. It's a rejection worse than any from a boy could ever have been.

Gilly chooses her friends very carefully after that.

23

"Fuck my life!" Todd hissed and stuck his fingers in his mouth as he knelt by the stove to poke at the logs. "Burned myself."

Gilly looked up from the magazine crossword puzzle she was working on. "Do you have to drop the f-bomb with everything you say?"

Todd looked up from the fire and dusted off his hands on the thighs of his already dirty jeans. He'd been wearing the same pair for the past few days. Gilly had a few unworn shirts from the stash he'd bought her and had done some laundry in the bathtub, but Todd was apparently far less concerned with recycling his clothes. His forehead furrowed.

"Huh?"

"You curse all the time."

"I do?"

"Yes," Gilly said patiently. "Almost every sentence you're saying *fuck* or *shit* or something like that."

Todd shrugged. "So?"

"Well…can't you think of a better way to express yourself?" Gilly prompted. "You know, Todd, words don't have to be big to be effective."

"No." He held out his forefinger and thumb a scant inch apart. "Sometimes they're really tiny and they work great. Like, for instance, *fuck*."

She cocked an eyebrow at him. Todd stood. He put his hands on his hips, looking down at her.

"You've said it," he told her. "I heard you."

"Well, yes, I've said it, but I don't say it all the time."

"Maybe you should say it more." He grinned. "Fuck! Say it. It feels really good. Besides, the more you say it, the less scary it is. Go on."

"I'm not scared of saying it. I just choose to express myself with different word choices." God, she sounded prissy even to herself.

"Ooh." Todd fluttered his fingers over his heart. "Fancy."

She bit the inside of her cheek, but not in anger. "The more you say it, the less effective it actually becomes. You should try it. Using something else."

"What do you want me to stay instead?"

"Fudge?"

Todd laughed aloud. "Oh, right. That's so cool. 'Hey baby, wanna fudge?' Wow, I bet I'd get laid so much my dick would fall off."

"Gross!"

"Slow your roll, Gilly, jeez. You act like you never heard a dude talk about his dick before. And don't tell me you haven't, because we all do it."

Seth had, indeed, talked about his "junk" on more than one

occasion, but Gilly wasn't going to talk about that with Todd. "Use whatever words you want. I'm just saying that society will look at you less askance if you clean up your mouth."

As soon as she said it, Todd's grin faded. "Yeah. Because society really gives a fuck about my mouth."

"You never know," Gilly said, "what makes an impression."

Todd pointed at his chest. "See this? See me, standing right here in front of you?"

"You're hard to miss since you are standing right there," she said.

"Yeah, well, let me tell you something. I could put on a suit and tie and slick my hair back and shave, and I'm still always going to be a guy society looks upon like an ass can'ts, whatever the fuck that is."

"*Askance.* It's like..." She demonstrated with her expression.

"Scared?"

"No. Not... More like this." She tried again, raising her brows and parting her lips.

He laughed. "Yeah. Scared. Like I might mug you."

"Well..." She looked him up and down but didn't finish the thought.

Todd's smile faded. He stalked to the window and looked out, silent for a few minutes. "It's snowing again."

"Again?"

He pointed out the window. "Yeah."

Beyond the glass, she could see nothing but white. Gilly turned her attention back to the puzzle and shrugged. She needed an eleven-letter word for a noun meaning "anything abominable; anything greatly disliked or abhorred" and "mother-in-law" didn't fit. She knew because she'd tried.

She tapped the pencil, worn to a soft-nosed nub, against her chin. "Nothing we can do about it."

Todd paced a little bit in front of the stove, stopping every now and then to peer out the window again. He discovered a ball in some drawer, along with a suction-cupped basketball hoop. He took shot after shot, making most of them but occasionally needing to dive after the ball as it bounced wildly along the floor or rolled under the couch where she was sitting.

Gilly forced herself to concentrate on the crossword puzzle, though Todd's constant motion agitated her. The third time she had to lift her feet so he could get beneath them, she fixed him with a glare Todd didn't seem to notice. Cheek pressed to the worn carpet, one long arm snaking under the couch to grab the ball, his ass in the air, he didn't look so threatening. In fact, she thought suddenly, catching sight of the knife in the sheath on his belt, his face was at just the right place to kick.

"Gotcha." Todd got up, ball in hand, and the moment, such as it was, passed.

She filled in another few words and sighed. Now would've been a good time for the use of the word she'd told Todd to find a substitute for. Todd, tossing the ball back and forth from hand to hand, looked down at the paper.

"Abomination," he said.

"What?"

"Abomination." There was a pause as he waited, mouth quirked, for her to reply, but he spoke before she did. "Even has more than four letters."

Gilly filled in the letters carefully. "Abomination."

It was sort of the same thing as mother-in-law.

She hated crossword puzzles, normally. She wasn't good

at figuring out definitions from vague clues and vocabulary had never been her strongest talent. She knew what words meant when she read them, but thinking of them when she needed to use them often left her grasping. Still, it was better than sitting staring at the wall, which is what she'd have been reduced to, otherwise.

Or, she thought, biting the familiar spot to keep from growling, she could pace up and down like a caged animal and totally annoy everyone else in the room. Todd had lost interest in the makeshift basketball game and now wandered from window to window, looking out and muttering. That was bad enough, but when he plopped onto the couch beside her and put his feet on the coffee table, then started jiggling them so the entire couch shook, Gilly'd had enough.

"Todd!"

He jumped, looking guilty, and thumped his feet to the floor. "Sorry."

Gilly closed the magazine with a sigh. "Can't you sit still? It's like you're being electrocuted."

Todd frowned and shrugged. "I'm fucking bored as fuck. What do you want me to do?"

She sighed again. "Take a nap. Sew that hole in your shirt. Better yet, wash the shirt, it's disgusting."

Todd looked down at the front of it and ran his fingertips over the mother-of-pearl snap buttons. "I like this shirt."

"Obviously, since you've worn it for the past three days."

"Aw, Gilly," Todd said with a grin. "You noticed."

She sighed. "Just...do something that doesn't involve you annoying me!"

"Is there anything that wouldn't annoy you?" Todd got up from the couch. He shifted on his feet, looking for all the world like a cat ready to pounce on a mouse. Everything about him reminded her of some feral creature. He went to the window again. "I'm so fudging bored!"

Gilly fixed him with an impatient stare. "What do you want me to do about it?"

"You like Monopoly?"

Actually, she loved the game, but hadn't played for years. A house with small children was no place for a game with a myriad of tiny pieces. Todd went to the large armoire in the corner and pulled out the familiar box.

"We could play," he said.

"I'm busy."

The idea was tempting. She was more than a bit bored herself, but Gilly forced her attention back to the magazine. She couldn't allow herself to relax with him or she'd be lost, and yet each passing moment in his company made it harder and harder to hold him at a distance. Not when he asked her to do innocent things like play Monopoly.

"Your head hurting again?"

She shook her head. Her fingers fluttered on the magazine's slick pages. Todd sat down across from her and pulled the magazine from her hands.

"Hey!"

"Play with me, Gilly."

"No."

He sighed. "Shit."

Gilly snatched back the crumpled pages and turned her face from him. "Leave me alone, Todd."

"Just one game. C'mon. I'll let you pick whatever piece you want. Top hat, race car, thimble, whatever. Hell, you can even roll first."

"I said no!" The words spit from her mouth like bullets from a gun.

He recoiled, his mouth twisting. A spark that didn't look like anger glimmered in his eyes, but Gilly didn't flinch. She lifted her chin, daring him to protest.

"Christ, you're a bitch," he said.

Gilly put the magazine on the coffee table between them and stood up, hands on her hips. "Why do men always say that when they don't get what they want?"

Her head spun a little at the speed of her retreat, but she managed to walk away with some semblance of dignity. That he was right didn't bother her. He'd called her a growling dog, too. If being a bitch meant she could survive this ordeal, then she'd be one.

Todd's voice stopped her at the foot of the stairs. "Is that what your husband calls you?"

She stiffened. "Seth has never called me a bitch."

"Not to your face," Todd muttered.

Gilly bit back a retort. There'd been days when she knew her frustration spilled out in sharp words, her tongue a keener weapon than any knife. She knew she'd send her husband from her with his pride smarting, his love for her the only reason he'd kept his own replies civil. She knew it when it happened and had felt helpless to stop it, and she knew it now.

She did with Todd what she'd so often felt incapable of doing with Seth—she held her tongue. Gilly went up the stairs and changed into her nightclothes: thick socks, heavy sweatpants, the flannel nightgown she hated but wore because it kept her warm. She got into bed and pulled the covers up to her chin. Daylight still filtered through the window, but through the densely falling snow the light was diffuse enough to ignore. She closed her eyes and waited for him to come and demand she get out of bed, but he didn't.

Much later, when night had fallen, she woke to the sound

of Todd's boots on the stairs. For once, she'd slept without dreaming. Within minutes the light he'd brought with him went out and they lay in the dark again. Together but separated by more than just the low half-wall. After a time, she heard his soft, slow breathing, and knew he slept.

She desperately had to pee. Gilly blinked against the dark. Since she'd gone to bed so early, she hadn't brought a light. She pressed her thighs together, but the dull, cramping ache in her bladder meant there was no way she'd be able to make it until morning.

She swung her legs out of bed and shivered instantly. Without constant stoking, the woodstove quickly stopped heating the cabin. The shivering didn't help her need to pee, and she took a few deep breaths to convince her body she was going to make it to the bathroom without embarrassing herself.

Darkness would make the trip hazardous, and Gilly had a vision of herself tripping over something. Falling and wetting herself at the same time. Once upon a time she'd been able to go without bathroom breaks for hours, but not since having babies. She'd almost embarrassed herself enough times to know better than to tempt fate. Only the dimmest glimmer of light shone in through the windows on either end of the room, not enough to see by. She'd have to make it by memory.

Think about it. Picture the room in your mind. You can find your way to the stairs, no problem. Just take one step at a time.

Gilly walked with her hands held out like a sleepwalker. Instead of lifting her feet high, she slid them along the floor, shuffling to prevent herself from tripping. Her thighs bumped the edge of the dresser and her hands felt empty space in front of her. She shuffled forward.

Her eyes had adjusted to the darkness, not enough to see anything clearly but enough to let her know approximately where she was going. From the opening in the partition, there was a clear space between the rows of beds all the way to the steep stairwell. If she could make it all the way there without falling down them, she'd do all right.

Once at the stairs, Gilly gripped the railing hard. Step by step. Downstairs a soft red glow from the stove's vents gave her some meager light, but she used the wall to guide her to the bathroom where she sat with an audible sigh.

On the way back through the living room, she paused. Her house was never this quiet. There was always the ambient hum of appliances, the sound of occasional traffic and the dog, who could never be content to simply sleep but had to yip and pant and scrabble in constant doggie dreams. This cabin was silent, not even any wind outside blowing snow against the walls.

Yet this felt familiar, being awake while everyone else slept. She had spent many nights wandering the house in the dark, unable to sleep. Sometimes because she was simply waiting to be woken, sometimes because of an overwhelming need to check on everything one last time. Sometimes because no matter how exhausted she was, she couldn't go to bed until toys that would simply be dumped again in the morning had been put away, or that last load of laundry tossed in the washer. The dishes soaking in the sink scrubbed and dried and put away so she didn't have to face them in the morning.

Gilly always felt like the only member of her household who cared if any of those tasks were completed. It didn't stop her, though. Those were things she could control, make happen. Now she tipped her face to the ceiling. This nighttime wandering felt familiar, but she couldn't let herself forget that it wasn't.

She climbed the steps, the journey up in darkness somehow easier than it had been going down. Todd's breathing grew louder as she got closer. She picked out his form in the darkness, a huddled lump in the middle bed on the right-hand side. The moon had risen and by chance or luck a pale shaft of moonlight managing to trickle through the window highlighted the curved metal headboard. Gilly glimpsed a tuft of dark hair on the white pillow.

He shifted as she drew near and flung one long arm above his head. Now the soft light seemed to almost caress the curve of his jaw, the line of his lips. He muttered something, softly, and Gilly froze.

She drew closer to the bed, watching the way his mouth pursed with his breath. In sleep, with the covers shielding most of his body from her, he looked far less threatening. He didn't look like a man, really. More like an overgrown boy.

"Mama." He spoke with a child's voice, timid, small and broken of heart.

What was this? The man who'd held her at knifepoint and threatened to kill her was asking for his mother? It might have been comical if not for the utter desolation in his voice, if not for the way the word caused her nipples to peak and her heart to ache with remembrance of baby voices crying out her name in the night just that way.

Three short steps on whispering feet took her to the side of his bed, and she took them without thinking twice. Automatic, the way she did at home when the murmur of a child caught her ear. Todd spoke the word again, this time with a sigh. Tears glittered like fallen diamonds on his cheeks as he shifted again in the bed.

Gilly reached out a hand to brush the hair from his forehead, to wipe away the tears shining on his face. She stopped herself just before she touched his skin, before she could condemn herself to pity and kindheartedness. Todd took in a hitching breath and whispered one last time, “Mama.” Then he began to snore softly, and Gilly finished her journey in the dark without hearing him speak again.

24

Todd was quiet in the morning, shadows beneath his dark eyes. He toyed with his lighter, snapping it again and again as it sparked, until the sharp, gassy smell of the fluid tickled a sneeze from Gilly's nose. He didn't offer a "God bless you."

"The funniest thing I ever seen was a fat lady in a bikini trying to do the limbo," Todd said suddenly.

At the sheer incongruity of his statement, Gilly turned from the sink where she was washing her breakfast plate. "Where did you see that?"

"At the beach. I only went one time." Todd leaned back in his chair, rocking. "Laughed so hard I pissed my pants and… the people I was with got mad and took me home."

She watched him tilt the chair, waiting for him to tumble backward. By luck or skill he kept the chair hovering in place while he balanced. He was graceful that way. Comfortable and competent with his body in a way he wasn't with his intellect.

Todd looked at her. "What's the funniest thing you ever seen?"

Gilly shrugged. It didn't seem that conversation should be so easy, no matter how much he made it so. "I don't know."

Todd sighed dramatically. "You're never any fun."

His comment stung. "*Young Frankenstein.* That's a funny movie."

Todd rolled his eyes. "Not a movie. What's the funniest thing you ever seen in your real life? Bet it ain't as funny as a fat lady in a bikini trying to do the limbo."

He was challenging her again, and Gilly rose to the bait. "When I was just out of college, I bought a new mattress from this factory outlet store. When I went to pick it up, the guy from the store helped me put it in the back of this van I'd borrowed. He tried carrying it on his back, but he got stuck, and then the mattress fell on him and only his legs were sticking out...."

Todd raised both eyebrows. Gilly frowned. "What? It was funny. I guess you had to be there."

"I made you smile." Todd thumped his chair down onto all four legs. "See?"

Gilly pushed her mouth back into the frown, but it was too late. "I wasn't smiling at you."

"You got a nice smile." Todd winked.

Oh, how she wanted and needed him to be loathsome to her! Gilly thought of the way his hand had felt when he hit her mouth, drawing blood. The memory was still vivid enough to make her put a hand to her lips. It was also enough to wipe the smile from her face.

"I wasn't smiling." Her denial was transparent, but Gilly didn't care.

"Are you this much fun at home, too?" Todd pulled a

crumpled pack of cigarettes from his T-shirt pocket and scowled to find it empty. He tossed it onto the kitchen table and stood. His gaze swept her up and down. "Maybe they don't miss you as much as you think they do."

He stomped into the pantry while Gilly, stunned, stared after him. In the months before he'd taken her, Gilly had felt more often like screaming than laughing. She thought hard, tears springing to her eyes, about the last time she had laughed with her children. Really laughed. It had been a long time. There had been too many days when her palms hurt from clenching her fists too hard to keep from striking out, too many nights when the last words she uttered were not "I love you," but "for God's sake, go to sleep!"

People always vowed to change, if given a second chance. Gilly was no different, no better. She sat rigid, her back as straight as a poker, and vowed that if she was allowed to return to them, she would cherish her family as something more precious than diamonds. Later, when most of her time with Todd had begun to fade into a series of hazy memories, this moment at the kitchen table would forever stand out as clear as crystal. She wouldn't spend the rest of her life without yelling at her kids or arguing with her husband; such a thing would be impossible and impractical. But when those moments came, the times of anger and grief, it was the moment at Todd's kitchen table she always recalled, and that was usually enough to make her put out her hands and forgive.

"I know you want to hate me," Todd said from the doorway, a fresh pack of cigarettes in one fist. "I know you want to, real bad. But admit it. You just can't."

"You're wrong." Her voice stuttered, giving away her emotions.

"You just ain't that hard." Todd dismissed her protest like

it meant nothing. "And if you do hate me, it isn't because of what I done, really. It's because of what you done. So you're mad at yourself."

His observation was the truth, but Gilly wasn't about to admit it to him. "Don't try to psychoanalyze me. You're not smart enough to get inside my head."

He smoothed a hand through his hair. "Shit, Gilly, you seem like a sad, uptight bitch to me. Why the hell would I want to get inside your head?"

She exploded. "Just shut up!"

"Ooh." Todd raised his hands in mock fear. "That's a smart comeback. Wish I could think of something that smart."

Gilly left the table and stalked to the living room, but there was no place to escape him. She paced the wooden planks, wishing suddenly she smoked so she could have the comfort of a cigarette to occupy herself.

She was hard enough to hate, she thought spitefully, watching him as he set out a game of solitaire on the dining table. And she had every reason to hate him. But she also had every reason to hate herself.

Thinking of the evil he'd committed against her, holding her at knifepoint, slapping her face, should have been enough to keep the fires of her hatred burning. Gilly, however, feared that Todd was right about her. She wasn't hard enough to keep hating, not in the face of kindness and good humor. Not even when she should.

Relationships were like machines. Gears fit together, turning to make the machine work. Boss, roommate, parent, child, spouse. The cogs moved, the gears turned or stuck and needed to be oiled. Todd was none of these to her and yet there was no denying they had a relationship, and that it was as much a machine as any other. If they couldn't find some way to make it work, it would break down. A day before, Gilly would've said without question she didn't want to make it work. Now she wasn't sure she could stop herself.

"I don't like to tell anyone," Gilly said, "but I like to watch videos of people falling down."

Todd sat back in the chair, cigarette dangling. "Yeah?"

"Yeah." She nodded.

"Well..." Todd paused as though considering this. "That *is* funny, sometimes. When someone falls. Even if they get hurt, you know, it's funny to see it happen."

"It's wrong to laugh at someone who's hurt, but I can't help it."

Both of Todd's eyebrows lifted. "That's messed up."

"I know," Gilly said, but with a sense of relief, as if she'd confessed to some sort of crime. "It's awful. I'm a terrible person."

"Nah. Or if you are, you're not the only one," Todd pointed out. He shuffled the cards back and forth so fast they became a blur and then again in an intricate pattern. Seeing her look, he paused. "I worked in a casino for a while, too...before."

She wasn't surprised. She took the chair across from him. "So deal something out."

She hated the wary way he looked at her, as though waiting for her to change her mind. Todd shuffled the cards, then caught them all in one hand to take his cigarette from his lips with the other. He tapped the cards into a tidy pile on the table.

"What do you want to play?"

"I don't care. I'm not good at anything," Gilly said.

"I bet you're great at fifty-two pickup."

She made a face. "Yeah, I'm also not that stupid."

"No," Todd said quietly. "I know you're not."

They passed the day that way, hours of cards. He taught her games she'd never known and even a trick or two. By the end of the day, they were not friends but no longer enemies.

25

"What's in that file you keep peeking at?" Gilly turned from where she'd been poking the woodstove to catch Todd sifting through his papers again.

"Nothing." He wasn't in a friendly mood today, which perversely had made Gilly bright and chipper.

"Something you need to throw in the fire?" she asked suspiciously, because he seemed to keep dancing around that decision. "We could use something in there."

"No!"

Gilly blew out a gust of air. "Sorry."

Todd stuffed the papers back in the file and put them on top of the armoire, a gesture she could in no way misinterpret since the only way she could have reached up there was to stand on a chair. Gilly poked the logs one last time and watched them crumble into glowing ruby embers. She sat back on her heels, holding her hands out to the warmth.

"Want to play some cards again?" she asked, to make him

turn away from the window where he stared out into the darkness.

"No."

"Best out of three...?" she began, her tone lightly teasing, in a better mood than she'd been in the weeks since he'd brought her here.

"Just shut the fuck up, okay?" Todd snapped.

Gilly wilted like a flower without water, then set her jaw. "Fine."

Todd was agitated, rocking on the balls of his feet, lighting cigarettes from the ends of others. He shrugged into his ratty sweatshirt and pulled a large plaid hunting jacket over top. "I'm going out."

"Out where?" Gilly got to her feet, alarmed. "It's freezing out there."

"I've got to get out of here!" His eyes looked through her without seeing her. He took one last drag on his smoke before dropping it to the floor and stubbing it out with the toe of his boot.

Gilly recognized the edge of panic in his voice, but could not imagine what had caused it. "Todd..."

He slapped himself in the face. Gilly stopped, stunned. A runner of blood appeared at the corner of Todd's mouth, and he didn't even bother to wipe it away. He slapped the other side. His bent his head, his dark hair hanging to obscure his face.

"What's wrong with you?" This new behavior frightened Gilly more than any other had. She stepped toward him, not thinking, and grabbed his arm.

Todd flung off her touch and fled out the door. He disappeared into the night, leaving only footprints in the snow to show where he had gone. Gilly stood in the doorway, mindless of the frigid night air against her skin for a full few minutes as she searched the darkness for him. He was gone.

Gilly shivered and went inside, closing the door behind her. The sight of Todd's blood had left her with a chill that even sitting by the fire could not chase away. What had made him do that?

Something in that ragged file of papers had upset him. She had to know what it was. Without a second thought, Gilly grabbed one of the dining table chairs and dragged it over to the huge armoire in the corner.

Someone, a long time ago, had lovingly carved the armoire to fit the cabin's corner space. The massive piece rose nearly to the ceiling, its heavy doors shielding four deep drawers and eight roomy shelves. Todd, easily taller than six-two, had no problem tucking the file away on top of the armoire, but Gilly at almost a foot shorter wasn't nearly tall enough to reach. Even with the chair, and standing on her tiptoes, she couldn't quite grab the file. She strained, fingers scrabbling, but all that happened was the chair wobbled and she nearly fell.

The door banged open, and cold air swirled in. Startled and guilty, Gilly jumped from the chair. Todd slammed the door behind him and shrugged out of his coat. He stamped the snow from his boots.

There was no hiding what she'd been doing. Gilly waited for his reaction. Todd stared at her for a long time, so long that the silence became uncomfortable and Gilly had to break it.

"You came back."

His slanting grin lacked its usual luster. "You think I wouldn't?"

"I didn't know." Gilly took the chair back to the table and

hung his snow-covered coat over the back of it. "Are you okay?"

"Nope," Todd said with a trace of his former cheeriness. "But I'm used to it."

"I can make some tea," Gilly said, surprising herself with the offer.

She must have surprised him, as well, because he cocked his head to stare at her thoughtfully. "Thanks."

She nodded, uncertain exactly what had passed between them but knowing something had begun to change. As she headed for the kitchen to boil water, he called after her.

"Don't look in that file," Todd said. "There's some pretty awful shit in there. Especially for someone like you."

Someone like her? But Gilly was afraid to ask, and so he didn't tell.

26

"I've been waiting for a girl like you..." Seth sings this loudly and off-key. He's had too much to drink. He's not charming when he's drunk. He might be charming all the rest of the time, but not when he's drunk. Or maybe it's her, maybe it's just that she doesn't like it.

A girl like you, Seth sings again, lifting his glass toward her.

Karaoke sounded like a good idea when she agreed to go along with a bunch of other people from the office and some of their friends, and some random strangers who'd ended up coming along. Gilly doesn't like to sing, not in public, anyway, and has been more than content to sit and watch.

Seth is a friend of her boss's wife. Gilly met him at a barbecue a few months ago, and he's shown up fairly often at group dates like these. He's always been nice. They have something in common, both of them Jews in a widely Christian area. He's handsome and funny, when he's not drinking and making an ass of himself singing in falsetto.

Tonight she was supposed to have a date with Joe, but he stood her up. Well, he called to cancel. That wasn't any better. He thinks Gilly loves him, but she doesn't.

Later, though, she's glad Joe passed on the night. Gilly realizes Seth's not drunk. Sure, he's had a couple of beers, but it's not alcohol that gets him up there to sing and dance and make a fool of himself. He just doesn't care if people think he's a goofball.

She likes that about him, Gilly realizes, the third or maybe it's the fourth time they go out like that. She likes Seth. She offers him her number without thinking too much about it. Not a big deal, really. He'll call or he won't.

But Seth holds the number in his hand as though she's given him something precious. "I didn't think..."

Gilly's been laughing, having fun with friends. This didn't seem like something important until just now, but watching Seth look at her she understands it's all become very significant, indeed. "You didn't think what?"

"I didn't think a girl like you would go out with a guy like me. That's all."

"What," she says, laughing, "is a girl like me?"

Seth's answer is a kiss, soft and lingering.

He never does give her an answer other than that.

27

Whatever had been bothering him the night before had left him. Gilly watched him carefully, trying not to let him know she was doing it. Todd might call himself dumb, but he noticed her scrutiny.

"I'm okay today," he told her. "I'm not going to freak out on you or anything like that."

"Whatever," Gilly said as though she didn't really care. "Want to play some checkers?"

"Sure." Todd got out the board and checkers from the armoire and put them on the coffee table in front of the woodstove.

They played three games, and Todd won every one. After the third victory, he lit a fresh cigarette and gave Gilly a sideways, thoughtful glance. She pretended not to notice as she set the board up again.

"How come you were letting me win?"

Gilly feigned ignorance. "I wasn't letting you win."

He snorted. “Yeah, you were.”

Gilly forced herself to look offended, though he *had* caught her out. “Why would I do that?”

For once, Todd let the cigarette burn without smoking it. “You tell me.”

Gilly sighed. “I didn’t want you to get upset again.”

“And you thought if I lost a stupid game of checkers, I’d get whacked-out again?” Todd’s eyebrows disappeared behind his bangs and shook his head. “I’m a piece of work, I know, but I ain’t that bad.”

Now she was on the defensive. “I just thought…”

“You do that for your kids? Let them win so they don’t get upset?”

“Sometimes.” Gilly fiddled with the checkers.

“You think that helps them?”

“I don’t think it hurts them,” Gilly said.

Todd rolled his neck on his shoulders, cracking it, and stretched out his impossibly long legs. “The world is shit, Gilly, and the sooner they learn that, the better off they’ll be.”

Gilly thought of her sweet babies, her innocent darlings. “I don’t agree.”

He fixed her with a look. “It’s true.”

“If the world is such shit, like you say, then I want to protect them as long as I can. Keep them safe.” Gilly waved her hand over the checkerboard. “My kids are little, still. There’s plenty of time for them to learn the world isn’t always a happy place.”

He snorted. “They’ll grow up thinking everything’s got to go their way.”

“They will not.” She frowned at his casual dismissal of her parenting choices. “They’ll grow up with self-confidence and security.”

"You going to let them win off you all the time?"

Gilly shook her head. "Of course not."

"How old?" Todd crumpled his package of cigarettes, but didn't light another one. "Your kids, I mean."

"Five and two." Gilly closed her eyes briefly at the thought of them, and the sight of their faces in her mind had her smiling instead of crying.

"I was five when my mother..." He stopped himself. "When she died."

Instant pity flooded Gilly. "I'm sorry."

He shrugged it off, though clearly the memory wasn't dismissed. "Not your fault. What are their names?"

He was deliberately changing the topic, but Gilly let him. "Arwen and Gandy."

Todd pulled a funny face. "Arwen and Gandy? What kind of names are those?"

Gilly had been asked that question so many times it could no longer offend. "They're names from Tolkein. Gandy's real name is Gandalf."

"What's Toll-keen?"

"J.R.R. Tolkein," Gilly explained. "He wrote *The Hobbit, The Lord of the Rings.* Seth, my husband, he's really into the Middle Earth series."

She thought he might laugh, but he only nodded. "Oh, yeah. I seen that movie."

"They were books first."

"Figures someone like you would name their kids after someone from a book."

"Someone like me?" Gilly furrowed her brow at him. "You keep saying that. What does that mean?"

"You know." Todd began stacking the small wooden disks

with swift and efficient movements, making a tower. "Smart. High-class. Rich."

Gilly shook her head, though his assessment of her was complimentary. "Oh, God. No, Todd."

He looked at her from beneath the fringe of bangs and grabbed her hand. He turned it over so that her engagement ring glittered. "Looks pretty high-class to me. And you must've been smart to catch a man who could buy a rock like that."

"This ring was my grandmother's." Gilly took her hand away and rolled the diamond with the back of her finger. "She brought it with her when her family fled Europe to escape the Nazis."

Todd tapped the pile he'd made, and the checkers scattered across the board. "You mean like Anne Frank? See, that's a book, too. I had to read it in school."

"That's not just a book. It was real," Gilly said. "And Anne Frank did not escape."

Suddenly, uncomfortably, she was forcibly reminded of her situation. She could see in Todd's eyes that he, too, had not missed the parallel. He cleared his throat.

"That was different," he said.

"Yeah." She refused to look at him. On her finger, the diamond winked. "Anne Frank was hidden away to save her life. It was completely different than this."

"Gilly..." His voice trailed off.

She shrugged, mimicking him. Gilly picked up the checkers and replaced them, snapping the small wooden pieces onto the board with firm gestures. "Let's play again."

This time, she won.

28

She didn't try to lose any more games. Sometimes she won and sometimes she lost, but victory or defeat were fair results. At least Uncle Bill had stocked the cabin with plenty of board games and decks of cards. They wouldn't lack for that form of entertainment.

"What did you plan to do here all by yourself?" Gilly asked as they set up the board for another game, this time Monopoly.

Todd picked out the little silver shoe he claimed gave him good luck and set it on Go. "Nothing."

"What do you mean nothing? How can you do nothing? What does that even mean?" Gilly dealt the money and laid out the property cards.

Todd gave her fierce look. "I came up here to be by myself... and do nothing."

Gilly persisted, her curiosity piqued. "There's no TV, no DVD, no internet...."

"Didn't have any of that anyway."

She grimaced. "How could you live without internet?"

Some days, the internet was her sole adult entertainment. The television ran constantly on the kiddie channels during the day and at night she was often too tired to watch any more than an hour of whatever reality TV show Seth had chosen before falling asleep. On the worst days she had a few minutes here and there to check her email, maybe chat online with a friend. On the best days she wasted hours surfing sites, looking at photos with funny captions, watching videos of people falling down.

"I didn't have a computer. Besides, online's for porn and shopping," Todd said succinctly. "I can buy a skin mag cheaper, and I don't shop."

Gilly gaped. "I don't look at porn!"

Todd rolled his eyes.

"I don't!"

"Everyone looks at porn." He shrugged. "Anyone who says they've never looked at porn is full of shit."

Gilly's mouth worked on a reply that came out stuttering with affront. "I don't look at porn."

"Never once?" Todd leaned back in his chair, tipping it again. He looked her up and down, and under his scrutiny Gilly's cheeks heated, even though she was telling the truth. "Not even one time?"

"No!" She shook her head. "First of all, my kids are with me almost all the time. I can't have them looking at something like that. It's my job as their mother to make sure they don't see anything like that. My daughter uses the computer to play games. I have parental controls to block all that stuff."

"Yeah? What about your husband? I bet he looks at porn."

"Seth has his own laptop," Gilly said stiffly. "I don't think he looks at porn."

"Even if he doesn't talk about it, he's got a dick, right? Then he looks at porn. I guarantee it." Todd closed his fist on air and jerked it. "Nothing to be scared of."

Gilly rolled the dice and moved her piece, the top hat, five spaces to land on her own property. "I'm not scared of it. If he looks at porn, I don't know about it, okay? And that's the way I'd like to keep it."

She couldn't keep her lip from curling with distaste at the idea of her husband masturbating to video clips of huge-breasted, spread-eagled women in trashy shoes. Todd laughed and took his turn, also landing on one of her properties. Gilly collected his money without hesitation or remorse.

"So, you shop, then."

Gilly straightened a row of houses on the property closest to her, thinking about buying a hotel the next time around. "Hmm?"

"You don't watch porn. You must shop."

She laughed. "You think I have so much money I can shop all day?"

"Don't you?"

To him, she realized, it must seem like it. The engagement ring. The truck, now totaled. The money from the ATM. He didn't know they ate rice and beans so often because it was worth it to her to sacrifice fancy, gourmet meals to spend a week at the beach in a house nicer than the one they lived in full-time. Todd didn't know how some months the choice between dinner and a movie lost to a pair of shoes for Arwen, or about the number of payments Gilly still had to make on her mother's medical bills that had gone uncovered by insurance. He didn't know about the money she squirreled away every month against a time when something might unexpectedly break or get lost, how she hoarded paper towels and toilet paper and ramen noodles against the impending apocalypse.

"You know it's not money that makes a person rich, Todd."

"Oh, fuck, here we go with the Chinese fortune cookie shit."

"F—" she began and stopped herself.

Todd laughed. "Go ahead and say it. You know you want to. Fuck you, fuck me. Fuck everyone."

She flipped him off, not giving him the satisfaction of saying it aloud. "I don't have enough money to spend all day shopping online. Okay?"

"So, you don't shop. You don't watch porn. What do you do? Connex?" Todd made air quotes around the term and rolled his eyes again.

"Sometimes."

"Lame." He snorted.

Gilly bristled. "What do you know about it, if you don't have one?"

"I don't," Todd said off handedly, "have anyone to Connex with."

"What about all your alleged friends?"

"They don't do lame shit like that. They're too busy committing felonies," he said with a straight face.

She thought he might be kidding but this time couldn't really be sure. "Nice."

He laughed. "Connex sucks."

"How can you say it sucks if you've never done it?" Gilly had nearly five hundred "friends" on Connex and knew maybe about a third of them personally.

"I don't want to do it. Have a bunch of friends—" again

with the air quotes "—reading about when I take a dump and how many times a day I jerk off?"

"You're so crude," she said, though truthfully that was pretty close to what a lot of the people on her list did status updates about.

He made a jerking-off motion with curled fingers. "Dear Connex, today I shot my load four times. I wanted to try for five, but I ran out of lube."

"Todd."

He laughed again. "Yeah, really. People don't give a shit about that stuff. What's the point?"

"To connect with people who share similar interests. It's why they called it Connex." Gilly had no idea why she was defending a website she thought was sort of stupid, too.

"I don't have similar interests to anyone."

"I'm not surprised."

Todd blinked. Then grinned. "You're such a bitch."

Gilly wasn't insulted this time; he'd sounded almost fond. "It's called social networking for a reason. To be social. I stay home with my kids all day long. If I didn't do something online, talk to people, I'd go…"

"Crazy?" he prompted after half a minute when she stalled.

"Yes. I'd go crazy." Gilly fussed with her houses again.

She thought of the sound of muffled sobs behind a bedroom door and the cloying scent of spilled perfume. The sting of splintered glass in her feet. This, like the mysteries of her bank account, wasn't something Todd knew or would ever know.

"Who do you talk to?"

"Oh…family. People I went to school with or used to work with. I belong to a few groups for things I like."

"Like what?"

Gilly looked at him. "Authors. Television shows. Rock bands. Whatever."

Todd snorted and rattled the dice in his palm but didn't throw them. "Huh. That sounds like a fuckton of boring."

"Hey," Gilly said, annoyed. "You asked, didn't you? I'm not going to tell you things if you're going to make fun of me once you know."

Too late, she'd admitted she'd tell him things. Todd grinned as Gilly scowled. He handed her the dice.

"Besides," she added. "It's not just the people and the groups. There are games to play. And other things to do."

"Like what?"

"Oh. Take surveys. Are you going to roll those dice or what?"

He rolled, took his turn. "Surveys for what?"

She didn't want to admit her shameful secret, that she whored herself for "seeds" in her favorite Connex game, Farmburg. "Anything."

Todd nodded and helped himself to two hundred bucks for passing Go. "Yeah, right. For cash. I had a friend who got a bunch of stuff doing that. Crap, mostly. But some money."

"I don't do it for money." Though she had heard stories about people who'd won big.

"The fuck would you do an online survey for, if not money?" Todd looked up at her, brow furrowed.

Gilly sighed. No reason not to tell him. Stranded in a mountain cabin with a stranger who'd abducted her at knife-point, after tossing her kids out a vehicle window, she really shouldn't be worried about telling him she had an addiction to a silly online game. "For seeds."

"Huh?" Todd brushed hair from his eyes and tipped his

chair back, going to his pocket for a cigarette he stuck in his mouth but didn't light. "What kind of seeds?"

"For a game," she said, and took the dice, rolling. She landed on Boardwalk, as-yet-unowned, and crowed. "Yes! I'm buying it."

Todd passed her the card. "So you do surveys for… seeds."

Gilly settled her card amongst the others and looked up at him. "Yeah. You need seeds to plant, to get crops. To expand your farm and level up."

Todd raised an eyebrow.

"It's fun," Gilly said.

"Sooo…" Todd drew out the word, long and slow. "How many surveys do you do?"

"I don't have a lot of time, you know," Gilly began defensively, and stopped at another of Todd's raised-eyebrow looks. "Maybe three or four."

"A day?"

"Yes."

Or five. Once a memorable ten while Gandy napped and Arwen had a playdate. Her wrist had begun to ache from scrolling through the choices and the seeds had been spent in fifteen minutes. She'd had to filter out junk mail for the next six weeks.

"I'll be damned." All four legs of Todd's chair hit the floor. "Surveys are your porn."

"Shut up!" Gilly gasped, horrified. "Gross."

Todd grinned, unapologetic, and pointed at her. "They are."

"You're disgusting!"

"Well, yeah, maybe," Todd said. "But that don't make me wrong."

Gilly lifted her chin and gave him a cool glare. "It's your turn."

They rolled the dice, moved their pieces around the board, collected the paper cash when they passed Go. There was a suspicious absence of Go To Jail cards in this set, but Gilly didn't question it. She played for keeps, though, trying to strategize while Todd gambled his way around the board picking up properties at random without seeming to care about the cost or location.

"I'll trade you the Electric Company for Indiana and Illinois." Gilly already owned Kentucky and was itching to get hotels on those spots.

"Nope."

"C'mon, Todd. When I land on it, I'll have to pay you four times the number I roll on the dice."

Todd snorted, the unlit cigarette still dangling from his lower lip. "Nope."

"Electric Company and Water Works. Ten times the roll of the dice when you own both."

"No fucking way, Gilly. I'm dumb but I'm not that dumb." He made another of those jerking-off gestures. "You'll put hotels on those bitches and I'll land on them every fucking time."

"You won't," she scoffed, though she had to give him grudging admiration for outplaying her. He'd been merrily buying up properties, keeping her from owning more than two per set, therefore making it impossible for her to complete them. "It's statistically impossible for you to land on it every time."

"Yeah, well, you can forget it." His hair fell over his eye.

"Fine," she said. "But I'm buying Park Place and putting hotels up, and you can kiss my ass."

"Ooh, scary."

She was angrier than she should've been about a game and understood it wasn't that at all. Her cheek hurt when she bit it and hurt worse when she rubbed the sore spot with her tongue over and over to keep from saying something she didn't mean. But to her surprise, the mantra of *Count to ten, Gilly,* didn't start. She didn't need it. She snorted a little under her breath and looked up to Todd's curious glance.

"It's just a game," she said.

He studied her. "Well…yeah."

She shrugged. "I mean, it's *just* a game."

She looked around the room, then got up to go to the window. More snow. She snorted louder this time and pressed her forehead to the glass, relishing the chill.

Just a game. Slow your roll, Gilly. Chill out.

"Are we gonna finish the game, or what?"

She looked over her shoulder. "I guess so. Nothing else to do, right?"

Todd gave her a strange look and half got to his feet. "Gilly, you're not gonna freak out on me again, are you? Run out in the snow?"

She shook her head, took her seat. "No. I'm okay. Let's play."

They did for another few rolls of the dice, before Todd said, "What's he like?"

"Who? My husband?"

"Yeah."

She shrugged, concentrating on the board to keep emotion from overtaking her. "He's a good man. He's a good dad, fantastic with the kids. I love him very much."

"You're lucky, then. Really fucking lucky."

"Yes," Gilly said. They played in silence for a minute before the words rose to her lips, unbidden and undeniable. She'd never said this aloud before, not even to her girlfriends sitting around a coffee table, bitching about their husbands. "He doesn't listen to me."

The dice, tipped from Todd's hand, rolled across the board and came to rest. Snake eyes. He didn't move his piece right away; she felt his eyes on her and didn't want to meet them, but did.

"I mean, I think he hears me. He just doesn't listen."

Todd moved his racing car to an open property but didn't look to see the cost or offer to buy it. He didn't even glance toward the thin piles of paper money he'd carefully laid out in front of him. He gathered the dice again, rolling them in his palm. They clattered like bones against the board and he moved again, this time to one of his own properties.

"He's a good man," Gilly repeated in a low voice.

"What doesn't he listen to you about?"

Gilly picked up the dice, warm from Todd's palm. Her fingers curled over the plastic. "Never mind. Forget it."

It was wrong to talk about her husband like that with Todd. It was a betrayal. Gilly rolled the dice. They played the game.

She lost.

29

At home, just as it was never totally quiet, the house was never fully dark. Too many night-lights and appliances with clocks. Navigating her house in the night meant hopscotching from shadow to faint green glow. Gilly was the one who rose in the night and paced the floors, listening. Never Seth.

He never listened for the sound of the subtle shift in a child's breath that predicted a cough or a cry, or the dreaded, always-at-three-in-the-morning puke. He never listened for the dog's claws clicking toward the garbage can on the hardwood floor of the kitchen, or the neighbor's revving engine that meant their teenage son had finally returned. Seth went to bed and slept, sprawling and snoring. He probably didn't even know about the nights Gilly spent awake, checking the locks and the stove burners, or leaning over her children's beds just to make sure they still breathed.

He didn't listen to any of those things, and Seth didn't listen to her. Saying it to Todd had been like some bitter confession she could still taste hours later as she lay in the dark and stared up at a ceiling she couldn't see. Gilly swallowed hard now, her ears popping with the effort. She burrowed deeper into the blankets and curled on her side in a bed that would've been too small to share with her husband and was infinitely too vast when she was in it alone.

She loved her husband. He was a good man. A wonderful father, a loving husband. If he didn't listen to her, maybe it was because she didn't make herself heard. Or he couldn't understand that when she told him something it was real and true, not empty words said for the sake of conversation.

If Seth thought she was joking when Gilly told him she was going to lose her mind if he didn't replace the garbage bag after emptying the trash, or put a new roll of toilet paper on the holder when he'd used the last scrap, whose fault was that? His for not taking her seriously, or hers for not impressing upon him how utterly serious she was? Or hers, for allowing such minor, small things to eat away at her? It didn't matter now. Their marriage was a machine, the gears and cogs turning or sticking. What more could she ask for? What more could she expect?

"How'd you meet him?" Todd's voice parted the darkness.

Gilly lifted her head, turning her face toward him but not her body. "My husband?"

"Yeah. How'd you meet him?"

She settled back into the blankets, shrugging them higher on her shoulders. "A friend introduced us."

"At a party?"

"Yes." She paused, curiosity winning. "How'd you know?"

She heard him shifting in his sheets and imagined a shrug. "Lots of people get introduced at parties."

"It was a barbecue at his boss's house. His boss's wife was my friend." Gilly paused again, the dark room a perfect screen for the movie of her memories.

Seth had been wearing a pink polo shirt and khaki shorts, a beer in the hand he hadn't held out for her to shake. His hair had been too long for her taste, his smile nice enough, but Gilly hadn't been looking at him "like that."

"Did you like him right away?"

Gilly blinked away the vision of the first time she'd seen the man she'd marry. "No. God, no."

Todd laughed a little louder. "Huh?"

"I was with someone else. I thought he was okay, but I wasn't interested in him that way."

"So how you'd end up together?"

Was this wrong, to talk about this with Todd? She hadn't thought about it for years. The kids weren't old enough to ask about it, and the story had never seemed romantic enough to retell. "We went out a bunch of times with friends."

"And then you hooked up with him?"

Gilly smiled, bittersweet, at the memory. "Not that first time. I was still seeing the other guy, the one I'd gone to the barbecue with. I thought I liked him, but…he turned out to be sort of a jerk."

"What did he do to you?" Todd's voice broke on a yawn and triggered one from her.

"Oh, the usual stuff."

"Knocked you around? Stole shit from you? Ran around on you?"

"No! Is that what you think the usual stuff is?" Gilly shifted in her blankets, indignant.

"Sure. If you don't like a dude, yeah, I mean, that's some bad stuff, right?" He paused. "I mean…you don't think that's okay, do you?"

"Of course it's not. *You* don't think that's okay, do you?"

"No. Of course not. A man who hits a woman isn't much of a man," Todd said in a low voice.

They both ignored the fact they'd hit each other, and more than once.

"He didn't hit me. He probably did run around on me, yes. Mostly he didn't call when he said he would, stood me up. That sort of thing." Gilly frowned as she remembered. "I didn't even like him that much, that guy. He thought I was in love with him, though, which made it even worse."

"Huh?"

Gilly sighed. "If he'd treated me badly knowing I didn't really love him, that would've been one thing. But if he thought I was in love with him and he still did that stuff… that's worse. That it didn't matter how I felt about him. I went out with Seth, finally, because that other guy had promised to call and didn't."

"And you knew he was the guy for you."

She smiled a little at the certainty in Todd's voice. "Oh…I don't know about that. I didn't know right away, that's for sure."

"You didn't?"

"No. I don't think anyone can ever know right away."

More shifting and rustling from his side of the room. "You don't believe in love at first sight and all that shit?"

"No. Do you?"

"Fuck no." Todd's laugh grated, rusty and sharp. "Love's just another word for sucker."

"Oh, Todd." Gilly bit back a laugh. "That's not true. Haven't you ever…haven't you had…?"

She trailed to a stop. They weren't giggling girlfriends at a sleepover. She burrowed deeper into the blankets.

Todd stayed silent long enough Gilly thought he'd gone to sleep. "What? Like a girlfriend?"

"Someone," Gilly amended at the way he'd sneered the word.

Todd made a low, derisive noise. "Girls like men with money."

"That's not the only thing women like about men." The urge to defend her gender was automatic and not necessarily sincere.

"Well, let me put it like this. They don't like guys without money as much as they like guys with cash," Todd said. "It don't matter if you're nice to 'em. Hell. Some of 'em like it better when you're mean, so long as you've got bank."

The question tripped off her tongue before she could stop it. "So, no girlfriend, ever?"

"I had girlfriends." Todd sounded angry at first, then, quieter. "I had one, once…."

She waited.

"Her name was Kendra. I met her at work."

"At the diner?"

"No." He sounded gruff. "This was a long time ago, before the diner. I was working for a landscaping company. Planting trees, hauling brush, that sort of shit."

"Did she work for the landscaping company?"

More silence. She thought he'd fallen asleep. "No. She was…the daughter of a customer."

He didn't really have to say more than that. Gilly could guess the outcome. She made a sympathetic noise, anyway, not necessarily to encourage him but not trying to put him off, either.

"I broke up with her," Todd said.

"Oh." It was so not the scenario she'd imagined—irate customer waving off "the help" to protect his daughter's virtue.

"Yeah, I know," Todd said in a voice dripping with sarcasm, showing he guessed what she'd been thinking. "Who'd have guessed it would be me who bailed, huh?"

"I didn't say anything."

"You didn't have to."

Another few minutes of silence until Gilly said, tentatively, "What happened?"

"She wanted to get married."

"Oh." It wasn't the first time she'd heard about a relationship ending because the woman had wanted more of a commitment than the man. "And you didn't want to."

"Fuck no!" Todd sounded as thoroughly disgusted as if she'd suggested he eat feces.

There didn't seem much to say after that. Gilly closed her eyes and noticed no difference in the darkness behind her lids than when she'd been staring. During the past few years, there'd been many nights Gilly had greeted her husband at the door with her car keys already in one hand, her purse in the other, so desperate to get out of the house by herself she manufactured errands to run. There'd been far fewer times lately that she'd greeted him the way she had in the early days of their marriage, with a kiss and a hug and questions about his day.

Those days seemed faraway now. All of them. The good and the bad, both. The cliché would've been that if she had the chance to greet him at the door again, she'd choose the kiss rather than escape, but listening to the soft sound of Todd's snoring slipping through the chill and black, Gilly wasn't quite able to convince herself it was true.

30

Gilly hadn't watched the television show *Lost* in a long time, not since the end of the second season when the show had totally, well…lost her. Yet there was a moment during the show's first season she would never forget—the part when Hurley's CD player finally gave up and died. She couldn't remember what the character had said to commemorate the occasion, but the words that came out of her mouth were definitely not allowed on network television.

She tugged the headphones from her ears and thumbed the iPod's controls. Nothing. Totally dead. Worse, she'd been listening to a song she didn't even like. She'd wasted the last few minutes of music time on garbage.

Todd had gone outside to bring in some wood for the stove. Now he came in and dumped the logs into the bin. Snorting and stamping, he slapped his bare hands against his thighs and blew into his curled fingers. He looked up at the sound of her curse and raised both eyebrows.

"It's dead," Gilly said in a tone more appropriate to the loss of a pet than an inanimate piece of electronic equipment. She held up the iPod.

Todd toed off his boots and left them to drip snow onto the floor by the door. He shivered, still rubbing his hands together and shook his hair, coated with a light mist of flakes from the seemingly constant snowfall. "That sucks, huh?"

"Yes. It does." Gilly got up, put the iPod on the table.

She hadn't wept in weeks, but she wanted to cry now. Instead she scrubbed furiously at her eyes until they stung and her breath caught in her throat. "It's just an iPod," she said.

She felt him watching her but Todd said nothing, just disappeared into the kitchen. She heard him rummaging around in the drawers. He was back before she had time to even turn around.

"Here." Todd held out a handful of batteries. "There's an old CD player in the cupboard. It should work."

She didn't move toward him to take what he offered. After half a minute Todd sighed, shoulders slumping, and rolled his eyes. He went to the cupboard himself, pulled out the boom box. He brought it to the table and set it beside the iPod, then flipped the CD player on its side to pry open the back and fill the empty slot with the batteries.

"I took them from the flashlight," he said. "If you don't fucking listen to something, I'm going to be pissed off."

The threat sounded empty. Gilly was too touched by the gesture to do more than stare, anyway. Todd sighed again, heavier this time, and stomped upstairs. She heard the scrape of a drawer, then his feet on the stairs. He brought her the CD case he'd rescued from the truck.

"Here." Todd opened it. "Pick something."

Gilly unzipped the case and flipped through the plastic

pages. The sight of the silver discs, such a vivid link to her life, made her throat burn. She gave herself a mental shake and forced the feeling away. "Like what?"

Todd took the case from her and looked through the choices. His forehead wrinkled in consternation. "What the hell is this stuff?"

Gilly bit a smile, knowing instantly the reason for his question. Her taste in music was eclectic, to say the least, her iPod filled with everything from classical to reggae. She rarely listened to CDs anymore except in the truck, and the discs she'd chosen to keep in there had all been chosen for their "singability." She had to be able to belt out the lyrics, sing with abandon, and generally make the kind of fool of herself that she could only do in the privacy of her vehicle with no one to hear but the kids.

"Hedwig and the Angry Inch? The Rocky Horror Picture Show? Phantom of the Opera?" He faked a gag. "Don't you have anything good?"

"Hey. All of those CDs are good."

Todd flipped some more pages. "*One Hundred and One Silly Kids Songs?* The Wiggles? Jesus, Gilly."

She smiled. "You might like it."

Todd rolled his eyes and pulled out another disc. "Simon and Garfunkel. Jason Manns, who the hell is he? Oh, hell, no. Spare me that folk shit. Okay, this is better. The Doors. Greatest hits. Sweet."

"That's my husband's..." Gilly stopped herself. She didn't want to talk about Seth with Todd any more than she already had. "But we can listen to it."

Todd punched the button on the small CD player and inserted the disc. In a few seconds, the first opening strains of "The End" came out of the speakers. He grabbed the bowl of popcorn he'd made earlier and sat down on the couch, long legs stretched out on the coffee table, head back on the cushions.

"This is good."

The music made Gilly restless. At the window, she peered out into the rapidly falling night. More snowflakes, light now but promising to get heavier, drifted down. She hadn't been outside in nearly a month. Todd's footprints still broke the span of white, but with the new snow coming down it wouldn't be long until they disappeared, too.

Jim Morrison's achingly clear voice spouted poetic lyrics that reminded her of college parties, lights dim in the basement of some fraternity house, warm beer and cigarette smoke. The song made her think of Seth, too, who'd owned the CD before they'd met. He'd taken her to see the film *The Doors,* Val Kilmer playing a perfect Morrison, at some college art department film series on their fourth date. He'd bought her popcorn and nonpareils, and later had licked the salt and chocolate from her fingers before leaning over in the dark movie theater to kiss her. Gilly touched the frosted window and watched her fingertips make small, clear ovals in the rime.

She missed him. Missed his strength, his quiet humor. She missed the way he put up with her sniping and complaining, and the way he laughed with her at silly old movies. She missed the scent of him, fresh soap and water, and the way he never failed to squeeze her when she passed him.

She had no tears, not now, not when they would serve no purpose. Watching the snow outside, it seemed impossible it would ever melt. That she would ever be able to get away from this place. It seemed as though she might be here forever, listening to a dead man sing and watching darkness swallow the world.

"What do you think he means, anyway?" Todd's voice broke her concentration, and Gilly jumped a little.

Her fingers skidded in the frost, leaving slashed marks like wounds on the glass. "Who?"

"Morrison." Todd crunched some popcorn. "The killer picks a face from the ancient gallery and all that shit. What's that mean, do you think?"

Gilly tore her gaze from the window to contemplate the man on the couch. "I suppose you could take it to mean that…well…" She struggled to put her thoughts into words. *Her* thoughts, not anything she'd read that someone else had postulated. "That there's a killer in all of us. Or that we can choose our actions. I think he means we can choose the face we wear."

"Gilly." Todd gave her a look. "The fuck's that mean? Choose your face. You get the face you're born with."

"Not your real face." She made a circle with her finger, outlining her features. "Not your eyes and nose and mouth, not like that. The face you put on for people. For the rest of the world. I think he meant you choose that face."

Todd cocked his head. "Huh. You think that's true?"

She nodded. "Yes. I do."

Her answer seemed to satisfy him, because he nodded thoughtfully. But then Todd said, "That's a bunch of crap."

Gilly sniffed. "Why'd you ask if you didn't want to know?"

"I asked what you thought. Doesn't mean I have to agree. What about the rest of it?" Todd reversed the CD for a few seconds until the passage started again. "The blue bus and all that stuff?"

Gilly pondered, aware that for whatever reason, he expected her to have an answer. "Life is a journey?"

She waited for his scoffing.

Todd glanced at her. "Hell, it sure ain't one I want to take on a bus. You ever take a trip on a bus, Gilly?"

She had, several times, to visit a college boyfriend. "Sure." The memory made her smile. "Bus stations are scary."

"You got that right." Todd cocked his head to listen to the music. "Morrison was one fucked-up dude."

"Some people think he was a great poet for his time," Gilly said, uncertain why his casual assessment of the long-dead rock star should affect her at all, much less cause her to rise to his defense. Hell, she didn't even like Morrison all that much, despite his sexy ways and liquid lyrics.

Todd turned up the volume. "The dude wanted to kill his father."

"And fuck his mother," Gilly said matter-of-factly, and was completely unprepared for Todd's reaction.

His face went pale, and his mouth gaped. He turned his attention from the small CD player and stared at her with stunned disgust. He even went so far as to take a step back.

"What?"

Gilly took her own step back from the force of his glare. "That's what he says at the end there…well, at least, that's what people think he meant to say…."

"People are sick!" Todd shuddered. "For crissakes, Gilly, that's sick."

Gilly chewed on her response before saying anything. This was not the first time the topic of motherhood had set him off. And he had mentioned that his mother died. Gilly wasn't sure what to say.

Todd shuddered again and ran a hand over his hair. "You think he really wanted to do that?"

"I don't know," she admitted. "Maybe it's an urban legend

or a rumor, but that's what I always thought he meant. It would fit with the whole Oedipus thing, with wanting to kill his father…."

She stopped at Todd's blank look.

"I told you before, I ain't smart."

She hadn't meant to throw his lack of education in his face. "Oedipus is an old story about a man who accidentally kills his father and marries his mother."

"How in the hell do you accidentally kill your father to marry your mom?"

On the CD, "The End" became "Touch Me." She wished he'd asked about that song. It would've been way easier to interpret.

Gilly sighed, not sure she remembered all the details and not up to the task of teaching the Greek classics. "It's complicated."

"Yeah, I bet."

"It's Greek," she said, like that made a difference.

Todd rolled his eyes. "They have good salad and shitty stories."

It took her a minute before she realized he was making another one of his jokes. A giggle almost squeezed out of her throat, but she pinched it off. She might not be able to hate him, but Gilly wasn't ready to laugh with him.

"It wouldn't kill you to laugh," Todd said, as if reading her mind.

But Gilly thought it might do just that. She got up and turned off The Doors and slipped in *Hedwig and the Angry Inch*. "Enough Morrison."

Todd listened to the first few words of the song that came on, and looked as shocked as he had when she told him what Jim Morrison wanted to do to his mother.

"What the…?" He was too stunned even to utter his favorite curse word.

Gilly had chosen the track on purpose to shock him. She felt another giggle coming on, a nasty one this time, but she satisfied herself with an evil grin. "His sex-change operation got botched. It's pretty self-explanatory."

Though she'd removed the CDs from their plastic jewel cases to put them in the travel case, she'd also put in the inner sleeves. Todd pulled out the one for Hedwig and stared in utter amazement at the photo of the man in a bright yellow wig and tons of glam makeup screaming into a microphone.

"Is that a dude?"

"Yes," Gilly said. "I guess you've never seen the movie."

Todd gave her a look. "This is from a movie? Figures."

"It was a good movie," Gilly replied somewhat wistfully. It had been a long time since she'd watched a movie.

Todd waved the travel case. "Why do you listen to this shit. You got a thing for guys in makeup, or what?"

"I guess I have a thing for the underdog." The self-assessment surprised her. Bat Boy. Hedwig. Even poor, misunderstood tragic antihero Frank-N-Furter. All underdogs who met bad ends when the world they lived in rejected them for being who they were.

"If you like the underdog," Todd said, "then you should practically be in love with me."

Without looking at him, Gilly took the CD out and put it back in the travel case. She slid another into the player and hit Play. She thought he'd grumble, but she didn't care. When the music began, she went to the window and pressed her face against the glass to look out at the snow. It was the same view. The same snow. Constant, not changing. As was all of this.

Todd, quiet, took a place beside her at the window. Gilly

straightened up, her forehead cold from where it had rested on the glass. They stared out into the darkness, but all Gilly could see was their reflection, blurry. Her and Todd.

"This song," he said, after it had played nearly all the way through.

She looked at him, not in the mirror made by the light inside shining to the outside, but at his face. His real face. "What about it?"

"This one's right," Todd said. "The part where he says I told the truth, didn't come here to fool you. That's a good song."

It ended. Todd left her side and messed around with the CD player's buttons. It was a song Gilly loved, though not the lyric he'd quoted. She thought of the part that made the most sense to her—love was not a victory march.

"C'mon," she told him as the song began again. "I'll make us something to eat."

31

Board games and their dozens of tiny pieces were scattered all over the place. Gilly looked around the room and frowned. "This place is a pigsty."

Todd looked up from the couch, where he'd been silently contemplating the ceiling for the past fifteen minutes. "So clean it up."

Her fingers itched to do just that, but she refused to be a slave to this house. "*You* clean it up."

"I'm relaxing."

"Relaxing implies rest," Gilly said sourly. "Like you've been actually working."

Todd scratched his head with his middle finger, and Gilly fumed. She envied him the ability to sit and stare at nothing for an hour at a time. She crossed her arms and glared.

"Is it nice?" she asked another fifteen minutes later when Todd hadn't moved and she'd been unable to stop herself from putting away the Monopoly game.

Todd looked at her, then. "Is what nice?"

She gestured at the ceiling. "Being entertained by the ceiling? Is that an advantage to being a meathead?"

"I guess it is." Todd smirked.

A strand of hair had come loose from her ponytail, and she grimaced as she tucked it back. She'd bathed every day since he'd forced her out of bed, quick rinses bent over the tub, using tepid water. Nothing thorough or luxurious.

"I want a bath."

Todd flapped a languid hand toward the bathroom. "Go ahead. Who's stopping you?"

In the bathroom, door closed, Gilly flipped him off but felt no better for the gesture. If anything, she felt petty and stupid again, which only made her grouchier. A hot bath would fix her temper. Hot baths could fix a lot of things.

She turned on the taps, which sputtered and spit and groaned but let loose a flood of water that rang against the bottom of the iron tub like Jamaican kettledrums. She grimaced as she stripped out of her clothes and felt the prickly stubble of her armpits and legs. Greasy hair, unshaven legs, no wonder she felt gross and grumpy.

The water had filled the tub only halfway when she thought to run a hand under the stream. It would've been generous to call it lukewarm. Gilly wilted and dipped her fingers into the water in the tub's bottom. That was hot enough, but not deep enough.

She turned off the faucet and yanked on her clothes, then opened the door. "Todd. The hot water's not working."

He looked over his shoulder at her. "Oh. Yeah."

"What do you mean, 'oh, yeah'?" She put her hands on her hips.

He gave her a shrug that had become familiar. "Water

heater's probably fucked. And shit, Gilly, it's not like we have a fuckton of propane. Maybe we're running out. In which case we really are fucked."

She swallowed a bitter retort at that. "Really?"

Another shrug.

"Todd!" she cried, exasperated, and left the bathroom to face him. "Are you serious? Why didn't you say anything?"

She hated the grin and the wicked glint in his eyes that told her he enjoyed teasing her. She hated the fact he knew he was getting under her skin even more. She tried forcing her expression to smooth with little success.

"You said you wanted a bath. What was I going to do? Tell you no?"

"I don't want it," she said with tense jaw and narrowed eyes, "if it means we're going to run out of propane. I've suffered with sponge baths up to now. I could get by with it."

Todd got up, stretching to his full height and looked down at her. "This is a hunting cabin. Dudes mostly don't go for long bubble baths. We always had enough hot water for a couple of showers. The water heater's small and it's old. It probably needs time to refill, that's all."

She wanted to punch his arm. Or someplace more tender. "And if it's the propane tank?"

He shrugged a third time. "Then we go without lights and have to use the hand pump outside for water, if that bitch hasn't frozen solid. Heat'll be fine so long as we have wood for the stove."

"You don't sound too worried about it!"

Todd looked at her this time. "Would it matter if I was? Nothing I can do about it. You can't, either."

"How do you check?"

He jerked a thumb at the window. "Tank's out back. There's

a gauge." He paused. "Last time I checked, there was plenty, should get us through until spring anyway. Uncle Bill always made sure to top off the tank before winter."

Her mouth tightened. "The last time you…so you know how much we have? We're not close to running out?"

"Nah. I don't think so." Todd grinned, eyes glinting again.

"You're an asshole," Gilly muttered, arms linked tight across her chest.

"Aw, hey."

"Hey, nothing! I was…worried," she admitted, hating it.

"I'm sorry," Todd said.

He sounded as if he meant it, but Gilly wasn't going to take his apology. "You could've told me that before I tried filling the tub."

Todd's brows went up as the corners of his mouth turned down. "How was I supposed to know the hot water'd run out before you could fill the tub? The fuck you think I am, psychic?"

"Well, I know you're not as funny as you think you are!"

Todd's frown tightened. He slouched back to the couch, feet on the table. "Fuck you. Go take a bath. Freeze your tits off. The fuck I care?"

She was not going to freeze, and she *would* have a hot bath. Gilly went to the kitchen and filled the largest pots she could find with water. Also the kettle. While the water boiled, she sorted through the last few fresh items in the refrigerator. She took an apple and some cheese and went to the pantry for a box of wheat crackers.

By the time she'd finished peeling and slicing the apple and cubing the cheese, the water was boiling. Grabbing a set of oven mitts, she carried the pots to the cast iron bathtub and poured them in. She refilled the containers and set them to boil again.

Todd watched her with undisguised interest. "You going to fill up the whole tub that way?"

Gilly put her snack on a plate and sat at the kitchen table to wait for the water. "Yes."

He snorted. "It'll get cold before you're done."

She didn't think so. The tub would hold in most of the heat, and she hoped that by the time the tub had enough water in it for soaking, the boiling water would have become cool enough to bathe in but not too cold. And if it wasn't, it would be simple enough to add some cold water to it.

When she dumped the second set of pots, the tub water was still steaming. However, she needed more water, and faster. Gilly dug around in the bottom cupboards while the next batch of water heated. She found several large, deep stockpots. They were incredibly heavy when she finally got them filled, and she didn't try to put them on the stove. She put them on the woodstove.

"You're wasting good propane," Todd told her.

Gilly shrugged, an echo of him, not worried now that he'd told her there was enough propane to last until spring. "I need a bath. I *want* a bath."

She ate the rest of her food and took another set of pots to the bathroom. The water in the tub had cooled considerably, but was still luxuriously warm. The pots on the woodstove began to boil next.

Gilly lugged gallon after gallon of boiling water to the tub. She burned her wrists and hands when the water slopped over the sides, and she hurt her back lifting the heavy pots. But she did it.

When she finally shed her clothes and sank up to her chin in the water, she was sure she'd caused herself permanent injury. Every part of her body throbbed and ached even worse than after she'd wrecked the truck. To finally feel clean, though… well, she thought the pain was worth it.

Water had always soothed her. She preferred showers to baths, usually. She loved the way the hot water made steam and pounded down all around her, blocking out the noise of a whining child or the phone or any other of a dozen disturbances. This wasn't as nice as a shower, but it was wonderful all the same.

Floating. Gilly was floating. She'd drifted off to sleep, letting her body slip almost completely beneath the water. Only her face stuck out, just far enough for her to breathe. She didn't dream, wasn't far enough down for that. Gilly simply floated.

Sweet summer corn.

She didn't know why that came into her mind, but now it was all she could think about. Corn on the cob slathered with butter and salt, fresh from the farm stand. The last time she'd eaten corn, she'd bought it from the side of the road. A young Mennonite girl, hair in long braids, her feet bare, had taken the money and counted sufficient change in her head faster than Gilly could've done with a calculator. She'd taken it home and boiled it to eat with burgers on the grill, sliced tomatoes from the garden and home-sliced French fries she'd seasoned with sea salt and fresh-ground pepper.

Gilly's mouth watered as she drifted in the bath, eyes closed. Thinking of summer. Heat. Her stomach rumbled.

Gilly's mother had loved sweet corn. Even in the worst times, when she insisted all she could drink was cola—heavily laced with rum, but nobody was supposed to know it—her mother could be tempted to eat sweet corn. At the end it was all she would eat. Her mother had loved it so much Gilly sometimes felt she should hate it just to be ornery, be different, or because remembering how much her mother had loved it was too painful.

But Gilly didn't hate it. She wanted some, right now, even though it was out of season and she wasn't at home. She was… someplace else, far away, craving something she couldn't have.

The water cooled, and her body protested. Gilly left the haze of sleep to which she'd so gratefully succumbed, and opened her eyes. And screamed.

Todd stood over her. How long had he been watching? Gilly scrambled upright, sloshing water over the side of the tub, wetting the legs of his jeans. Her hands were inadequate for the task, but she tried futilely anyway to cover herself.

He stepped back, expression unreadable. "I thought you drowned. I thought you were dead."

"Go away!" Gilly cried, hunching forward to protect her body from his emotionless eyes.

"Get out of the tub now, Gilly." Todd left the bathroom.

There would be no more peace for her here. Gilly shivered from more than the chilly air as she got out of the water and dried herself. Her fingers had gone pruney, but her stomach rumbled. She could still taste the memory of sweet corn, but it had gone sour on her tongue.

32

"No more eggs for breakfast. These are the last." Gilly cracked the last two into the challah dough.

Todd stubbed out his cigarette into the puddle of tea in his saucer until Gilly, with a sigh, pushed an ashtray from the cupboard across the table at him. "It's okay. I like your bread."

"Thanks." The word slipped off her tongue far more easily than it would have even a few days before.

She finished kneading the dough and left it on the counter to rise, then went to the sink and cleaned her hands with a scant palmful of soap, mindful of the emptying bottle. Outside, the winter sun glared brilliantly off the still-immense piles of snow. No sign of any melting, and the temperatures hadn't dropped so none seemed likely anytime soon.

Gilly let out a long, hard sigh.

Todd got up to put his dishes in the sink. He leaned against the counter and stretched, cracking his neck. "I need a new pillow."

The ghost of a grin painted Gilly's mouth. "Let me run out and get you one."

Todd didn't laugh. He rolled his head on his neck with a grimace and a bit of a groan. "It always kinks up on me like this after a while. It's from a car wreck I was in. Feels like someone stabbed me with an ice pick."

Gilly raised her eyebrows at him and held up her hands, wiggling the fingers. "Don't look at me."

"Wow. Ha-ha-ha. You know you ain't as funny as you think you are?" Todd rubbed the junction of his shoulder and neck with his fingertips.

Gilly brushed past him and went to the living room, restless. She'd read all the magazines and finished the crossword puzzles. She picked up one of the magazines anyway and sat down with it.

"Will you rub it for me?"

"What? No!" Gilly shrank away from Todd, who'd suddenly appeared before her.

"Please?" He grimaced again. "It really hurts bad."

He sank to the floor in front of her and sat cross-legged. He let his head hang down, and the thick dark hair parted, exposing his neck. A downy line of dark fuzz dusted his skin there.

Gilly stared at him but didn't touch him. "I can't do that. I'm…I'm not any good at massage."

He shot her a grin over his shoulder. "I seen you kneading that bread. Just do the same on my neck. C'mon. Right there."

He waited, and Gilly faltered. She did not want to touch him. And yet, she was tired of being the growling dog. Her defenses were slipping in the face of Todd's constant forgiving spirit.

Gilly put her hands on Todd's shoulders and felt the knots there. "You're really tense."

"No shit."

She spread out her fingers, resting them lightly on the bare skin of his neck. His hair brushed her knuckles. His arms pressed against the inside of her calves.

Todd let out a low, guttural groan as she began the massage. She faltered a moment at the sound but then continued, working the muscles the way she kneaded her dough. He hung his head, allowing her to access the sides of his neck and shoulders.

"That feels good."

Todd relaxed and went boneless under her fingers, but Gilly remained tense. This didn't feel right. At last she had to pull away. Gilly got up from the chair and surreptitiously wiped her hands on the seat of her jeans as she went to the kitchen.

Todd followed. "Why'd you stop?"

"I have to check the bread dough." A blatant lie. Gilly lifted the damp cloth to peek at the rising dough, which didn't need her attention. Her face felt flushed with the untruth, her palms sweaty.

Todd was behind her. She was aware of him, how he towered over her, how the aura of his strength surrounded her. He was so much bigger, taller and broader, that she was made tiny. Gilly turned to leave, to make her escape. His hand on her arm stopped her.

"What's wrong?" Todd asked.

"Nothing."

She shrugged the lie and pushed past him into the living

room. It wasn't enough. She needed more distance. Gilly went upstairs and sat on her bed.

"What's the matter with you?" Todd had followed her but stopped at the top of the stairs.

"I have a headache." The third lie slipped out. She lay down, facing away from him, on top of the covers.

"That's what you're supposed to tell your husband, not me."

She didn't look at him, just made a disgruntled sound.

Todd sighed. He wasn't wearing boots and his tread was lighter than usual across the bare floor. "Sorry. I know that wasn't funny. Hey, Gilly, c'mon. Look at me."

She refused. "I'm tired. Let me take a nap."

His weight dented the bed. She still didn't turn. Gilly closed her eyes, willing him to go away. His hand weighted her shoulder, but his touch was gentle. Inquiring, not demanding.

"What did I do?" he asked, in a low voice unlike his normal tone. "Talk to me. Please?"

"You didn't do anything." Gilly rolled into a tight ball, knees to her chest. "I told you, I'm just tired. I have a headache. That's all. Let me sleep."

He sighed and did not remove his hand. "You're acting like I done something real bad to you. Something scary. And I didn't even touch you."

Gilly sat, twisting her body away from him and scooting across the double bed as far as she could to get out of his reach. "No, I touched you."

Todd rolled his head on his neck again. No popping or cracking of the joints this time. No grimace of pain. "Yeah, thanks. It was great."

She shivered. "You don't understand."

His gaze flickered. He tried to joke. "I got cooties, huh?"

She didn't even smile. "I don't want to touch you. Anymore. Ever."

"It's okay to hit me, but not to help me," Todd said, with a touch to his cheek where the faint line of the earlier injuries she'd inflicted still remained. "Making me bleed is okay, though, huh? That's just fine?"

She looked down at her betraying hands. "You couldn't possibly understand."

Todd's mouth thinned. "Christ, Gilly. I didn't ask you to give me a hand job."

"Stop it!" She clapped her hands over her ears. "Stop!"

She could still hear his voice, low, and angry. "Still got to be that growling dog, huh?"

She took her hands away from her ears. "Can you blame me?"

He was not, she realized with some alarm, angry. Todd was upset. His mouth trembled, and did she see a glint of tears in his eyes? He hung his head, making it impossible for her to be sure.

"You act like touching me was going to burn your hands or something." Todd splayed his fingers on his thighs, then gripped the denim of his jeans as though he was trying to stop from clenching his fists. "Like I'm dirty."

Touching him with compassion had made her *feel* dirty. Gilly didn't deny it. She watched him with wide eyes, waiting to see what he would do.

"Is that what you think?" He looked at her with naked honesty in his face. "I'm dirty to you?"

Gilly remained silent. Todd sighed again. He set his jaw, waiting for her to talk to him.

"You ain't going to say anything?"

She shook her head slowly. Todd got up from the bed and left the room. A few moments later, she heard a tremendous crash that nearly startled her into falling off the bed. More crashes followed, interspersed with cursing.

Gilly crept beneath her covers, shaking, and tried to warm herself. She could close her eyes, but even putting the pillow over her head wasn't enough to drown out the noise. She bit her lip to keep from crying out at every bang and crash.

The silence that followed was worse than the crashing. She waited, aching from breathlessness, to hear the sound of his footsteps on the stairs. She fell asleep waiting for it.

A cry woke her from another dream of roses. Gilly shot straight up in bed, heart pounding so hard she saw bright flashes of light in front of her eyes. The room had fallen into blackness while she slept.

She pressed her hands to her mouth, shaking, listening for the cry to come again. In the first few moments of wakefulness she'd again thought she was home, listening for one of her children. Maybe she would always think that. Now she remembered where she was, knew it couldn't be Arwen or Gandy, but still strained to hear the cry.

It came again from downstairs, lower this time, a sound so filled with grief and agony it brought sympathetic tears to Gilly's eyes. She swung her legs over the bed, waiting to hear it again. It did, the low, destitute cry of a child who's given up on his mother ever coming to comfort him.

It was Todd.

She did not have to go to him. It would've been easy enough to close her ears to his anguish, to roll over in bed and force herself back into sleep. His suffering did not have to become her own. She owed him nothing. Yet she got out of bed and sought him, because listening to his pain without offering solace went against every instinct she had. Gilly couldn't close her heart.

She made her way down the dark stairs. He'd lit candles, not a propane lantern, and the flickering light turned his skin to gold. Todd sat in front of the fire, his familiar pile of crumpled and stained papers in front of him. He held the red folder, creased and also stained, and bulging with what looked like newspaper clippings. The scraps of yellowing newsprint fell from the folder to his lap, covering his knees. Todd rocked from side to side, muttering.

"Todd?"

He whipped around to face her. His eyes were red rimmed and awful looking, like pools of blood surrounding the darkness of his pupils. His cheeks, grown pale from so many days without the sun, had bloomed with two red roses. His mouth worked, and his hands opened helplessly. The rest of the folder fell to the floor. He pressed the heels of his hands to his eyes, fingers tipped with raw, chewed nails.

"Oh, Todd." She said his name softer the second time. Gentler.

He held out the papers to her, a sheaf of clippings falling to the floor like dirty snowflakes. He didn't speak. Gilly forgot all that had passed between them and went to him, knelt beside him. She took the papers.

Squinting in the candlelight, she read the first article. A black-and-white photograph filled most of the page. Five children encircled a woman whose mouth twisted in an insincere smile. She held the sixth, smallest child, a small boy with smooth dark hair and wearing bibbed overalls, in her lap. The headline above the photo didn't match the picture of familial bliss.

One of Six Survives

Gilly was slammed back in time to elementary school. The story had been huge back then with its gruesome details and tragic ending. The worst kind of legend, based on truth but grown from repeated whispers in the hallway, the bathroom, the playground. Everyone knew what had happened. They said if you went up to the church where she'd done it, you could see their ghosts.

"Oh, my God," Gilly breathed. "You're that boy?"

She sifted through the rest of the pile, catching bits of the story here and there. Though she'd been too young to follow the story in the papers or on the news, what she'd heard in school had been pretty accurate.

Boy survives mother's wrath. Five children slain. Mother dies by own hand.

"She said we were going to see Jesus," Todd said in a voice filled with rust and razor blades. "I thought she meant church. She took us there sometimes, when she thought we were being bad, and she'd make us sit in those little benches and pray. The little church back there in the woods. The one her family built way back a couple hundred years ago."

Gilly knew the place. It had always had a reputation of being haunted, even before Todd's mother had killed her children there. A set of famed murderers, the last criminals to be hanged in Pennsylvania, had been buried in the cemetery. It had been a place to go at midnight on Halloween, a place to scare yourself stupid.

"She put us in the Fuego, even though there wasn't enough seat belts for us all. She always made us wear our seat belts. But not that night. Katie and Mary sat in the front with her. Stevie, Joey, Freddy and me were in the back. Stevie was my oldest brother." Todd pointed to the tallest boy in the photo.

"My Grandma Essie sometimes called Mama Fertile Myrtle, because she had us six kids in ten years. Daddy left around the time I was born, just run off with the truck-stop waitress from Ono, but we all lived with Grandma and Uncle Bill."

He took a deep, shuddering breath that didn't seem to calm him. Gilly's legs had gone to rubber, and she was thankful she was already kneeling instead of standing. The details of the story had rushed back to her as soon as he began speaking. It had been told in horrified yet fascinated whispers, passed from mouth to ear like a game of telephone. Particulars had been exaggerated, some lost, but the sadness of it hadn't been diluted. Even as a kid Gilly had wanted to cry when she heard it.

"She told us to be real quiet, and we'd get to see a star shower." Todd looked into the fire, the flames reflected in his eyes. "'Hush up,' she said. 'You'll see Jesus in the stars.' Katie started to cry because she had to go to the bathroom, and Mama kept telling her to hush up, hush up now. It was cold out there in the dark, and spooky, too. Stevie held my hand because he knew I was afraid. He was always good like that, I remember. He'd push me on the swings when nobody else would. He let me lay down next to him under the old blanket that still smelled like puke from when Freddy threw up on it, and we looked out the big glass hatchback up to the sky. But I didn't see stars.

"I looked, though. I looked hard. Mama left the car running, and she got out once and did something to the tailpipe, but I didn't know what she was doing. She was laughing and talking to herself, like something was really funny. Then she started crying, too. After a while, we started to get sleepy, and Mama said 'It's not enough.' Then she took out the knife."

Todd stopped. His hands drifted up to bury themselves in

his hair, like squeezing his head would press out the rotten memories. He let out a low moan, and though it came from a man's throat, it was a little boy's cry.

"There was so much blood," he said. "And the smell of it, like lightning, like biting on a penny, I couldn't breathe. She took Katie first, and Mary didn't even cry when Mama did her, too. Joey tried to get away but she grabbed him by the shirt and hauled him up front, and she did him, too. Right across the throat, like killing chickens.

"Freddy screamed, and when she was fighting with him, Stevie started kicking at the glass. Stevie was my oldest brother, but he was still just a kid, and that glass wouldn't break. Freddy fell on the backseat like he was broke, just like the doll Katie got one year for Christmas that fell down the stairs. Mama was reaching for us, and all the time she was singing. 'Go to sleep, little baby,' she sang, that song she used to sing when we was wakeful and wouldn't go down at night for her.

"She caught Stevie by the hair, but he was near as big as her, and he pulled away. She couldn't get into the backseat too easy, not with Freddy in the way, gurgling and kicking. Stevie grabbed the jack from alongside us and he whacked that glass window with everything he had. The glass fell in on us. It got in my hair, all sticky and gummy, and all over my clothes.

"Mama yanked Freddy out of the way and went for Stevie. She looked like she'd dipped herself in black paint, and all's I could see was her eyes and her teeth as she grinned. She grabbed Stevie by the back of his shirt, but he pushed me through the hatchback like I wasn't nothing more than air. 'Run, Todd!' he hollered. Then he couldn't say anything else. I fell over the bumper and landed on my head, and that was the only time I saw any stars that night. I was froze to the ground, couldn't run. I heard her scream, and then it was quiet. I stayed there all night, until the cops came."

"Oh…" No endearment seemed right, no matter how much he needed one. "Oh, Todd."

She put her hand on him, and it landed upon a piece of lined notebook paper. Todd looked at her, then down to the paper. He took it from her and opened it, smoothed it out, handed it back.

"She left a note," he said.

Gilly didn't want to see what sort of words a woman who killed her children might have thought important enough to leave behind, but she took the paper. She smoothed it as Todd had done. In the dim candlelight she'd have been happy not to be able to read it, but she could.

Nothing stays clean. Three words only, written in a rounded, careful hand in dark ink gone faded with time. *Nothing stays clean.*

Gilly imagined that would be true for a mother with six children each only a year or so apart. She thought of her own two children and the swath of destruction they left in their path. No, nothing ever did stay clean.

Gilly didn't forget what Todd had done. She didn't forget her vow to escape him in any way she could. She simply put those things aside. She dropped the folder without care, not bothering to notice if the pages in it scattered on the floor. She opened her arms to him in invitation, and without hesitation.

"Come here, Todd," Gilly said, and enfolded him in her arms to weep there until his sobs faded away, and at last, he slept.

33

The next morning, Gilly helped Todd clean up the mess he'd made. Together they swept up broken glass and the shattered remains of one of the dining table chairs. Gilly piled all the papers, the newspaper clippings and the note, inside the battered red file and handed it to him.

"Burn it," Todd told her.

She did without hesitation. Then she went to the kitchen sink to wash her hands, because touching those papers had left her feeling as though she'd laid her hands down in the fly-blown corpse of something only recently dead. Todd waited until she had washed, rinsed, then dried her hands.

"I never told anybody that stuff before." His gaze was earnest, not shifty. "Lots of people knew, but I never told nobody that story. Not the cops, not the Social Services zombies, not the people in the hospital or even my uncle Bill. You're the first person I ever told that story to."

Would she rather have lived her entire life without hearing

that? Definitely yes. But she had heard it, and hearing it, could never forget it. Gilly put the towel back on the hanger.

"Did telling it make you feel better?"

The shaggy head moved from side to side, then hesitantly, up and down. "I don't know for sure. I guess so."

"Sometimes, getting something like that off your chest can make a world of difference." Gilly meant what she said but it still sounded wrong. Sort of patronizing, which wasn't what she felt at all. It was daytime television psychobabble. There was no way talking about what had happened could ever make it better.

"You ever have something bad like that happen to you?" Todd's left hand went habitually to his pocket for the package of cigarettes.

Gilly thought of her mother's "vacations," which were better in many ways than the silent dinners or the bouts of screaming that became weeping. At least, when her mother was in the psychiatric hospital or in rehab, life moved in an orderly fashion. With her mother home, nothing was standard, nothing was reliable. Everything was chaos. Time and prescription drugs had cleared her mother's mind and helped her stop drinking. Before she died of cirrhosis at age fifty-six, Gilly's mother had actually become a woman she felt she could be proud to call "mom."

"No," Gilly said. "Nothing so bad as that."

"Uncle Bill used to say all families had their dirty little secrets." Smoke filtered from Todd's mouth while he spoke. "Ours was just dirtier than most."

"God gives us what we can handle." Again, Gilly wished she could say something more meaningful. Something real that would actually help him, not something regurgitated and lame. "It doesn't seem fair, but that's how it is."

"Pfft. I stopped believing in God when I was five years old. Not sure I can start now."

What kind of God would allow a mother to slaughter her children? Would allow a child to witness it? The same God who would allow a man to take a mother from her children, and a mother to let him take her.

"I guess that doesn't matter, as long as God believes in you." Even as she said them the words tasted false. Sanctimonious. She didn't blame him for rolling his eyes.

Todd's laugh was an ugly sound. "Bullshit. God doesn't believe in fuckall. Do *you* believe that, Gilly? Really?"

"I don't know, Todd." It was the truth. Gilly'd spent her share of years wondering about the existence of a higher power. She'd decided believing in God was easier than not, but the real truth was, she spent very little time praying. Religion had become a set of holidays and habits, not of faith.

"You don't even believe in Jesus."

That was true, too. Gilly shrugged. "Yeah, so? You think Jesus is the only way to believe in God?"

"It's the only way I know about."

"Well," Gilly said gently, because she wasn't trying to lecture or condemn him, "it's not."

Todd shook his head and scrubbed at his face with the back of his hand. He wouldn't look at her just now. Gilly found herself wanting to take his chin in her hand the way she did with Gandy when he'd made a mess and knew he was in trouble.

"She used to tell us Jesus suffered the little children. Whatever the fuck that meant. I don't think it meant what she thought it meant, anyway. But we…they…suffered. Didn't they?"

Gilly thought the one who'd suffered most had been Todd,

the one left behind. The pain the other children had felt had, at least, been blessedly brief. He'd had to live with the pain for his entire life, and there didn't seem any way Gilly could see for something like that to ever fade.

"They were scared." Todd said. "That was the last thing they had in them. Fear."

He did look at her then, brown eyes bright with tears that didn't seem to shame him. Gilly thought of how she'd cradled him the night before, but comfort that seemed all right to give in the dark wasn't the same now the sun had come up. Things had changed between them, but not as much as that.

She could be sincere, though. "I'm sorry, Todd."

His lip curled at her sympathy, and he backed away. "Forget it. It was a long time ago."

He hadn't forgotten it, and how could he, ever? Gilly hadn't forgotten it and she hadn't lived it. She'd never forget it now, either.

Todd turned his back. Walking away. He was giving up on her, and though Gilly didn't necessarily want the responsibility of trying to help him, she found herself speaking anyway.

"When I was about nine years old, my dad started traveling for business. Before that he'd worked normal hours, nine to five or so. He was always home for dinner. But his job changed…actually, he lost his job. He was fired." Gilly drew in a sharp breath. "That's the first time I've ever told anyone that."

Todd cocked his head and drew out a cigarette he held between his thumb and forefinger but didn't light. He didn't say anything. He offered her the comfort of a listening ear the way she'd done the night before, without trying to diminish any part of what she was saying.

"Anyway. He started traveling. Days at a time. Three, four.

Or he'd get up early in the morning and be gone until after I went to bed. I didn't know it at the time, but he probably didn't have to work so hard...it was easier for him, I think. Than being at home."

Todd put the cigarette in his mouth and lit it, nodding. His eyes squinted shut against the smoke. He took care to blow it away from her face.

"I was an only child. My mom had been pregnant a couple times before and after me, but hadn't carried to term. It was something with her uterus, it was tipped or something." Gilly had spent the bulk of both her pregnancies worried she'd miscarry the way her mother had, even though there were no indications it was likely.

"So it was just you and your mom?"

"Yes."

"What happened when your dad started traveling?"

Gilly needed something to do with her hands while she told this story and found it in the task of making tea. They'd both drunk a lot of tea over the past few weeks. She filled the kettle and settled it on the burner before turning back to him.

"Well, my mom didn't like it when he was gone. She relied on my dad for a lot. Everything, really. She didn't work. I mean, she had worked, but when I was born she decided to stay home. She hadn't had a baby for other people to raise, she always said." Gilly's voice hitched on that, remembering long hours with her mother reading stories or playing dolls.

From the cupboard she took a mug and added sugar. Holding the mug kept her focus on something other than the story. She felt the weight of Todd's gaze and didn't want to face him, but did.

"It's why I stayed home with my kids."

"Because of your mom?"

"Yes. Because I hadn't had them for other people to raise." Tears burned the back of her eyes and she blinked to keep them from overflowing. This wasn't the time for weeping. This was the time for telling.

Todd smiled faintly. "I had a foster mom once. She stayed home, too. She was nice. She's the one who taught me how to bake cookies."

It was good to hear someone had been kind to him. The kettle whistled and she poured hot water over the tea bag, then took the mug to the table to sit. He followed.

"When my dad was gone, my mom was always more… nervous."

Nervous.

It was what her mother had always called it.

"She drank a lot when she was nervous," Gilly continued in a voice as flat and emotionless as she could make it. It was the only way to get through this. "She was too nervous to cook or clean the house. Mostly she stayed in bed all day."

"I bet that sucked."

That was succinct. Gilly smiled a little. "Yeah. It did. I got myself up in the morning to go to school, and when I got home, she'd still be in bed, all the curtains closed. She kept the bottle in her nightstand. What a fucking cliché."

She surprised herself, but said it again. "A cliché. A fucking stereotype. It was like she'd put herself in some Tennessee Williams play. Pathetic!"

The mug warmed her hands, even though she had no desire to drink the tea. It sloshed, burning her fingers. Gilly didn't let go of the mug; if she did, she might make a fist. If she made a fist, she might use it to punch something. A wall, the door, herself.

She could tell Todd didn't know Tennessee Williams, but it didn't matter. He understood what she meant. He nodded. Gilly kept talking.

"One day, I was late coming home from school. I'd gone to a friend's house to play. I didn't tell my mom, or even call. I knew she wouldn't get out of bed to answer the phone, and we didn't have an answering machine. God. That was so long ago."

"I've never had one," Todd offered with a laugh. "Hell. I never even got a cell phone."

Both of them contemplated the turning of time and technology for a moment.

"I knew she'd worry about me," Gilly said softly. "I think I wanted her to."

"What happened?"

"I got home. She was in her room. I could smell something bad, really strong. I went in, and..." Gilly swallowed hard against the memory and had to close her eyes for a minute to clear her brain. To make it just a memory, not something she was reliving. It was hard.

Todd breathed out. Gilly breathed in. She opened her eyes.

"She'd smashed all her perfume bottles. And the bottle of booze. She'd broken the mirror on her vanity table, too. There was glass everywhere. I ran into the room in bare feet—Mom always insisted on taking off our shoes in the house, even when she wasn't keeping up with the cleaning. Anyway, I ran in, right onto the glass. It cut my feet pretty bad." Gilly gripped the mug. "She wasn't cut at all."

"Of course she wasn't." Todd sneered. "She'd have been careful, right?"

Gilly looked up at him, no longer surprised at his insight.

"Yes. She was careful not to hurt herself. She was crying, though. Blaming my dad for being gone, me for being late. Saying over and over again how nobody loved her. Not enough. I went to her on bleeding feet and tried to tell her I loved her, but it wasn't enough. Nothing was. Not when she was…nervous."

"Shit. No wonder you don't drink."

He had a way of summing it up her husband had never managed. It felt disloyal to think that, but it was true. Seth couldn't comprehend what it had been like for her, growing up. Seth's parents believed they meant well and were interminably pushy and self-centered, but nevertheless "normal." If any family could ever be considered nondysfunctional, which Gilly doubted.

"I needed four stitches in my foot. I called the ambulance myself. She wanted to drive me. I wouldn't let her. I knew she'd been drinking."

Todd leaned the chair, balancing, his hands laced behind his head. "You were a smart little kid."

"Yeah. Well. You see why I laugh when you say someone 'like' me."

His chair came down. "But you don't laugh."

Gilly could now sip from the mug, the story finished and tea cool. "Hmm?"

"You don't laugh," Todd pointed out. "Not ever. I've never heard you laugh."

Gilly met his eyes. "I have nothing to laugh about right now."

Todd's eyes narrowed, his mouth pursed, but he gave her a curt nod. "Oh. Right. Stupid me."

If only whatever this was between them could be balanced as easily as he balanced his chair, she thought as he pushed away from the table and left the kitchen. She didn't go after him. Gilly sat and drank her tea, even though it had gone cold, instead.

34

They'd given up on the radio. Even with batteries stolen from the CD player it picked up nothing more than static. Todd finally snapped it off and blew a ring of smoke into the air.

"Must be the snow," he commented with a wave to the window. Outside, more snow fell as dusk began coating the trees. "Messing up the signal."

Gilly nodded. She walked from one end of the room to the other, pacing. Going stir-crazy. Weeks of regular snow had kept them indoors, and her last foray outside had made her leery about going out even for a few minutes. A line from a television production of *Pride and Prejudice* suddenly came to her.

"Won't you join me in a turn about the room? It's so refreshing."

Todd looked at her as if she'd lost her marbles. A wild gust of laughter threatened to burst out of her mouth, but Gilly bit it off like a piece of licorice, chewed and swallowed her mirth though it stuck in her throat. She waved a hand at him.

"It's from a book."

"You and books," Todd said.

"You should read one sometime," Gilly told him loftily.

Todd snorted. "I've read books. Stroke books."

Gilly wrinkled her nose. "Todd. Gross."

He laughed, loud and long, and pointed at her. "Gotcha. No, seriously, I've read books."

She didn't read as much as she used to. Not enough time. She missed it, though. "Yeah? Like what?"

Todd shrugged. "I like horror. And science fiction."

"Me, too." Gilly perched on the edge of the chair. "Like what?"

Todd gave her another look. "You want me to tell you about what books I read?"

"Yes. Maybe I've read them, too. We could talk about them."

"The fuck you think this is, *The Oprah Show?*" Todd laughed again and shook his head. "Right."

"Never mind. Don't tell me." Gilly sighed and started pacing again.

To the window. To the door. To the kitchen, where she filled a glass with water and drank only half before dumping it down the drain.

Todd gave her another look but settled back onto the couch. Again, she envied him the ability to sit for long periods of time doing nothing. Now, however, she did not cruelly assume the skill came from his lack of intelligence. Now she imagined the trait had grown within him out of necessity.

"I liked this book called *Swan Song,*" Todd offered. "You ever read that one?"

"No." Gilly turned from the sink and looked at him from under the hanging cabinets dividing the living room from the kitchen, then came around to lean in the doorway. "What's it about?"

"Nuclear war. Bunch of bombs go off and then the people have to survive nuclear winter. It scared the shit out of me as a kid," Todd said with a grin. "I read it about four times. Took me for-fucking-ever, though. It's really long."

"I wish I had a book now," Gilly said.

Todd looked around, frowning. "Yeah. Sorry. Uncle Bill wasn't much of a reader, and I didn't think about it when… well. You know."

She did know and didn't really want to go over all that ground again. She left the doorway to look out the front windows. Snow and more snow. She sighed.

Her stomach growled, but the thought of actually eating made her want to gag. A twinge of headache ran behind her eyes, telling her to sit down and close them or suffer the consequences. Gilly made a place for herself on one of the couches, plumped the sagging cushions, rescued a crocheted afghan from one of the drawers in the armoire. She laid her head back, letting her body sink into the barely comfortable couch.

"What's your favorite book?" Todd asked.

"I have so many, I'm not sure I could pick one."

"If you had to," Todd said.

She turned her head to look at him on the couch's other end. "Oh. Maybe the collected works of Ray Bradbury. Something like that. I could read all those stories over and over again."

"Ray Bradbury!" Todd's eyes lit. "Electric Grandmother."

"You know it?"

"Yeah, sure. I used to wish for one." Todd was silent for a moment, and when he spoke again his tone wasn't sad or wistful, just resigned. "Of course I never had one, I mean, even if they were real I'd never have been able to get one. But I always thought it would be great to have."

"Yeah," Gilly said.

They fell into companionable silence.

Did she sleep, or only dream? In the silence, and with only the flickering red-gold light from the woodstove to illuminate the room, Gilly didn't know for sure. This was different from earlier, when she'd sought the realm of sleep to escape reality. Now she embraced the reality of being here, the snow outside, the man slouched at the other end of the couch. Cigarette smoke tickled her nose, and the glowing ember of the tip of Todd's Marlboro winked at her.

Only a few weeks ago she'd never have sat this way with him. Things were different now. After what he'd told her, how could they not? Gilly rescued stray kittens, donated her time and money to the local soup kitchen, was always the first to weep at the tragedies she saw on the evening news. She couldn't have hardened her heart against Todd any more than she could've refused to go to her children when they wept for her in the night.

She knew the date only because she could see it on the dial of her watch. February, the coldest and dankest month. The one with Valentine's Day right in the middle, a made-up holiday people needed just to get through—and someone had made it shorter, too, knowing that February just couldn't be borne for thirty days. It was only February.

But March would come soon, and with it, warmer days. Days when the snow would melt and she could…she could…

Gilly opened her eyes to the yellow glow of the propane lantern and the sight of Todd banking the fire for the night. She would not think of March now, not when she could do nothing to hasten its arrival.

"Ready for bed?" Todd asked her.

She rose lazily from her self-made nest and nodded, surprised to find herself tired after the hours of inactivity. "Yes."

He climbed the stairs in front of her, leading the way with the light so she would not trip. He gave her the lantern to put on her dresser, then turned away without being asked to give her privacy while she dressed for bed.

"Good night," she called across the partition as she turned out the light. It was the first time she'd ever said the words to him.

Later, his moans woke her from dreamless sleep. Gilly blinked in the darkness, confused for a moment before remembering where she was. She heard the shuffling of sheets, the whisper of bare feet on the wooden floor.

She didn't need the light to know he was there. Todd hesitated in the opening of the partition. Gilly had been woken countless times by just such an apparition, albeit one usually much smaller, but with the same intent.

She flipped back the covers and slid over, whispering: "It's all right. You can come in."

Anxiety filled her for one moment, for despite all he'd shared with her, Todd was not a child. He slid in beside her, his own heat radiating like an oven even though he'd been standing in the frigid air.

"I have bad dreams, sometimes," he whispered.

"It's okay." Gilly pushed him onto his side so she could curl against his back. She pressed her cheek to the softness of his T-shirt, took the warmth he provided and prepared to offer comfort of her own. “So do I.”

35

Todd laid the yellow three on top of the blue three, and crowed, "Uno!"

Gilly sighed dramatically. "I don't have any threes…or any yellows…"

He hooted and rapped the table with his hands, managing to do a victory dance while still seated. Gilly pretended to reach for the draw pile, but then drew back.

"Oh, wait," she said. "I do have this wild card…the one that says Draw Four."

She put the multicolored card on the pile and smirked. "Uno. The color is red."

Todd narrowed his eyes at her. "You suck."

Gilly rolled her eyes. "And you're a poor loser."

"No, I ain't." Todd grinned, and Gilly had to look away so as not to let herself be taken breathless with how the smile swept his face into beauty. "I can still win."

He proved it by picking up four cards and slapping down a

red skip card, followed by a yellow skip card. Gilly, who could no longer use her remaining red card, had to draw from the pile.

"Me and Uncle Bill had some pretty good Uno tournaments," Todd said as he gathered up the scattered cards to reshuffle. "Don't feel bad."

"I don't."

He shot her a glance. "What would you be doing if you was home, now?"

The question startled her. "What?"

Todd dealt another hand of cards. "What would you be doing?"

Gilly crossed her hands on the table and stared down at them. "I wouldn't be playing Uno."

He waited for her to speak. She heard the soft rise and fall of his breathing and became intensely aware of his gaze upon her. Hot, like a flame held too close to her skin.

"It's ten-thirty on a Sunday morning," Gilly said. "I would probably be at the synagogue, watching the door during Hebrew School."

His puzzled look showed her he didn't understand.

"The synagogue is always locked," Gilly explained. "During Hebrew School hours, a parent volunteers to sit in the office to push the button to open the door for anyone who needs to get in."

"Why's it locked? I thought churches were always open."

"Unfortunately, some people don't have the same open minds as others about religion," Gilly said lightly, and raised her head to see Todd looking confused. "There were some threats to the synagogue. The congregation decided it was better to lock the doors for safety."

"That's fucked-up."

"Yeah, well, it's a fucked-up world."

Todd rearranged his cards. "And after that? What would you do then?"

She thought, her throat tightening but glad to talk of it. "I'd take Arwen, and we'd go to the grocery store for some things. Come home. Fix lunch. Clean the house. Do laundry. Maybe we'd go to the movies, if there was something good for the kids. Maybe we'd go out to dinner, or order a pizza. Sunday's family day."

Todd put down his cards, got up from the table and went to the window. From the tense line of his shoulders, Gilly could tell something had upset him. She carefully gathered the cards and put them back into their box.

"It sounds real nice," Todd said finally.

"It is."

He turned to her. "Your kids are lucky. You're a good mom."

A good mother wouldn't be here. Gilly rested her head in her hands for a moment, plagued by a sudden onset of weariness that made her want to cry. The moment passed, leaving behind only a vague nausea that unsettled her stomach.

She hadn't disagreed aloud, but now Todd argued with her silence. "You are. You give your kids stuff...love and stuff."

She didn't say, *Of course.* For Todd, there could be no *Of course* about it. What was natural and expected from a mother hadn't existed for him.

She motioned for him to sit back at the table. She took his hand, held his arm out flat against the wood. She pushed his sleeve up, gently, and touched the inked pattern. She knew what it meant now.

"One of six," she murmured.

This time, Todd didn't jump away from her. Below her

fingertips, his pulse jumped. Gilly touched the tattoo again before withdrawing.

"I used to be one of six," Todd said, voice hoarse, eyes bright. "But then I was the only one."

"What happened to you, after?" Gilly asked quietly.

He hunched his broad shoulders. "They took me to the hospital. But there was nothing wrong with me. The blood… it wasn't mine. They made me sleep there."

"Alone?"

"There was a big room, with a bunch of kids…." He stopped. "But they were all there because they were sick. Some of them were crying because it hurt them. I didn't cry."

Gilly bit the inside of her cheek, the spot tender with old scars from many bites. "What about your Grandma? Uncle Bill?"

Todd shuddered, then seemed to catch himself. "They called my Grandma to tell her what happened. Grandma…had a bad heart, Gilly."

The story grew worse. Gilly put her hand over his. "Oh, Todd."

His sigh was like the bitter wind outside. "I didn't know she died until they came to take me away. They took me to a foster home. It smelled like cat piss and baby puke. They didn't let me take my nonnie…" He looked embarrassed. "My blanket. You know, like babies have? But I was five. They didn't let me have it."

Her heart broke a little more at the picture of Todd as a child. "And then what?"

She didn't prompt him out of her own need to listen to the story. They were past that, anyway. Todd needed to tell her these things. She would never have thought she'd want to understand him. But that was before.

"They sent me to another place, after a while. They brought me some of my stuff, but they didn't know they gave me some of Freddy's stuff, too. His shirts. One shirt he had, it had the Dallas Cowboys on it. I always wanted it, but he'd never let me wear it. They brought me that shirt, and I put it on, and it still smelled like Freddy. I wouldn't let the foster mom wash it. She got real mad at me. Finally, when I was at school, she took it and threw it away. Because it stank so bad, she said. She didn't know it was all I had of my brother."

Her throat closed. She remembered cleaning Arwen's room of its collection of broken toys, discarded playthings, clothes that had become too small. Junk her daughter had loved and wept to discover gone.

"How many homes?" Gilly asked.

Todd ran a hand through his hair and looked at her sideways. "A lot. I started being bad. I don't know why, except being bad made me feel better. I didn't *want* to be bad. I just was."

Just as he didn't want to keep her. He just was. Gilly didn't point that out, though she was pretty sure he was thinking it, too.

"The Social zombies started making me go to a shrink. I had four different homes in two years before they put me in the group home. I lived there until I was twelve."

Gilly waited for the rest of the story. She sat patiently, without moving. Watching him. The weak February sun cast lines on his cheeks, highlighting the dark scruff with hints of gold.

"I almost burned it down." Todd waited for her response, which Gilly purposefully masked. "They sent me to the hospital for that."

"For attempted arson?"

He shook his head. "For attempted suicide. I poured gasoline on myself and tried to light a match." He laughed. "Damn wind kept blowing the fucking thing out. They said it was a suicide attempt. I don't know. It probably was."

"How many times did you try?" Gilly asked, horrified yet fascinated.

"On purpose?" He thought a moment. "Three on purpose. Fire. Pills, twice. How many times just by doing stupid shit, hoping it would be the last time I had the chance? A lot more."

Todd stood and lifted his shirt over his head. It was the first time she'd seen him completely bare, and her heart thudded in her throat at the intimacy of the sight. His chest was smooth, dark nipples surrounded by a smattering of sleek black hairs. Muscles corded in his biceps and shoulders as he moved, though his stomach was soft. The white scar rippled across his belly; Gilly flinched at the sight though she'd seen it before. A smaller, deeper scar dimpled the flesh next to his navel.

Todd pointed to both of them. "I crashed my car doing eighty around a curve when I was seventeen. This is where they took out my spleen. This is where they stuck a tube in me to drain out all the bad shit."

Gilly made a sad noise.

"But I always fucked it up," Todd said with forced lightness. "Couldn't even kill myself right. Stupid fucking loser. Always fucked it up, let someone find me...."

"Maybe...maybe you didn't really want to die," Gilly said. "Maybe..."

"Don't give me that cry for help shit, Gilly." Todd shook his head and pulled his shirt back on. "I wanted to die. I'm just too fucking stupid to pull it off."

"What changed your mind? What made you decide living would be better?"

He looked at her with his sideways glance. "What makes you think I did?"

"You're here," she pointed out. "Not in the ground."

Todd lifted the edge of his shirt. His hand went to his waist, and he unsnapped the leather holster. He pulled out the knife. The blade glinted in the sunlight as he turned it from side to side so she could see every inch of the long blade.

"Once you asked me what I came up here planning to do." Todd let the blade rest lightly on the skin of his forearm. When he took it away, a thin line of blood remained.

"You told me 'nothing.'"

"I lied," Todd told her. "Did you ever feel so bad you wanted to die?"

She had not. Even during the worst times in her youth, she'd clung to the idea of life with desperation. If she lived, she knew she would grow up and eventually get away from the horror of living with her mother. If she died then, she'd die with grief in her heart.

But it wasn't hard for her to understand the pain that must've driven Todd to thoughts of suicide. Gilly, who could perhaps imagine better than some people how a mother's betrayal affected a child, could only begin to imagine how deeply Todd's mother's death had messed him up. She'd never wanted to die, but she knew too well the craving for oblivion.

"I ain't never been good at anything," Todd said. "Not in school. Not even shop. I can't make things. I ain't good with my hands. Can't hold a job for shit. Can't even rob a damn liquor store without getting caught."

His litany urged her to murmur "It can't be that bad," even as she knew it must be.

"Girls don't like me," Todd continued. "No chick wants to hang out with a dumbass like me with no job, no money, a jail record. Least, not any girl I'd like to hang with. Not nice girls…not like you."

Gilly put the cards back in the box, guessing their game was over. She didn't remind him of the girl he'd said wanted to marry him. In her palm, the box of cards felt slick and cool. Heavier than it looked.

"You know that's not true, Todd."

"You're not nice?"

She looked up at him, their eyes meeting with neither flinching away. Gilly shook her head a little. The inside of her cheek felt torn and raw; she chewed it anyway in lieu of an answer.

Todd studied her. He reached in his pocket, stroking the crinkly wrapping of his pack of cigarettes, but didn't pull one out. "You're good, Gilly. I'm not."

"Oh, Todd."

How many times had she said this, now? How many more would his name come from her lips that way? Gilly's chair rocked, but she didn't get up. She clenched the cards tight, tighter. "You have this idea about me, but you don't really know me at all."

He reached across the table and flicked the ends of her hair, unsecured in its usual ponytail. Then her sleeve, her shirt the one she'd been wearing the day he got into the passenger seat beside her. "Look at you."

"It has nothing to do with what I look like."

"I know that." Todd's quiet dignity was a splinter in her skin, stinging. "Anyway. I figured, if I kept going on the way I was, I was going to get sent back to jail. Guys like me just don't turn their lives around, Gilly. I'm not smart enough to do it, and I can't work hard enough, either." He paused, looking out the window. "A guy like me…I figure I was gypped out of a lot of good stuff, and it really pisses me off."

His expression darkened, and his hands clenched on the table. "Seems like I been in some sort of jail all my life, Gilly. And I swore I'd never go back. They…they do stuff to you in jail."

He didn't elaborate with words, only with a shudder and a grimace of disgust. "Worse even than some of the homes I was in. They hurt you in jail. I figured…fuck. I figured there'd been a lot of shit in my life I didn't get to choose. I thought it was time I got to decide what happened to me."

"That's why you didn't care about the truck. About being found. You didn't intend to be caught."

She thought he might get angry. Todd touched the knife on the table between them. His fingers tightened on the handle, and he tilted the blade again to catch a ray of weak February sunshine. It was the kind of knife a hunter used to gut a deer. It was the knife he'd pointed at her throat on that evening what seemed a lifetime ago. Now he moved it back and forth and made something pretty with it, sunshine in stripes on the table.

"You know how easy this knife cuts?" he said quietly. "It's real sharp. I made sure of that. It won't snag on anything. It'll just cut. Human skin's not even an inch deep, you know that? But most people who cut themselves to die, they do their wrists. The blood clots."

He drew the flat of the knife crossways over his wrist, then up from the heel of his hand to his elbow. "You're supposed to go down the lane, not across the street. You ever hear that?"

"No."

"It works better that way. But you know what works even better than that?" He looked at her.

She looked back. "Todd, don't."

He put the flat of the blade to his throat, then turned it so the edge pressed lightly. His skin dented. "Cutting the carotid artery would fuck you up pretty good. It's how I'd do it. I thought it all out. One quick slice, and it would be all over. No coming back from that, really. You'd have to be one lucky prick to get through that."

He looked at the knife. "I've never been lucky."

Gilly had nothing more to say than that. Any words she'd find would be empty. Useless.

Todd put the knife back in its sheath on his belt and pulled his shirt down over it. He put his head in his hands for a moment. When he looked back at her, his face was bleak. "I figured I deserved it, you know? Just once. To decide what happened to me."

She couldn't disagree with that, but she tried. "It doesn't have to be…"

"No. Look at you, sitting there. Tell me I'll get out of this, Gilly. Tell me you'd be able to convince anyone I didn't take you on purpose. Hell, see if that even matters if it was by accident. I still did it. I still took the truck, I still took you. Tell me anything you could say would make a difference." He tilted his head, studying her. "Tell me you'd say anything, anyway. Tell the police you ran away with me, right? You'd never."

"I have no idea what I'll say," she told him honestly. "But I could tell them it was a mistake. It *was* a mistake, Todd."

"There isn't any room in my life for more mistakes."

She believed him when he said he couldn't survive another stay in jail. "Why didn't you do it?"

"You," Todd said simply. "I didn't do it because of you."

"I couldn't have stopped you." And wouldn't have, not when he'd first taken her. Now? Now Gilly wasn't sure what she would do should he take the knife from the table and slash at himself with it.

She'd bind his wounds, she thought suddenly. She would do what she could to save him, if she could. She wouldn't let him die in front of her any more than he'd allowed *her* to perish in what had been as much a suicide attempt as he'd planned.

Todd shook his head. "At first, you had me so rattled I didn't know what to do. Then, you were so sick…I couldn't just let you die up here. Couldn't have that one more mess on my head, you know?"

She nodded. "Yes."

Todd tugged on his shirt hem, covering up the scars no mother's love had ever soothed. He went to the window and looked out at the blinding whiteness of the snow. "I'm not so sure I want to die anymore, Gilly."

Gilly didn't ask him what had changed his mind. She didn't want to hear his answer, didn't want to accept responsibility for his decision not to take his life. But she thought maybe she already had.

"Tea?" she asked instead, because that was safe.

Todd didn't turn from the window. "Yeah. Sure."

Gilly boiled the water, and they sat at the table and drank cup after cup until it was gone. Their silence was not hostile. It was the quiet of two people who didn't need to speak to know what the other was thinking.

36

Todd refused to listen to any more of what he termed "that freaky music." So they stuck to The Doors, some Simon and Garfunkel, and an old Guns N' Roses CD Gilly'd forgotten she had.

Gilly found a thousand-piece jigsaw puzzle in one of the armoire drawers, and she set it up on the dining room table. She didn't like jigsaw puzzles any better than crosswords, as a rule, having neither the patience nor the time to devote to their creation. But here she had nothing but time, even if her patience hadn't grown. The puzzle was a hard one, an intricate mess of swirling colors without rhyme or reason. Gilly hated it, loathed it, despised, abominated and abhorred it…but every piece set into its proper place gave her an immense satisfaction that had quickly become addictive.

She glanced up from the puzzle to see Todd in a corner of the room, whaling away on an air guitar to "Welcome to the

Jungle." His dark hair fell across his face as he strummed the imaginary instrument.

"Wyld Stallynz," she murmured to herself, but he heard her.

With no embarrassment, he turned to her. "What?"

"You remind me of that movie with Bill and Ted," Gilly said.

He could always surprise her. With a cock of his head and a smile, a mere hand gesture, Todd transformed himself into the character from the movie.

"Bogus! Party on, dude!"

"You've seen the movie, I take it," Gilly said dryly.

Todd struck a pose with his invisible guitar. "Yeah. Never thought I looked like Ted, though. That dude is good-looking."

"You're—" Gilly clipped the words and looked down to her puzzle, her cheeks heating.

She didn't want him to get the wrong idea, not when their co-existence was so precarious. She picked up a piece, set it against one, fitted it beside another. When she finally looked at him, his face was stormy.

"Don't make fun of me," he said. "I know I'm an ugly cuss."

With another man she might've thought he was fishing for a compliment or trying to make her uncomfortable. Gilly bit her lip and sighed, cursing her own inconstant tongue. She set the puzzle pieces down.

"Did someone tell you that?"

He shrugged in a way that showed her the answer was yes. Gilly tapped her fingers on the table. The people in Todd's life hadn't been very kind.

"You're not ugly." Gilly touched the puzzle lightly. "I don't know who told you that, but they were wrong."

"Monkey boy," he muttered, and the way he said it showed it had not been a term of endearment. "Big hands, big feet. Always tripping over myself. Always making a mess of things. I wasn't little and blond and cute like Ricky Buckwalter, who stole money from the housemother's purse and bought weed."

"Todd, you aren't ugly." Gilly put firmness into her voice, the voice of authority.

He gave her his sideways glance and the ghost of a smirk. "Right, I'm a regular fucking Keanu Reeves."

Todd didn't have that actor's smoothness, his ethereal beauty. The resemblance was slight, a similarity in the eyes and the hair, in the curve of his jaw. His grin had the same goofy light as Ted Logan in *Bill and Ted's Excellent Adventure,* but Todd was not that man. He was Todd himself. Unique.

Gilly shook her head. "Bogus."

"Shit." Todd frowned. "If I looked that good I'd have been swimming in pu—girls. Ah, well. Girls…shit. All's they want is to get married, have babies…and I know I won't ever do that."

"Why not?" Gilly ran her fingers over the puzzle pieces, hoping for some intuition that would lead her to the one that would fit next. It was hard work, this puzzle. Took a lot of thought. It was why she liked it even though she hated it at the same time.

"Like I'd make somebody a good father," Todd said scornfully. "Right."

Gilly, puzzle piece in hand, looked at him thoughtfully. "Maybe you would be a good father, because you would have learned all the things not to do. You'd do the opposite."

"Bad seed."

"What?"

Todd pointed at himself. "I got bad seed. You think I ought to go out and spread that around? Think of what I come from, Gilly. You think any kid deserves a dad like me?"

"There are plenty of people who come from worse who don't give a damn how many kids they spawn. Lots of people don't deserve to be parents, but they go ahead and have kids anyway."

"I guess I did at least one good thing with my life, then," Todd said with a grin. "I always used a rubber and I never knocked anybody up."

"Well, amen to that," Gilly said, and fit another piece into the puzzle. She let out a hoot of pleasure. "Yeah!"

"You've got a pretty smile," Todd told her in a wistful tone that froze Gilly's hand over the scattered pieces on the table.

"Go put in another CD," she told him without looking up. "I'm tired of Guns N' Roses."

He did as she asked, and didn't mention her smile again.

37

"I'm bored!" Todd groaned and flopped onto the couch. He flung his arm over his head. "Damn, Gilly! I'm so fucking bored I could get a hard-on watching paint dry."

She grimaced. "Ew."

Todd sighed and squirmed to look at her. "Why do you always say 'ew' like that?"

"Because you're crude when you talk about sex."

He gave a snort of laughter. "Sorry. You want me to talk about surveys?"

She ignored his wiggling eyebrows, though the thought of surveys being her porn seemed funnier now, in retrospect. "Find something to do."

"Like what?"

"It's not my job to entertain you," Gilly said calmly.

She'd said that often, at home, up to her ears in laundry and dinner and the scrubbing of toilets. What excuse did she have here? She left the horrendous puzzle and peered out the front window.

The sun was bright. It looked warm, though she knew the temperature outside remained bitter. Still, with layers of clothes…

"Can't we go outside?" she said.

Todd sat up. "It's colder than a vanilla ice cream cone up a polar bear's ass out there!"

Gilly rolled her eyes. "So? We've been cooped up in here for too long." She wrinkled her nose. "It stinks in here. We should go outside, get some fresh air."

"Are you nuts?" He got up from the couch and crossed to the window. "What do you want to do out there?"

"I don't know," Gilly said. "We could build a snowman."

Todd barked out a laugh. "Yeah, right."

"Okay, a snow woman," Gilly said. "We can give her great big boobs if you want. Like Pam Anderson."

Todd's laugh was more genuine this time. "I never built a snow woman. Or a snowman."

"What?" Gilly looked at him in surprise. "Never?"

Todd shifted uncomfortably. "There was never anyone… I never…"

She put her hand on his arm. "It's okay. I get it."

She suddenly felt very bad for him. Worse even than before. As if sensing her pity, Todd scowled.

Suddenly desperate to go outside, Gilly quickly changed the subject. "I guess it's about time, right? C'mon. Let's do it."

She could see his growing excitement with the idea. He was as transparent as Arwen and Gandy. His grin faded for a minute, as he looked down at her feet.

"You don't have boots."

She'd forgotten. It had been weeks since she'd entertained

the idea of running away. Gilly faced him squarely. "Did you throw my boots away?"

Todd hesitated. He looked from her feet to the window, then raised his gaze to hers. "No. I just took them away so you couldn't—"

She cut him off, wanting for the moment to forget his reasons. "But you have them."

He nodded, slowly. "But, Gilly..."

She reached out and took his hand. "Todd. I won't run away. Not now. How far would I get, even with boots? The snow is three feet deep out there, deeper in the drifts. I don't even know where I am."

She wasn't convincing him. His warm fingers twitched against her palm. He bit at his lower lip, worrying it. When he looked her again, she could tell he was going to say no.

"I got to know..."

"What, Todd?"

He sighed. "I want to know you won't run away..."

"I won't. I told you that."

He made a face of frustration. "No. Not because of the snow, or any of that. Just...because."

Gilly dropped his hand and took a step back. "You want me to say I won't run away because I don't want to?"

Slinking dog faced growling dog.

"Yeah."

"No." Gilly's voice was ice. "I can't say that. You know I can't."

He reached for her hand, but she pulled it away. "How come?"

"I would be lying."

His face turned hard. "Then stay inside."

All at once the need to go outside burned inside her brighter than any desire she'd had for months. Any desire she could ever remember, as a matter of fact. Gilly drew herself up, not nearly as tall as Todd but making herself bigger. "You'd spite yourself to hurt me?"

"If that's what you want to call it," Todd told her.

"We're both bored," Gilly said in a low voice. "We both want this. We both *need* this."

"Yeah? Maybe I need a lot of things. Going outside to play in the snow ain't one of them."

She turned from him to hide the tears of angry frustration. "Fine. Be a stupid asshole."

"Don't call me that!" His hand gripped her shoulder, turning her.

She yanked herself from his grasp. "Don't you raise your hand to me!"

His eyes were flat, black, obsidian. The eyes of a snake. She had time to marvel again at how quickly he could change, but then he'd grabbed her. Pulled her close.

"Tell me," he ordered.

"No!"

"Why not?"

She wasn't proud of her temper. She could blame tight quarters and circumstance for it, but in the end would know it was simple bitterness with no excuse. It was just her. The way she was built. It didn't matter what triggered it, Gilly had the choice to hold her tongue and didn't.

She sneered and dug where it would hurt the most. "You really *are* stupid if you can't even figure that out."

"You're still thinking about it? Getting away? Fucking up my life?"

"You fucked up your life, not me!" Gilly twisted fruitlessly in his grip. "Don't you blame me! Blame yourself!"

"You'd have them send me back to jail in one second, wouldn't you?" His breath was hot on her face. "One fucking second."

"I thought," Gilly said harshly, "you were going to kill yourself before that could happen. And why not? Maybe that would be the best thing for you!"

He pushed her away from him so hard she stumbled backward. "The fuck are you trying to do? You want to make me so mad I—"

"Don't you threaten me!" Gilly cried. She'd twisted her ankle and it throbbed, but she refused to even wince. "Don't you dare!"

"Quit riding me! Get off my back!" Todd advanced on her.

He was like a great wolf, snarling. Gilly stood her ground. Toe to toe, he towered over her, but Gilly didn't move.

If anything, she forced herself to stand taller. Look him in the eyes. "You want me to lie to you? I give you honesty, and you want lies?"

"Why not?" Todd said. "It's all I've had my whole damn life."

He pushed past her and disappeared into the pantry. A moment later he returned, her boots in his hand. He threw them at her feet.

"Go outside," he said. "Make a fucking snowman."

She did not go out into the snow, and they didn't speak to each other the rest of the day. The boots lay where Todd had thrown them on the floor. Gilly didn't touch them.

Stubborn, he'd called her. He was right. He hadn't returned her boots to her out of kindness but disdain.

Besides, even with her boots, her fashionable but useless

boots, she couldn't expect to make it out of here. Not for a while. Not if she was smart.

Oh, the thought crossed her mind. Of layering her clothes, packing food and drink. Of somehow rendering Todd incapable of stopping her and hiking out of here…

Of dying in the woods, in the snow. Of never making it home. She was stubborn, but she was also afraid. Once she started, there'd be no going back…and what if she failed?

38

The first contraction ripples over her belly like fingertips, tickling. Not painful, not yet. That will come later. Later, Gilly will sweat and scream and moan and lie glassy-eyed with agony in a big bed with smooth sheets. But just now she puts her hands to the watermelon her stomach has become and she smiles.

It's going to happen, finally. Nine months of waiting, six months of trying before that. The baby's coming.

A little boy? A little girl? She and Seth have both agreed it won't matter, though in her deep and secret heart Gilly has prayed for a daughter. It's important to her, to have a daughter. To be a mother to a daughter. A son would be fine; she will love a son. But she really wants a daughter.

She quit her job last month in preparation for the baby coming, already planning to stay home and raise her child because, after all, she wasn't bearing this baby for someone else to raise. She's spent the past month getting the nursery ready, even if Jewish tradition says you're not supposed to do anything until the baby's born. Bad luck or some such thing, but Gilly doesn't believe in luck.

Little socks, little shoes, tiny little caps and blankets in yellows and soft greens. Things suitable for either boy or girl. Seth doesn't know that Gilly found a perfect little dress outfit complete with matching cap and ruffled diaper cover on a trip to the baby outlet, or that she bought it and tucked it away here beneath the stacks of burp cloths and onesies.

It was only a few dollars, less than ten. On sale. But perfect, just the thing she'd buy to dress her daughter in. If she has one. And as another contraction tightens across her stomach and echoes deep inside her, Gilly puts her hands on the dresser she'll use as a changing table, and she prays once more to whoever will listen that the baby on its way is a girl.

Seth is at work. She won't call him just yet. The pain isn't bad and she's had Braxton Hicks several times already. Gilly folds tiny clothes instead. She tests out the rocker and imagines how it will be when she sits there at three in the morning with her baby in her arms.

She plans to nurse and now she cups her breasts, thinking how heavy they are. What will it be like to feed a child from them? It's sort of a disgusting idea, actually, but it seems the right one. Just as she's not having this baby for someone else to raise, knowing that her body naturally will make something to sustain her child seems the right choice to make.

Oh, she knows it won't be easy. She'll have to be the one getting up at all hours since Seth won't be able to feed the baby. But it'll be all right. It's going to be marvelous.

By evening she's sick to her stomach and has been on the toilet all day long. Everything in her guts wants to come out. The midwife assures her this is normal, her body's way of getting ready to give birth, but to Gilly it feels like a bad case of food poisoning.

When Seth gets home unexpectedly late, she's already packed and ready to go. She snaps at him when he takes too long changing his clothes and making a sandwich. When he fumbles with the suitcase they're taking to the birth center. When he pulls out of the driveway without putting on his seat belt.

This is a time when they're supposed to feel closer to each other than ever, but everything he does is a splinter of glass in all her tender places. The way he laughs with the midwives, joking about the drive. How he lingers in the hall instead of bringing her suitcase to her so she can get into the soft nightgown she's going to wear. Gilly presses her lips together and makes fists of her hands, wanting to tell him to move his fucking ass, but instead she breathes in deep. Out slowly. In and out, concentrating on the pain, willing herself to get through it.

Nothing she has read or watched or listened to prepared her for this. Natural birth? What a fucking joke. What is natural about being torn apart from the inside out? What is natural about stinking fluid gushing out of her as she squats once more on the toilet, groaning and pale faced, her hands gripping the metal railings.

Birth is slippery and smelly, coated in blood. Labor takes forever. The contractions consume her—this pain doesn't sting like a wound, not an ache like a break or strain. This pain is white-hot, lava, it rips through her with dreadful regularity every minute and gives her no time even to breathe in between.

"Do you want something for the pain?" the nurse asks.

Stubborn, Gilly shakes her head. "No."

"You can go ahead and push," says the midwife sometime later, Gilly's not sure how long, from between Gilly's legs. The midwife's just used her fingers to decide if it's time. The intrusion was worse than the pain.

Push? Gilly pushes. Nothing happens.

"From your bottom," the midwife says unhelpfully. "Push from your bottom."

Gilly has no fucking idea what that even means. Exhausted, she strains. Nothing. The baby isn't coming. Not moving. The contractions keep coming and she bites down on the inside of her cheek to keep from screaming…but no baby.

There is the hush of whispered conversation that's not quiet enough for her not to overhear. Hey, morons, Gilly wants to say. I can hear you. They talk of a C-section, of calling in the on-call obstetrician for a consult.

She is going to have this baby no matter what. Not by cutting it out of her. She is going to push this child out of her body and make this pain stop. Gilly's never been more determined to do anything in her life.

But no matter how hard she tries to push from her bottom, whatever the fuck that means, what does that even mean? No matter how hard she pushes, or strains, how hard she grips the bed railings, no matter how many times Seth squeezes her hand and offers terrifically unhelpful encouragement, this baby will not come.

"I can't do it," Gilly says.

She's failed.

"You can do it," Seth tells her, patting her face.

She almost bites his hand. She wants to. Bite his fucking fingers off and spit them in his face for touching her now.

"I can't do it," she says again. She thinks she's shouting but really, it's only a whisper.

"Breathe," Seth offers.

She wants to kick him in the face for that.

The nurse beside her says to him, "The next time she pushes, you hold her knee back."

Seth looks confused. It's not fucking brain surgery, Gilly wants to tell him. She gets it. Hold her knees back so she can open up her birth canal and push this baby the fuck out of her vagina. But Seth doesn't get it, even when the nurse shows him.

The next contraction comes. The nurse puts both hands flat on Gilly's belly and pushes down. The midwife makes a tutting noise but doesn't stop her.

"Push now," the nurse says. "The baby will come."

And…it does. Gilly can feel the baby moving down and out of her. Something rips inside her. She wants to scream and bites it back, still stubborn. Her hand clutches Seth's so hard it goes numb and he winces. She doesn't care.

She pushes. The nurse presses down. The baby is coming, finally, and the midwife eases the child into the world as she's done with hundreds already.

But this baby is not like those. This is Gilly's baby. The midwife coos and there's a scuffle of activity as they clean the baby. Seth goes around to the foot of the bed and makes strange, excited noises. He might be saying something, but all Gilly can hear is the sound of an ocean roar.

"She's passing out," someone says.

There comes the insensitive and insulting sting of a needle. A rush of clarity. The pain eases, and she thinks she was crazy for not taking this sooner. Why would it have been a failure to take even this small comfort?

Then they put the baby, wrapped in a blanket, on her chest. Nobody's told her if it's the daughter she wanted or a son she'll love just as much. She stares with tear-blurred eyes at a tiny, ugly face, blotchy red and still coated in places with white, waxy goo.

"Who is it?" she asks. Not what. But who.

Her husband puts his hand on the baby's head, the other on Gilly's shoulder. "It's a girl. It's Arwen."

And Gilly trembles in the aftermath of birth, barely twitching as the midwife between her legs stitches her intimate places. Gilly stares in wonder at this small creature she created and carried and has now ejected from her body. She touches tiny eyebrows with the tip of her finger and waits to feel…something. Anything. She waits for the rush of emotion that has so often hit her over the past few months and feels only the weight of responsibility and reality. Fear.

Love doesn't come until later.

39

Todd greeted her over breakfast with a sunny smile that might have fooled someone…but not her. Gilly watched his guarded eyes.

Breakfast didn't sit well with her. She got up from the table to pace off the nausea, but when the cold sweat broke out on her forehead and spine, she knew it was no use. She vomited quietly in the bathroom, heaving until she had nothing left to bring up and then heaving some more. The world spun, and she clung to the worn linoleum floor as if that would keep her from flying off.

Gray faced and shaking, she splashed cold water on her face. After a few moments, she began to feel better. She rinsed her mouth and brushed her teeth with the purple sparkly toothbrush.

"You okay?" he asked when she came out.

Her voice was an old woman's, hoarse and raw and quavery. "Yeah."

She went to the table and sat down, staring at the half-finished puzzle with no desire to try to fit any of the pieces. The swirling, vibrant colors made her head ache. Gilly closed her eyes against the sight, feeling suddenly weary.

She felt the thump of something heavy hit the table. She opened her eyes to see her boots. She looked up.

"I'm sorry, Gilly."

She nodded, reached out and touched the leather. She'd bought these boots because she wanted something nice, something fashionable. Any single thing to make her feel less frumpy and matronly. More like…a woman. Now the effort seemed ridiculous, that a pair of shoes could make her feel anything. That she'd put so much value into something she wore rather than anything she did.

"Me, too," she said.

"I always had a temper. Guess I should've learned my lesson by now, huh?" Todd laughed without humor.

"I know about temper. It's okay." She meant the words the same as she'd meant the apology, but Todd looked at her as though she'd lied. "I lose mine, too."

His smile looked a little more natural. "No shit."

"I just can't hold it in sometimes." Gilly got up from the table. Sitting was making her feel worse, not better. She needed to walk. She didn't think she had to puke again…not quite.

Todd watched her as she went to the row of windows at the front of the house. She looked out each one. She turned to face the room. He hadn't spoken.

She didn't want to tell him about the days she went into her closet and stuffed her face into the racks of hanging clothes, screaming until her throat ripped and left her hoarse and sore. She didn't want to even think about those days. Gilly didn't want to tell Todd about the taste of blood she'd grown so used to, or the constant sore spot on the inside of her cheek from biting it.

"I don't want to be angry so much. I just am," Gilly said quietly. "Too much. It's too much, Todd."

"I make you angry?"

She threw out her hands and turned in a slow circle. "This place makes me angry. This situation. Everything about it makes me mad, Todd. You're part of it…I'm a part of it."

She looked at him. "I know I did this to myself, and I'm angriest about that. I wouldn't be here if I hadn't been so stupid. If I'd just gotten out of the truck at the gas station…"

She bit down on the words; chewed them into blood-tasting paste. Swallowed and waited for them to choke her. They went down smoother than she'd thought through a throat closed tight with emotion.

"Everything would've been different if you had," Todd said. "I know you're upset. But I'm not. Not really."

Of course he wouldn't be. Gilly took a deep breath, and another. One more. She counted slowly to ten while Todd watched her, and at the end of it, she held out her hand. He looked at it without taking it.

"I'll try not to lose my temper," Gilly said firmly, reaching to grab his hand and shake it. "If you do the same."

Todd's hand engulfed hers, as warm as the rest of him. He gave her a quizzical look. "Ooohkay."

"It will be better for us both. Easier to get along, if we both try. Deal?"

Todd squeezed her fingers and let them drop. He looked wary, then broke into a grin. "You are one weird woman."

"Deal?" she repeated.

"Sure," Todd said. "It's a deal."

40

Gilly watched the gray sky, thinking that if she saw one more snowflake come down she would lose her mind. So far the clouds had kept their contents inside. She pressed her fingers to the window, feeling the cold.

"I'd like to go for a walk," she blurted.

Todd's calm response showed no indication of surprise. "You're crazy."

"I know." Gilly looked back outside, twisting her neck to catch a glimpse of blue sky that simply wasn't there. "But I need to get outside, Todd. I have to. I'm going to explode if I don't, and trust me, you don't want to see that."

He didn't argue with her, just flapped a hand in her direction. He was whittling a piece of firewood. She didn't think he actually meant to make something from it, at least nothing she could tell.

"Fine. Go ahead."

Gilly went upstairs and layered herself with as many clothes as she could. She slipped her feet into thick socks, then put on the boots he'd given as a peace offering, and tied them. They pinched, tight on her feet. After so many weeks without shoes at all, her feet hurt from the constriction of the leather. The thick socks only made it worse.

She wouldn't be out long, she told herself. Not in this weather. Not with these clothes. But she had to get out of the cabin. Feel the fresh air on her face, breathe it deep into her lungs. She was stagnating.

Todd hadn't moved from his chair when she came downstairs. He sat in his usual position, head thrown back, face slack. He wasn't sleeping.

"I'm going," Gilly said.

"Be careful."

She paused to consider him, carefully. "Thanks. I will."

Stepping outside was a kick in the ass and a kiss on the cheek all at the same time. Bitter wind slapped at her face. She had no scarf, so struggled to pull her sweatshirt's neckline up over her mouth and nose. Her eyes instantly stung with tears that froze and burned. She'd never smelled anything so sweet.

Gilly hopped off the porch and into the knee-high snow. She would walk in this? She *was* insane. She struggled forward. The heavy snow weighed her down, but she pushed forward.

She didn't want to go back inside. Not with the fresh air whisking away the stink of all that had happened these past few weeks. Outside, she could almost forget where she was and what was happening. Close her eyes, picture herself on a ski slope somewhere…

That was no use. Skiing created warmth. Standing in the drifted snow there was only coldness. Gilly forced her foot forward, then the other. She'd taken two steps.

She glanced over her shoulder but could see nothing inside the cabin windows. She put her attention back to her feet, lifting one and then the other. Two more steps.

"Just once around the house," she told herself through gritted teeth. "Once around. Then back inside."

The cabin was so small, it didn't seem like such a daunting task. Gilly, who could carry two bags of groceries and a tired toddler, should be able to forge a path around the house. Just once.

"Yeah, right," she muttered and clapped her hands together sharply, though the sound was muffled. "Right. Let's go."

As with most things, the first step was the hardest. She forced her feet forward again anyway. The snow clung in great white clots to her sweatpants and the bootlaces. She'd added a good pound to each of her legs just from the clumping snow, which was heavy and wet.

Heart attack snow. Make sure you take a break when you're shoveling. You don't want to end up in the E.R.

Gilly blinked for a moment, distracted by her father's voice. He hardly ever popped into her mind like this, not like her mother, who Gilly seemed doomed to never escape. It had been a while since she'd talked to him. She'd spoken to him in September, for Rosh Hashanah. Maybe for the last time.

She pushed the thought from her mind and shifted her weight forward, yanking her foot free of the heavy snow and putting it down. One step. Then another.

She could do this. She *had* to do it. She was well aware her mind had twisted again, that her compulsion was anything but healthy. But, shit, she thought, tilting her head to the sky and drinking in the frigid, fresh air like wine, didn't it feel good?

She let out a whoop of joy, then tossed a double handful of

snow into the air. It fell down around her with solid thumps, creating pockets in the drifts. No tiny, dainty flakes here. This snow was serious. She looked up to the gray sky again, daring it to open up. Gilly stuck out her tongue and did as much of a dance as she could while up to her knees in snow that felt like wet sand.

Ten arduous steps took her to the edge of the house. Already her thighs burned, her calves ached. Her feet, which before had felt pinched and aching in the boots, had gone numb. Her hands, wrapped in layers of thick socks in lieu of the gloves Todd had not provided, were okay as long as she clenched and unclenched the fingers to keep them warm. Her face above the sweatshirt was numb, too.

Outside she was frozen, but inside Gilly felt warm. She'd spent too many days idle, too many hours lying on the couch. Her body ached with the efforts she forced upon it, but she felt exhilarated, too. She was moving! Doing something, not just being done to. Powerful, not powerless. Active, not passive. This was more than exercise. It was freedom.

She trudged ahead until she could touch the corner of the house. Now she faced the side with the lean-to and pantry. Green and black shingles, many rotted or missing, covered the walls of the small addition to the cabin. Three rickety steps led up to it.

She'd tossed buckets of black water off those steps. They'd made dirty ice underneath the white snow. She would have to walk carefully. She didn't want to break an ankle. She lifted her feet one at a time, shook them free of their load of snow and dropped them. On this side of the house, the snow wasn't as deep. Perhaps the wind had blown more of it to other parts of the yard. There was a bit of path, too, from Todd's trips to the woodpile. She was crossing it, not moving along it, but her legs were grateful for the respite.

The door to the lean-to opened as she stood there. Todd, wearing no coat, no hat, just the same familiar hooded sweatshirt, was already lighting up a cigarette. He snapped his lighter closed and tucked it in his front jeans pocket, then jerked his chin toward her.

"Hey."

"Hey." She sounded breathy, winded.

"How's it going?"

Gilly stretched, not wanting to lose her momentum or get chilled. "Good. Fine. Great, as a matter of fact."

"You coming back in?"

"Not yet." She stepped off the path of beaten-down snow into the depths of a small drift and sank up to her shins. "Still walking."

"It's cold as fuck out here, Gilly."

She glanced over her shoulder at him. She was already nearing the house's second corner. She had a rhythm starting, and she grinned. It seemed to take him aback, because he flinched.

"Crazy bitch," Todd muttered. He went inside and closed the door firmly. The scent of smoke lingered for only half a second before the wind whisked it away.

Gilly looked at the sky and, laughing, did her best Todd imitation. "Fucking insane."

She pushed on. Five more steps. She experimented, taking small half steps interspersed with lunging strides. She stopped to rest after just a few steps. Her breath whistled in her throat, her mouth parched, and she scooped a handful of snow to melt on her tongue.

Gilly had never understood those people who risked their

lives to climb mountains or explore wastelands. One of Seth's favorite shows was that one about the man who put himself out into the wilderness and survived by eating insects and drinking urine. Gilly didn't even like to read about that sort of thing, much less watch it on television. So what on earth was possessing her to live it now?

Without looking at her watch she could only guess at the amount of time she'd been out here already, but it hadn't been too long. Perhaps half an hour. Thirty minutes to move a few hundred feet!

Sweat streamed down her back and froze on her forehead. She sucked in gusts of air, burning her lungs and enjoying it. Determination fueled her. It would be so easy to give up. Gilly forced herself to move forward two more steps, the weight of the snow even heavier on her legs now that she'd taken a few minutes to rest.

If she gave up now, it would be a failure she could never forgive herself for. Somehow, for some stupid reason, making her way around this cabin had fixed itself in her mind as something important. Sacrifice for redemption…for penance? An idea completely at odds with what she believed, totally against her faith.

However, knowing what she was doing was crazy didn't make Gilly change her mind. She set her jaw, biting at the thick fabric of her sweatshirt to keep it from slipping down off her face. She lifted her legs, the muscles burning, and set them down. Two more steps.

By the time she made it around the cabin's second corner, her mood had changed from exhilaration to doubt. She reached out to touch the side of the cabin. Like a talisman, touching the rough shingles gave her strength.

Evening, by her reckoning, was a few hours away, but the

sky had grown dark enough to make it seem as though night were beginning to fall. She had to finish this journey before that happened. She might be crazy, but she wasn't insane enough to stay out here after dark.

Gilly had only seen the back of the cabin through the windows. Once out here, the humped and hilly landscape of snow seemed as foreign to her as an alien planet. She made it to a dilapidated picnic table, heaped high with snow, with a minimum of huffing and puffing and steadied herself on its snow-covered top.

Gilly glanced to the windows, half-expecting to see Todd's broad silhouette checking on her again, but all she saw was the glow of the lights he must've recently lit. She paused long enough to sit on the table's bench seat and wiggle her toes inside the boots. She could still feel her feet pushing against the leather, though all other sensation had numbed. The foolishness of this undertaking struck her as she thought of blackened and amputated toes.

Don't think of it. You'll be okay. Just keep moving.

She whacked the snow off her bottom and looked at the cabin. Through the windows she saw Todd moving. It looked warm in there, and though she wasn't cold yet—not really, aside from her toes—she was tired and hungry and worn-out.

"Move your ass," she said aloud. "C'mon, Gilly. You came out here and wanted to do this. Don't be a baby."

Time ceased ticking as she stumbled through the mounds of whiteness. One foot in front of the other, lifting and plunging. The sound of her breath came loud in her ears, like a freight train. Like the roar of a lion. It gave her strength, that sound, and when she opened her mouth and let out a scream of triumph as she touched the cabin's third corner, she didn't care how crazy or bestial she sounded. Her shriek echoed off the trees, startling a rabbit from its hiding place beneath the thick undergrowth. The sound of it, though it had come from her own throat and of her own volition, frightened Gilly, too.

She was almost there. The world tilted in front of her eyes, but Gilly managed to bring it back into focus. No fainting out here, not even if it meant she could lie down in the deep, soft snow. Sleep had never been so appealing, but to sleep here meant certain death. She must keep moving.

Had she ever done anything this physically hard? Gilly thought again of childbirth, the never-endingness of it, the fact that once begun she could not have stopped it if she tried. There are moments in life that once started cannot be stopped; she would have to see this through to completion as surely as she'd given birth to her children. There was no going back. Only forward.

She gathered her strength again, feeling it ebb with every moment she remained still. Her body screamed a protest when she forced her foot forward. Gilly stumbled, the first time since she'd stepped off the porch earlier this afternoon, and hit the snow.

It engulfed her, enveloped her, wrapped her in clouds of stinging softness. Whiteness filled her eyes, her nose, her throat while she coughed and gagged. She was drowning in it.

Gilly got her feet beneath her and pushed with her hands, lifting herself out of the drift with an effort she could only classify as superhuman. She shivered, then quaked with reaction and cold.

"C'mon," she muttered, slapping her hands together. "Stupid, Gilly! Stupid to do this!"

But even as her body stung and ached, and the bitter wind

tore at her flesh, Gilly didn't feel stupid. She was almost done. She would do this, and in doing it become stronger.

She forged ahead, battling her weakness with grunts and curses. She touched the fourth corner of the cabin, viewed the front porch, and found no strength for screams this time. Instead she gathered her breath and forced herself to drag herself through the snow.

"To the steps," she breathed. "Then I'm done."

And she made it to the steps, though without recall of how she did it. Every painful step of the trip around the house was clear like ice in her brain, but not the final steps. She simply found herself inside the front door, shedding her clothes, and realized she'd done it.

Her hands wouldn't loosen her clothes. Gilly staggered to the dining room table, knocking puzzle pieces to the floor. She didn't have the strength to do more.

The room felt blessedly, unbearably hot. She raised her face to the warmth, letting it seep into her as she tried to shed her sodden, frozen clothes.

"Get out of that stuff," Todd told her.

Gilly looked up, feeling the goofy grin paint itself on her face. "I did it. All the way around the house!"

"You're a real jerkoff, Gilly, do you know that?"

She should've felt worse for her adventure. Should've been cringing and whimpering as the heat leached into her frozen bones. Instead, Gilly felt joyous. Exuberant. She almost, but not quite, laughed.

The almost-laugh sobered her. "I need to warm up."

"I heated some water for you."

"What?" His statement was so unexpected, she blurted the question though she had heard him perfectly.

"It should still be hot," Todd told her. He held up one hand to show her a splash of red across it. "Burned myself just for you, so you better fucking enjoy it."

Enjoy it? Gilly almost bent down and kissed Todd's feet for the kindness. "Thank you, thank you, oh, God. Thank you!"

She didn't need his help to make it to the bathroom, and once inside, even managed to slide out of her layers of clothes. Naked, she worked her fingers and toes and was relieved to see they looked all right.

Sliding into the hot water made her cry out, moan, whimper. In seconds her body adjusted to the temperature, and it became paradise. He'd filled the tub nearly to overflowing, a task that must've taken him nearly the same amount of time for her to make it around the cabin.

Gilly sank into the water, letting it heal her. No one would probably ever understand why she'd done it. She wasn't sure she understood, herself. But she had, and it was something she would never forget. Gilly grinned and sank beneath the water.

By all rights, when she got out she should have been stiff and sore. That would come later, maybe, when her muscles tightened as she slept. Now, though, she felt just fine. Relaxed. Even…content. Not with her situation, which she could be resigned to but not content with. Content with herself. It was a feeling she hadn't had in a long, long time.

"Todd?"

His answer came garbled and muffled. "Yeah?"

"Can you bring me something to wear?"

She heard him pound up the stairs and then down. The door creaked. His hand appeared with a pile of dry clothes. The door closed again.

Gilly dressed, combed her hair, brushed her teeth. She

peered at her windburned cheeks in the mirror and noted the sparkle in her eyes. She bared her teeth at the image and then ignored it.

She walked out into a candlelit haven. The smell of something delicious wafted from the kitchen, and her stomach grumbled. She was starving.

"What's for...?" Gilly stopped, stunned.

Todd had set the table. Though the candles were utilitarian and white, they highlighted pretty china plates and silverware on a delicate flowered cloth. He turned from the stove as she came into the kitchen.

"I hope you're hungry," he said.

She nodded, not trusting herself to speak. Todd motioned for her to sit, and she did, sliding into the chair that had become hers by habit. She touched the silverware, the plates, the tablecloth.

Todd had brushed his hair. It swept off his face to curl softly behind his ears and to his shoulders. The permanent scruff of his beard had been shaved. He wore a black turtleneck shirt and jeans, and his feet were bare.

Gilly saw all these things because she could not look away from him. Todd's smile was brief before it disappeared. The cautious look in his eyes was belied by his confident stance.

"Happy Valentine's Day, Gilly."

Her heart met her stomach as one sank and the other leaped to her throat. She bent her head to stare at the plate, no longer able to look at him.

Oh, no. Oh, God.

"It's only macaroni and cheese," Todd said, "but it's the good kind. Shells. It's the best of what's left. I thought you might like it."

He'd also made canned potatoes, soft and white, and added

slivers of some kind of potted meat the origin of which she knew better than to question. He'd added a plate of saltines painted with grape jelly. Her stomach, which had been growling only moments before, twisted at the sight of the haphazard dinner. She picked up her fork anyway.

"You were out there a real long time," Todd said. "I thought I might have to go out for you."

"No," Gilly said faintly, raising a forkful of cheesy pasta to her lips. "I was okay."

"I don't have any candy, but I made a white cake for dessert. Box mix. Didn't have eggs, but I think it turned out okay."

"Good." She chewed carefully, still unable to look at him.

"Gilly."

She raised her gaze to his. In the candlelight, his eyes were the color of warm caramel. The black turtleneck emphasized the darkness of his hair and the paleness of his skin. He could've passed for a gothic novel's vampire lover, save he had no fangs.

"I never did this for anyone before. It's probably shit compared to what you're used to."

"I…we…don't celebrate Valentine's Day," Gilly said. His brow furrowed. She explained further. "The holiday started as a way to honor Saint Valentine…many Jews don't recognize Christian saints."

Todd slid into his chair and rested his hands on the table. "So you never got cards or chocolates or stuff like that?"

Gilly shook her head. "Not usually, no."

He grinned. "Then it's a first for you, too."

"Todd…"

"Please, Gilly," Todd said softly. "Just this once, for tonight. Can you let me be nice to you?"

Something inside her broke, agonizing in its painlessness. Gilly sighed, brushing her forehead with the fingertips of one hand. She was helpless to deny him, despite the strength she had gained only hours before.

"All right. Sure."

The smile lit up his face, creasing his cheeks and sending sparks to flare in the chocolate-colored eyes. He forked a bite of macaroni and cheese but seemed unable to eat it. Todd wriggled in his seat like a puppy thrilled with praise from its master.

It was only a meal. She would think no further than that. Just this once, for a reason she could not explain and would not ponder, she would let him be nice to her.

He charmed her over the sorry meal. Todd had already proved himself to be insightful. When he wasn't self-conscious about being stupid, he actually turned out to be knowledgeable on a lot of subjects, and Gilly told him so.

"Nah. It's just a bunch of stupid shit nobody cares about. Just trivia." He mixed potatoes and macaroni and cheese without eating it.

"No, it's not," she insisted. "It's not just trivia, Todd. Being smart isn't always about what big words you can spout out or how fast you can do math, you know."

He shrugged. "I guess I've just…lived more, or something. Done a lot of stuff. Hey, that's one good thing about never hanging on to a job, I guess. I learned how to do a lot of stuff. But I'm still stupid."

He had indeed lived a lot more than she ever had. She didn't envy him the experience. "Doing stupid things doesn't mean you're stupid, Todd."

"No?" His brows arched beneath the fringe of his dark hair. "What does it mean?"

"Well. It means you're...not...it just means...you need to think before you act." She nodded firmly, the voice of authority.

The food disappeared as they talked. At the end of the meal, Todd presented the cake with a flourish, though it was flat and crumbly without the eggs for the batter. It tasted strongly of cinnamon and honey, two flavors Gilly didn't like. She ate it anyway, and praised him for the effort.

Todd gave her his curious puppy look. "You're being nice."

"Do you want me to stop?"

"No." He shook his head. "Ain't so hard, is it?"

That it wasn't difficult would've frightened her had Gilly allowed it. Instead, she put it from her mind, too. A thought for a later time.

They'd never assigned each other chores, each usually taking care of their own meal prep and cleanup, but tonight Todd cleared and washed the dishes, insisting she sit.

"Happy Valentine's Day," he insisted at her protest that he'd done enough by preparing the meal. "Take a load off."

Gilly had never really minded missing out on the national day of romance. Seth had been fond of reminding her that every day in their marriage was a celebration of their love. Gilly didn't always agree, particularly on the days when the children's hijinks had shortened her temper and Seth breezed in late from work asking "What's for dinner?" Still, she didn't miss the overpriced chocolates and bouquets of flowers that were heavy on guilt and lacking in sentiment. Her husband told her he loved her every day, and didn't need the words on a greeting card to do it.

Because she didn't share Valentine's Day with Seth, sharing it with Todd somehow didn't seem like betrayal. At least not so far, with his innocuous offering of food and service. Gilly sat on the couch, watching the play of candlelight on the ceiling.

She shivered and wanted the chill to come from the room's lowering temperature and not from her sudden anxious anticipation. She got up to put some more logs on the fire, and took the last three from the battered wicker basket next to the stove. They were almost out of wood.

"We need more wood," Gilly called.

Todd appeared beside her, startling her. "The pile out back's all, gone," he said, using the typical Pennsylvania Dutch phrasing that usually made her cringe. "I didn't have time to cut more today."

Gilly hadn't realized their supply was so low. She felt stupid for not noticing. "Oh."

Todd poked at the logs she'd put on. Red sparks hissed in the fire. The logs popped and complained at their fiery fate.

"I'll cut some more tomorrow."

He'd leaned across her to reach the poker. Now they faced each other from no more than a few inches apart. The red and orange flames reflected in his eyes, and Gilly knew she didn't imagine the questions she saw there.

Self-consciously, she got to her feet and moved away. She wasn't certain exactly where she meant to go when there was no place to escape. His voice, low and uncertain, froze her solid.

"Gilly…"

She murmured a reply. "Hmm?"

He sighed. She closed her eyes and her teeth found the inside of her cheek. She prayed he wouldn't find the courage to ask her the question she'd seen glimmering in his eyes. He cleared his throat, and she tensed. Waiting.

"Gilly, would you dance with me?"

It wasn't the question she'd expected, though not much better. Gilly turned to face him, her face a careful, neutral mask. "What?"

He got to his feet, all arms and legs, gangly. "Dance? I'm not any good. But would you…?"

"Dance with you?" Gilly murmured. She allowed his touch on her fingers, her thoughts elsewhere. Her breath caught in her throat before coughing out. "Oh, Todd."

"Please?"

What harm could it do? She knew even as she nodded her reply that she was dooming herself. And him. No good could come from this. But…could harm? What could giving him this one thing hurt?

"Great!"

For once the radio didn't let them down. Todd tuned in a station playing classic golden oldies. *Smoke Gets In Your Eyes* made way for *Unchained Melody.*

They moved to a clear spot on the floor. He didn't know where to put his hands, and Gilly showed him. They were large and encircled her waist in a way that made her feel he could squeeze her in half with little effort. The top of her head just barely reached his shoulder. Gilly was not a small woman, but once again he'd made her tiny.

"I told you I'm not good," Todd said.

"You're doing fine," Gilly whispered, her throat dry.

His innate grace took the place of his inexperience. The songs playing on the radio flowed one into the other with no more than a few seconds of break between them. Todd and Gilly danced, their movements slow but unhesitating.

He pulled her slowly, hesitantly closer. His hands didn't stray from her hips. The puff of his breath ruffled her hair.

She knew this had been a mistake. This didn't mean the same things to her as it must to him. This was Reg Gampey all over again. This was giving someone something he wanted because she felt so bad about something else she didn't know how to say no.

But then she'd been a kid. She was a woman now. She shouldn't let pity move her into doing something she knew would end badly.

The slow songs kept playing. Todd and Gilly kept dancing. She rested her hands on his shoulders and just barely kept her face from touching even the soft flannel of his shirt.

She was reminded of middle-school dances where the girls and boys were too scared to even touch. But this wasn't quite like that. In middle school Gilly had known the mechanics of what sex was but hadn't had a clue about what it could be. Even later, in high school, when dancing close often led to making out in shadowy corners, there'd still been an innocence to sharing a dance that was missing here.

At last the music stopped. An announcer spoke. The moment broke.

Gilly tried to pull away, but Todd's hands stayed her. Her head dropped. She saw the floor, his bare feet, the ragged hem of his jeans.

"Gilly?"

"No, Todd."

For an instant she sensed anger. His fingers clutched at her waist, then relaxed. He tried again.

"Gilly..."

"No." Her voice came more firmly this time. Definite. She moved out of his embrace, clutching her elbows and turning from him.

"Look at me?"

Because it was a plea and not a demand, she obliged. She could hardly bear the look of longing on his face. Gilly swallowed, hard, and shook her head again.

"Don't ask, and I won't have to tell you no again."

"Why?" The question was simple, and the answer should've been simpler, but was not.

"My mother used to tell me, 'be happy with what you have,'" Gilly said at last. "Be happy with what you have, Todd."

He looked around the cabin, at her, and then down at himself. "What I have? That looks like a whole lot of nothing."

She moved, still trembling, to the stairs before changing her mind. She didn't want to lead him up there, where the line of beds would be all too tempting. She went instead to the dining room table and one of her puzzles but couldn't find rest there, either. Finally, she turned and faced him squarely.

"I can't change things," she told him. "And I wouldn't if I could. I have too much to lose and nothing to gain."

His face broke, his head dropped. His knees buckled for an instant before he caught himself and made his way to a chair. Todd buried his face in his hands, his sigh soft but as loud and mournful as the howling of wolves. He pressed the heels of his hands to his eyes.

"Is it wrong to want just one thing? One good thing?" He spoke so low she could've pretended not to hear him.

But she did hear him, every word.

"No. But I'm not it."

"You could be. If you wanted to."

"But I don't want to, Todd." She hated the words the second they came out, even though she meant them.

"See? I am stupid."

He hadn't moved from the chair. She was still by the table.

A vast distance separated them, too far for her to touch him, but she put out her hand anyway.

"You're not—"

He cut her off with a low noise from deep inside him. Gilly stopped, uncertain. Todd looked up at her.

"Go away," he told her, and she went.

41

The gears had jammed, the machine ground to a halt. Todd replied when she spoke to him, but only in the gruffest, briefest words. Gilly didn't really blame him. There wasn't much more to say. She should've been grateful for it and could only be sad.

They fixed lunch at the same time but not together, bound by mutually growling stomachs if nothing more. Long weeks of confinement meant they'd worked out a routine in the kitchen. A step here, a dodge there. Today she zigged when he zagged, and Gilly found herself with both hands pressed to his chest to keep them from colliding.

He pushed her away, gently but firmly. "Don't touch me."

Now she understood how it must've felt for him when she'd said those same words. "Todd."

"Don't." He jerked his hands away, lifting them out of her reach as though she'd tried to take one, then moved around her to grab his plate. He turned his back on her to take a seat at the kitchen table.

Gilly had fixed herself the last handful of wheat crackers and some squares of defrosted lunch meat that was a little too pink to be turkey. Was it only weeks ago she'd refused a plate of eggs mixed with bacon? She'd have eaten it, now. They were far from starving but they'd had an unspoken agreement to cut back on their meals. Their stomachs, like the pantry and fridge, were emptier every day.

At the table across from him, Gilly attempted to start a conversation that Todd shut down with one-word answers. They ate in uncompanionable silence. Her food tasted bad because of it.

"Don't blame me for what I can't change," she blurted finally, unable to help herself.

He lifted his eyebrows at her and leaned back in the kitchen chair, tipping it. The smoke from his cigarette wreathed his features, made them softer, even as his scowl became harsher. He said nothing.

"I can't," Gilly whispered, and got up from the table. She left her plate.

Behind her she heard the thump of all four chair legs hitting the floor, but she didn't turn. The scent of his cigarette smoke tickled her nose, but she refused to cough. She went to the bathroom and ran the cold water, splashed her face again and again until her eyes burned and her face turned red.

When she came into the living room, he'd gone upstairs. She heard the sound of his footsteps on the creaking wooden floor. She tilted her head toward the ceiling, but he didn't seem to be coming back down. This time, Todd was the one who'd escaped upstairs.

"I can't change things, damn it!" she cried to the ceiling,

her fists clenched in impotent anger. Even as she said it, she could taste the lie on her tongue. Could not and would not were two separate things altogether.

Gilly pressed the heels of her palms to her eyes, willing away the urge to cry. She owed him no tears. If she wept it should be for Seth, for Arwen, for Gandy. Perhaps even for herself. But not Todd. Not over this.

All at once, she couldn't breathe. Her throat burned with the effort, and Gilly sank onto the sofa. She pushed her hands against her chest, feeling and hearing the thunder of her heart.

"I'm sorry," she whispered. He couldn't hear her, but that didn't matter. She knew she'd said it.

42

"Coming to bed?" This is Seth's code for wanting to make love.

Gilly looks at the pile of bills as-yet-unpaid. From the laundry room, the dryer buzzes with a load of sheets and towels, with one last load in the washer ready to be transferred. It's only a little after nine o'clock, and she could easily stay up until eleven without suffering too much in the morning. Two whole hours with a house sleeping around her—how much she could finish in that solitude!

"I have to finish a few things first."

He comes up behind her to kiss her neck. Gilly stiffens. The inside of her cheek burns and stings as she bites, though at least she doesn't taste blood. Not yet.

"Come to bed," her husband says as his hands come around to cup her breasts even though she's told him time and again that nursing made them too sensitive for her to enjoy being grabbed that way. "I'm horny."

She isn't.

Her mind races, calculating if she can satisfy him with a quick hand-job at the desk so he'll go away and leave her alone. He's already taking her hand and rubbing his crotch with it. Seth thinks this will make her want to have sex with him, when all it really does is make her want to grab as hard as she can and yank.

It wasn't always this way. Gilly remembers a time when she was the one chasing her husband for sex, he the one complaining about being tired. That was before children, though, back in the days when she had nobody to take care of but herself. When she could stay up until midnight and still get seven hours of uninterrupted sleep. Back when her belly had been smooth and curved, not loose and doughy and road-mapped with scars.

She has friends whose husbands don't like to screw the way they used to—something about their wives gaining weight or being matronly, something about being unable to look at them as lovers any longer. She should be thankful her marriage is still strong, that her husband watched two children come out of her vagina and still finds her not only just attractive but sexy enough to chase around the house.

He shouldn't have to chase her.

At the very least, she shouldn't mind when he catches her.

But she does, and Gilly sighs as Seth whispers in her ear again, adding a stroke of tongue to her earlobe that makes her shudder with nothing resembling passion.

"Come to bed," Seth says.

Gilly does, because appeasing him has become one more thing on a long list of chores she needs to complete before the night is through. She goes through the motions and the noises, wanting to please him because she does love him, after all, this man who quickly turns to snoring beside her in their bed. He doesn't notice when she gets up to go back downstairs and finish the chores she'd left undone so she could take the time to satisfy him.

"Don't forget to take your pills," Todd says from the bathroom when Gilly at last finishes the last load of laundry, closes the checkbook,

and heads for a hot, steamy shower. She wants to stay in the water for a long time, letting it beat on her neck and shoulders, blocking out the world. She stops, instead, to listen to him say, "They're on the counter. You're sick, remember? The antibiotics."

As the steam begins to fill the room, Gilly thinks she ought to scream. There's a stranger in her house. He's staring at her like he knows her. Not a stranger, after all.

Gilly doesn't scream.

But she did wake up, heart pounding and stomach sick. She rushed to the bathroom to hover over the toilet, hoping she wouldn't vomit and yet somehow relieved when she couldn't hold it back. She was in there for a long time and when she came out, unlike all the others, Todd didn't ask her if she was okay.

43

Gilly wasn't used to being the bad guy, and she definitely didn't like it. Three days had passed since Todd had asked her to dance. Early on in all of this, she'd have thought it better if they didn't speak, but they'd gone beyond that now. Todd turned his back on her when she entered a room and ignored her when she spoke. He'd even taken to sleeping downstairs on the couch so they didn't have to share the room upstairs. It was killing her.

She'd spent the morning tidying just to keep herself busy, but at last she turned to him. "Are you ever going to talk to me again?"

Todd said nothing.

"Please?" Gilly said, exhausted. She sank into a chair across from him. "C'mon, Todd. Please. Don't do this."

Todd got up when she sat down, but before he could escape Gilly had snagged his sleeve. He set his jaw and deliberately pulled it from her grip. He didn't look at her.

"I'm going to get some wood." He might've been talking to himself for all the attention he gave her.

"Do you need some help?"

He fixed her with a look so contemptuous and bitter she recoiled from it the way she would've if she'd stumbled on a snake in a woodpile. Without answering, he shrugged into an extra sweatshirt and pulled his hood up over the fall of silky dark hair. Then he stomped outside.

It always seemed to come back to sex, with men. Whether they wanted it and didn't get it, or got it but not enough of it, it led to more arguments and hard feelings than anything else Gilly could think of. In the beginning she'd been afraid Todd meant to rape her—and that would've been about power, not sex. Now it was simply about longing, and somehow that made it so much more frightening.

She couldn't repair the hurt she'd caused him. Any apologies she made would ring false, and Gilly wasn't sure she could convince him of the difference between being sorry she couldn't give him what he wanted and sorrow that her decision had caused him pain.

She cradled her head in her hands for a minute, willing her headache to subside. The rolling of her stomach had woken her early this morning. She'd been sick again. She didn't want to contemplate what that might mean.

She watched Todd from the window as he trudged through the thigh-deep snow. She gained some small measure of satisfaction from seeing that he didn't have a much easier time wading through the snow than she had. He disappeared into the woods.

He'd only taken a small hand ax. Guilt nudged her when she glanced at the empty wicker basket next to the woodstove. She hadn't ever thought about where the wood came from, or wondered what would happen when the stockpile outside the lean-to disappeared. Then again, neither of them had expected so much snow, or to be here this long.

She busied herself with her puzzle, nearly completed now, but could find no pleasure in it. She heard the thump of wood against the back of the house, and jumped. Todd didn't come back inside.

More time passed. Gilly finished the puzzle, but her triumph was empty. She sat at the table and stared at the brightly colored picture she'd made. Then she took it all apart.

She heard another load of wood thump against the house. She looked at her watch. An hour had passed. Plenty of time for him to have cut enough wood to last a few days. She went again to the window, and was just in time to see Todd vanish again into the woods.

Gilly went to the back door and gaped at the size of the pile. How had he managed to cut and carry all of that in so short a time, and alone? Her gaze followed the trampled path in the snow to where it led to the trees.

Heart attack snow.

What if Todd had gone out there alone and fallen ill? Hurt himself? What if the ax had slipped and he was lying in a pool of his own frozen blood? What if he was exhausted and hypothermic?

What would she do out here, alone, without him?

Gilly boiled water, found a mug, dunked a tea bag. She added extra sugar. While it steeped she wrestled herself into several layers of clothing and forced her feet into her boots. As an afterthought, she found the large deep stockpot, filled it, and put it on top of the woodstove.

She carried the mug carefully through the path Todd had made and into the woods. She found him seated on a fallen tree, the ax resting at his side. His breath plumed out in front of him. His hair had frozen, stiff with sweat, into random spikes.

"Here." She handed him the mug.

He took it with cold-reddened hands. "Thanks."

"You've been out here a long time."

"We needed wood."

She glanced at the pile at his feet. "I think we have enough."

"I needed to work." He cupped the mug with his hands and tested the still steaming liquid with the tip of his tongue.

"It's cold out here," Gilly said. "Why don't you take a break?"

"Why don't you get the fuck out of my face?" he replied evenly, and handed her back the mug. "Don't you get it, Gilly? I *need* to work."

His gaze swept her from head to toe, burning her even through the many layers. She nodded quickly, her cheeks heating, and took the cup. She hurried back through the snow and into the cabin.

Inside, she tore her top layer of clothes off and flung them to the floor. She splashed frigid water on her hot face. Dripping and gasping, Gilly pushed back from the sink and dried herself with the hem of her shirt.

She let herself rest at the table. She put her head in her hands. Stifled a groan.

The thud of logs against the pile outside again startled her into standing. In another moment, the back door opened. Todd stomped in, scattering clods of snow onto the linoleum. He blew into his hands. His teeth started to chatter.

"You need to get those wet clothes off…I didn't have time to fill the tub like you did for me…but I heated some water…."

She was babbling, and realized it. Gilly closed her mouth abruptly. "Come sit over on the couch."

He did. Gilly found a smaller pan and set it on the floor in front of him. She added enough cold water to make the temperature bearable and got up. "Take off your boots."

Todd bent, but she could clearly see that his fingers were too numb to work the laces. Gilly knelt and did it for him. He groaned as she pulled off the battered hiking boots, and then the socks beneath. His toes were ice cubes.

"I'll make some more tea."

He caught her hand as she turned and tugged her close to him. "Now you're being nice to me again. I don't get it."

At first, Gilly couldn't form her answer into words. She held his icy feet between her hands to warm them a bit before she slipped them into the hot water. He hissed and clenched his fists, but didn't protest.

"Todd," Gilly said finally with a sigh. "Being nice doesn't have to mean…"

She stopped, mouth working as she tried to put her thoughts into speech. "I can take care *of* you without caring *for* you."

She raised her gaze to his face and instantly wished she hadn't. Beneath the ruddy color from the cold, he'd gone pale. His mouth set in a thin line.

"I guess you can," he said.

"I have a home," Gilly said. "I have a family. And I will get back to them someday. Whether you want to believe it or not. I believe it. I have to."

He nodded twice, sharply. "You still want to get away from me."

"How can you ask me that?" Gilly reached for a towel, lifted his feet from the water, dried them. "Todd, can you expect anything else from me?"

He leaned forward, grasped her upper arms. His eyes searched hers. "Yeah. I think I can."

Gilly shook her head. "No. You can't. It's too much to expect. Even for you."

"What's that mean? Even for me? Even for a dumbass like me, you mean?"

"That's not what I meant, and you should know that," Gilly said. "I meant that no matter what I know..."

His fingers tightened. She restrained a wince. "You pity me."

"I empathize with you, Todd. There's a difference."

His grip softened, but not by much. His gaze did, too. "I ain't asking for so much. Am I, really?"

"It's too much."

He shook her a little, and the role of power had shifted. Now kneeling at his feet felt subservient instead of caretaking. Gilly started to get to her feet, but Todd's grasp stopped her.

"What *can* you give?"

She looked at him, then waved her hand at his feet. "This. It's all I have for you, Todd."

He gave a low, growling laugh. "You want to be my fucking mother?"

"Interesting choice of words," Gilly murmured.

"You shut...you shut your mouth." He pushed away from her, got up, took long, limping strides to the edge of the room before turning back to her. "Is that what you think of me?"

Gilly shook her head, her knees hurting on the bare floor. She got up. "No, of course not."

He drew a cigarette from the crumpled pack and threw the empty paper to the floor. The smoke seeped from his nostrils in slow, twin tendrils, Fog. He picked a bit of tobacco off his tongue with one finger, turned and spit onto the floor. When he looked at her, Gilly wanted to turn away from the bluntness in his eyes.

"What, then?" he shouted. "The fuck am I to you, then, Gilly? Because I know I'm something to you."

Todd's voice dipped low and soft. Hopeful. "I am, right?"

She couldn't answer and he seemed to take her silence as assent.

"I never met anyone like you, Gilly." Todd's smile was lopsided. "You…you're clean. When I'm around you, I feel clean, too."

"Then let me stay that way," Gilly said. "Please."

Todd shook his head and bent his head to stare up at her through the sheaf of his dark hair. "I don't think I can."

"You have to."

He shook his head. "I ain't that good a person, Gilly."

A drop of cold sweat trickled down her spine, but she refused to shiver. "You can be. If you try."

Todd drew deep on his cigarette, watching her. Thinking. When she saw he wasn't going to say anything else, Gilly took the basin into the kitchen and emptied it. They did not continue the conversation.

44

What did he mean to her? The answer wasn't "nothing." Gilly knew it, even if she wasn't going to tell him. She thought about what it might be through the night as she fought sleep so she wouldn't have to face her dreams. She'd sought refuge in them before, but now they only made everything hurt worse.

For the first time ever, Gilly waited for the sound of her mother's voice to ring in her head, and it didn't come. She could hear her mother's words, but it wasn't like she was there, speaking them, and they were only memory, time-faded and inexact.

Roses, she thought, prompting with no response. What had her mother said about roses? What had she said about… love?

No. Not that. It was impossible.

Love had many shapes, but this was not and could not be one of them. She couldn't love Todd. It was wrong. It was a perversion of the very word. Whatever she felt for him—and she could admit it was something, yes, she could do that, it was most emphatically not love.

She felt as responsible for him as she did for her children, yet she didn't feel maternal toward him. She believed he knew her as well as her husband did, but she didn't feel romantic toward him, either. Everything about Todd was chaos and conflict.

She heard his step on the stairs, the shuffle of his feet along the floor to his bed. The creak of the springs. She waited for the soft sigh of his snore, which she'd missed while he was avoiding her by sleeping on the couch. Instead, she heard him murmur her name.

"Yes, Todd."

His reply came with the shuffle of feet on the floorboards and a shadow standing, hesitating, in the space between the partition. There was no moon, or it hadn't yet risen, and all she could see was the black, hunched shape of his shoulders. She heard his breathing.

She tensed.

He came closer and sat, close enough to touch her if he wanted but not touching her. He was always so warm, tonight no exception. She could feel him even through the blankets.

"I told you about Kendra," Todd said.

"Yes. Your girlfriend. She wanted to get married and you didn't." Gilly shifted in the covers, turning onto her side to face him though she couldn't see anything more than the shape of him.

"Yeah. See, the thing about Kendra, was that she wasn't like the other girls I'd ever been with. I mean, I never really had a lot of girlfriends. Just some girls I got with every once in a while when I could. But when I met her, it was different. She was nice. She lived in a nice house. She had a job."

"What did she do?"

"She taught kindergarten." Todd laughed harshly. "Can you believe that, Gilly? Me with a fucking kindy teacher. She spent all day with little kids. And she went out with me at night. I bet if those parents had known what she was up to, they wouldn't have been so happy."

Gilly was a parent. If she'd found out her daughter's teacher was dating a convict, she'd have had trouble with it, no doubt. "It was her social life, not any of their business."

"Yeah, well. You know how people are."

"Yeah. I do."

Todd shifted and the bed dipped a little as he half turned toward her. "She had the prettiest laugh. And she laughed a lot when she was with me. I laughed, too. When I was with Kendra, I felt..."

Gilly waited.

"Luminescent," Todd said finally. "You know that word?"

"Yes. I do."

"It's a good one."

She smiled in the dark. "A very good one."

"One of Uncle Bill's favorites," Todd said off handedly. "But that's how I felt when I was with Kendra."

"So what happened?"

"She wanted to get married. And I just couldn't do it. She said it would all work out and everything would be okay, but I couldn't do it."

Gilly put out her hand. Her fingertips grazed his back. She kept them there, barely touching.

"She didn't really know me," Todd said. "She loved me, though. But I didn't lose her. I pushed her away."

Gilly put her hand flat on his back, but it fell away when Todd stood. She missed his heat right away and shivered. He moved, and the floorboards creaked.

"I shouldn't have asked you for more," Todd said.

Then he went back to his bed.

45

Todd slid a hand through his hair in irritation. "Damn it."

Gilly looked up from the list she was writing. "What?"

"My hair." Todd blew upward, causing the strands to lift off his forehead. "It's too long."

She looked at him critically. It hung past the edges of his shoulders and obscured the crows' wings of his eyebrows. "It sure is."

He snorted. "I hate dirty hair."

She put a hand up to her own hair, pulled back into a ponytail for the same reason. Neither of them had been much concerned about washing their hair. It was hard enough taking a bath.

He tugged at a handful. "It's driving me crazy."

"I could cut it for you." She meant the offer casually, not thinking he would take it.

Todd's eyes lit. "Yeah?"

Gilly shrugged. "Sure. I can't promise you how pretty it will turn out, but I can do it. I cut my kids' hair all the time."

"Cool!" Todd went to the kitchen and began rummaging around in one of the drawers. He came back with his trophy held high: a large pair of scissors. "Here."

She took the dull and ancient tool and looked at it skeptically. "I don't know about this."

"Just try. I can't stand it."

"Okay, so long as you're not planning on entering any beauty pageants." She motioned to him. "Sit down."

He sat so she could stand behind him, and his head still came up to her chin. Gilly snapped the scissors open and shut a few times and touched Todd's hair. It was dirty, but still smooth. She ran it through her fingers, catching the snags.

"Ouch!"

"Sorry." She tried again, with the same response. "It's too tangled."

"Cut the knots out."

"No," Gilly said sternly. "You'd look horrible. I have to comb it first. And I think I should wash it."

He protested, but only feebly. Gilly led him to the bathroom and bent him over the bathtub. He yelped as the lukewarm water hit his scalp, but didn't fight to get away.

Gilly worked quickly, mindful of how quickly the hot water ran out. She soaped Todd's head and rinsed it, then used a palmful of conditioner. It was the last in the bottle.

She finished, and he wrapped his head in a towel. They returned to the living room, moving the chair closer to the fire. She combed his hair until it lay smooth and shining against his scalp and hung straight to the middle of his back.

"It seems a shame to cut it. You have such nice hair, Todd."

"Sissy hair," he said. "I have girl's hair."

"No," Gilly admonished. "Just because it's long doesn't make it girl's hair."

"It's too pretty," Todd said in a mocking tone. "Faggot hair."

Gilly shook her head, thinking of one of her best friends from college. Mark would've said the very same thing, only with envy in his tone. Mark's partner wore his hair long and straight, like Todd's, but Mark kept his short in a buzz cut to disguise a receding hairline.

Todd twisted to look at her. "You think that's funny?"

His vehemence took her aback. "No."

"My uncle Bill was a fag," Todd said, his face stony. "And he was the best man who ever was. If you got a problem with that you'd better keep it to yourself."

"Todd." Gilly cut him off. She laid her hand on his shoulder. "I don't."

He wet his lips. "Some people do."

"I'm not some people."

He nodded. "Yeah. Right."

She pushed his head until he looked forward again, and brandished the scissors. "If you want me to cut it, I'll cut it."

"Do it."

In a few minutes, the deed was done. Todd's hair lay in loose curls all over the towel draped across his shoulders and the floor. He ran a finger through the short, cropped strands.

"Feels nice," he commented.

The short hairstyle emphasized the line of his cheekbones and curve of his jaw. He'd grown thinner, Gilly noted. His scalp showed white in places, and a few tiny silver hairs glittered in places she hadn't noticed before.

"All done." Before she could stop herself, Gilly reached out and stroked his cheek. Then, not wanting to make a scene, she pretended she was merely brushing some stray hairs from his face.

He pressed his face against her hand and closed his eyes for a minute. Gilly took her hand away. She busied herself with tidying up.

When he wasn't looking, she gathered a hank of his hair and twisted it together before slipping it into her pocket. She couldn't have said what compulsion had made her do it; she didn't want to dwell on it. Later, she took it out and put it in her dresser drawer. She didn't look at it again, but she always knew it was there.

46

"What are you doing?"

Gilly looked down at the piece of paper now mostly filled with lines of her sloping handwriting. "Writing a list."

Todd bent to look over her shoulder. "A list of what?"

Gilly moved her hand to show him. "Things I want to do. Or that I've never done."

"Shit, it would take a lot more than one piece of paper for me to do that."

Gilly looked at what she'd written. "This is just a start."

"What do you got on it?"

For a moment, she didn't want to tell him. Her list, like her laugh, was private. A piece of herself. But then, unlike her laughter, Gilly shared what she'd written.

"'Take my kids to the beach,'" she read. "They've never seen the ocean. I'd like to see Gandy get out of diapers. See Arwen start first grade."

"Are they all about your kids?" Todd's voice was carefully neutral.

Gilly looked over the list and read some more aloud. "'Learn to play the piano. Go scuba diving. Research my family tree.'"

She continued. "'Buy Seth the golf clubs he's been wanting. Finish painting Arwen's bedroom.'"

"You have a lot of stuff on your list."

She ran her fingers over the ink. "Yes. I do."

He didn't offer her false comfort. Gilly knew he wouldn't say she'd do those things someday. He didn't believe she ever would. All at once, the thought she'd never hold her children in her arms again made her start to cry.

The sobs tore from her throat with a force and vehemence that left her gasping. A hot fist clutched her heart, squeezed it, made her moan. She no longer had the strength to grasp the paper, and it floated from her fingers. Gilly buried her face in her hands, breathless with sobs, agonized in her grief.

"Hey," Todd said, and then again. "Hey. Shh. Shh, Gilly, it's okay."

She felt his arm curl around her shoulders, and he drew her close to him. The flannel of his shirt was soft against her cheek. The scent of tobacco permeated him, underlying the scent of fresh air he always seemed to carry with him.

Gilly pushed away from him but was too weakened by grief to move far. His arms held her, loosely but firmly, in his comforting grasp.

"I love them!" she sobbed, spitting the words against his chest. "Ah, God, I miss them!"

He rocked her, slowly, as she had once rocked him. He smoothed her hair. She felt the touch of his lips on her forehead. Gilly sagged into Todd's embrace, not welcoming it but helpless to fight it.

"I miss them," she whispered raggedly, her throat raw from tears. Her fingers clutched a handful of flannel shirt. "My family."

"Don't cry, Gilly."

The tears were tapering off into sniffles. He let her pull away from him. Her eyes ached, swollen and hot.

"I want to see my children again."

He shook his head slowly, back and forth, once. "If you go back, they'll make you tell them what happened. They'll make you tell them where I am. *Who* I am. They'll send me back to jail. And I won't go."

The truth of his statement was undeniable, but Gilly didn't care. She railed at him, flailing her arms. "You son of a bitch! Didn't you hear me? I want to see my children! Don't you understand? I miss my kids!"

"I understand," Todd growled, catching her hand in mid-strike and holding it. His voice softened. "I know, Gilly. What do you want me to do about it?"

"Tell me you'll let me go home."

Todd shook his head. "Can't."

"Just tell me," she said. "Even if you don't mean it!"

He shook his head again.

"Then do what you came up here to do," she said through gritted teeth and yanked her hand from his grasp.

His eyes flickered. "I can't. I could've before. But now I can't."

"You," she said with deliberate cruelty, "are afraid."

He frowned. "Shut up!"

"You're chickenshit!" Gilly cried. "You're a pussy!"

"Shut up, Gilly, or so help me…"

"Or what?" she asked and held out her hands. "What? You'll hit me? You'll kill me?"

"Shut up," he said for a third time, his voice low. He turned from her. "Just shut your mouth."

"If I knew that I would never see my kids or Seth again, I would kill myself," Gilly said with a faint contemptuous sneer. "And I wouldn't be afraid, either."

"Oh, no?" Todd's hand went to the leather sheath on his belt. He unbuckled the huge knife and drew it out. "Then do it. Here you go. Take it."

She didn't.

He put the knife away. "I didn't think so. Not so easy, is it, when it comes right down to it?"

Her smile felt hot and wild, plastered to her face. "I believe I will get back to my family, Todd."

He bowed his head. "I can't let you do that. You know that."

"You won't have a choice," Gilly said.

March

47

For the first morning in a long time, Gilly's stomach didn't hurt. She got out of bed without the rumble and roil of nausea, and that alone was enough to put a smile on her face. The bright morning sunshine, too, lifted her spirits. Its yellow glow meant warmth. Soon, the days would get longer, the sun hotter. Soon, she thought, as she opened the pantry to look for food, the snow would melt entirely.

Todd had risen before her. He said nothing as she prepared pancakes from a boxed powder mixed with water. Even the smell of the food didn't make him stir from his seat. An ashtray overflowed beside him.

"Ugh." Gilly wrinkled her nose as she sat down across from him with her plate of pancakes. "Todd, do you have to do that at the table?"

Silently he got up and went through the pantry. She heard the back door open and close. When he returned, the ashtray was empty.

"Want some pancakes?" she asked around a full mouth.

He shook his head. Brooding. Gilly took a deep breath, not sure what she was going to say, but ready to say it anyway. He cut her off with a short hand gesture.

"Hush."

She chewed, though now the golden cakes stuck in her throat. She washed them down with a glass of cold, clear water, then stabbed another. She was starving.

"My life has always been shit," Todd said. "Can you blame me for wanting to turn it around, now?"

"Of course not. But you broke the law, Todd. You can't expect it to be without consequences." She sipped water, paused, searched his face. "I'm sorry, but that's the way it is."

He grimaced. "Do you really think I deserve to go back to jail? Is that what you want?"

Did she want that? "I don't know."

"Why didn't you get out of the truck when I gave you the chance?" he asked. "None of this would've happened if you'd just got out of the damn truck."

"One of life's greatest mysteries," Gilly told him. "I don't know that, either. It was wrong."

"So now we're both fucked."

She got up and put her empty plate in the sink. "Maybe."

"Those were my last smokes," he told her. "All gone. No more."

"Smoking is a bad habit," Gilly said.

"Bad seems to be the only kind I have," Todd replied. "Let's play a game."

48

More days passed that way, with board games and puzzles, but Todd didn't seem to have the patience to pay attention to any one thing for long. Gilly couldn't blame him. Aside from her kamikaze jaunt around the house and his trips outside to cut wood, neither of them had left the tiny cabin for more than a few minutes.

He shuffled the cards again but only halfheartedly dealt out the hand. Gilly didn't take them. She got up from her chair and stared out the window.

"Looks like a nice day," she commented.

He sighed and reached up to run a hand through his now short hair. "Yeah."

"Come outside with me."

He rolled his eyes. "Didn't we talk about that before?"

Gilly looked back out the window. "The sun is shining. It looks a little warmer outside. It's better than staying in here all day."

"Okay."

Gilly grinned. "You mean it?"

"Yeah, yeah, I mean it. I'll help you build your damn snowman." He stood and stretched, seeming impossibly tall.

"Snow woman," Gilly corrected. "With huge boobs."

Todd laughed and shook his head. "Jeez. Okay."

"C'mon," Gilly said, and reached over to take his hand. "It'll be fun."

But a few hours later, with snow in her face and up her shirt, Gilly didn't think it was so fun. Todd, however, was having a blast. Now he laughed in her face while he held a huge handful of sopping snow ready to throw at her.

"You're bigger than I am!" Gilly cried, wriggling. "Not fair!"

"If you can't play with the big boys," Todd said with an evil grin, "don't start the game."

Perhaps throwing that first snowball hadn't been such a smart idea. Gilly was willing to admit that. Taunting him hadn't been so smart, either.

"Get off me," she gritted out, feeling another inch of snow creep beneath her layers of clothes. They'd stomped it down in a lot of places, but most of it was still up to her knees.

He did, then held out a hand to help her up. "You started it."

His dripping face was evidence of that. Gilly slapped at the snow on her clothes, then lifted her face to the sunshine. Thank God it was warmer today than it had been last week. It hadn't made a lot of difference in the depth of the snow… not yet. But it would.

She waved her hand at the huge snow woman they'd built. "Aren't you ashamed to act this way in front of your girlfriend?"

Todd trudged over and slapped a couple of handfuls onto the already gigantic chest. "She can't be my girlfriend unless her hooters are bigger."

Gilly shook herself so the snow slipped out from under her clothes. "If they get any bigger she won't be able to walk."

"She's made out of snow," Todd said. "She can't walk anyway."

For a moment she wasn't sure he knew she'd been joking, but the devilish twinkle in his eyes proved otherwise. "You're a smart-ass."

He bowed, low, with a sweeping gesture of his hand. "Yeah. I know."

Gilly felt a burble of laughter welling up in her throat, but quenched it. "I'm cold. Let's go back in."

The noise reached them both at the same time; she knew it by the way Todd stood suddenly, head cocked, face turned toward the woods. A low, buzzing rumble. It had been so long since Gilly had heard anything like it she couldn't, at first, figure out what it was.

Todd had no trouble. "Snowmobile."

Her guts clenched, the snow-packed earth beneath her feet tripping her so she stumbled. Todd grabbed her arm to hold her up. His fingers pinched hard even through the layers. He wasn't looking at her, but Gilly had no doubt he was completely, totally aware of her.

The buzzing came closer.

"Get inside." Todd yanked Gilly so hard she stumbled again, her feet tangling. He didn't even give her the chance to get up before he was dragging her.

Snow got up inside her shirt, cold and stinging, and Gilly swung at him. "Todd, stop it!"

He waited, but only the barest moment before grabbing her

with his other hand, too, and hoisting her over his shoulder. Dangling this way, her hair in her face and the blood rushing to her head, Gilly couldn't even scream. She clutched the back of his sweatshirt as Todd stumbled. She closed her eyes and prayed they wouldn't fall.

He banged open the door to the lean-to and put her down. Gilly wobbled, the world spinning. Her flailing hands knocked a couple of cans from the decimated pantry shelves and a moment later, Todd had done the same but on purpose.

"Shit," he muttered. "Shit, shit, shit."

"Todd—"

Without even looking at her, he pushed her back against the wall opposite the shelves hard enough to knock the breath from her. He reached a long arm into the shadows of the shelves behind the supplies and pulled. The shelf moved aside, exposing a narrow closet.

"No!" Gilly cried.

Todd looked at her. "Get in there."

"No, Todd!"

He grabbed her arm and pulled her close, gaze boring into hers. "It's where Uncle Bill hung meat to cure. It's been empty a long time. It won't even smell bad. Get in there and be quiet."

The revving rumble of the snowmobile's engine was much, much louder. Gilly shivered. Time had turned to syrup again. She shook her head.

The motor cut off. Gilly tensed; Todd went stiff. Gilly strained to hear the crunch of boots on snow.

"If you don't get in there, if you make a sound, I will kill whoever's out there. And then I'll kill you," Todd said flatly. "And then I'll do myself, too."

He pushed her into the closet and slid the door closed. It

wasn't dark or warm. Stripes of light shafted in through the gaps between the wallboards, the only solid surface being the back of the door through which he'd pushed her. Large hooks hung from the ceiling and lined the boards, stained from long-ago kills. He was right, it didn't smell bad, no matter how many corpses had hung here. In fact, the only scent tickling her nose was the faintest whiff of gasoline from outside and the lingering undercurrent of wood smoke. The stove vented into this space, or around it, or something, maybe to aid in curing the meat. She didn't know. She didn't care. Gilly pressed her fingers to the wall and looked through a crack.

It was a ranger.

Todd opened the back door and went out into the snow. The ranger was admiring the snow woman, and he turned with a grin as Todd walked up. Gilly pressed her forehead to the boards, trying to see.

"Hey," Todd said.

"Hi, sir. How's it going?"

"Good. Fine." Todd didn't even glance toward the cabin. "What can I do for you?"

"Just doing a routine check. We're making a run on all the places out here that back up to the state game lands. Making sure everyone's got what they need."

"I do," Todd said.

She'd never heard him sound like that—cool but friendly. Todd had ceased to be a stranger to her, but his voice was utterly alien just then. The ranger didn't notice, and why would he? Todd wasn't acting suspicious. The ranger had no idea she was there, and wouldn't, unless she screamed.

Even from here she could see the leather sheath on Todd's belt. She knew too well the length of the blade inside. With his hands on his hips it would take him a second to whip out the knife. Did the ranger have a weapon? Even if he had a gun, would he be able to draw it before Todd stabbed him?

Gilly stayed quiet.

"That's quite a snowman. Snow lady." The ranger laughed and looked around at the cabin.

What would he see? Gilly clutched at the wood, not caring about what blood might have darkened it in the past. The snow, trampled. Smoke coming from the chimney. No vehicle.

No vehicle.

Notice. How did Todd get here without a car? Please, notice.

"How about this snow, huh?" The ranger kicked at some of it. "Worst we've had in as long as I can remember. Lots of folks buried back here. Got a fellow a few miles up on Timberline Road, he's got a plow. I could send him over if you need it."

"Ah…no, thanks. I'm okay. Snow can't last forever, right? And I stocked up good before the storms started."

The ranger took another look around the yard and swung his gaze back to Todd. "You all alone out here, sir?"

"Ah…no. My wife's with me." In profile, Todd's grin was just as transforming as it was full-on—the ranger seemed calmed by it, anyway. "Sort of a…honeymoon."

The ranger laughed and tipped a finger to his hat. "Gotcha. Don't want to be disturbed, huh?"

"You got it."

"But you've got a working phone? Someone to call in case of an emergency? I see you don't have a vehicle here, sir."

"Had to park it at the end of the lane," Todd said easily, evenly, breezily. "Though it's not there, now, my wife's brother's borrowing it for a couple weeks until we get back. He'll come pick us up on a snowmobile if he has to. Like the one you have. What is that, a Bearcat five-seventy?"

The ranger looked over his shoulder. "Yep."

"Sweet." Todd walked over to it farther from the house. He shot a glance over his shoulder, seeming to look right into her eyes, then turned to openly admire the snowmobile.

The men talked about vehicle specs while Gilly shivered. This wasn't the way it had been at the gas station, when she'd lost her senses. Now she wanted to scream out, to batter the door open with her fists.

He said he'd kill the ranger. Then you. Then himself. Even if he doesn't…what will happen if you scream and the ranger doesn't hear you? What if he does and he manages to keep Todd from attacking him? What if Todd doesn't kill him, and the ranger gets away? What would happen then, Gilly?

Gilly turned her back to the crack she'd been peeking through and slid down the wall to bury her face in her hands. Shuddering with cold and anxiety, she wept. Her tears froze on her lashes.

You know what would happen.

You have to take care of what you love, Gillian. Even if it makes you bleed.

After another few minutes, she heard the snowmobile's buzz moving away. A minute after that, Todd opened the door and pulled her out. His eyes were wide and staring, a little crazy. When he pulled her against him, hugging her tight, Gilly was too surprised to stop him. They breathed together, in and out. His hand stroked down her back. She pulled away.

"Thank you, Gilly. Thank you."

"C'mon," Gilly said tensely. "Let's have some tea. I think there are some cookies left, too."

"Maybe you should lay off the cookies," Todd joked as they went into the kitchen. "I about busted myself lifting you."

Gilly, nerves already strung tight, gaped at this sad attempt at humor. Her hands flew to the mound of her stomach. Even beneath the layers of clothes she could feel a small, round bulge. Her face had grown thin, her arms and legs, too, but her belly had not. Her face heated. "That's an awful thing to say!"

She stormed into the bathroom and stripped off her clothes, tossing them into a pile on the floor. The small mirror above the sink could not reflect her entire body, so she had to rely on her own eyes and the movement of her hands as she felt her stomach.

She cupped her breasts in her hands, felt their weight and the way they ached. She slid her palms over the rounded curve of her belly. Still small. But there.

Gilly pawed through the depleted supplies Todd had bought for her so many weeks ago. Shampoo. Soap. Toothbrush. Toothpaste. No tampons, no sanitary napkins. And she hadn't noticed, had she? Hadn't paid attention to something missing that she hadn't needed to use? And she hadn't needed those monthly reminders of her fertility, because…

I'm pregnant. Oh, my God. No.

"Gilly? You okay?" Todd rapped on the door and tried the handle, but Gilly grabbed it tight before he could open it.

"I'll be out in a minute."

She was not okay. Not at all. Gilly bit the familiar sore spot inside her cheek to stifle a moan. She sank to the floor, mindless of the cold air that had her skin humped into prickly gooseflesh. She knelt in the pile of sopping wet clothes and pressed her hands to her face.

Not this. Not now, when Arwen starting first grade and Gandy graduating from diapers meant she would begin to have some of her life back.

A baby? Breastfeeding, diaper explosions, sleepless nights?

Soft, sweet heads that smelled of baby soap. Tiny fingers and toes. The first toothless grin.

She was not a woman who "oohed" and "aahed" over babies in the grocery store or on the street. Both her pregnancies had been fraught with illness, complications and hard, relentless labor. The beauty of her children more than made up for the pain, but she'd vowed after Gandy's forty-eight-hour labor and birth that she'd never go through it again.

"Damn, damn," she swore softly. Goose bumps as hard as rocks pebbled her skin. She had nothing dry or warm to put on. "Todd...?"

He'd already anticipated her. The door edged open, and his hand appeared. He gave her underwear, socks, T-shirt, sweatshirt, sweatpants. Layers of warmth that would do nothing to chase away the chill. She took them with thanks, dried herself, slipped them on.

"You okay?" he asked when she finally ventured forth from the bathroom. He looked at her face and guessed the answer before she could reply. "You puke again? Are you sick?"

Gilly sat on the ugly plaid chair. "I'm pregnant."

The stunned look on his face would've been comical if she'd been in a better mood. For several long moments, Todd appeared unable to speak. Finally he ran a hand over his face, then up through the cropped remains of his hair.

"The fuck?" he asked.

"What the fuck, indeed," Gilly replied. She plucked at the front of her sweatshirt, peeling away bits of the logo with her fingernails.

"Jesus, Gilly. Pregnant? But...we...I mean..."

Todd struggled for the words, and Gilly decided to help him. "Not you. Seth. My husband. I was sick and needed antibiotics...they interfere with birth control pills."

Todd's hand reached naturally for his pocket, but found nothing except an empty cigarette package. He tossed it to the floor, then got up. He paced in front of her, finally turning to face her.

"What are you going to do?"

"Do?" Gilly asked. "There's not much to do, is there?"

"Whoa." Todd's voice turned gruff. "A baby. Damn, that's a big pile of shit, huh?"

The casual echo of her own earlier thoughts seemed heartlessly cruel. Gilly burst into tears. She felt foolish even as she wept, even as Todd handed her a hankie to wipe her face. Now the tears made sense, though, her hormones racing.

In seconds her tears had disappeared, replaced by weary hilarity. "A baby!" she said, not quite able to bring herself to laughter. "Oh. My. God."

Todd sat down on the couch nearest her and reached for her hand. "Gilly."

He said her name as though there should be more, but nothing else came.

"Oh, my God," Gilly replied, wiping at her face.

"I'll take care of you."

She lowered the cloth from her eyes to stare at him. "Surely you must see this changes everything."

He shook his head. "It doesn't have to. Stay here with me. Let me take care of you."

"What?" Gilly forced herself up from the chair. She couldn't make sense of what he'd just said. "What exactly do you want?"

"Have your baby with me," Todd said, a note of growing desperation in his voice. "Just…just say you'll stay here with me. We can raise it together."

"Are you out of your fucking mind?" Gilly shrieked. She

backed away from him, toward the stairs. The horror of his suggestion raced through her. "Are you crazy?"

"Don't you call me that!" Todd was across to her in two strides. His fingers closed around her upper arms, holding her. "Just don't!"

Gilly didn't fight him. She didn't strike back. The child swimming in her belly made that impossible. She had more than herself to care for now. Protective instinct surged forth, overwhelming her. She'd *thought* she'd do anything to get back to her children, but now, to protect the life growing inside her, she *knew* she would. Whatever it took.

Lie. Cheat. Steal.

Kill.

"I'm sorry," she whispered and let him pull her closer again.

"I just wanted to tell you something." He didn't wait for her to reply before continuing. "I want you to know…I didn't mean it. About the ranger, or you. I would never…I'd never hurt you, Gilly. Not ever."

"I know you wouldn't."

"Do you?"

"Of course, Todd." Cheek pressed to the soft flannel of his shirt, she nodded. "I know you."

"And you'll stay with me, right?"

"All right," Gilly said in a voice as cold as the icicles hanging from the roof outside. "Okay, Todd. I'll stay with you."

She did know him, she thought as he let her go with one last squeeze. Todd was a rose. He'd be beautiful if tended properly, but would always have thorns.

49

"I'm pregnant, not disabled," Gilly told Todd, who'd just insisted on bringing her lunch to the couch. "Really, it's better for me to be active."

"You sure?" His worried expression was so sincere, it scraped at Gilly's heart.

She touched his cheek. "I'm sure."

He set the tray he'd prepared on the table. "Don't you got to have good food, though? Milk and eggs and shit? Vitamins?"

"Well, yes. I should." Gilly eyed the plate of boxed macaroni and cheese made with water instead of butter and milk. He'd sprinkled some peanuts on top. "But we don't have those things."

"Won't it hurt the baby?"

She'd had no doctor's appointments, no checkups. She'd been battered and stressed. She'd suffered trauma. But she couldn't allow herself to dwell on those things. Not when she had no way of changing them.

"I'll be fine. Women have been having babies for thousands of years."

"And lots of them died," Todd said.

Gilly's hands fisted at the bluntness of his words. "Todd!"

He shrugged, then sat down beside her. "I don't know anything about pregnant ladies. I just don't want anything bad to happen to you."

"I'll be fine," she said tightly, though images of blood-soaked sheets filled her mind. Her womb twinged in memory, and a sharp pain stabbed between her legs. Cold sweat trickled down her spine.

Todd put his arm around her. "Do you think it will be a boy or a girl?"

"I don't know." She shook herself mentally, though the image had been so vivid she could practically smell the copper tang of blood.

"If it's a boy," Todd said slowly. "Do you think we could name him Bill?"

The very thought of naming her child after Todd's dead uncle turned her stomach. Gilly smiled. "Of course."

His answering smile was like the sun parting rain clouds. "Cool!"

He got up and took the tray to the kitchen. Gilly poked a fork at the urine-colored pasta, but didn't eat it. She touched the small bulge of her tummy, knowing it was too early to feel anything but imagining the flutter of movement anyway. She had to care for this child. She ate the macaroni, every last bite of it.

Later, when the afternoon had passed into evening, Todd

brought out a pair of white candles and set them on the counter. "I thought you might want these."

Gilly looked at him in surprise. She'd allowed the past few Sabbath evenings to pass without lighting candles to commemorate them. She'd been unable to perform the rituals that usually so calmed her. Lighting the candles had made her ache for her family too much.

"Thank you." Gilly took the pack of matches and lit one, touching it to the first wick and then the other. She closed her eyes and waved her hands toward her face, then said the blessing aloud.

"Why do you do that thing with your hands?" Todd asked when she'd finished.

For a moment she didn't know what he meant. The habit of candle-lighting was so ingrained she didn't have to really think about any one part of it. Then she understood.

"You mean this?" She repeated the gesture.

"Yeah."

"When I do that," Gilly said with a sigh that came from her toes, "I'm gathering up all the bits of wonder I've found since last Shabbat and offering them up to Adonai. To God. All the blessings and things to be thankful for."

"What did you send up this week?" Todd asked her as innocently as any child.

Gilly touched her stomach. "This." She thought, then touched his shoulder. "And you, I guess."

She hadn't thought she would say such a thing until it popped out of her mouth. The awful and hilarious thing was, she meant it. Hate and love were two pages back to back in the same story. What she felt for him now was no different than what she'd felt in the beginning, and yet it was vastly, immensely dissimilar. As was everything inside her. Nothing could ever be the same.

Todd looked pleased. "Yeah?"

"Yeah," Gilly said. "Sure, Todd."

Even she couldn't be certain if she was lying.

50

Drip. Drip. Drip. The icicles on the porch grew longer every day. First the sun melted them enough to allow the water to drip from the ends, and when night came they froze. Now they looked like great, jagged teeth in the mouth of an enormous beast.

Was it better to be on the inside looking out, already consumed by the giant? Or to be outside, looking at the teeth ready to snap down on tender flesh? Gilly leaned her forehead against the window, pondering.

"Want to play a game?" Todd asked.

"No." Gilly's hands caressed her belly absently. Her thoughts were on the baby. Boy or girl, this time?

"There's another puzzle in the cabinet. I'll help you put it together. It's got trains on it."

"No, thanks."

Todd let out a frustrated sigh. "C'mon, Gilly. Let's do something!"

She blinked, focusing on him. "I don't feel like doing anything."

He groaned. "Damn it!"

In the light of her hormonal glow, his childishness was endearing rather than annoying. Gilly smiled and rolled her eyes. "What game would you like to play?"

Todd crossed to the large armoire and opened the doors. "Monopoly. Life. Checkers. Battleship…ah, shit, half the pieces are missing out of that one. Shit. We've played all these a million times."

It certainly felt as though they had. "What's up on that shelf, up there?"

Gilly pointed. Despite his height, Todd stood too close to the shelves to see to the back of the ones above his head. From her vantage point across the room, though, Gilly saw some boxes tucked back in the shadows. Perhaps more games, or another puzzle. Something fresh to them, anyway, and something to relieve the tedium.

Todd reached up and stuck his hand back along the shelf. He still wasn't quite tall enough to grab it. "Grab me a chair, will you?"

Her attention now was piqued. Gilly took him one of the tottery dining chairs and held the back of it while he stood on top. Todd peered back into the shelf and grabbed one of the boxes, handed it down to her and stepped from the chair.

"What is it?" Todd asked.

Gilly brushed at the thick coating of dust. The wooden box was fairly large, big enough to need two hands to hold it properly. She sniffed. Cedar. Gilly smiled. Seth always said no tourist trap would be complete without a display of cedar boxes and moccasins.

"I'm not sure." Gilly cracked open the lid, which squealed on its hinges. "Pictures?"

"Let me see." Todd took the box from her and flipped through the sheaf of yellowed photographs and pieces of paper. He stopped, the color draining from his face. "Oh."

"What is it?"

He held up one. "My mother."

Gilly took his elbow and led him to one of the couches. "Here. Sit down. Let's look at them."

Todd shoved the box away from him. Paper scattered across the battered coffee table. "No! I don't want to look at her!"

Gilly gathered them up gently and tucked them back into the box. "They're only pictures, Todd. They can't hurt you."

He shook his head, fingers going to the cigarettes that weren't there and then running through the length of hair that was no longer long. His feet jittered on the nasty shag carpet. Gilly put a hand on his arm to soothe him, and he quieted suddenly.

"We can look at them together. It'll be okay." Gilly pulled out the one on top and held it so he could stare down at it if he chose.

At first he shook his head, but then he nodded his assent. He took the photo from her. "That's my mom."

The young woman in the picture looked vastly different from the haggard zombie in the newspaper clippings. Her smile was genuine here, her eyes bright.

"She's pretty," Gilly said.

"Yeah." Todd touched the smiling face.

"You look like her."

He looked surprised. "You think so?"

Gilly studied the dark-eyed woman whose hair fell in sheaves to her waist. "Yes. I do."

He put the picture aside and picked up the next. "Uncle Bill with Mom."

The siblings faced the camera, smiling, heads together and arms around each other's waists. They wore bathing suits, the colors of their vintage style still noxiously vivid even though time had faded their intensity. Todd's mother's belly peeked out from the opening of her bikini, perhaps in pregnancy?

Todd confirmed the thought. "My brother Stevie, probably."

He sifted through more of the pictures. He lifted one and let out a sigh that was half moan. "There we all are."

The picture, taken a few years earlier than the one featured in the paper, clearly showed the decline of Todd's mother. Her face had gone from smiling and pretty to glassy-eyed and rigid. Her arms encircled a blue wrapped bundle. Her hair, once dark and shining, had been cropped short and lay flat against her head. Tiny red sores clustered in one corner of her mouth.

"The baby…that's me." Todd showed her another photo, of only the children grouped around the blue bundle. He touched the faces of each of his brothers and sisters, naming them. "Stevie. Freddie. Mary. Joey. Katie."

One hand went to his face to cover his eyes. His shoulders heaved. He wept.

Gilly, uncertain, put a hand on his arm. Todd bent and buried his face in her neck. His face was hot on the skin of her throat. His tears splashed her, burning.

She held him tightly, not knowing what to say and so comforting him as best she could with her silence. She put one hand to the back of his head, stroking the shorn strands. His hands clutched her.

"We were just kids!" he sobbed against her, his words nearly unintelligible.

"It wasn't your fault."

He still wept. "We were only little kids! Why? What did we do that was so bad that she wanted to kill us?"

"It wasn't you," Gilly repeated more firmly. "Todd, your mother was mentally unstable. She was in pain. She couldn't decide what was right and wrong, or she would have never—"

"I should've died there, too," he whispered. "Along with Stevie and the others. I wasn't no better then them! I ain't never been better!"

"Todd!" She shook him until he sat up. "Listen to me!"

She used her "Mommy means business" voice, the one guaranteed to stop a rampaging toddler in his tracks seconds before grocery store disaster. It worked on Todd, too. He knuckled his eyes, but stopped protesting.

"There is nothing you could have done to stop your mother," Gilly said. "She was sick. You were only five years old. You and your brothers and sisters didn't do anything to make her do what she did. You didn't deserve it. She was wrong."

"She didn't love us…." He sighed, scrubbing at his face. "Why didn't my mom love me?"

Without thinking, Gilly put her hand on her stomach. "She must have loved you, Todd. There's no way she couldn't have. But what she did…as sick as it was…she probably did it out of that love. She must have thought you would be better off…"

Her explanation trailed off, insufficient.

"That ain't love," Todd said fiercely. "You love your kids.

You told me you'd do anything to stop them from getting hurt. You'd never do what she did!"

"No. I wouldn't."

He lifted another photograph, another of his mother while still young and pretty. "Look at her there, Gilly. See how she looked before she had us?"

"Mothers love their babies—"

"*Some* mothers love their babies," Todd interrupted. "Some don't know how to."

"Maybe that's true," she conceded. "But that's not your fault. Stop blaming yourself. You were only a kid! You're still..."

He would always be a child where this was concerned. Always a wounded, damaged boy who'd been left for dead by the person who was supposed to love him more than anything in the world. Gilly swallowed hard.

"It's not your fault," she repeated. "None of it."

"This must've been Uncle Bill's box," Todd said. "He never showed it to me."

"Maybe he thought it would upset you too much."

Todd stared off into the distance. "Nobody ever talked about them, you know? Nobody ever said their names. It was like they didn't just die, they never even were born. I didn't have anything even to remember them by. If I'd had this box maybe things would've been at least a little different. If I'd had this instead of a file full of newspaper clippings and a note."

He shrugged, hand going absently to his pocket and falling away again when it found no cigarette package there. "Maybe it would've been a little easier."

She doubted it. "Maybe."

He took out a faded piece of ruled notebook paper. "Uncle Bill wrote this. I recognize the writing."

It was a poem, and not a very good one. What it lacked in creative imagery it made up for in emotion. Todd read the first few lines aloud.

"'She's pretty like the red rose, with skin as soft as butterfly wings. Hair as dark as the night that has to shield our love.'"

He frowned, turning the paper over. "I didn't know Uncle Bill wrote poems."

And to women, no less, Gilly thought, remembering that Todd had claimed his uncle to be homosexual. "People usually manage to surprise us."

He read to the bottom of the page. "For Sharon. That's my mother."

"Are you sure Uncle Bill wrote this?"

Todd put the paper back into the box. "Hell if I know. But this is his box and it sure looks like his writing. Why would he have somebody else's poem in it?"

He opened a creased envelope, looked over the lined paper, and handed it to Gilly without a word. Todd got up from the couch, spilling the box's contents. Gilly read the letter, written in a looping, uneducated hand, the same from the note he'd shown her weeks before.

Bill,

The test shows positive. Im knocked up again & this time we know for shore who the dad is, huh? We said it wuldn't happen again but God knows more than us and so we are caught again. Stevie is ok but what if this one ain't right?

The letter continued, mostly into ramblings about God and Jesus and whether or not the child she carried would be normal or deformed. Gilly's hands shook as she set the paper down, and her stomach twisted in a way that had nothing to do with morning sickness. If she'd read the letter correctly, Bill Lutz and Sharon Blauch had created two children, Stevie and Todd. Sharon didn't name the father of her other four children, but Gilly assumed from the woman's disjointed words that they hadn't been Bill.

"I…I thought you said he was gay," she finally said, wishing after she spoke to take the words away.

Todd hadn't gone far, just to the window. Now he turned to look at her. "He was."

"But…" She stopped, unable to say anything more.

"He fucked men and he knocked up his sister," Todd said. "And I guess he was my father. Shit."

He pulled up his sleeve and looked at the tattoo. "I thought I was one of six. I guess I was just one of two, huh? One of fucking two."

His voice broke on that, and Gilly's heart broke a little listening to it. He crossed to her and gathered the pile of pictures and letters. He took the one of himself as an infant, surrounded by his smiling siblings, and put it in the pocket that used to hold his smokes. He stuffed the rest into the box and returned it to the armoire, where he slid it back onto the highest shelf.

"Some things," Todd said, "just aren't right to know."

51

Gilly eyed the empty basket by the woodstove and debated getting some more logs from the pile outside the back door. The longer it took her to decide, the less she felt like heaving herself up from the couch and going outside. And really, she comforted herself, it was downright balmy in here. With the warmth outside now, they didn't even need a fire at all.

Todd set a plate of crackers and aerosol cheese in front of her. "Here."

She grimaced.

He looked serious. "All we got for snacks. Better eat it. Besides, Gilly, it's cheese. Good for you and the baby."

He hadn't asked again to call the child after his uncle. Gilly picked up the plate and looked at it critically. "Todd, this stuff has more sodium and chemicals in it than anything else. I don't think it even came from a cow."

He snatched one of the crackers and tucked into his mouth,

chewing solemnly. "Yeah, but this and a handful of Slim Jims is like eating a piece of heaven."

Gilly snorted. "There's no accounting for taste."

Her stomach rumbled, and she ate a cracker. She was taking her mother's advice and being happy with what she had. Which wasn't much.

"When the snow melts, I'll hike out to the main road and hitch a ride to town. Get us a truck. Buy some stuff."

The utter improbability of what he proposed made Gilly stuff another cracker in her mouth to keep from laughing out loud. His face showed he was serious. He meant that she should stay with him. Have her baby here in this cabin. Raise it together like some perverted Little House in the Big Woods family.

"I know you don't think it's going to work," Todd said in a low voice.

"Oh, Todd." Gilly took a deep breath. "Don't talk about it. There's nothing we can do about it right now, anyway."

"I'm a fucking moron, ain't I?" His self-deprecating question had the lilt of humor in it, but Todd wasn't smiling. "A foron. A stupid foron."

"I don't think so."

"You don't want to stay with me," Todd said matter-of-factly. "No matter what you said before."

Gilly faced him, the taste of slick processed cheese bitter on her tongue. "So, what are you going to do about it?"

"Nothing." Todd met her eyes. "I told you before I couldn't ever let you go. But I know you think about getting away. I know you're going to try."

Had she really thought she could continue to lie to him? That she could convince him of her willingness to stay and raise her child with him? She'd underestimated him.

"Yes. When the snow melts." Gilly touched his hand. "I have to."

"Even if you promised not to tell them anything, they'd come here, wouldn't they? They'd find me. Even if I ran, I guess they would. I'd have no chance, huh?"

"I don't think so. And I couldn't promise you I wouldn't say anything. I'd have to, you know. Tell them something."

"I'd go to jail. Or I'd cut myself and bleed to death up here, all alone. Not much of a choice." He poked at one of the crackers, then swallowed it.

Gilly rested her hands on her belly. "No. I'd say it's not."

"A good person would give up, let you go. I wish I was a good person." He said suddenly, "But I just ain't!"

"People can change."

Todd shook his head. "Tell me again that you'll stay here with me."

"I'll stay here with you," Gilly said.

He stretched out beside her and put his head in her lap. "Wouldn't it be nice if that were true?"

She threaded her fingers through his hair. "Sure it would."

He closed his eyes and nestled close to her. Gilly stroked his hair, watching the sun paint lines on the planes of his face. When he slept, she watched the rise and fall of his chest. How hard would he hang on to life, she thought, when she tried to take it away?

52

Todd was balancing a straw on the end of his nose. Arms out at shoulder height, fingers spread, he bobbed and weaved, trying to keep the straw from falling. The sight was completely ridiculous, especially since he went about the feat with so much determination.

"I seen this on TV once," he said as the straw hit the floor again. "You're supposed to watch the end. Then you can balance it."

He watched the end all right, but since the straw was so short, watching it crossed his eyes. Gilly bit her lip against a giggle. Todd caught the gesture from the corner of his eye and let the straw fall off without retrieving it.

"Aren't you ever going to laugh? Not ever?"

Gilly shook her head. "I don't think so."

"Not ever again?"

Not here, with him. Gilly just shook her head again, unwilling to answer. Todd scowled and left the kitchen.

A few minutes later, she heard him call her name. She looked across to the living room to see what her college roommate had fondly called a "moon." Gilly clapped her hands over her eyes in mortification.

"Todd!"

"Make you laugh?"

"No!" she cried, and covered her eyes.

"Shit."

She peeked through her fingers to see him tucking in his shirt. "That was really uncalled-for."

"I just wanted to see if I could make you laugh." Todd sauntered closer. "Figured the sight of my hairy a—"

"Todd! For goodness' sakes!" Gilly felt a burble of hilarity in her chest, but it didn't come out. She smiled, but kept her laughter to herself as she had vowed to do.

"Whatever." He shrugged, then waggled his eyebrows. "It sure made your cheeks go all pink."

Gilly rolled her eyes. "I guess it did."

Todd leaned against the half wall, ducking his head to peer under the hanging cabinets at her. "Tell me something."

"About what?" she asked, thinking he had something specific in mind.

He waved his hand at her. "I don't know. Just something. Anything."

"Are we going to tell stories, is that it?"

Todd didn't smile back. "I figure you know a hell of a lot about me. Thought maybe I ought to get to know you."

"There isn't much to tell." Gilly thought. That wasn't really true, was it? She had lots of stories, none quite so tragic and horrendous as Todd's, but tales of her life that showed why she had become the woman she was.

"What about your family?" Todd tapped the counter restlessly, and she could tell he was missing his smokes.

"I told you about my family."

"Not all of it."

Gilly came around the counter and motioned with her head for him to follow her to the couch. "You sure you want to know?"

"What the hell else is there to do?"

Todd flopped onto the couch and spread out his arms and legs, then patted the seat beside him. Gilly looked at the couch across from him but sat where he'd indicated. His thigh touched hers, but there was no point in moving away. Not now. They'd come too far for her to play at coyness, or to pretend she didn't recognize their closeness.

She looked outside, where snow still covered every surface though the sun had risen high in the sky. "My family. Okay. Well, my mother was an alcoholic with paranoid and depressive tendencies. She spent a lot of time in the hospital when I was in my early teens. By the time she got on the proper medication and stopped drinking, I was in college. She died before my children were born."

"Do you miss her?"

Unexpected tears stung her eyes. "Sometimes. Yes. I miss her."

Todd made a low noise. "Even though she was all messed up?"

Gilly's memories could in no way compete with Todd's for heartbreak, but her childhood and adolescence had been far from the sweetness and light of a television sitcom. "Yes. Even though she was all messed up."

He bit at his nails, a habit he'd taken up since running out of cigarettes. "Why do you think that is?"

"Because she was my mother," Gilly said in surprise, as though the answer should be obvious. Well, it should be. But she understood his question, and why he asked it. "Because… no matter how much bad she gave me, I loved her."

"Because she was your mom."

"Yes."

Todd sighed heavily, leaning his head back on the couch. A moment later he slouched down to rest it on Gilly's shoulder. He'd washed his hair that morning, cursing and shouting at the cold water, but now the cropped strands smelled faintly of citrus. It tickled her cheek.

"What made you decide to have kids?" Todd reached over and took her hand. He turned it palm up and traced the lines there. "Did you think you'd be a better mother than yours?"

"Oh, no," Gilly said. "I wasn't sure I'd be a good mother at all. I didn't think I knew how." She trailed off, picturing her children. "I'm still not sure I know how."

"But you love your kids."

"Of course. You know I do."

"And you're going to have another one," Todd said, resting his hand on her belly.

Gilly snorted. "Not on purpose, believe me."

"But you'll love it, right?" He peered up at her, the slinking dog look returning after long absence. "Even though you didn't want it?"

Gilly placed her hand over his. "Yes. I will love this child. And I will protect it."

"I never wanted kids." The weight of his hand was not unwelcome on her stomach. "I knew I'd fuck them up. Bigtime."

"Understandable that you would feel that way." Gilly leaned her head back and closed her eyes.

"Do you think I could be a good father?"

She cracked open one eye to look down at him, but his attention was focused on her stomach. "It's not something anyone can know until it happens."

"Funny thing is," he said, "I think I might like to try. I think I could be okay at it."

"You do?"

"Yeah." Now he looked at her, a light of excitement in his eyes. His hand rubbed slow, hypnotizing circles on her stomach. "How long until it comes?"

Gilly thought. "Six or seven months."

"My birthday is in November," Todd told her. "Maybe it'll come on my birthday."

"You never know." The slow rhythm of his hand was putting her to sleep. The conversation had become dreamlike. Unreal. She knew what he was asking but could not answer him.

"Stay with me," he whispered, and she was awake as instantly as if someone had popped a balloon in her ear. "Let me show you. Help me be good, Gilly."

"Only you can make that choice, Todd."

"I think I could love a baby. A kid."

"They're hard not to love," Gilly said.

They fell silent together, and she thought of mothers who didn't love their children, and those who loved them in the wrong way. Perhaps Todd was thinking of that, too. But since he didn't speak, Gilly didn't know.

53

The sound of rushing water had been constant over the past few days. Bright sunshine every day. Warmth. The snow was melting, finally. Not quite there yet. And then…

Gilly gasped when she saw green. Grass, showing through one of the bare patches from where they'd rolled the snowman. She pressed her face to the glass, unable to believe it. Only one small patch, and only in the places they'd already mostly cleared. But there.

"Spring," she murmured, then said a blessing. "*Baruch HaShem.* Thank you, God."

It was time to get prepared.

Her hands went to her belly automatically as she thought. She would still need appropriate clothes. Food. Water. She didn't know how long it would take to hike the road, if she even could, but…she would do it, now. She had to.

She heard Todd's heavy tread upstairs, and turned from the window as he came down. "Todd…"

But she couldn't tell him that the snow was melting, not with so much joy in her voice. She wouldn't be able to hide it. She couldn't be deliberately cruel to him. Not anymore.

He looked at her curiously. "Yeah?"

"Nothing," Gilly replied with a smile that felt as though it stretched across her entire face.

She wanted to run outside, to throw herself down in the tiny emerald patch, to rub her face and hands all over it. Her hands shook with the desire, so intense she had to shove her hands in her pockets to stop their trembling. She forced herself to look away from it. To pretend it wasn't there.

"It's hot in here," Todd said. "I won't even have to light the stove today."

Gilly nodded and walked on stiff legs to the dining table. She'd begun another puzzle, this one of a thousand different kinds of lollipops. Her fingers patted the scattered pieces, but she did not place any. She would not, if God was willing, finish this puzzle.

It was almost time for her to go home.

54

"I'm so hungry I could eat a bowl of cigarette butts with a hair in it." Gilly groaned and grabbed her stomach. "Hurry up with those potatoes!"

"Calm down." Todd brandished his knife. "They've got a million eyes in them, all over the place."

"You're going to cut off your fingers. Use a paring knife."

Todd concentrated on gouging out another eye, then tossed the edible potato into the pot with the others. "This is the sharpest knife we got."

"Just be careful, that's all. I don't want to have to stitch you up." Gilly went to the window over the sink. It seemed that for almost three months, all she'd done was look, from one window or the other, out at the white wasteland of imprisonment.

No more. Water ran from the gutters with a sound like a running brook. Large patches had rotted in the snow, revealing the brown and green of earth underneath. At the edge of the woods, the first shoots of crocuses poked their purple and yellow heads up to reach the sun.

She couldn't sit still. Gilly paced constantly, like a tiger in a cage. Each day she'd woken to brilliant sunshine was one she was closer to release.

"That's the last of the oil," Todd said, setting a pot of it on the stove.

She'd been craving French fries since yesterday. Today, Todd had pulled out the last crinkly sack of potatoes that had weathered the winter. Some of them had been salvageable.

In contrast to Gilly's edginess and constant monitoring of spring's progress, Todd was actively ignoring the season's change. He had to notice, had to see, but Gilly didn't mention the decreasing blanket of snow outside and neither did he.

His nightmares had returned, and his cries often woke her from her own dreams. The fields of roses had stopped blooming. Now she dreamed of rows and rows of barren, thorn-ridden stems. Each time she soothed him and herself back to sleep with wordless lullabies. It was easy to do, in the dark, with his tears wetting her shoulder. Easy to pretend he was just another child to care for.

In the light of day, it was different. She watched him without looking at him. Saw how his face had grown thinner and haggard over the past few days, while her own in the mirror glowed with vibrant, unvoiced joy. If she was kinder to him then, it was because she was helpless to be anything else.

Their time together was running short. She knew it, and he had to know it, too. Every hour that passed took her farther away from him, though she hadn't gone anywhere at all.

"Stay with me," he asked her in the night, and her lie hung between them like the strands of a caterpillar's silk. "Stay with me," he whispered with increasing desperation, but only in the dark. In the light, Todd no longer asked.

Gilly turned from the window, powerless to stop the smile stretching her lips. Sunshine filled her soul, her heart, even her womb, where the life inside gave her the strength she would need to do what she must. When he saw her face, Todd flinched, but recovered.

"Almost done," he said, and waved the huge knife at her and the potato. "French fries, coming right up."

"Yummy!" Gilly cried. Seeing the early spring flowers had made her positively giddy.

The potato slipped from Todd's fingers and landed on the floor. He reached for it, smacking his head on the table with a resounding thud and a muffled curse. The accident did what his silly jokes and awkward wordplay had not.

Gilly laughed.

The delight that filled her from the soft spring breeze now burst from her throat in a load guffaw. The noise was loud. It startled both of them. And it didn't stop.

Gilly laughed until her sides ached and tears streamed down her face. Todd, who could have been offended by her making such fun of his misfortune, merely gazed at her gape-mouthed. He reached up to rub the lump on his forehead, and hit himself in the eye with the potato.

Gilly laughed harder. Todd met her with a smile, then a chortle. He joined her hilarity. They laughed together, and it was all right. She gave him the last secret part of herself she'd been holding back, and it didn't matter.

Todd put the knife on the table to hold his sides in laughter. Gilly's eyes fell on it, the blade so huge and glinting. Her laughter stopped. She met Todd's gaze.

In that last moment, his smile faded. His eyes closed briefly and when they opened, she saw he knew what she meant to do. There was no future for Todd if Gilly left this place. There could be no future for her if she stayed.

She had nothing more for him than this, a cruelty that was in fact a simple mercy.

The knife was heavy in her hand, but her aim was true. She slashed once. Todd went to his knees in front of her as if he was praying, hands to his throat. Crimson jetted between his fingers.

The knife fell, turning over and over, and clattered to the floor beside her, but Gilly didn't pay attention. She went to her knees, too, arms reaching to catch him as he slumped.

Not long ago she'd asked herself how hard he'd hold on to life when she took it away. She had her answer now. Todd didn't struggle or fight. His back arched as his life ran out over his hands and hers. As she cradled him against her, fingers stroking in his hair.

She sang to him, the same lullabies from their long nights together, all mixed up yet somehow making sense. A long stream of words and melody, broken now and again by the relentless hitch of her breath as she fought sobs. She didn't make it through one verse.

There was more blood than she'd expected, gouts of it, splattering the floor and legs of the table. It painted everything, the color too bright. Unreal. Too real.

And too short. She'd had months to convince herself she'd do this to survive. It took only seconds to make it happen. She'd thought she would do this for herself, but in the end she did it for him.

Todd's lips moved, though he had no voice. He clutched at her. He drew her close, and she let him. She kissed his forehead and looked into his eyes as he mouthed two words she didn't have to hear to understand.

"You're welcome," Gilly said.

And then Todd died.

55

"See, Arwen. Roses don't like to get their feet wet. Just a little bit of water." Gilly handed her daughter the watering can and looked up at the warm spring sunshine.

"I like red roses," Gandy said matter-of-factly.

No more baby words for him. He spoke in full sentences now and no longer needed a blankie. Arwen had shot up two inches and a dress size. Sometimes Gilly looked at the two of them and couldn't believe how much they'd changed.

Baby Tyler in the sling across her chest let out a small, muffled wail and Gilly reached to unbutton the flap of her nursing shirt so he could reach her breast. The tingle of her milk letting down had started at the first whimper and her youngest son latched on, sucking hard while she cupped the back of his tiny head. Gilly, sitting on a blanket in the sunshine with her children beside her, surveyed the yard where last year only dandelions had grown.

She'd planted roses.

Red roses, all of them, different varieties and shades but every one of them red. She'd worked hard in the garden, digging and turning the soil, making raised beds in the places where it was too boggy and moist for roses to thrive. She'd spent hours on her efforts and would see no results until they bloomed, but that was all right. She could wait.

"Mama?"

"Yes, baby." She smoothed Arwen's hair back from her forehead.

"I missed you."

Gilly shifted Tyler so she could pull Arwen into her lap. She didn't have to ask when. Arwen had had more trouble with what had happened last year than Gandy. She still woke from nightmares, sometimes. Gilly cradled her daughter close, even when the baby let out a "meep" of protest before getting back to the business of nursing.

"I know you did, baby. But Mama's here now."

"And you won't go away again, right?"

"No."

Gandy, who'd taken the watering can to fill it from the spigot, was having trouble with it now. His sturdy legs weren't as chubby as they'd been last year. He'd stretched up. He set the can down and furrowed his brow to give it a hard stare before picking it up again. Water sloshed as he struggled, but he finally got it back to the bush they'd last planted.

"Good job, Gandy." Gilly waved at her son. "Come here. Mama needs a squeeze."

All three of them crowded onto her lap and Gilly held them as close as she could. She breathed them. These, her children, whom she loved so dearly.

"That man won't ever come back, will he?" Arwen insisted.

"No."

"Because he's dead," Gandy offered.

There would always be pieces of the story Gilly wouldn't tell anyone, ever, about those three months. Nobody had ever questioned what she'd said about how Todd had held her against her will, or that he'd died by his own hand. She thought he'd forgive her that.

She hadn't given her children all the details, though she knew some day they might ask. "Yes. His name was Todd. And he died."

Gandy struggled to his feet, eager to be off and away. Arwen snuggled closer for a moment, plucking at the sling and petting the top of her baby brother's head. Gilly's thighs cramped but she held her daughter tight.

"Do you miss him, Mama?" Arwen asked, looking into Gilly's face. "Do you ever miss that man?"

Gilly stroked her hand down Arwen's hair. She looked out across the roses, bare now but promising beauty. She watched her son running and felt her infant taking nourishment from her body. She looked into her daughter's eyes.

The crunch of tires on the driveway made them both look up. A familiar gray Volvo was pulling into the garage, Arwen already tumbling off Gilly's lap in her eagerness.

"It's Daddy! I'm going to give him what I made in school!" Arwen cried, and ran, her brother following.

Gilly got to her feet and watched her husband gather their children into his arms for hugs and kisses. He lifted Gandy upside down, sending the boy into fits of giggles, then bent to take the linked necklace of paper rings Arwen had made in first grade. Seth lifted his hand to her, waving, his grin familiar and beloved and just for her.

"Yes," Gilly murmured with only the roses as witness. "Sometimes, I do."

And then she went to her husband, whom she greeted with kisses, and together with their children they went inside. This was her family. Precious and fragile and beloved.

This was the life she'd made, and she'd never again lose sight of what it meant.

★★★★★

ACKNOWLEDGMENTS

As always, I could write without music, but I'm ever so grateful I don't have to. Much appreciation goes to the following artists, whose songs made up the playlist for this book. Please support their music through legal sources.

"Give It Away"—Quincy Coleman
"Take Me Home"—Lisbeth Scott and Nathan Barr
"Everything"—Lifehouse
"This Woman's Work"—Kate Bush
"You've Been Loved"—Joseph Arthur
"Iris"—Goo Goo Dolls
"Look After You"—The Fray
"The End"—The Doors
"One Last Breath"—Creed
"A Home for You"—Kaitlin Hopkins, Deven May
"Over My Head"—Christopher Dallman

And a special thanks to Jason Manns, whose version of "Hallelujah" wasn't there when I started this book but was there all through the end.